Crime is not a term most of us would link with that gentlest of humorists, P.G. Wodehouse, but it is a fact that, perhaps affected by a boyhood diet of the latest exploits of Sherlock Holmes as they came off the presses, he was rarely able to keep his characters within the law. In this collection, the *heroes and heroines* indulge in gunplay, theft, assault with sharp instruments, arson, fraud, and extortion; we shrink from revealing what the bad guys get up to. Bertie Wooster, Jeeves, Lord Emsworth, any number of Mulliner friends-and-relations, and the arch-fiendess Roberta (Bobbie) Wickham stand shown at last in their true criminous colors.

P.G. WODEHOUSE
available in IPL editions:

IF I WERE YOU
FULL MOON
SERVICE WITH A SMILE
WODEHOUSE ON CRIME

and

WHO'S WHO IN WODEHOUSE
edited by Daniel Garrison

WODEHOUSE ON CRIME
A Dozen Tales of Fiendish Cunning

P.G. Wodehouse

Edited and with a preface by D.R. Bensen
Foreword by Isaac Asimov

LIBRARY OF CRIME CLASSICS®

MISTER E'S™

INTERNATIONAL POLYGONICS, LTD.
NEW YORK CITY

Anne

Amor e cor gentile
son una
cosa

CONTENTS

Foreword
THE
LOVABLE
CRIMINALITY
OF
P. G. WODEHOUSE
by Isaac Asimov

P. G. WODEHOUSE, AS WE ALL KNOW, CREATED A
world of his own; or, rather, forced one to live past its time.
He took Edwardian England, purified it of its grosser elements, and kept it alive by some alchemy, of which only he
knew the secret, right into the Vietnam era.

And in doing so, he imbued every aspect with lovability.

Do some of his characters seem like wastrels? Semi-idiots?
Excrescences on the face of society?

Undoubtedly, but, one and all, each worthless idler would
rather die by torture than sully a woman's name, however
indirectly and involuntarily. All would engage, at a moment's
notice, in any act of chivalry and kindness, though it meant
the loss of all their worldly goods (all five pounds of it) or,
worse yet, though it meant a rip in their perfectly-creased
trousers.

It is because of my admiration for these deadbeats that I
have had an ambition that has plagued me steadily for forty
years. I want to dine at the Drones Club.

It's no use telling me there's no such organization. Somewhere, in some magic place in London, I know it must exist

— and oh to be there, in April or any other month.

In moments of high spirits, Wodehouse tells us, the gilded lordlings of the Drones Club cannot control their exuberance, and "a goodish bit of bread is thrown about." I want to be there and throw bread. I want to bean someone with a crusty roll.

Think how lovable a world must be where throwing a crusty roll in a private club is what high spirits lead to. Consider Frederick Altamont Cornwallis Twistleton, Earl of Ickenham.

With reference to him, a Drone has more than once remarked: "I don't know if you know what is meant by the word 'excesses' but that is invariably what Lord Ickenham commits when he finds himself in London."

And what are these excesses? Why, typically they consist of impersonating some bounder in order that the kindly Ickenham might help a damsel in distress.

To be sure Lord Ickenham, Galahad Threepwood, and several others are constantly being thrown out of nightclubs, but the reason for it is never described. I suspect it is because they throw crusty rolls at a headwaiter who well deserves it.

There are outright villains in Wodehouse's accounts who are mean, self-centered and penny-pinching, such as H. C. Purkiss, who is Bingo Little's boss, or Ivor Llewellyn, that quintessence of Hollywood magnatehood; but these are usually so plagued by indigestion, high blood pressure, and ferocious wives that one is satisfied at once that they are adequately punished each day for anything they do.

It is admittedly hard to love Oofy Prosser, the Drones Club millionaire, but he can be forgiven for the sake of his case of terminal acne. It is even more difficult to love Percy Pilbeam, the well-known private detective, but to possess a face which, under all disguises, inspires unanimous mistrust is punishment enough.

This book you have in your hand, however, deals with a special subdivision of Wodehousian activity — that of crime.

Can there be crime in the never-never-land of P. G. W. idyllatry?

Certainly! The tales are saturated with it, and even that does not weaken our love.

Consider the misdemeanor of pinching a policeman's helmet. This is the particular specialty of young Bertram Wooster, the most lovable of all Wodehouse's characters and one who combines a negligible intelligence with an absolutely perfect ability to tell a complicated story. (Since I am so much more intelligent than Bertie, why is my ability at telling a complicated story somewhat less than perfect? I suppose that that is one of those cosmic questions which could be answered even by Einstein only with a thoughtful, "er . . . ah. . . .")

To be sure, the helmet-pinching almost always takes place on the occasion of Boat Race Night which, I take it, is the time when Oxford and Cambridge engage in some obscure contest. Apparently, all the graduates of either school (and all Wodehouse wastrels have passed through Oxford untouched by human thought) are honor-bound to get tipsy, whether they want to or not.

Then, too, the mildness of the crime is accentuated by the fact that no one in his right mind cares if a Wodehouse policeman or constable (routinely fat, obtuse and intent on laying siege to the hearts of innocent housemaids) is rendered helmetless.

Finally, the act is sometimes inspired by the righteous sense of retaliation of some fiery young woman (Stephanie Byng and Roberta Wickham spring instantly to mind) who long to bring the gray hairs of a particular constable with sorrow to the grave — after that constable, for instance, has cited the dog Bartholomew for chewing thoughtfully on the ankle of said constable with teeth that bite like the serpent and sting like the adder. Under these circumstances, the fiery young woman qualifies as a damsel in distress, and by the Wodehousian code all must rally to her defense.

There are, however, worse crimes. You can't throw a rock

anywhere in Wodehouse without hitting someone who is pinching silver cow creamers or prize pigs. These are valuable things, and their theft qualifies as grand larceny. Long prison sentences are in order if the malefactor is caught.

But consider the motives. It is always made abundantly clear that Sir Watkyn Bassett has no right to a cow creamer. In the first place, it has been obtained dubiously, and in the second place, his character disqualifies him. Bertie's aunt, Dahlia Travers (the good and deserving aunt) would argue that point at the top of her voice, if you asked her — or if you did not — salting it with a ripe fox-hunting expletive (never specified) that you could hear in the next county.

Again, the prize pig, when stolen, is usually stolen in order to stiffen the cooked-spaghetti spine of Clarence, Lord Emsworth, so that he might withstand the haughty stare of his sister, Lady Constance (the daughter of a hundred Earls) and come to the aid of a damsel in distress.

More awe-inspiring are the crimes against the code of the gentleman.

It is taken for granted that any gentleman would cheat any tradesman, and do so without a second's remorse. After all, tradesmen are created only so that they might be cheated by their betters.

However, no gentleman would dream of backing down on a debt of honor to a fellow gentleman. You might cheat a bounder, in other words, but never a fellow cheater.

There are reasons for that. If a bookie catches you cheating, the very worst that can happen is that some large bruiser (usually named Horace — a simple-minded soul with a one-word vocabulary: "R") will scoop out your insides with his bare hands. Cheating a gentleman, however, will cause you to be asked to resign your club.

Consequently, many of Wodehouse's accounts deal with the nobbling of contestants in important sporting events such as the egg-in-the-spoon race or the choirboys' open (to which all can enter whose voices have not yet broken as of Lammas-tide last). And I need not mention the vile actions taken in connection with the Great Sermon Handicap.

In fact, when one stops to think of it, there is rarely a story in the entire Wodehouse opera which doesn't feature crime.

In this one, Stanley Featherstone Ukridge labors to cheat an honest, hardworking insurance company by the arranging of fraudulent accidents. In that one, Jno. Horatio Biggs kidnaps his victim and feeds him bread and water to enforce his vile demands. Over there, Sir Murgatroyd Sprockett-Sprockett is plotting arson for the sake of insurance.

Unfortunately, very few of these criminals receive their comeuppance. To be sure, their plots often fail, but virtually never, whether their plots fail or succeed, do they feel the large hand of a policeman (with or without a helmet) upon a shoulder — let alone being forced to face the baleful glance of a magistrate at the Bosher Street Police Court, or getting two weeks without the option. In most cases, in fact, they reach the end of the story in triumph.

But I said "virtually never." Every once in a while, the prime Wodehousian crime of pinching a policeman's helmet gets its punishment. Indeed, there is no record of Bertie Wooster actually carrying through the crime successfully. There he is, up before the steely stare of Sir Watkyn Bassett, magistrate (who laid the foundations of his ample fortune — including his cow creamer — by hanging on to the five-pound fines he assesses like glue, for, as Bertie astutely observes, five pounds here and five pounds there mount up). In that case, Bertie has to pay the five pounds out of *his* ample fortune, even though, as he hotly remarks, a wiser magistrate would have been content with a simple reprimand.

To be sure, on one occasion, Oliver Randolph Sipperley is forced to go to jail — actually spend time in the chokey, old horse — but that is the exception that emphasizes the rule.

But read this collection — and see for yourself.

PREFACE

AS DR. ASIMOV'S INTRODUCTION SUGGESTS, IT would be impossible to present a full collection of those of P. G. Wodehouse's stories which are concerned with crime. It would be a book of thousands of pages, with a spine about two and a half feet wide, which would make for awkward reading. Almost any short story or novel selected at random will turn out to involve an offense, misdemeanor or felony, as an important part of the plot; and this is to say nothing (which indeed Dr. Asimov does) of professional criminals such as Soapy and Dolly Molloy, Fanny Welch in *The Small Bachelor*, Aileen Peavey in *Leave It to Psmith*, and the several American gangs in *Laughing Gas*, *The Little Nugget* and *Psmith, Journalist*, among others.

Asimov, as befits a trained scientist venturing into a new area, contents himself with describing his observations of a phenomenon, and does not attempt to account for it. An editor is allowed, and expected to take, more leeway; and I propose here to go into the question of why this amiable and blameless man chose to steep his works in crime.

My notion is that, fittingly enough for one of the most

professional writers of this century, the two main influences were, one directly and one indirectly, literary.

The direct influence is surely that of Conan Doyle. Wodehouse's letters tell us that as a youth he used to wait in ill-concealed agitation for the next *Strand* containing a Sherlock Holmes story. Now consider Holmes. "Consulting detective," indeed! The man solved crimes, true; but he also *committed* them with a good deal more flair than his adversaries. "A Scandal in Bohemia" shows him performing quasi-arson and burglary; and blackmail, assault, and abetting of theft, suicide, and even murder do not cause him to turn a hair. And certainly a man who deliberately urges Dr. Watson to provide himself with a loaded firearm must be considered to be criminally reckless. The effect of the Holmes stories must then be seen as strongly baleful.

The second — the indirect — influence is that of Dr. Thomas Arnold who was, if not the actual inventor, the chief propagandist, of the English public-school system. Something over half a century after he flourished, one of the many offshoots of his ideas was Dulwich College, which Wodehouse attended. These institutions, ostensibly intended to provide military, political, academic, commercial and clerical leaders for the late-Victorian Empire, were in fact remarkably similar to well-run minimum-security prisons of the present day and afforded their inmates a sound education in guerrilla warfare on authority and in circumvention of any and all rules. (On reflection, one might say that any contradiction between the stated aim and the result may be illusory.)

The youthful Wodehouse, his mind inflamed by Sherlock Holmes's high-handed ways with the law, was thrust into a hotbed of iniquity, Dulwich, at which nothing was thought of clandestine visits to the tuck-shop (to U.S. readers, candy store or soda fountain), evasion of boundary restrictions, subversion and terrorism (within the scope afforded by the school), and even midnight feasts of sausages toasted on a pen nib over a candle. Anything goes, if you can get away with it, was the public-schoolboy's motto.

No one exposed from his tenderest years to these malign forces could expect to escape them entirely. It is to Wodehouse's credit that, though proceeding directly from Dulwich to employment in a London bank, he did not use his honed criminal skills to become an embezzler or a loan officer, let alone to seek wider employment for them by standing for Parliament or embarking upon a military or mercantile career. One may imagine him, at the turn of the century, asking himself, "Have I got it in me to rake in the big bucks by becoming a Napoleon of Crime? No? Very well, then, I'll write about it in several score short stories and novels, pausing by the way to toss off a few unforgettable song lyrics — I mean to say, one can be Plum Wodehouse or one can be James Moriarty, and there's no middle ground, is there?"

We can only be grateful for the choice he made.

D. R. Bensen
Croton-on-Hudson, March, 1981

STRYCHNINE
IN
THE
SOUP

FROM THE MOMENT THE DRAUGHT STOUT ENtered the bar-parlour of the Anglers' Rest, it had been obvious that he was not his usual cheery self. His face was drawn and twisted, and he sat with bowed head in a distant corner by the window, contributing nothing to the conversation which, with Mr. Mulliner as its centre, was in progress around the fire. From time to time he heaved a hollow sigh.

A sympathetic Lemonade and Angostura, putting down his glass, went across and laid a kindly hand on the sufferer's shoulder.

"What is it, old man?" he asked. "Lost a friend?"

"Worse," said the Draught Stout. "A mystery novel. Got half-way through it on the journey down here, and left it in the train."

"My nephew Cyril, the interior decorator," said Mr. Mulliner, "once did the very same thing. These mental lapses are not infrequent."

"And now," proceeded the Draught Stout, "I'm going to have a sleepless night, wondering who poisoned Sir Geoffrey Tuttle, Bart."

"That Bart. was poisoned, was he?"

"You never said a truer word. Personally, I think it was the Vicar who did him in. He was known to be interested in strange poisons."

Mr. Mulliner smiled indulgently.

"It was not the Vicar," he said. "I happen to have read *The Murglow Manor Mystery*. The guilty man was the plumber."

"What plumber?"

"The one who comes in chapter two to mend the shower-bath. Sir Geoffrey had wronged his aunt in the year '96, so he fastened a snake in the nozzle of the shower-bath with glue; and when Sir Geoffrey turned on the stream the hot water melted the glue. This released the snake, which dropped through one of the holes, bit the Baronet in the leg, and disappeared down the waste-pipe."

"But that can't be right," said the Draught Stout. "Between chapter two and the murder there was an interval of several days."

"The plumber forgot his snake and had to go back for it," explained Mr. Mulliner. "I trust that this revelation will prove sedative."

"I feel a new man," said the Draught Stout. "I'd have lain awake worrying about that murder all night."

"I suppose you would. My nephew Cyril was just the same. Nothing in this modern life of ours," said Mr. Mulliner, taking a sip of his hot Scotch and lemon, "is more remarkable than the way in which the mystery novel has gripped the public. Your true enthusiast, deprived of his favourite reading, will stop at nothing in order to get it. He is like a victim of the drug habit when withheld from cocaine. My nephew Cyri —"

"Amazing the things people will leave in trains," said a Small Lager. "Bags . . . umbrellas . . . even stuffed chimpanzees, occasionally, I've been told. I heard a story the other day—"

My nephew Cyril (said Mr. Mulliner) had a greater passion for mystery stories than anyone I have ever met. I attribute this to the fact that, like so many interior decorators, he was a fragile, delicate young fellow, extraordinarily vulnerable to any ailment that happened to be going the rounds. Every time he caught mumps or influenza or German measles or the like, he occupied the period of convalescence in reading mystery stories. And, as the appetite grows by what it feeds on, he had become, at the time at which this narrative opens, a confirmed addict. Not only did he devour every volume of this type on which he could lay his hands, but he was also to be found at any theatre which was offering the kind of drama where skinny arms come unexpectedly out of the chiffonier and the audience feels a mild surprise if the lights stay on for ten consecutive minutes.

And it was during a performance of *The Grey Vampire* at the St. James's that he found himself sitting next to Amelia Bassett, the girl whom he was to love with all the stored-up fervour of a man who hitherto had been inclined rather to edge away when in the presence of the other sex.

He did not know her name was Amelia Basset. He had never seen her before. All he knew was that at last he had met his fate, and for the whole of the first act he was pondering the problem of how he was to make her acquaintance.

It was as the lights went up for the first intermission that he was aroused from his thoughts by a sharp pain in the right leg. He was just wondering whether it was gout or sciatica when, glancing down, he perceived that what had happened was that his neighbour, absorbed by the drama; had absent-mindedly collected a handful of his flesh and was twisting it in an ecstasy of excitement.

It seemed to Cyril a good *point d'appui.*

"Excuse me," he said.

The girl turned. Her eyes were glowing, and the tip of her nose still quivered.

"I beg your pardon?"

"My leg," said Cyril. "Might I have it back, if you've finished with it?"

The girl looked down. She started visibly.

"I'm awfully sorry," she gasped.

"Not at all," said Cyril. "Only too glad to have been of assistance."

"I got carried away."

"You are evidently fond of mystery plays."

"I love them."

"So do I. And mystery novels?"

"Oh, yes!"

"Have you read *Blood on the Banisters*?"

"Oh, *yes!* I thought it was better than *Severed Throats.*"

"So did I," said Cyril. "Much better. Brighter murders, subtler detectives, crisper clues . . . better in every way."

The two twin souls gazed into each other's eyes. There is no surer foundation for a beautiful friendship than a mutual taste in literature.

"My name is Amelia Bassett," said the girl.

"Mine is Cyril Mulliner. Bassett?" He frowned thoughtfully. "The name seems familiar."

"Perhaps you have heard of my mother. Lady Bassett. She's rather a well-known big-game hunter and explorer. She tramps through jungles and things. She's gone out to the lobby for a smoke. By the way" — she hesitated — "if she finds us talking, will you remember that we met at the Polterwoods'?"

"I quite understand."

"You see, mother doesn't like people who talk to me without a formal introduction. And, when mother doesn't like anyone, she is so apt to hit them over the head with some hard instrument."

"I see," said Cyril. "Like the Human Ape in *Gore by the Gallon.*"

"Exactly. Tell me," said the girl, changing the subject, "if you were a millionaire, would you rather be stabbed in the back with a paper-knife or found dead without a mark on you, staring with blank eyes at some appalling sight?"

4

Cyril was about to reply when, looking past her, he found himself virtually in the latter position. A woman of extraordinary formidableness had lowered herself into the seat beyond and was scrutinising him keenly through a tortoiseshell lorgnette. She reminded Cyril of Wallace Beery.

"Friend of yours, Amelia?" she said.

"This is Mr. Mulliner, mother. We met at the Polterwoods'."

"Ah?" said Lady Bassett.

She inspected Cyril through her lorgnette.

"Mr. Mulliner," she said, "is a little like the chief of the Lower Isisi — though, of course, he was darker and had a ring through his nose. A dear, good fellow," she continued reminiscently, "but inclined to become familiar under the influence of trade gin. I shot him in the leg."

"Er — why?" asked Cyril.

"He was not behaving like a gentleman," said Lady Bassett primly.

"After taking your treatment," said Cyril, awed, "I'll bet he could have written a Book of Etiquette."

"I believe he did," said Lady Bassett carelessly. "You must come and call on us some afternoon, Mr. Mulliner. I am in the telephone book. If you are interested in man-eating pumas, I can show you some nice heads."

The curtain rose on act two, and Cyril returned to his thoughts. Love, he felt joyously, had come into his life at last. But then so, he had to admit, had Lady Bassett. There is, he reflected, always something.

I will pass lightly over the period of Cyril's wooing. Suffice it to say that his progress was rapid. From the moment he told Amelia that he had once met Dorothy Sayers, he never looked back. And one afternoon, calling and finding that Lady Bassett was away in the country, he took the girl's hand in his and told his love.

For a while all was well. Amelia's reactions proved satisfactory to a degree. She checked up enthusiastically on his proposition. Falling into his arms, she admitted specifically that he was her Dream Man.

Then came the jarring note.

"But it's no use," she said, her lovely eyes filling with tears. "Mother will never give her consent."

"Why not?" said Cyril, stunned. "What is it she objects to about me?"

"I don't know. But she generally alludes to you as 'that pipsqueak.'"

"Pipsqueak?" said Cyril. "What *is* a pipsqueak?"

"I'm not quite sure, but it's something mother doesn't like very much. It's a pity she ever found out that you are an interior decorator."

"An honourable profession," said Cyril, a little stiffly.

"I know; but what she admires are men who have to do with the great open spaces."

"Well, I also design ornamental gardens."

"Yes," said the girl doubtfully, "but still —"

"And, dash it," said Cyril indignantly, "this isn't the Victorian age. All that business of Mother's Consent went out twenty years ago."

"Yes, but no one told mother."

"It's preposterous!" cried Cyril. "I never heard such rot. Let's just slip off and get married quietly and send her a picture postcard from Venice or somewhere, with a cross and a 'This is our room. Wish you were with us' on it."

The girl shuddered.

"She would be with us," she said. "You don't know mother. The moment she got that picture postcard, she would come over to wherever we were and put you across her knee and spank you with a hair-brush. I don't think I could ever feel the same towards you if I saw you lying across mother's knee, being spanked with a hair-brush. It would spoil the honeymoon."

Cyril frowned. But a man who has spent most of his life trying out a series of patent medicines is always an optimist.

6

"There is only one thing to be done," he said. "I shall see your mother and try to make her listen to reason. Where is she now?"

"She left this morning for a visit to the Winghams in Sussex."

"Excellent! I know the Winghams. In fact, I have a standing invitation to go and stay with them whenever I like. I'll send them a wire and push down this evening. I will oil up to your mother sedulously and try to correct her present unfavourable impression of me. Then, choosing my moment, I will shoot her the news. It may work. It may not work. But at any rate I consider it a fair sporting venture."

"But you are so diffident, Cyril. So shrinking. So retiring and shy. How can you carry through such a task?"

"Love will nerve me."

"Enough, do you think? Remember what mother is. Wouldn't a good, strong drink be more help?"

Cyril looked doubtful.

"My doctor has always forbidden me alcoholic stimulants. He says they increase the blood pressure."

"Well, when you meet mother, you will need all the blood pressure you can get. I really do advise you to fuel up a little before you see her."

"Yes," agreed Cyril, nodding thoughtfully. "I think you're right. It shall be as you say. Good-bye, my angel one."

"Good-bye, Cyril, darling. You will think of me every minute while you're gone?"

"Every single minute. Well, practically every single minute. You see, I have just got Horatio Slingsby's latest book, *Strychnine in the Soup*, and I shall be dipping into that from time to time. But all the rest of the while. . . . Have you read it, by the way?"

"Not yet. I had a copy, but mother took it with her."

"Ah? Well, if I am to catch a train that will get me to Barkley for dinner, I must be going. Good-bye, sweetheart, and never forget that Gilbert Glendale in *The Miss-*

ing Toe won the girl he loved in spite of being up against two mysterious stranglers and the entire Black Moustache gang."

He kissed her fondly, and went off to pack.

Barkley Towers, the country seat of Sir Mortimer and Lady Wingham, was two hours from London by rail. Thinking of Amelia and reading the opening chapters of Horatio Slingsby's powerful story, Cyril found the journey pass rapidly. In fact, so preoccupied was he that it was only as the train started to draw out of Barkley Regis station that he realized where he was. He managed to hurl himself on to the platform just in time.

As he had taken the five-seven express, stopping only at Gluebury Peveril, he arrived at Barkley Towers at an hour which enabled him not only to be on hand for dinner but also to take part in the life-giving distribution of cocktails which preceded the meal.

The house-party, he perceived on entering the drawing-room, was a small one. Besides Lady Bassett and himself, the only visitors were a nondescript couple of the name of Simpson, and a tall, bronzed, handsome man with flashing eyes who, his hostess informed him in a whispered aside, was Lester Mapledurham (pronounced Mum), the explorer and big-game hunter.

Perhaps it was the oppressive sensation of being in the same room with two explorers and big-game hunters that brought home to Cyril the need for following Amelia's advice as quickly as possible. But probably the mere sight of Lady Bassett alone would have been enough to make him break a lifelong abstinence. To her normal resemblance to Wallace Beery she appeared now to have added a distinct suggestion of Victor McLaglen, and the spectacle was sufficient to send Cyril leaping toward the cocktail tray.

After three rapid glasses he felt a better and a braver man. And so lavishly did he irrigate the ensuing dinner with hock, sherry, champagne, old brandy and port, that at the conclusion of the meal he was pleased to find that his diffidence had completely vanished. He rose from the table feeling equal to asking a dozen Lady Bassetts for their consent to marry a dozen daughters.

In fact, as he confided to the butler, prodding him genially in the ribs as he spoke, if Lady Bassett attempted to put on any dog with *him,* he would know what to do about it. He made no threats, he explained to the butler, he simply stated that he would know what to do about it. The butler said "Very good, sir. Thank you, sir," and the incident closed.

It had been Cyril's intention — feeling, as he did, in this singularly uplifted and dominant frame of mind — to get hold of Amelia's mother and start oiling up to her immediately after dinner. But, what with falling into a doze in the smoking-room and then getting into an argument on theology with one of the under-footmen whom he met in the hall, he did not reach the drawing-room until nearly half-past ten. And he was annoyed, on walking in with a merry cry of "Lady Bassett! Call for Lady Bassett!" on his lips, to discover that she had retired to her room.

Had Cyril's mood been even slightly less elevated, this news might have acted as a check on his enthusiasm. So generous, however, had been Sir Mortimer's hospitality that he merely nodded eleven times, to indicate comprehension, and then, having ascertained that his quarry was roosting in the Blue Room, sped thither with a brief "Tally-ho!"

Arriving at the Blue Room, he banged heartily on the door and breezed in. He found Lady Bassett propped up with pillows. She was smoking a cigar and reading a book. And that book, Cyril saw with intense surprise and resentment, was none other than Horatio Slingsby's *Strychnine in the Soup.*

The spectacle brought him to an abrupt halt.

"Well, I'm dashed!" he cried. "Well, I'm blowed! What do you mean by pinching my book?"

Lady Bassett had lowered her cigar. She now raised her eyebrows.

"What are you doing in my room, Mr. Mulliner?"

"It's a little hard," said Cyril, trembling with self-pity. "I go to enormous expense to buy detective stories, and no sooner is my back turned than people rush about the place sneaking them."

"This book belongs to my daughter Amelia."

"Good old Amelia!" said Cyril cordially. "One of the best."

"I borrowed it to read in the train. Now will you kindly tell me what you are doing in my room, Mr. Mulliner?"

Cyril smote his forehead.

"Of course. I remember now. It all comes back to me. She told me you had taken it. And, what's more, I've suddenly recollected something which clears you completely. I was hustled and bustled at the end of the journey. I sprang to my feet, hurled bags on to the platform — in a word, lost my head. And, like a chump, I went and left my copy of *Strychnine in the Soup* in the train. Well, I can only apologize."

"You can not only apologize. You can also tell me what you are doing in my room."

"What I am doing in your room?"

"Exactly."

"Ah!" said Cyril, sitting down on the bed. "You may well ask."

"I *have* asked. Three times."

Cyril closed his eyes. For some reason, his mind seemed cloudy and not at its best.

"If you are proposing to go to sleep here, Mr. Mulliner," said Lady Bassett, "tell me, and I shall know what to do about it."

The phrase touched a chord in Cyril's memory. He recollected now his reasons for being where he was. Opening his eyes, he fixed them on her.

"Lady Bassett," he said, "you are, I believe, an explorer?"

"I am."

"In the course of your explorations, you have wandered through many a jungle in many a distant land?"

"I have."

"Tell me, Lady Bassett," said Cyril keenly, "while making a pest of yourself to the denizens of those jungles, did you notice one thing? I allude to the fact that Love is everywhere — aye, even in the jungle. Love, independent of bounds and frontiers, of nationality and species, works its spell on every living thing. So that, no matter whether an individual be a Congo native, an American song-writer, a jaguar, an armadillo, a bespoke tailor, or a tsetse-tsetse fly, he will infallibly seek his mate. So why shouldn't an interior decorator and designer of ornamental gardens? I put this to you, Lady Bassett."

"Mr. Mulliner," said his room-mate, "you are blotto!"

Cyril waved his hand in a spacious gesture, and fell off the bed.

"Blotto I may be," he said, resuming his seat, "but, none the less, argue as you will, you can't get away from the fact that I love your daughter Amelia."

There was a tense pause.

"What did you say?" cried Lady Bassett.

"When?" said Cyril absently, for he had fallen into a daydream and, as far as the intervening blankets would permit, was playing "This little pig went to market" with his companion's toes.

"Did I hear you say . . . my daughter Amelia?"

"Grey-eyed girl, medium height, sort of browny-red hair," said Cyril, to assist her memory. "Dash it, you *must* know Amelia. She goes everywhere. And let me tell you something, Mrs. — I've forgotten your name. We're going to be married, if I can obtain her foul mother's consent. Speaking as an old friend, what would you say the chances were?"

"Extremely slight."

"Eh?"

"Seeing that I *am* Amelia's mother. . . ."

Cyril blinked, genuinely surprised.

"Why, so you are! I didn't recognize you. Have you been there all the time?"

"I have."

Suddenly Cyril's gaze hardened. He drew himself up stiffly.

"What are you doing in my bed?" he demanded.

"This is not your bed."

"Then whose is it?"

"Mine."

Cyril shrugged his shoulders helplessly.

"Well, it all looks very funny to me," he said. "I suppose I must believe your story, but, I repeat, I consider the whole thing odd, and I propose to institute very strict enquiries. I may tell you that I happen to know the ringleaders. I wish you a very hearty good night."

It was perhaps an hour later that Cyril, who had been walking on the terrace in deep thought, repaired once more to the Blue Room in quest of information. Running over the details of the recent interview in his head, he had suddenly discovered that there was a point which had not been satisfactorily cleared up.

"I say," he said.

Lady Bassett looked up from her book, plainly annoyed.

"Have you no bedroom of your own, Mr. Mulliner?"

"Oh, yes," said Cyril. "They've bedded me out in the Moat Room. But there was something I wanted you to tell me."

"Well?"

"Did you say I might or mightn't?"

"Might or mightn't what?"

"Marry Amelia?"

"No. You may not."

"No?"

"No!"

"Oh!" said Cyril. "Well, pip-pip once more."

It was a moody Cyril Mulliner who withdrew to the Moat Room. He now realized the position of affairs. The mother of the girl he loved refused to accept him as an eligible suitor. A dickens of a situation to be in, felt Cyril, sombrely unshoeing himself.

Then he brightened a little. His life, he reflected, might be wrecked, but he still had two-thirds of *Strychnine in the Soup* to read.

At the moment when the train reached Barkley Regis station, Cyril had just got to the bit where Detective Inspector Mould looks through the half-open cellar door and, drawing in his breath with a sharp, hissing sound, recoils in horror. It was obviously going to be good. He was just about to proceed to the dressing-table where, he presumed, the footman had placed the book on unpacking his bag, when an icy stream seemed to flow down the centre of his spine and the room and its contents danced before him.

Once more he had remembered that he had left the volume in the train.

He uttered an animal cry and tottered to a chair.

The subject of bereavement is one that has often been treated powerfully by poets, who have run the whole gamut of the emotions while laying bare for us the agony of those who have lost parents, wives, children, gazelles, money, fame, dogs, cats, doves, sweethearts, horses, and even collar-studs. But no poet has yet treated of the most poignant bereavement of all — that of the man half-way through a detective story who finds himself at bedtime without the book.

Cyril did not care to think of the night that lay before him. Already his brain was lashing itself from side to side like a wounded snake as it sought for some explanation of Inspector Mould's strange behaviour. Horatio Slingsby was an author who could be relied on to keep faith with his public. He was not the sort of man to fob the reader off in the next chapter with the statement that what had made Inspector Mould look horrified was the fact that he had suddenly remembered that he had forgotten all about the letter his wife had given him to post. If looking through cellar doors disturbed a Slingsby detective, it was because a dismembered corpse lay there, or at least a severed hand.

A soft moan, as of some thing in torment, escaped Cyril. What to do? What to do? Even a makeshift substitute for *Strychnine in the Soup* was beyond his reach. He knew so well what he would find if he went to the library in search of something to read. Sir Mortimer Wingham was heavy and country-squire-ish. His wife affected strange religions. Their literature was in keeping with their tastes. In the library there would be books on Ba-ha-ism, volumes in old leather of the Rural Encyclopædia, "My Two Years in Sunny Ceylon," by the Rev. Orlo Waterbury . . . but of anything that would interest Scotland Yard, of anything with a bit of blood in it and a corpse or two into which a fellow could get his teeth, not a trace.

What, then, coming right back to it, to do?

And suddenly, as if in answer to the question, came the solution. Electrified, he saw the way out.

The hour was now well advanced. By this time Lady Bassett must surely be asleep. *Strychnine in the Soup* would be lying on the table beside her bed. All he had to do was to creep in and grab it.

The more he considered the idea, the better it looked. It was not as if he did not know the way to Lady Bassett's room or the topography of it when he got there. It seemed to him as if most of his later life had been spent in Lady Bassett's room. He could find his way about it with his eyes shut.

He hesitated no longer. Donning a dressing-gown, he left his room and hurried along the passage.

Pushing open the door of the Blue Room and closing it softly behind him, Cyril stood for a moment full of all those emotions which come to man revisiting some long-familiar spot. There the dear old room was, just the same as ever. How it all came back to him! The place was in darkness, but that did not deter him. He knew where the bed-table was, and he made for it with stealthy steps.

In the manner in which Cyril Mulliner advanced towards the bed-table there was much which would have reminded Lady Bassett, had she been an eye-witness, of the furtive prowl of the Lesser Iguanodon tracking its prey. In only one respect did Cyril and this creature of the wild differ in their technique. Iguanodons — and this applies not only to the Lesser but to the Larger Iguanodon — seldom, if ever, trip over cords on the floor and bring the lamps to which they are attached crashing to the ground like a ton of bricks.

Cyril did. Scarcely had he snatched up the book and placed it in the pocket of his dressing-gown, when his foot became entangled in the trailing cord and the lamp on the table leaped nimbly into the air and, to the accompaniment of a sound not unlike that made by a hundred plates coming apart simultaneously in the hands of a hundred scullery-maids, nose-dived to the floor and became a total loss.

At the same moment, Lady Bassett, who had been chasing a bat out of the window, stepped in from the balcony and switched on the lights.

To say that Cyril Mulliner was taken aback would be to understate the facts. Nothing like his recent misadventure had happened to him since his eleventh year, when, going surreptitiously to his mother's cupboard for jam, he had jerked three shelves down on his head, containing milk, butter, home-made preserves, pickles, cheese, eggs, cakes, and potted-meat. His feelings on the present occasion closely paralleled that boyhood thrill.

Lady Bassett also appeared somewhat discomposed.

"You!" she said.

Cyril nodded, endeavouring the while to smile in a reassuring manner.

"Hullo!" he said.

His hostess's manner was now one of unmistakable displeasure.

"Am I not to have a moment of privacy, Mr. Mulliner?" she asked severely. "I am, I trust, a broad-minded woman, but I cannot approve of this idea of communal bedrooms."

Cyril made an effort to be conciliatory.

"I do keep coming in, don't I?" he said.

"You do," agreed Lady Bassett. "Sir Mortimer informed me, on learning that I had been given this room, that it was supposed to be haunted. Had I known that it was haunted by you, Mr. Mulliner, I should have packed up and gone to the local inn."

Cyril bowed his head. The censure, he could not but feel, was deserved.

"I admit," he said, "that my conduct has been open to criticism. In extenuation, I can but plead my great love. This is no idle social call, Lady Bassett. I looked in because I wished to take up again this matter of my marrying your daughter Amelia. You say I can't. Why can't I? Answer me that, Lady Bassett."

"I have other views for Amelia," said Lady Bassett stiffly. "When my daughter gets married it will not be to a spineless, invertebrate product of our modern hot-house civilization, but to a strong, upstanding, keen-eyed, two-fisted he-man of the open spaces. I have no wish to hurt your feelings, Mr. Mulliner," she continued, more kindly, "but you must admit that you are, when all is said and done, a pipsqueak."

"I deny it," cried Cyril warmly. "I don't even know what a pipsqueak is."

"A pipsqueak is a man who has never seen the sun rise beyond the reaches of the Lower Zambezi; who would not know what to do if faced by a charging rhinoceros. What, pray, would you do if faced by a charging rhinoceros, Mr. Mulliner?"

"I am not likely," said Cyril, "to move in the same social circles as charging rhinoceri."

"Or take another simple case, such as happens every day. Suppose you are crossing a rude bridge over a stream in Equatorial Africa. You have been thinking of a hundred trifles and are in a reverie. From this you wake to discover that in the branches overhead a python is extending its fangs towards you. At the same time, you observe that at one end of the bridge is a crouching puma; at the other are two head hunters — call them Pat and Mike — with poisoned blow-pipes to their lips. Below, half hidden in the stream, is an alligator. What would you do in such a case, Mr. Mulliner?"

Cyril weighed the point.

"I should feel embarrassed," he had to admit. "I shouldn't know where to look."

Lady Bassett laughed an amused, scornful little laugh.

"Precisely. Such a situation would not, however, disturb Lester Mapledurham."

"Lester Mapledurham!"

"The man who is to marry my daughter Amelia. He asked me for her hand shortly after dinner."

Cyril reeled. The blow, falling so suddenly and unexpect-edly, had made him feel boneless. And yet, he felt, he might have expected this. These explorers and big-game hunters stick together.

"In a situation such as I have outlined, Lester Mapledur-ham would simply drop from the bridge, wait till the alligator made its rush, insert a stout stick between its jaws, and then hit it in the eye with a spear, being careful to avoid its lashing tail. He would then drift down-stream and land at some safer spot. That is the type of man I wish for as a son-in-law."

Cyril left the room without a word. Not even the fact that he now had *Strychnine in the Soup* in his possession could cheer his mood of unrelieved blackness. Back in his room, he tossed the book moodily on to the bed and began to pace the floor. And he had scarcely completed two laps when the door opened.

For an instant, when he heard the click of the latch, Cyril supposed that his visitor must be Lady Bassett, who, having put two and two together on discovering her loss, had come to demand her property back. And he cursed the rashness which had led him to fling it so carelessly upon the bed, in full view.

But it was not Lady Bassett. The intruder was Lester Mapledurham. Clad in a suit of pyjamas which in their general colour scheme reminded Cyril of a boudoir he had recently decorated for a Society poetess, he stood with folded arms, his keen eyes fixed menacingly on the young man.

"Give me those jewels!" said Lester Mapledurham.

Cyril was at a loss.

"Jewels?"

"Jewels!"

"What jewels?"

Lester Mapledurham tossed his head impatiently.

"I don't know what jewels. They may be the Wingham Pearls or the Bassett Diamonds or the Simpson Sapphires. I'm not sure which room it was I saw you coming out of."

Cyril began to understand.

"Oh, did you see me coming out of a room?"

"I did. I heard a crash and, when I looked out, you were hurrying along the corridor."

"I can explain everything," said Cyril. "I had just been having a chat with Lady Bassett on a personal matter. Nothing to do with diamonds."

"You're sure?" said Mapledurham.

"Oh, rather," said Cyril. "We talked about rhinoceri and pythons and her daughter Amelia and alligators and all that sort of thing, and then I came away."

Lester Mapledurham seemed only half convinced.

"H'm!" he said. "Well, if anything is missing in the morning, I shall know what to do about it." His eye fell on the bed. "Hullo!" he went on, with sudden animation. "Slingsby's latest? Well, well! I've been wanting to get hold of this. I hear it's good. The *Leeds Mercury* says: 'These gripping pages...'"

He turned to the door, and with a hideous pang of agony Cyril perceived that it was plainly his intention to take the book with him. It was swinging lightly from a bronzed hand about the size of a medium ham.

"Here!" he cried, vehemently.

Lester Mapledurham turned.

"Well?"

"Oh, nothing," said Cyril. "Just good night."

He flung himself face downwards on the bed as the door closed, cursing himself for the craven cowardice which had kept him from snatching the book from the explorer. There had been a moment when he had almost nerved himself to the deed, but it was followed by another moment in which he had caught the other's eye. And it was as if he had found himself exchanging glances with Lady Bassett's charging rhinoceros.

And now, thanks to this pusillanimity, he was once more *Strychnine in the Soup*-less.

How long Cyril lay there, a prey to the gloomiest thoughts, he could not have said. He was aroused from his meditations by the sound of the door opening again.

Lady Bassett stood before him. It was plain that she was deeply moved. In addition to resembling Wallace Beery and Victor McLaglen, she now had a distinct look of George Bancroft.

She pointed a quivering finger at Cyril.

"You hound!" she cried. "Give me that book!"

Cyril maintained his poise with a strong effort.

"What book?"

"The book you sneaked out of my room?"

"Has someone sneaked a book out of your room?" Cyril struck his forehead. "Great heavens!" he cried.

"Mr. Mulliner," said Lady Bassett coldly, "more book and less gibbering!"

Cyril raised a hand.

"I know who's got your book. Lester Mapledurham!"

"Don't be absurd."

"He has, I tell you. As I was on my way to your room just now, I saw him coming out, carrying something in a furtive manner. I remember wondering a bit at the time. He's in the Clock Room. If we pop along there now, we shall just catch him red-handed."

Lady Bassett reflected.

"It is impossible," she said at length. "He is incapable of such an act. Lester Mapledurham is a man who once killed a lion with a sardine-opener."

"The very worst sort," said Cyril. "Ask anyone."

"And he is engaged to my daughter." Lady Bassett paused. "Well, he won't be long, if I find that what you say is true. Come, Mr. Mulliner!"

Together the two passed down the silent passage. At the door of the Clock Room they paused. A light streamed from beneath it. Cyril pointed silently to this sinister evidence of reading in bed, and noted that his companion stiffened and said something to herself in an undertone in what appeared to be some sort of native dialect.

The next moment she had flung the door open and, with a spring like that of a crouching zebu, had leaped to the bed and wrenched the book from Lester Mapledurham's hands.

"So!" said Lady Bassett.

"So!" said Cyril, feeling that he could not do better than follow the lead of such a woman.

"Hullo!" said Lester Mapledurham, surprised. "Something the matter?"

"So it was you who stole my book!"

"Your book?" said Lester Mapledurham. "I borrowed this from Mr. Mulliner there."

"A likely story!" said Cyril. "Lady Bassett is aware that I left my copy of *Strychnine in the Soup* in the train."

"Certainly," said Lady Bassett. "It's no use talking, young man, I have caught you with the goods. And let me tell you one thing that may be of interest. If you think that, after a dastardly act like this, you are going to marry Amelia, forget it!"

"Wipe it right out of your mind," said Cyril.

"But listen —!"

"I will not listen. Come, Mr. Mulliner."

She left the room, followed by Cyril. For some moments they walked in silence.

"A merciful escape," said Cyril.

"For whom?"

"For Amelia. My gosh, think of her tied to a man like that. Must be a relief to you to feel that she's going to marry a respectable interior decorator."

Lady Bassett halted. They were standing outside the Moat Room now. She looked at Cyril, her eyebrows raised.

"Are you under the impression, Mr. Mulliner," she said, "that, on the strength of what has happened, I intend to accept you as a son-in-law?"

Cyril reeled.

"Don't you?"

"Certainly not."

Something inside Cyril seemed to snap. Recklessness descended upon him. He became for a space a thing of courage and fire, like the African leopard in the mating season.

"Oh!" he said.

And, deftly whisking *Strychnine in the Soup* from his companion's hand, he darted into his room, banged the door, and bolted it.

"Mr. Mulliner!"

It was Lady Bassett's voice, coming pleadingly through the woodwork. It was plain that she was shaken to the core, and Cyril smiled sardonically. He was in a position to dictate terms.

"Give me that book, Mr. Mulliner!"

"Certainly not," said Cyril. "I intend to read it myself. I hear good reports of it on every side. The *Peebles Intelligencer* says: 'Vigorous and absorbing.'"

A low wail from the other side of the door answered him.

"Of course," said Cyril, suggestively, "if it were my future mother-in-law who was speaking, her word would naturally be law."

There was a silence outside.

"Very well," said Lady Bassett.

"I may marry Amelia?"

"You may."

Cyril unbolted the door.

"Come — Mother," he said, in a soft, kindly voice. "We will read it together, down in the library."

Lady Bassett was still shaken.

"I hope I have acted for the best," she said.

"You have," said Cyril.

"You will make Amelia a good husband?"

"Grade A," Cyril assured her.

"Well, even if you don't," said Lady Bassett resignedly, "I can't go to bed without that book. I had just got to the bit where Inspector Mould is trapped in the underground den of the Faceless Fiend."

Cyril quivered.

"*Is* there a Faceless Fiend?" he cried.

"There are two Faceless Fiends," said Lady Bassett.

"My gosh!" said Cyril. "Let's hurry."

THE
CRIME
WAVE
AT
BLANDINGS

THE DAY ON WHICH LAWLESSNESS REARED ITS ugly head at Blandings Castle was one of singular beauty. The sun shone down from a sky of cornflower-blue, and what one would really like would be to describe in leisurely detail the ancient battlements, the smooth green lawns, the rolling parkland, the majestic trees, the well-bred bees and the gentlemanly birds on which it shone.

But those who read thrillers are an impatient race. They chafe at scenic rhapsodies and want to get on to the rough stuff. When, they ask, did the dirty work start? Who were mixed up in it? Was there blood, and, if so, how much? And — most particularly — where was everybody and what was everybody doing at whatever time it was? The chronicler who wishes to grip must supply this information at the earliest possible moment.

The wave of crime, then, which was to rock one of Shropshire's stateliest homes to its foundations broke out towards the middle of a fine summer afternoon, and the persons involved in it were disposed as follows:

Clarence, ninth Earl of Emsworth, the castle's owner and

overlord, was down in the potting shed, in conference with Angus McAllister, his head gardener, on the subject of sweet peas.

His sister, Lady Constance, was strolling on the terrace with a swarthy young man in spectacles, whose name was Rupert Baxter and who had at one time been Lord Emsworth's private secretary.

Beach, the butler, was in a deck chair outside the back premises of the house, smoking a cigar and reading Chapter Sixteen of *The Man With The Missing Toe*.

George, Lord Emsworth's grandson, was prowling through the shrubbery with the air gun which was his constant companion.

Jane, his lordship's niece, was in the summerhouse by the lake.

And the sun shone serenely down — on, as we say, the lawns, the battlements, the trees, the bees, the best type of bird and the rolling parkland.

Presently Lord Emsworth left the potting shed and started to wander towards the house. He had never felt happier. All day his mood had been one of perfect contentment and tranquillity, and for once in a way Angus McAllister had done nothing to disturb it. Too often, when you tried to reason with that human mule, he had a way of saying "Mphm" and looking Scotch, and then saying "Grmph" and looking Scotch again, and after that just fingering his beard and looking Scotch without speaking, which was intensely irritating to a sensitive employer. But this afternoon Hollywood yesmen could have taken his correspondence course, and Lord Emsworth had none of that uneasy feeling, which usually came to him on these occasions, that the moment his back was turned his own sound, statesmanlike policies would be shelved and some sort of sweet-pea New Deal put into practice as if he had never spoken a word.

He was humming as he approached the terrace. He had his programme all mapped out. For perhaps an hour, till the day had cooled off a little, he would read a Pig book in the library. After that he would go and take a sniff at a rose or two and possibly do a bit of snailing. These mild pleasures were all his simple soul demanded. He wanted nothing more. Just the quiet life, with nobody to fuss him.

And now that Baxter had left, he reflected buoyantly, nobody did fuss him. There had, he dimly recalled, been some sort of trouble a week or so back — something about some man his niece Jane wanted to marry and his sister Constance didn't want her to marry — but that had apparently all blown over. And even when the thing had been at its height, even when the air had been shrill with women's voices and Connie had kept popping out at him and saying, "Do *listen*, Clarence!" he had always been able to reflect that, though all this was pretty unpleasant, there was nevertheless a bright side. He had ceased to be the employer of Rupert Baxter.

There is a breed of granite-faced, strong-jawed businessman to whom Lord Emsworth's attitude towards Rupert Baxter would have seemed frankly inexplicable. To these Titans a private secretary is simply a Hey-you, a Hi-there, a mere puppet to be ordered hither and thither at will. The trouble with Lord Emsworth was that it was he and not his secretary who had been the puppet. Their respective relations had always been those of a mild reigning monarch and the pushing young devil who has taken on the dictatorship. For years, until he had mercifully tendered his resignation to join an American named Jevons, Baxter had worried Lord Emsworth, bossed him, bustled him, had always been after him to do things and remember things and sign things. Never a moment's peace. Yes, it was certainly delightful to think that Baxter had departed forever. His going had relieved this Garden of Eden of its one resident snake.

Still humming, Lord Emsworth reached the terrace. A moment later, the melody had died on his lips, and he was rocking back on his heels as if he had received a solid punch on the nose.

"God bless my soul!" he ejaculated, shaken to the core.

His pince-nez, as always happened when he was emotionally stirred, had leaped from their moorings. He recovered them and put them on again, hoping feebly that the ghastly sight he had seen would prove to have been an optical illusion. But no. However much he blinked, he could not blink away the fact that the man over there talking to his sister Constance was Rupert Baxter in person. He stood gaping at him with a horror which would have been almost excessive if the other had returned from the tomb.

Lady Constance was smiling brightly, as women so often do when they are in the process of slipping something raw over on their nearest and dearest.

"Here is Mr. Baxter, Clarence."

"Ah," said Lord Emsworth.

"He is touring England on his motor bicycle and, finding himself in these parts, of course he looked us up."

"Ah," said Lord Emsworth.

He spoke dully, for his soul was heavy with foreboding. It was all very well for Connie to say that Baxter was touring England, thus giving the idea that in about five minutes the man would leap on his motor bicycle and dash off to some spot a hundred miles away. He knew his sister. She was plotting. Always ardently pro-Baxter, she was going to try to get Blandings Castle's leading incubus back into office again. Lord Emsworth would have been prepared to lay the odds on this in the most liberal spirit. So he said "Ah."

The monosyllable, taken in conjunction with the sagging of her brother's jaw and the glare of agony behind his pince-nez, caused Lady Constance's lips to tighten. A disciplinary light came into her fine eyes. She looked like a female lion tamer about to assert her personality with one of the troupe.

"Clarence!" she said sharply. She turned to her companion. "Would you excuse me for a moment, Mr. Baxter? There is something I want to talk to Lord Emsworth about."

She drew the pallid peer aside, and spoke with sharp rebuke.

"Just like a stuck pig!"

"Eh?" said Lord Emsworth. His mind had been wandering, as it so often did. The magic word brought it back. "Pigs? What about pigs?"

"I was saying that you were looking like a stuck pig. You might at least have asked Mr. Baxter how he was."

"I could see how he was. What's he doing here?"

"I told you what he was doing here."

"But how does he come to be touring England on motor bicycles? I thought he was working for an American fellow named something or other."

"He has left Mr. Jevons."

"What!"

"Yes. Mr. Jevons had to return to America, and Mr. Baxter did not want to leave England."

Lord Emsworth reeled. Jevons had been his sheet anchor. He had never met that genial Chicagoan, but he had always thought kindly and gratefully of him, as one does of some great doctor who has succeeded in insulating and confining a disease germ.

"You mean the chap's out of a job?" he cried aghast.

"Yes. And it could not have happened at a more fortunate time, because something has got to be done about George."

"Who's George?"

"You have a grandson of that name," explained Lady Constance with the sweet, frozen patience which she so often used when conversing with her brother. "Your heir, Bosham, if you recollect, has two sons, James and George. George, the younger, is spending his summer holidays here. You may have noticed him about. A boy of twelve with auburn hair and freckles."

"Oh, George? You mean George? Yes, I know George. He's my grandson. What about him?"

"He is completely out of hand. Only yesterday he broke another window with that air gun of his."

"He needs a mother's care?" Lord Emsworth was vague, but he had an idea that that was the right thing to say.

"He needs a tutor's care, and I am glad to say that Mr. Baxter has very kindly consented to accept the position."

"What!"

"Yes. It is all settled. His things are at the Emsworth Arms, and I am sending down for them."

Lord Emsworth sought feverishly for arguments which would quash this frightful scheme.

"But he can't be a tutor if he's galumphing all over England on a motor bicycle."

"I had not overlooked that point. He will stop galumphing over England on a motor bicycle."

"But — "

"It will be a wonderful solution of a problem which was becoming more difficult every day. Mr. Baxter will keep George in order. He is so firm."

She turned away, and Lord Emsworth resumed his progress towards the library.

It was a black moment for the ninth Earl. His worst fears had been realised. He knew just what all this meant. On one of his rare visits to London he had once heard an extraordinarily vivid phrase which had made a deep impression upon him. He had been taking his after-luncheon coffee at the Senior Conservative Club, and some fellows in an adjoining nest of armchairs had started a political discussion, and one of them had said about something or other that, mark his words, it was the "thin end of the wedge." He recognised what was happening now as the "thin end of the wedge." From Baxter as a temporary tutor to Baxter as a permanent secretary would, he felt, be so short a step that the contemplation of it chilled him to the bone.

A shortsighted man whose pince-nez have gone astray at the very moment when vultures are gnawing at his bosom seldom guides his steps carefully. Anyone watching Lord Emsworth totter blindly across the terrace would have foreseen that he would shortly collide with something, the only point open to speculation being with what he would collide.

28

This proved to be a small boy with ginger hair and freckles who emerged abruptly from the shrubbery carrying an air gun.

"Coo!" said the small boy. "Sorry, Grandpapa."

Lord Emsworth recovered his pince-nez and, having adjusted them on the old spot, glared balefully.

"George! Why the deuce don't you look where you're going?"

"Sorry, Grandpapa."

"You might have injured me severely."

"Sorry, Grandpapa."

"Be more careful another time."

"Okay, big boy."

"And don't call me 'big boy.'"

"Right ho, Grandpapa. I say," said George, shelving the topic, "who's the bird talking to Aunt Connie?"

He pointed — a vulgarism which a good tutor would have corrected — and Lord Emsworth, following the finger, winced as his eye rested once more upon Rupert Baxter. The secretary — already Lord Emsworth had mentally abandoned the qualifying "ex" — was gazing out over the rolling parkland, and it seemed to his lordship that his gaze was proprietorial. Rupert Baxter, flashing his spectacle over the grounds of Blandings Castle, wore — or so it appeared to Lord Emsworth — the smug air of some ruthless monarch of old surveying conquered territory.

"That is Mr. Baxter," he replied.

"Looks a bit of a— —," said George critically.

The expression was new to Lord Emsworth, but he recognized it at once as the ideal description of Rupert Baxter. His heart warmed to the little fellow, and he might quite easily at this moment have given him sixpence.

"Do you think so?" he said lovingly.

"What's he doing here?"

Lord Emsworth felt a pang. It seemed brutal to dash the sunshine from the life of this admirable boy. Yet somebody had to tell him.

"He is going to be your tutor."

"Tutor?"

The word was a cry of agony forced from the depths of the boy's soul. A stunned sense that all the fundamental decencies of life were being outraged had swept over George. His voice was thick with emotion.

"Tutor?" he cried. *"Tew*-tor? Ter-YEW-tor? In the middle of the summer holidays? What have I got to have a tutor for in the middle of the summer holidays? I do call this a bit off. I mean, in the middle of the summer holidays. Why do I want a tutor? I mean to say, in the middle of . . ."

He would have spoken at greater length, for he had much to say on the subject, but at this point Lady Constance's voice, musical but imperious, interrupted his flow of speech.

"Gee-orge."

"Coo! Right in the middle — "

"Come here, George. I want you to meet Mr. Baxter."

"Coo!" muttered the stricken child again and, frowning darkly, slouched across the terrace. Lord Emsworth proceeded to the library, a tender pity in his heart for this boy who by his crisp summing up of Rupert Baxter had revealed himself so kindred a spirit. He knew just how George felt. It was not always easy to get anything into Lord Emsworth's head, but he had grasped the substance of his grandson's complaint unerringly. George, about to have a tutor in the middle of the summer holidays, did not want one.

Sighing a little, Lord Emsworth reached the library and found his book.

There were not many books which at a time like this could have diverted Lord Emsworth's mind from what weighed upon it, but this one did. It was Whiffle on *The Care of the Pig* and, buried in its pages, he forgot everything. The chapter he was reading was that noble one about swill and bran mash, and it took him completely out of the world, so much so that when some twenty minutes later the door suddenly burst open it was as if a bomb had been exploded under his nose. He dropped Whiffle and sat panting. Then, although his pince-nez had followed routine by flying off, he was able by some subtle instinct to sense that the intruder was his sister Constance, and an observation beginning with the words "Good God, Connie!" had begun to leave his lips, when she cut in short.

"Clarence," she said, and it was plain that her nervous system, like his, was much shaken, "the most dreadful thing has happened!"

"Eh?"

"That man is here."

"What man?"

"That man of Jane's. The man I told you about."

"What man did you tell me about?"

Lady Constance seated herself. She would have preferred to have been able to do without tedious explanations, but long association with her brother had taught her that his was a memory that had to be refreshed. She embarked, accordingly, on these explanations, speaking wearily, like a schoolmistress to one of the duller members of her class.

"The man I told you about — certainly not less than a hundred times — was a man Jane met in the spring, when she went to stay with her friends, the Leighs, in Devonshire. She had a silly flirtation with him, which of course she insisted on magnifying into a great romance. She kept saying they were engaged. And he hasn't a penny. Nor prospects. Nor, so I gathered from Jane, a position."

Lord Emsworth interrupted at this point to put a question.

"Who," he asked courteously, "is Jane?"

Lady Constance quivered a little.

"Oh, Clarence! Your niece Jane."

"Oh, my *niece* Jane? Ah! Yes. Yes, of course. My niece Jane. Yes, of course, to be sure. My — "

"Clarence, please! For pity's sake! Do stop doddering and listen to me. For once in your life I want you to be firm."

"Be what?"

"Firm. Put your foot down."

"How do you mean?"

"About Jane. I had been hoping that she had gotten over this ridiculous infatuation — she has seemed perfectly happy and contented all this time — but no. Apparently they have been corresponding regularly, and now the man is here."

"Here?"

"Yes."

"Where?" asked Lord Emsworth, gazing in an interested manner about the room.

"He arrived last night and is staying in the village. I found out by the merest accident. I happened to ask George if he had seen Jane, because I wanted Mr. Baxter to meet her, and he said he had met her going towards the lake. So I went down to the lake, and there I discovered her with a young man in a tweed coat and flannel knickerbockers. They were kissing one another in the summerhouse."

Lord Emsworth clicked his tongue.

"Ought to have been out in the sunshine," he said disapprovingly.

Lady Constance raised her foot quickly, but instead of kicking her brother on the shin merely tapped the carpet with it. Blood will tell.

"Jane was defiant. I think she must be off her head. She insisted that she was going to marry this man. And, as I say, not only has he not a penny, but he is apparently out of work."

"What sort of work does he do?"

"I gather that he has been a land agent on an estate in Devonshire."

"It all comes back to me," said Lord Emsworth. "I remember now. This must be the man Jane was speaking to me about yesterday. Of course, yes. She asked me to give him Simmons' job. Simmons is retiring next month. Good fellow," said Lord Emsworth sentimentally. "Been here for years and years. I shall be sorry to lose him. Bless my soul, it won't seem like the same place without old Simmons. Still," he said, brightening, for he was a man who could make the best of things, "no doubt this new chap will turn out all right. Jane seems to think highly of him."

Lady Constance had risen slowly from her chair. There was incredulous horror on her face.

"Clarence! You are not telling me that you have promised this man Simmons' place?"

"Eh? Yes, I have. Why not?"

"Why not! Do you realize that directly he gets it he will marry Jane?"

"Well, why shouldn't he? Very nice girl. Probably make him a good wife."

Lady Constance struggled with her feelings for a space.

"Clarence," she said, "I am going out now to find Jane. I shall tell her that you have thought it over and changed your mind."

"What about?"

"Giving this man Simmons' place."

"But I haven't."

"Yes, you have."

And so, Lord Emsworth discovered as he met her eye, he had. It often happened that way after he and Connie had talked a thing over. But he was not pleased about it.

"But, Connie, dash it all — "

"We will not discuss it any more, Clarence."

Her eye played upon him. Then she moved to the door and was gone.

Alone at last, Lord Emsworth took up his Whiffle on *The Care of the Pig* in the hope that it might, as had happened before, bring calm to the troubled spirit. It did, and he was absorbed in it when the door opened once more.

His niece Jane stood on the threshold.

Lord Emsworth's niece Jane was the third prettiest girl in Shropshire. In her general appearance she resembled a dewy rose, and it might have been thought that Lord Emsworth, who yielded to none in his appreciation of roses, would have felt his heart leap up at the sight of her.

This was not the case. His heart did leap, but not up. He was a man with certain definite views about roses. He preferred them without quite such tight lips and determined chins. And he did not like them to look at him as if he were something slimy and horrible which they had found under a flat stone.

The wretched man was now fully conscious of his position. Under the magic spell of Whiffle he had been able to thrust from his mind for awhile the thought of what Jane was going to say when she heard the bad news; but now, as she started to advance slowly into the room in that sinister, purposeful way characteristic of so many of his female relations, he realized what he was in for, and his soul shrank into itself like a salted snail.

Jane, he could not but remember, was the daughter of his sister Charlotte, and many good judges considered Lady Charlotte a tougher egg even than Lady Constance or her younger sister, Lady Julia. He still quivered at some of the things Charlotte had said to him in her time; and, eyeing Jane apprehensively, he saw no reason for supposing that she had not inherited quite a good deal of the maternal fire.

The girl came straight to the point. Her mother, Lord Emsworth recalled, had always done the same.

"I should like an explanation, Uncle Clarence."

Lord Emsworth cleared his throat unhappily.

"Explanation, my dear?"

"Explanation was what I said."

"Oh, explanation? Ah, yes. Er — what about?"

"You know jolly well what about. That agent job. Aunt Constance says you've changed your mind. Have you?"

"Er . . . Ah . . . Well . . ."

"Have you?"

"Ah . . . Well . . . Er . . ."

"Have you?"

34

"Well . . . Er . . . Ah . . . Yes."

"Worm!" said Jane. "Miserable, crawling, cringing, gelatine-backboned worm!"

Lord Emsworth, though he had been expecting something along these lines, quivered as if he had been harpooned.

"That," he said, attempting a dignity which he was far from feeling, "is not a very nice thing to say. . . ."

"If you only knew the things I would like to say! I'm holding myself in. So you've changed your mind, have you? Ha! Does a sacred promise mean nothing to you, Uncle Clarence? Does a girl's whole life's happiness mean nothing to you? I never would have believed that you could have been such a blighter."

"I am not a blighter."

"Yes, you are. You're a life blighter. You're trying to blight my life. Well, you aren't going to do it. Whatever happens, I mean to marry George."

Lord Emsworth was genuinely surprised.

"Marry George? But Connie told me you were in love with this fellow you met in Devonshire."

"His name is George Abercrombie."

"Oh, ah?" said Lord Emsworth, enlightened. "Bless my soul, I thought you meant my grandson George, and it puzzled me. Because you couldn't marry him, of course. He's your brother or cousin or something. Besides, he's too young for you. What would George be? Ten? Eleven?"

He broke off. A reproachful look had hit him like a shell.

"Uncle Clarence!"

"My dear?"

"Is this a time for drivelling?"

"My dear!"

"Well, is it? Look in your heart and ask yourself. Here I am, with everybody spitting on their hands and dashing about trying to ruin my life's whole happiness, and instead of being kind and understanding and sympathetic you start talking rot about young George."

"I was only saying —"

"I heard what you were saying, and it made me sick. You really must be the most callous man that ever lived. I can't understand you, of all people, behaving like this, Uncle Clarence. I always thought you were fond of me."

"I am fond of you."

"It doesn't look like it. Flinging yourself into this foul conspiracy to wreck my life."

Lord Emsworth remembered a good one.

"I have your best interests at heart, my dear."

It did not go very well. A distinct sheet of flame shot from the girl's eyes.

"What do you mean, my best interests? The way Aunt Constance talks, and the way you are backing her up, anyone would think that George was someone in a straw hat and a scarlet cummerbund that I'd picked up on the pier at Blackpool. The Abercrombies are one of the oldest families in Devonshire. They date back to the Conquest, and they practically ran the Crusades. When your ancestors were staying at home on the plea of war work of national importance and wangling jobs at the base, the Abercrombies were out fighting the paynim."

"I was at school with a boy named Abercrombie," said Lord Emsworth musingly.

"I hope he kicked you. No, no, I don't mean that. I'm sorry. The one thing I'm trying to do is to keep this little talk free of — what's the word?"

Lord Emsworth said he did not know.

"Acrimony. I want to be calm and cool and sensible. Honestly, Uncle Clarence, you would love George. You'll be a sap if you give him the bird without seeing him. He's the most wonderful man on earth. He got into the last eight at Wimbledon this year."

"Did he, indeed? Last eight what?"

"And there isn't anything he doesn't know about running an estate. The very first thing he said when he came into the park was that a lot of the timber wanted seeing to badly."

"Blast his impertinence," said Lord Emsworth warmly. "My timber is in excellent condition."

"Not if George says it isn't. George knows timber."

"So do I know timber."

"Not so well as George does. But never mind about that. Let's get back to this loathsome plot to ruin my life's whole happiness. Why can't you be a sport, Uncle Clarence, and stand up for me? Can't you understand what this means to me? Weren't you ever in love?"

"Certainly I was in love. Dozens of times. I'll tell you a very funny story — "

"I don't want to hear funny stories."

"No, no. Quite. Exactly."

"All I want is to hear you saying that you will give George Mr. Simmons' job, so that we can get married."

"But your aunt seems to feel so strongly — "

"I know what she feels strongly. She wants me to marry that ass Roegate."

"Does she?"

"Yes, and I'm not going to. You can tell her from me that I wouldn't marry Bertie Roegate if he were the only man in the world — "

"There's a song of that name," said Lord Emsworth, interested. "They sang it during the war. No, it wasn't 'man.' It was 'girl.' If you were the only . . . How did it go? Ah, yes. 'If you were the only girl in the world and I was the only boy' . . ."

"Uncle Clarence!"

"My dear?"

"Please don't sing. You're not in the taproom of the Emsworth Arms now."

"I have never been in the taproom of the Emsworth Arms."

"Or at a smoking concert. Really, you seem to have the most extraordinary idea of the sort of attitude that's fitting when you're talking to a girl whose life's happiness everybody is sprinting about trying to ruin. First you talk rot about young George, then you start trying to tell funny stories, and now you sing comic songs."

"It wasn't a comic song."

"It was, the way you sang it. Well?"

"Eh?"

"Have you decided what you are going to do about this?"

"About what?"

The girl was silent for a moment, during which moment she looked so like her mother that Lord Emsworth shuddered.

"Uncle Clarence," she said in a low, trembling voice, "you are not going to pretend that you don't know what we've been talking about all this time? Are you or are you not going to give George that job?"

"Well — "

"Well?"

"Well — "

"We can't stay here forever, saying 'well' at one another. Are you or are you not?"

"My dear, I don't see how I can. Your aunt seems to feel so very strongly . . ."

He spoke mumblingly, avoiding his companion's eye, and he had paused, searching for words, when from the drive outside there arose a sudden babble of noise. Raised voices were proceeding from the great open spaces. He recognised his sister Constance's penetrating soprano, and mingling with it his grandson George's treble "coo." Competing with both, there came the throaty baritone of Rupert Baxter. Delighted with the opportunity of changing the subject, he hurried to the window.

"Bless my soul! What's all that?"

The battle, whatever it may have been about, had apparently rolled away in some unknown direction, for he could see nothing from the window but Rupert Baxter who was smoking a cigarette in what seemed a rather overwrought manner. He turned back, and with infinite relief discovered that he was alone. His niece had disappeared. He took up Whiffle on *The Care of the Pig* and had just started to savour once more the perfect prose of that chapter about swill and bran mash, when the door opened. Jane was back. She stood on the threshold, eyeing her uncle coldly.

"Reading, Uncle Clarence?"

"Eh? Oh, ah, yes. I was just glancing at Whiffle on *The Care of the Pig!*"

"So you actually have the heart to read at a time like this? Well, well! Do you ever read Western novels, Uncle Clarence?"

"Eh? Western novels? No. No, never."

"I'm sorry. I was reading one the other day, and I hoped that you might be able to explain something that puzzled me. What one cowboy said to the other cowboy."

"Oh yes?"

"This cowboy — the first cowboy — said to the other cowboy — the second cowboy — 'Gol dern ye, Hank Spivis, for a sneaking, ornery, low-down, double-crossing, hornswoggling skunk.' Can you tell me what a sneaking, ornery, low-down, double-crossing, hornswoggling skunk is, Uncle Clarence?"

"I'm afraid I can't, my dear."

"I thought you might know."

"No."

"Oh."

She passed from the room, and Lord Emsworth resumed his Whiffle.

But it was not long before the volume was resting on his knee while he stared before him with a sombre gaze. He was reviewing the recent scene and wishing that he had come better out of it. He was a vague man, but not so vague as to be unaware that he might have shown up in a more heroic light.

How long he sat brooding, he could not have said. Some little time, undoubtedly, for the shadows on the terrace had, he observed as he glanced out of the window, lengthened quite a good deal since he had seen them last. He was about to rise and seek consolation from a ramble among the flowers in the garden below, when the door opened — it seemed to Lord Emsworth, who was now feeling a little morbid, that that blasted door had never stopped opening since he had come to the library to be alone — and Beach, the butler, entered.

He was carrying an air gun in one hand and in the other a silver salver with a box of ammunition on it.

Beach was a man who invested all his actions with something of the impressiveness of a high priest conducting an intricate service at some romantic altar. It is not easy to be impressive when you are carrying an air gun in one hand and a silver salver with a box of ammunition on it in the other, but Beach managed it. Many butlers in such a position would have looked like sportsmen setting out for a day with the birds, but Beach still looked like a high priest. He advanced to the table at Lord Emsworth's side, and laid his cargo upon it as if the gun and the box of ammunition had been a smoked offering, and his lordship a tribal god.

Lord Emsworth eyed his faithful servitor sourly. His manner was that of a tribal god who considers the smoked offering not up to sample.

"What the devil's all this?"

"It is an air gun, m'lord."

"I can see that, dash it! What are you bringing it here for?"

"Her ladyship instructed me to convey it to your lordship — I gathered for safekeeping, m'lord. The weapon was until recently the property of Master George."

"Why the deuce are they taking his air gun away from the poor boy?" demanded Lord Emsworth hotly. Ever since the lad had called Rupert Baxter a — — he had been feeling a strong affection for his grandson.

"Her ladyship did not confide in me on that point, m'lord. I was merely instructed to convey the weapon to your lordship."

At this moment, Lady Constance came sailing in to throw light on the mystery.

"Ah, I see Beach has brought it to you. I want you to lock that gun up somewhere, Clarence. George is not to be allowed to have it any more."

"Why not?"

"Because he is not to be trusted with it. Do you know what happened? He shot Mr. Baxter!"

"What!"

"Yes. Out on the drive just now. I noticed that the boy's manner was sullen when I introduced him to Mr. Baxter and said that he was going to be his tutor. He disappeared into the shrubbery, and just now, as Mr. Baxter was standing on the drive, George shot him from behind a bush."

"Good!" cried Lord Emsworth, then prudently added the word "gracious."

There was a pause. Lord Emsworth took up the gun and handled it curiously.

"Bang!" he said, pointing it at a bust of Aristotle which stood on a bracket by the bookshelves.

"Please don't wave the thing about like that, Clarence. It may be loaded."

"Not if George has just shot Baxter with it. No," said Lord Emsworth, pulling the trigger, "it's not loaded." He mused awhile. An odd, nostalgic feeling was creeping over him. Far-off memories of his hot boyhood had begun to stir within him. "Bless my soul," he said. "I haven't had one of these things in my hand since I was a child. Did you ever have one of these things, Beach?"

"Yes, m'lord, when a small lad."

"Bless my soul, I remember my sister Julia borrowing mine to shoot her governess. You remember Julia shot the governess, Connie?"

"Don't be absurd, Clarence."

"It's not absurd. She did shoot her. Fortunately women wore bustles in those days. Beach, don't you remember my sister Julia shooting the governess?"

"The incident would no doubt have occurred before my arrival at the castle, m'lord."

"That will do, Beach," said Lady Constance. "I do wish, Clarence," she continued as the door closed, "that you would not say that sort of thing in front of Beach."

"Julia did shoot the governess."

"If she did, there is no need to make your butler a confidant."

"Now, what was that governess's name? I have an idea it began with — "

"Never mind what her name was or what it began with. Tell me about Jane. I saw her coming out of the library. Had you been speaking to her?"

"Yes. Oh yes. I spoke to her."

"I hope you were firm."

"Oh, very firm. I said, 'Jane . . .' But listen, Connie, damn it, aren't we being a little hard on the girl? One doesn't want to ruin her whole life's happiness, dash it."

"I knew she would get round you. But you are not to give way an inch."

"But this fellow seems to be a most suitable fellow. One of the Abercrombies and all that. Did well in the Crusades."

"I am not going to have my niece throwing herself away on a man without a penny."

"She isn't going to marry Roegate, you know. Nothing will induce her. She said she wouldn't marry Roegate if she were the only girl in the world and he was the only boy."

"I don't care what she said. And I don't want to discuss the matter any longer. I am now going to send George in, for you to give him a good talking-to."

"I haven't time."

"You have time."

"I haven't. I'm going to look at my flowers."

"You are not. You are going to talk to George. I want you to make him see quite clearly what a wicked thing he has done. Mr. Baxter was furious."

"It all comes back to me," cried Lord Emsworth. "Mapleton!"

"What *are* you talking about?"

"Her name was Mapleton. Julia's governess."

"Do stop about Julia's governess. Will you talk to George?"

"Oh, all right, all right."

"Good. I'll go and send him to you."

And presently George entered. For a boy who has just stained the escutcheon of a proud family by shooting tutors with air guns, he seemed remarkably cheerful. His manner was that of one getting together with an old crony for a cosy chat.

"Hullo, Grandpapa," he said breezily.

"Hullo, my boy," replied Lord Emsworth with equal affability.

"Aunt Connie said you wanted to see me."

"Eh? Ah! Oh! Yes." Lord Emsworth pulled himself together. "Yes, that's right. Yes, to be sure. Certainly I want to see you. What's all this, my boy, eh? Eh, what? What's all this?"

"What's all what, Grandpapa?"

"Shooting people and all that sort of thing. Shooting Baxter and all that sort of thing. Mustn't do that, you know. Can't have that. It's very wrong and — er — very dangerous to shoot at people with a dashed great gun. Don't you know that, hey? Might put their eye out, dash it."

"Oh, I couldn't have hit him in the eye, Grandpapa. His back was turned and he was bending over, tying his shoelace."

Lord Emsworth started.

"What! Did you get Baxter in the seat of the trousers?"

"Yes, Grandpapa."

"Ha, ha . . . I mean, disgraceful . . . I — er — I expect he jumped?"

"Oh yes, Grandpapa. He jumped like billy-o."

The Crime Wave at Blandings 43

"Did he, indeed? How this reminds me of Julia's governess. Your aunt Julia once shot her governess under precisely similar conditions. She was tying her shoelace."

"Cool! Did *she* jump?"

"She certainly did, my boy."

"Ha, ha!"

"Ha, ha!"

"Ha, ha!"

"Ha, h — Ah . . . Er — well, just so," said Lord Emsworth, a belated doubt assailing him as to whether this was quite the tone. "Well, George, I shall of course impound this — er — instrument."

"Right ho, Grandpapa," said George, with the easy amiability of a boy conscious of having two catapults in his drawer upstairs.

"Can't have you going about the place shooting people."

"Okay, chief."

Lord Emsworth fondled the gun. That nostalgic feeling was growing.

"Do you know, young man, I used to have one of these things when I was a boy."

"Cool! Were guns invented then?"

"Yes, I had one when I was your age."

"Ever hit anything, Grandpapa?"

Lord Emsworth drew himself up a little haughtily.

"Certainly I did. I hit all sorts of things. Rats and things. I had a very accurate aim. But now I wouldn't even know how to load the dashed affair."

"This is how you load it, Grandpapa. You open it like this, and shove the slug in here, and snap it together again like that and there you are."

"Indeed? Really? I see. Yes. Yes, of course, I remember now."

"You can't kill anything much with it," said George, with a wistfulness which betrayed an aspiration to higher things. "Still, it's awfully useful for tickling up cows."

"And Baxter."

"Yes."

"Ha, ha!"

"Ha, ha!"

Once more, Lord Emsworth forced himself to concentrate on the right tone.

"We mustn't laugh about it, my boy. It's no joking matter. It's very wrong to shoot Mr. Baxter."

"But he's a — —"

"He is a — —" agreed Lord Emsworth, always fair-minded. "Nevertheless . . . remember, he is your tutor."

"Well, I don't see why I've got to have a tutor right in the middle of the summer holidays. I sweat like the dickens all through the term at school," said George, his voice vibrant with self-pity, "and then plumb spang in the middle of the holidays they slosh a tutor on me. I call it a bit thick."

Lord Emsworth might have told the little fellow that thicker things than that were going on in Blandings Castle, but he refrained. He dismissed him with a kindly, sympathetic smile and resumed his fondling of the air gun.

Like so many men advancing into the sere and yellow of life, Lord Emsworth had an eccentric memory. It was not to be trusted an inch as far as the events of yesterday or the day before were concerned. Even in the small matter of assisting him to find a hat which he had laid down somewhere five minutes ago, it was nearly always useless. But by way of compensation for this it was a perfect encyclopaedia on the remote past. It rendered his boyhood an open book to him.

Lord Emsworth mused on his boyhood. Happy days, happy days. He could recall the exact uncle who had given him the weapon, so similar to this one, with which Julia had shot her governess. He could recall brave, windswept mornings when he had gone prowling through the stable yard in the hope of getting a rat — and many a fine head had he secured. Odd that the passage of time should remove the desire to go and pop at things with an air gun. . . .

Or did it?

With a curious thrill that set his pince-nez rocking gently on his nose, Lord Emsworth suddenly became aware that it did not. All that the passage of time did was to remove the desire to pop temporarily — say for forty years or so. Dormant for a short while — well, call it fifty years — that desire, he perceived, still lurked unquenched. Little by little it began to stir within him now. Slowly but surely, as he sat there fondling the gun, he was once more becoming a potential popper.

At this point, the gun suddenly went off and broke the bust of Aristotle.

It was enough. The old killer instinct had awakened. Reloading with the swift efficiency of some hunter of the woods, Lord Emsworth went to the window. He was a little uncertain as to what he intended to do when he got there, except that he had a very clear determination to loose off at something. There flitted into his mind what his grandson George had said about tickling up cows, and this served to some extent to crystallise his aims. True, cows were not plentiful on the terrace of Blandings Castle. Still, one might have wandered there. You never knew with cows.

There were no cows. Only Rupert Baxter. The ex-secretary was in the act of throwing away a cigarette.

Most men are careless in the matter of throwing away cigarettes. The world is their ash tray. But Rupert Baxter had a tidy soul. He allowed the thing to fall to the ground like any ordinary young man, it is true, but immediately he had done so his better self awakened. He stooped to pick up the object that disfigured the smooth, flagged stones, and the invitation of that beckoning trousers' seat would have been too powerful for a stronger man than Lord Emsworth to resist.

He pulled the trigger, and Rupert Baxter sprang into the air with a sharp cry. Lord Emsworth reseated himself and took up Whiffle on *The Care of the Pig*.

Everybody is interested nowadays in the psychology of the criminal. The chronicler, therefore, feels that he runs no risk of losing his grip on the reader if he pauses at this point to examine and analyse the workings of Lord Emsworth's mind after the penetration of the black act which has just been recorded.

At first, then, all that he felt as he sat turning the pages of his Whiffle was a sort of soft, warm glow, a kind of tremulous joy such as he might have experienced if he had just been receiving the thanks of the nation for some great public service.

It was not merely the fact that he had caused his late employee to skip like the high hills that induced this glow. What pleased him so particularly was that it had been such a magnificent shot. He was a sensitive man, and though in his conversation with his grandson George he had tried to wear the mask, he had not been completely able to hide his annoyance at the boy's careless assumption that in his air-gun days he had been an indifferent marksman.

"Did you ever hit anything, Grandpapa?" Boys say these things with no wish to wound, but nevertheless they pierce the armour. "Did you ever hit anything, Grandpapa?" Forsooth! He would have liked to see George stop putting finger to trigger for forty-seven years, and then, first crack out of the box, pick off a medium-sized secretary at a distance like that! In rather a bad light, too.

But after he had sat for a while, silently glowing, his mood underwent a change. A gunman's complacency after getting his man can never remain for long an unmixed complacency. Sooner or later there creeps in the thought of Retribution. It did with Lord Emsworth. Quite suddenly, whispering in his ear, he heard the voice of Conscience say:

"What if your sister Constance learns of this?"

A moment before this voice spoke, Lord Emsworth had been smirking. He now congealed, and the smile passed from his lips like breath off a razor blade, to be succeeded by a tense look of anxiety and alarm.

Nor was this alarm unjustified. When he reflected how scathing and terrible his sister Constance could be when he committed even so venial a misdemeanour as coming down to dinner with a brass paper fastener in his shirt front instead of the more conventional stud, his imagination boggled at the thought of what she would do in a case like this. He was appalled. Whiffle on *The Care of the Pig* fell from his nerveless hand, and he sat looking like a dying duck. And Lady Constance, who now entered, noted the expression and was curious as to its cause.

"What is the matter, Clarence?"

"Matter?"

"Why are you looking like a dying duck?"

"I am not looking like a dying duck," retorted Lord Emsworth with what spirit he could muster.

"Well," said Lady Constance, waiving the point, "have you spoken to George?"

"Certainly. Yes, of course I've spoken to George. He was in here just now and I — er — spoke to him."

"What did you say?"

"I said" — Lord Emsworth wanted to make this very clear — "I said that I wouldn't even know how to load one of those things."

"Didn't you give him a good talking-to?"

"Of course I did. A very good talking-to. I said, 'Er — George, you know how to load those things and I don't, but that's no reason why you should go about shooting Baxter.'"

"Was that all you said?"

"No. That was just how I began. I — "

Lord Emsworth paused. He could not have finished the sentence if large rewards had been offered to him to do so. For, as he spoke, Rupert Baxter appeared in the doorway, and he shrank back in his chair like some Big Shot cornered by G-men.

The secretary came forward limping slightly. His eyes behind their spectacles were wild and his manner emotional. Lady Constance gazed at him wonderingly.

"Is something the matter, Mr. Baxter?"

"Matter?" Rupert Baxter's voice was taut and he quivered in every limb. He had lost his customary suavity and was plainly in no frame of mind to mince his words. "Matter? Do you know what has happened? That infernal boy has shot me *again!*"

"What!"

"Only a few minutes ago. Out on the terrace."

Lord Emsworth shook off his palsy.

"I expect you imagined it," he said.

"Imagined it!" Rupert Baxter shook from spectacles to shoes. "I tell you I was on the terrace, stooping to pick up my cigarette, when something hit me on the . . . something hit me."

"Probably a wasp," said Lord Emsworth. "They are very plentiful this year. I wonder," he said chattily, "if either of you are aware that wasps serve a very useful purpose. They keep down the leatherjackets, which, as you know, inflict serious injury upon — "

Lady Constance's concern became mixed with perplexity.

"But it could not have been George, Mr. Baxter. The moment you told me of what he had done, I confiscated his air gun. Look, there it is on the table now."

"Right there on the table," said Lord Emsworth, pointing helpfully. "If you come over here, you can see it clearly. Must have been a wasp."

"You have not left the room, Clarence?"

"No. Been here all the time."

"Then it would have been impossible for George to have shot you, Mr. Baxter."

"Quite," said Lord Emsworth. "A wasp, undoubtedly. Unless, as I say, you imagined the whole thing."

The secretary stiffened.

"I am not subject to hallucinations, Lord Emsworth."

"But you are, my dear fellow. I expect it comes from exerting your brain too much. You're always getting them."

"Clarence!"

"Well, he is. You know that as well as I do. Look at that time he went grubbing about in a lot of flowerpots because he thought you had put your necklace there."

"I did not —"

"You did, my dear fellow. I daresay you've forgotten it, but you did. And then, for some reason best known to yourself, you threw the flowerpots at me through my bedroom window."

Baxter turned to Lady Constance, flushing darkly. The episode to which his former employer had alluded was one of which he never cared to be reminded.

"Lord Emsworth is referring to the occasion when your diamond necklace was stolen, Lady Constance. I was led to believe that the thief had hidden it in a flowerpot."

"Of course, Mr. Baxter."

"Well, have it your own way," said Lord Emsworth agreeably. "But bless my soul, I shall never forget waking up and finding all those flowerpots pouring in through the window, and then looking out and seeing Baxter on the lawn in lemon-coloured pajamas with a wild glare in his —"

"Clarence!"

"Oh, all right. I merely mentioned it. Hallucinations — he gets them all the time," he said stoutly, though in an undertone.

Lady Constance was cooing to the secretary like a mother to her child.

"It really is impossible that George should have done this, Mr. Baxter. The gun has never left this —"

She broke off. Her handsome face seemed to turn suddenly to stone. When she spoke again the coo had gone out of her voice and it had become metallic.

"Clarence!"

"My dear?"

Lady Constance drew in her breath sharply.

"Mr. Baxter, I wonder if you would mind leaving us for a moment. I wish to speak to Lord Emsworth."

The closing of the door was followed by a silence, followed in its turn by an odd, whining noise like gas escaping from a pipe. It was Lord Emsworth trying to hum carelessly.

"Clarence!"

"Yes? Yes, my dear?"

The stoniness of Lady Constance's expression had become more marked with each succeeding moment. What had caused it in the first place was the recollection, coming to her like a flash, that when she had entered this room she had found her brother looking like a dying duck. Honest men, she felt, do not look like dying ducks. The only man whom an impartial observer could possibly mistake for one of these birds *in extremis* is the man with crime upon his soul.

"Clarence, was it you who shot Mr. Baxter?"

Fortunately there had been that in her manner which led Lord Emsworth to expect the question. He was ready for it.

"Me? Who, me? Shoot Baxter? What the deuce would I want to shoot Baxter for?"

"We can go into your motives later. What I am asking you now is — did you?"

"Of course I didn't."

"The gun has not left the room."

"Shoot Baxter, indeed! Never heard anything so dashed absurd in my life."

"And you have been here all the time."

"Well, what of it? Suppose I have? Suppose I had wanted to shoot Baxter? Suppose every fibre in my being had egged me on, dash it, to shoot the feller? How could I have done it, not even knowing how to load the contrivance?"

"You used to know how to load an air gun."

"I used to know a lot of things."

"It's quite easy to load an air gun. I could do it myself."

"Well, I didn't."

"Then how do you account for the fact that Mr. Baxter was shot by an air gun which had never left the room you were in?"

Lord Emsworth raised pleading hands to heaven.

"How do you know he was shot with this air gun? God bless

my soul, the way women jump to conclusions is enough to ... How do you know there wasn't another air gun? How do you know the place isn't bristling with air guns? How do you know Beach hasn't an air gun? Or anybody?"

"I scarcely imagine that Beach would shoot Mr. Baxter."

"How do you know he wouldn't? He used to have an air gun when he was a small lad. He said so. I'd watch the man closely."

"Please don't be ridiculous, Clarence."

"I'm not being half as ridiculous as you are. Saying I shoot people with air guns. Why should I shoot people with air guns? And how do you suppose I could have potted Baxter at that distance?"

"What distance?"

"He was standing on the terrace, wasn't he? He specifically stated that he was standing on the terrace. And I was up here. It would take a most expert marksman to pot the fellow at a distance like that. Who do you think I am? One of those chaps who shoot apples off their sons' heads?"

The reasoning was undeniably specious. It shook Lady Constance. She frowned undecidedly.

"Well, it's very strange that Mr. Baxter should be so convinced that he was shot."

"Nothing strange about it at all. There wouldn't be anything strange if Baxter was convinced that he was a turnip and had been bitten by a white rabbit with pink eyes. You know perfectly well, though you won't admit it, that the fellow's a raving lunatic."

"Clarence!"

"It's no good saying 'Clarence.' The fellow's potty to the core, and always has been. Haven't I seen him on the lawn at five o'clock in the morning in lemon-coloured pajamas, throwing flowerpots in at my window? Pooh! Obviously, the whole thing is the outcome of the man's diseased imagination. Shot, indeed! Never heard such nonsense. And now," said Lord Emsworth, rising firmly, "I'm going out to have a look at my roses. I came to this room to enjoy a little quiet reading and meditation, and ever since I got here there's been a constant stream of people in and out, telling me they're going to marry men named Abercrombie and saying they've been shot and saying I shot them and so on and so forth. . . . Bless my soul, one might as well try to read and meditate in the middle of Piccadilly Circus. Tchah!" said Lord Emsworth, who had now got near enough to the door to feel safe in uttering this unpleasant exclamation. "Tchah!" he said, and adding "Pah!" for good measure made a quick exit.

But even now his troubled spirit was not to know peace. To reach the great outdoors at Blandings Castle, if you start from the library and come down the main staircase, you have to pass through the hall. To the left of this hall there is a small writing room. And outside this writing room Lord Emsworth's niece Jane was standing.

"Yoo-hoo," she cried. "Uncle Clarence."

Lord Emsworth was in no mood for yoo-hooing nieces. George Abercrombie might enjoy chatting with this girl. So might Herbert, Lord Roegate. But he wanted solitude. In the course of the afternoon he had had so much female society thrust upon him, that if Helen of Troy had appeared in the doorway of the writing room and yoo-hooed at him, he would merely have accelerated his pace.

He accelerated it now.

"Can't stop, my dear, can't stop."

"Oh yes you can, old Sure-Shot," said Jane, and Lord Emsworth found that he could. He stopped so abruptly that he nearly dislocated his spine. His jaw had fallen and his pince-nez were dancing on their string like leaves in the wind.

"Two-Gun Thomas—the Marksman of the Prairie—he never misses. Kindly step this way, Uncle Clarence," said Jane. "I would like a word with you."

Lord Emsworth stepped that way. He followed the girl

into the writing room and closed the door carefully behind him.

"You — you didn't see me?" he quavered.

"I certainly did see you," said Jane. "I was an interested eyewitness of the whole thing from start to finish."

Lord Emsworth tottered to a chair and sank into it, staring glassily at his niece. Any Chicago businessman of the modern school would have understood what he was feeling and would have sympathised with him.

The thing that poisons life for gunmen, and sometimes makes them wonder moodily if it is worth while going on, is this tendency of the outside public to butt in at inconvenient moments. Whenever you settle some business dispute with a commercial competitor by means of your submachine gun, it always turns out that there was some officious witness passing at the time, and there you are, with a new problem confronting you.

And Lord Emsworth was in a worse case than his spiritual brother of Chicago would have been, for the latter could always have solved his perplexities by rubbing out the witness. To him this melancholy pleasure was denied. A prominent Shropshire landowner, with a position to keep up in the county, cannot rub out his nieces. All he can do, when they reveal that they have seen him wallowing in crime, is to stare glassily at them.

"I had a front seat for the entire performance," proceeded Jane. "When I left you, I went into the shrubbery to cry my eyes out because of your frightful cruelty and inhumanity. And while I was crying my eyes out, I suddenly saw you creep to the window of the library, with a hideous look of low cunning on your face, and young George's air gun in your hand. And I was just wondering if I couldn't find a stone and bung it at you, because it seemed to me that something along those lines was what you had been asking for from the start, when you raised the gun and I saw that you were taking aim. The next moment there was a shot, a cry, and Baxter weltering in his blood on the terrace. And as I stood there, a thought floated into my mind. It was: What will Aunt Constance have to say about this when I tell her?"

Lord Emsworth emitted a low gurgling sound, like the death rattle of that dying duck to which his sister had compared him.

"You — you aren't going to tell her?"

"Why not?"

An aguelike convulsion shook Lord Emsworth.

"I implore you not to tell her, my dear. You know what she's like. I should never hear the end of it."

"She would give you the devil, you think?"

"I do."

"So do I. And you thoroughly deserve it."

"My dear!"

"Well, don't you? Look at the way you've been behaving. Working like a beaver to ruin my life's happiness."

"I don't want to ruin your life's happiness."

"You don't? Then sit down at this desk and dash off a short letter to George, giving him that job."

"But — "

"What did you say?"

"I only said 'But — ' "

"Don't say it again. What I want from you, Uncle Clarence, is prompt and cheerful service. Are you ready? 'Dear Mr. Abercrombie . . .' "

"I don't know how to spell it," said Lord Emsworth, with the air of a man who has found a way out satisfactory to all parties.

"I'll attend to the spelling. A-b, ab; e-r, er; c-r-o-m, crom; b-i-e, bie. The whole constituting the word 'Abercrombie', which is the name of the man I love. Got it?"

"Yes," said Lord Emsworth sepulchrally, "I've got it."

"Then carry on. 'Dear Mr. Abercrombie. Pursuant' — One p, two u's — spread 'em about a bit — an r, an s, and an ant — 'Pursuant on our recent conversation — ' "

"But I've never spoken to the man in my life."

"It doesn't matter. It's just a form. 'Pursuant on our recent conversation, I have much pleasure in offering you the post of land agent at Blandings Castle, and shall be glad if you will take up your duties immediately. Yours faithfully, Emsworth.' E-m-s-w-o-r-t-h."

Jane took the letter, pressed it lovingly on the blotting pad and placed it in the recesses of her costume. "Fine," she said. "That's that. Thanks most awfully, Uncle Clarence. This has squared you nicely for your recent foul behaviour in trying to ruin my life's happiness. You made a rocky start, but you've come through magnificently at the finish."

Kissing him affectionately, she passed from the room, and Lord Emsworth, slumped in his chair, tried not to look at the vision of his sister Constance which was rising before his eyes. What Connie was going to say when she learned that in defiance of her direct commands he had given this young man . . .

He mused on Lady Constance, and wondered if there were any other men in the world so sister pecked as he. It was weak of him, he knew, to curl up into an apologetic ball when assailed by a mere sister. Most men reserved such craven conduct for their wives. But it had always been so, right back to those boyhood days which he remembered so well. And too late to alter it now, he supposed.

The only consolation he was able to enjoy in this dark hour was the reflection that, though things were bad, they were unquestionably less bad than they might have been. At the least, his fearful secret was safe. That rash moment of recovered boyhood would never now be brought up against him. Connie would never know whose hand it was that had pulled the fatal trigger. She might suspect, but she could never know. Nor could Baxter ever know. Baxter would grow into an old white-haired, spectacled pantaloon, and always this thing would remain an insoluble mystery to him.

Dashed lucky, felt Lord Emsworth, that the fellow had not been listening at the door during the recent conversation.

It was at this moment that a sound behind him caused him

to turn and, having turned, to spring from his chair with a convulsive leap that nearly injured him internally. Over the sill of the open window, like those of a corpse emerging from the tomb to confront its murderer, the head and shoulders of Rupert Baxter were slowly rising. The evening sun fell upon his spectacles, and they seemed to Lord Emsworth to gleam like the eyes of a dragon.

Rupert Baxter had not been listening at the door. There had been no necessity for him to do so. Immediately outside the writing-room window at Blandings Castle there stands a rustic garden seat, and on this he had been sitting from beginning to end of the interview which has just been recorded. If he had been actually in the room, he might have heard a little better, but not much.

When two men stand face to face, one of whom has recently shot the other with an air gun, and the second of whom has just discovered who it was that did it, it is rarely that conversation flows briskly from the start. One senses a certain awkwardness — what the French call *gêne*. In the first half minute of this encounter the only thing that happened in a vocal way was that Lord Emsworth cleared his throat, immediately afterwards becoming silent again. And it is possible that his silence might have prolonged itself for some considerable time had not Baxter made a movement as if about to withdraw. All this while he had been staring at his former employer, his face an open book in which it was easy for the least discerning eye to read a number of disconcerting emotions. He now took a step backwards, and Lord Emsworth's aphasia left him.

"Baxter!"

There was urgent appeal in the ninth Earl's voice. It was not often that he wanted Rupert Baxter to stop and talk to him, but he was most earnestly desirous of detaining him now. He wished to soothe, to apologise, to explain. He was even prepared, should it be necessary, to offer the man his old post of private secretary as the price of his silence.

"Baxter! My dear fellow!"

A high tenor voice, raised almost to A in alto by agony of soul, has a compelling quality which it is difficult even for a man in Rupert Baxter's mental condition to resist. Rupert Baxter had not intended to halt his backward movement, but he did so, and Lord Emsworth, reaching the window and thrusting his head out, was relieved to see that he was still within range of the honeyed word.

"Er — Baxter," he said, "could you spare me a moment?"

The secretary's spectacles flashed coldly.

"You wish to speak to me, Lord Emsworth?"

"That's exactly it," assented his lordship, as if he thought it a very happy way of putting the thing. "Yes, I wish to speak to you." He paused, and cleared his throat again. "Tell me, Baxter — tell me, my dear fellow — were you — er — were you sitting on that seat just now?"

"I was."

"Did you by any chance overhear my niece and myself talking?"

"I did."

"Then I expect — I fancy — perhaps — possibly — no doubt you were surprised at what you heard?"

"I was astounded," said Rupert Baxter, who was not going to be fobbed off with any weak verbs at a moment like this.

Lord Emsworth cleared his throat for the third time.

"I want to tell you all about that," he said.

"Oh?" said Rupert Baxter.

"Yes. I — ah — welcome this opportunity of telling you all about it," said Lord Emsworth, though with less pleasure in his voice than might have been expected from a man welcoming an opportunity of telling somebody all about something. "I fancy that my niece's remarks may — er — possibly have misled you."

"Not at all."

"They may have put you on the wrong track."

"On the contrary."

"But, if I remember correctly, she gave the impression — by what she said — my niece gave the impression by what she said — anybody overhearing what my niece said would have received the impression that I took deliberate aim at you with that gun."

"Precisely."

"She was quite mistaken," said Lord Emsworth warmly. "She had got hold of the wrong end of the stick completely. Girls say such dashed silly things . . . cause a lot of trouble . . . upset people. They ought to be more careful. What actually happened, my dear fellow, was that I was glancing out of the library window . . . with the gun in my hand . . . and without knowing it I must have placed my finger on the trigger, for suddenly, without the slightest warning . . . you could have knocked me down with a feather . . . the dashed thing went off. By accident."

"Indeed?"

"Purely by accident. I should not like you to think that I was aiming at you."

"Indeed?"

"And I should not like you to tell — er — anybody about the unfortunate occurrence in a way that would give her — I mean them — the impression that I aimed at you."

"Indeed?"

Lord Emsworth could not persuade himself that his companion's manner was encouraging. He had a feeling that he was not making headway.

"That's how it was," he said after a pause.

"I see."

"Pure accident. Nobody more surprised than myself."

"I see."

So did Lord Emsworth. He saw that the time had come to

play his last card. It was no moment for shrinking back and counting the cost. He must proceed to that last fearful extremity which he had contemplated.

"Tell me, Baxter," he said, "are you doing anything just now, Baxter?"

"Yes," replied the other with no trace of hesitation. "I am going to look for Lady Constance."

A convulsive gulp prevented Lord Emsworth from speaking for an instant.

"I mean," he quavered, when the spasm had spent itself, "I gathered from my sister that you were at liberty at the moment — that you had left that fellow what's his name — the American fellow — and I was hoping, my dear Baxter," said Lord Emsworth, speaking thickly, as if the words choked him, "that I might be able to persuade you to take up — to resume — in fact, I was going to ask you if you would care to become my secretary again."

He paused and, reaching for his handkerchief, feebly mopped his brow. The dreadful speech was out, and its emergence had left him feeling spent and weak.

"You were?" cried Rupert Baxter.

"I was," said Lord Emsworth hollowly.

A great change for the better had come over Rupert Baxter. It was as if those words had been a magic formula, filling with sweetness and light one who until that moment had been more like a spectacled thundercloud than anything human. He ceased to lower darkly. His air of being on the point of shooting out forked lightning left him. He even went so far as to smile. And if the smile was a smile that made Lord Emsworth feel as if his vital organs were being churned up with an egg whip, that was not his fault. He was trying to smile sunnily.

"Thank you," he said. "I shall be delighted."

Lord Emsworth did not speak.

"I was always happy at the castle."

Lord Emsworth did not speak.

"Thank you very much," said Rupert Baxter. "What a beautiful evening."

He passed from view, and Lord Emsworth examined the evening. As Baxter had said, it was beautiful, but it did not bring the balm which beautiful evenings usually brought to him. A blight seemed to hang over it. The setting sun shone bravely on the formal garden over which he looked, but it was the lengthening shadows rather than the sunshine that impressed themselves upon Lord Emsworth.

His heart was bowed down with weight of woe. Oh, says the poet, what a tangled web we weave when first we practise to deceive, and it was precisely the same, Lord Emsworth realised, when first we practise to shoot air guns. Just one careless, offhand pop at a bending Baxter, and what a harvest, what a retribution! As a result of that single, idle shot he had been compelled to augment his personal staff with a land agent, which would infuriate his sister Constance, and a private secretary, which would make his life once again the inferno it had been in the old, bad Baxter days. He could scarcely have got himself into more trouble if he had gone blazing away with a machine gun.

It was with a slow and distrait shuffle that he eventually took himself from the writing room and proceeded with his interrupted plan on going and sniffing at his roses. And so preoccupied was his mood that Beach, his faithful butler, who came to him after he had been sniffing at them for perhaps half an hour, was obliged to speak twice before he could induce him to remove his nose from a Gloire de Dijon.

"Eh?"

"A note for you, m'lord."

"A note? Who from?"

"Mr. Baxter, m'lord."

If Lord Emsworth had been less careworn, he might have noticed that the butler's voice had not its customary fruity ring. It had a dullness, a lack of tone. It was the voice of a butler who has lost the bluebird. But, being in the depths and so in no frame of mind to analyse the voice production of butlers, he merely took the envelope from its salver and opened it listlessly, wondering what Baxter was sending him notes about.

The communication was so brief that he was enabled to discover this at a glance.

Lord Emsworth,
After what has occurred, I must reconsider my decision to accept the post of secretary which you offered me.
I am leaving the castle immediately.

R. Baxter.

Simply that, and nothing more.

Lord Emsworth stared at the thing. It is not enough to say that he was bewildered. He was nonplussed. If the Gloire de Dijon at which he had recently been sniffing had snapped at his nose and bitten the tip off, he could scarcely have been more taken aback. He could make nothing of this.

As in a dream, he became aware that Beach was speaking.

"Eh?"

"My month's notice, m'lord."

"Your what?"

"My month's notice, m'lord."

"What about it?"

"I was saying that I wish to give my month's notice, m'lord."

A weak irritation at all this chattering came upon Lord Emsworth. Here he was, trying to grapple with this frightful thing which had come upon him, and Beach would insist on weakening his concentration by babbling.

"Yes, yes, yes," he said. "I see. All right. Yes, yes."

"Very good, m'lord."

Left alone, Lord Emsworth faced the facts. He understood now what had happened. The note was no longer mystic. What it meant was that for some reason that trump card of his had proved useless. He had thought to stop Baxter's mouth with bribes, and he had failed. The man had seemed to accept the olive branch, but later there must have come some sharp revulsion of feeling, causing him to change his mind. No doubt a sudden twinge of pain in the wounded area had brought the memory of his wrongs flooding back upon him, so that he found himself preferring vengeance to material prosperity. And now he was going to blow the gaff. Even now the whole facts in the case might have been placed before Lady Constance. And even now, Lord Emsworth felt with a shiver, Connie might be looking for him.

The sight of a female form coming through the rosebushes brought him the sharpest shudder of the day, and for an instant he stood pointing like a dog. But it was not his sister Constance. It was his niece Jane.

Jane was in excellent spirits.

"Hullo, Uncle Clarence," she said. "Having a look at the roses? I've sent that letter off to George, Uncle Clarence. I got the boy who cleans the knives and boots to take it. Nice chap. His name is Cyril."

"Jane," said Lord Emsworth, "a terrible, a ghastly thing has happened. Baxter was outside the window of the writing room when we were talking, and he heard everything."

"Golly! He didn't!"

"He did. Every word. And he means to tell your aunt."

"How do you know?"

"Read this."

Jane took the note.

"H'm," she said, having scanned it. "Well, it looks to me, Uncle Clarence, as if there was only one thing for you to do. You must assert yourself."

"Assert myself?"

"You know what I mean. Get tough. When Aunt Constance comes trying to bully you, stick your elbows out and put your head on one side and talk back at her out of the corner of your mouth."

"But what shall I say?"

"Good heavens, there are a hundred things you can say. 'Oh yeah?' 'Is zat so?' 'Hey, just a minute,' 'Listen, baby,' 'Scram' . . ."

" 'Scram'?"

"It means 'Get the hell outa here.' "

"But I can't tell Connie to get the hell outa here."

"Why not? Aren't you master in your own house?"

"No," said Lord Emsworth.

Jane reflected.

"Then I'll tell you what to do. Deny the whole thing."

"Could I, do you think?"

"Of course you could. And then Aunt Constance will ask me, and I'll deny the whole thing. Categorically. We'll both deny it categorically. She'll have to believe us. We'll be two to one. Don't you worry, Uncle Clarence. Everything'll be all right."

She spoke with the easy optimism of youth, and when she passed on a few moments later seemed to be feeling that she was leaving an uncle with his mind at rest. Lord Emsworth could hear her singing a gay song.

He felt no disposition to join in the chorus. He could not bring himself to share her sunny outlook. He looked into the future and still found it dark.

There was only one way of taking his mind off this dark future, only one means of achieving a momentary forgetfulness of what lay in store. Five minutes later Lord Emsworth was in the library, reading Whiffle on *The Care of the Pig*.

But there is a point beyond which the magic of the noblest writer ceases to function. Whiffle was good — no question about that — but he was not good enough to purge from the mind such a load of care as was weighing upon Lord Emsworth's. To expect him to do so was trying him too high. It was like asking Whiffle to divert and entertain a man stretched upon the rack.

Lord Emsworth was already beginning to find a difficulty in concentrating on that perfect prose, when any chance he might have had of doing so was removed. Lady Constance appeared in the doorway.

"Oh, here you are, Clarence," said Lady Constance.

"Yes," said Lord Emsworth in a low, strained voice.

A close observer would have noted about Lady Constance's manner, as she came into the room, something a little nervous and apprehensive, something almost diffident, but to Lord Emsworth, who was not a close observer, she seemed pretty much as usual, and he remained gazing at her like a man confronted with a ticking bomb. A dazed sensation had come upon him. It was in an almost detached way that he found himself speculating as to which of his crimes was about to be brought up for discussion. Had she met Jane and learned of the fatal letter? Or had she come straight from an interview with Rupert Baxter in which that injured man had told all?

He was so certain that it must be one of these two topics that she had come to broach that her manner as she opened the conversation filled him with amazement. Not only did it lack ferocity, it was absolutely chummy. It was as if a lion had come into the library and started bleating like a lamb.

"All alone, Clarence?"

Lord Emsworth hitched up his lower jaw and said, yes, he was all alone.

"What are you doing? Reading?"

Lord Emsworth said, yes, he was reading.

"I'm not disturbing you, am I?"

Lord Emsworth, though astonishment nearly robbed him of speech, contrived to say that she was not disturbing him. Lady Constance walked to the window and looked out.

"What a lovely evening."

"Yes."

"I wonder you aren't out of doors."

"I was out of doors. I came in."

"Yes. I saw you in the rose garden." Lady Constance traced a pattern on the window sill with her finger. "You were speaking to Beach."

"Yes."

"Yes, I saw Beach come up and speak to you."

There was a pause. Lord Emsworth was about to break it by asking his visitor if she felt quite well, when Lady Constance spoke again. That apprehension in her manner, that nervousness, was now well marked. She traced another pattern on the window sill.

"Was it important?"

"Was what important?"

"I mean, did he want anything?"

"Who?"

"Beach."

"Beach?"

"Yes. I was wondering what he wanted to see you about."

Quite suddenly there flashed upon Lord Emsworth the recollection that Beach had done more than merely hand him Baxter's note. With it — dash it, yes, it all came back to him — with it he had given his month's notice. And it just showed, Lord Emsworth felt, what a morass of trouble he was engulfed in that the fact of this superb butler handing in his resignation had made almost no impression upon him. If such a thing had happened only as recently as yesterday, it would have constituted a major crisis. He would have felt that the foundations of his world were rocking. And he had scarcely listened. "Yes, yes," he had said, if he remembered correctly. "Yes, yes, yes. All right." Or words to that effect.

Bending his mind now on the disaster, Lord Emsworth sat stunned. He was appalled. Almost since the beginning of time, this superbutler had been at the castle, and now he was about to melt away like snow in the sunshine — or as much like snow in the sunshine as was within the scope of a man who weighed sixteen stone in the buff. It was frightful. The thing was a nightmare. He couldn't get on without Beach. Life without Beach would be insupportable.

He gave tongue, his voice sharp and anguished.

"Connie! Do you know what's happened? Beach has given notice!"

"What!"

"Yes! His month's notice. He's given it. Beach has. And not a word of explanation. No reason. No . . ."

Lord Emsworth broke off. His face suddenly hardened. What seemed the only possible solution of the mystery had struck him. Connie was at the bottom of this. Connie must have been coming the grande dame on the butler, wounding his sensibilities.

Yes, that must be it. It was just the sort of thing she would do. If he had caught her being the Old English Aristocrat once, he had caught her a hundred times. That way of hers of pursing the lips and raising the eyebrows and generally doing the daughter-of-a-hundred-earls stuff. Naturally no butler would stand it.

"Connie," he cried, adjusting his pince-nez and staring keenly and accusingly, "what have you been doing to Beach?"

Something that was almost a sob burst from Lady Constance's lips. Her lovely complexion had paled, and in some odd way she seemed to have shrunk.

"I shot him," she whispered.

Lord Emsworth was a little hard of hearing.

"You did what?"

"I shot him."

"Shot him?"

"Yes."

"You mean, *shot* him?"

"Yes, yes, yes! I shot him with George's air gun."

A whistling sigh escaped Lord Emsworth. He leaned back in his chair, and the library seemed to be dancing old country dances before his eyes. To say that he felt weak with relief would be to understate the effect of this extraordinary communication. His relief was so intense that he felt absolutely boneless. Not once but many times during the past quarter of an hour he had said to himself that only a miracle could save him from the consequences of his sins, and now the miracle had happened. No one was more alive than he to the fact that women are abundantly possessed of crust, but after this surely even Connie could not have the crust to reproach him for what he had done.

"Shot him?" he said, recovering speech.

A fleeting touch of the old imperiousness returned to Lady Constance.

"Do stop saying 'shot him?' Clarence! Isn't it bad enough to have done a perfectly mad thing, without having to listen to you talking like a parrot? Oh dear! Oh dear!"

"But what did you do it for?"

"I don't know. I tell you I don't know. Something seemed suddenly to come over me. It was as if I had been bewitched. After you went out, I thought I would take the gun to Beach —"

"Why?"

"I . . . I . . . Well, I thought it would be safer with him than lying about in the library. So I took it down to his pantry. And all the way there I kept remembering what a wonderful shot I had been as a child —"

"What?" Lord Emsworth could not let this pass. "What do you mean, you were a wonderful shot as a child? You've never shot in your life."

"I have. Clarence, you were talking about Julia shooting Miss Mapleton. It wasn't Julia — it was I. She had made me stay in and do my rivers of Europe over again, so I shot her. I was a splendid shot in those days."

"I bet you weren't as good as me," said Lord Emsworth, piqued. "I used to shoot rats."

"So used I to shoot rats."

"How many rats did you ever shoot?"

"Oh, Clarence, Clarence! Never mind about the rats."

"No," said Lord Emsworth, called to order. "No, dash it. Never mind about the rats. Tell me about this Beach business."

68

"Well, when I got to the pantry it was empty, and I saw Beach outside by the laurel bush, reading in a deck chair —"

"How far away?"

"I don't know. What does it matter? About six feet, I suppose."

"Six feet? Ha!"

"And I shot him. I couldn't resist it. It was like some horrible obsession. There was a sort of hideous picture in my mind of how he would jump. So I shot him."

"How do you know you did? I expect you missed him."

"No. Because he sprang up. And then he saw me at the window and came in, and I said, 'Oh, Beach, I want you to take this air gun and keep it,' and he said, 'Very good, m'lady.'"

"He didn't say anything about your shooting him?"

"No. And I have been hoping and hoping that he had not realized what had happened. I have been in an agony of suspense. But now you tell me that he has given his notice, so he must have done. Clarence," cried Lady Constance, clasping her hands like a persecuted heroine, "you see the awful position, don't you? If he leaves us, he will spread the story all over the county and people will think I'm mad. I shall never be able to live it down. You must persuade him to withdraw his notice. Offer him double wages. Offer him anything. He must not be allowed to leave. If he does, I shall never . . . Sh!"

"What do you mean, sh . . . Oh, ah," said Lord Emsworth, at last observing that the door was opening.

It was his niece Jane who entered.

"Oh, hullo, Aunt Constance," she said. "I was wondering if you were in here. Mr. Baxter's looking for you."

Lady Constance was distrait.

"Mr. Baxter?"

"Yes. I heard him asking Beach where you were. I think he wants to see you about something," said Jane.

The Crime Wave at Blandings 69

She directed Lord Emsworth a swift glance, accompanied by a fleeting wink. "Remember!" said the glance. "Categorically!" said the wink.

Footsteps sounded outside. Rupert Baxter strode into the room.

At an earlier point in this chronicle, we have compared the aspect of Rupert Baxter, when burning with resentment, to a thundercloud, and it is possible that the reader may have formed a mental picture of just an ordinary thundercloud, the kind that rumbles a bit but does not really amount to anything very much. It was not this kind of cloud that the secretary resembled now, but one of those which bursts over cities in the tropics, inundating countrysides while thousands flee. He moved darkly towards Lady Constance, his hand outstretched. Lord Emsworth he ignored.

"I have come to say good-bye, Lady Constance," he said.

There were not many statements that could have roused Lady Constance from her preoccupation, but this one did. She ceased to be the sportswoman brooding on memories of shikari, and stared aghast.

"Good-bye?"

"Good-bye."

"But, Mr. Baxter, you are not leaving us?"

"Precisely."

For the first time, Rupert Baxter deigned to recognise that the ninth Earl was present.

"I am not prepared," he said bitterly, "to remain in a house where my chief duty appears to be to act as a target for Lord Emsworth and his air gun."

"What!"

"Exactly."

In the silence which followed these words, Jane once more gave her uncle that glance of encouragement and stimulation — that glance which said "Be firm!" To her astonishment, she perceived that it was not needed. Lord Emsworth was firm already. His face was calm, his eye steady, and his pince-nez were not even quivering.

"The fellow's potty," said Lord Emsworth in a clear, resonant voice. "Absolutely potty. Always told you he was. Target for my air gun? Pooh! Pah! What's he talking about?"

Rupert Baxter quivered. His spectacles flashed fire.

"Do you deny that you shot me, Lord Emsworth?"

"Certainly I do."

"Perhaps you will deny admitting to this lady here in the writing room that you shot me?"

"Certainly I do."

"Did you tell me that you had shot Mr. Baxter, Uncle Clarence?" said Jane. "I didn't hear you."

"Of course I didn't."

"I thought you hadn't. I should have remembered it."

Rupert Baxter's hands shot ceilingwards, as if he were calling upon heaven to see justice done.

"You admitted it to me personally. You begged me not to tell anyone. You tried to put matters right by engaging me as your secretary, and I accepted the position. At that time I was perfectly willing to forget the entire affair. But when, not half an hour later . . ."

Lord Emsworth raised his eyebrows. Jane raised hers.

"How very extraordinary," said Jane.

"Most," said Lord Emsworth.

He removed his pince-nez and began to polish them, speaking soothingly the while. But his manner, though soothing, was very resolute.

"Baxter, my dear fellow," he said, "there's only one explanation for all this. It's just what I was telling you. You've been having these hallucinations of yours again. I never said a word to you about shooting you. I never said a word to my niece about shooting you. Why should I, when I hadn't? And, as for what you say about engaging you as my secretary, the absurdity of the thing is manifest on the very face of it. There is nothing on earth that would induce me to have you as my secretary. I don't want to hurt your feelings, but I'd rather be dead in a ditch. Now, listen, my dear Baxter, I'll tell you what to do. You just jump on that motor bicycle of yours and go on touring England where you left off. And soon you will find that the fresh air will do wonders for that pottiness of yours. In a day or two you won't know . . ."

Rupert Baxter turned and stalked from the room.

"Mr. Baxter!" cried Lady Constance.

Her intention of going after the fellow and pleading with him to continue inflicting his beastly presence on the quiet home life of Blandings Castle was so plain that Lord Emsworth did not hesitate.

"Connie!"

"But, Clarence!"

"Constance, you will remain where you are. You will not stir a step."

"But, Clarence!"

"Not a dashed step. You hear me? Let him scram!"

Lady Constance halted, irresolute. Then suddenly she met the full force of the pince-nez and it was as if she — like Rupert Baxter — had been struck by a bullet. She collapsed into a chair and sat there twisting her rings forlornly.

"Oh, and by the way, Connie," said Lord Emsworth, "I've been meaning to tell you. I've given that fellow Abercrombie that job he was asking for. I thought it all over carefully, and decided to drop him a line saying that pursuant on our recent conversation I was offering him Simmons' place. I've been making inquiries, and I find he's a capital fellow."

"He's a baa-lamb," said Jane.

"You hear? Jane says he's a baa-lamb. Just the sort of chap we want about the place."

"So now we're going to get married."

"So now they're going to get married. An excellent match, don't you think, Connie?"

Lady Constance did not speak. Lord Emsworth raised his voice a little.

"Don't you, Connie?"

Lady Constance leaped in her seat as if she had heard the last trump.

"Very," she said. "Oh, very."

"Right," said Lord Emsworth. "And now I'll go and talk to Beach."

In the pantry, gazing sadly out on the stableyard, Beach, the butler, sat sipping a glass of port. In moments of mental stress, port was to Beach what Whiffle was to his employer, or, as we must now ruefully put it, his late employer. He flew to it when Life had got him down, and never before had Life got him down as it had now.

Sitting there in his pantry, that pantry which so soon would know him no more, Beach was in the depths. He mourned like some fallen monarch about to say good-bye to all his greatness and pass into exile. The die was cast. The end had come. Eighteen years, eighteen happy years, he had been in service at Blandings Castle, and now he must go forth, never to return. Little wonder that he sipped port. A weaker man would have swigged brandy.

Something tempestuous burst open the door, and he perceived that his privacy had been invaded by Lord Emsworth. He rose, and stood staring. In all the eighteen years during which he had held office, his employer had never before paid a visit to the pantry.

But it was not simply the other's presence that caused his gooseberry eyes to dilate to their full width, remarkable though that was. The mystery went deeper than that. For this was a strange, unfamiliar Lord Emsworth, a Lord Emsworth who glared where once he had blinked, who spurned the floor like a mettlesome charger, who banged tables and spilled port.

"Beach," thundered this changeling, "what the deuce is all this dashed nonsense?"

"M'lord?"

"You know what I mean. About leaving me. Have you gone off your head?"

A sigh shook the butler's massive frame.

"I fear that in the circumstances it is inevitable, m'lord."

"Why? What are you talking about? Don't be an ass, Beach. Inevitable, indeed! Never heard such nonsense in my life. Why is it inevitable? Look me in the face and answer me that."

"I feel it is better to tender my resignation than to be dismissed, m'lord."

It was Lord Emsworth's turn to stare.

"Dismissed?"

"Yes, m'lord."

"Beach, you're tight."

"No, m'lord. Has not Mr. Baxter spoken to you, m'lord?"

"Of course he's spoken to me. He's been gassing away half the afternoon. What's that got to do with it?"

Another sigh, seeming to start at the soles of his flat feet, set the butler's waistcoat rippling like corn in the wind.

"I see that Mr. Baxter has not yet informed you, m'lord. I assumed that he would have done so before this. But it is a mere matter of time, I fear, before he makes his report."

"Informed me of what?"

"I regret to say, m'lord, that in a moment of uncontrollable impulse I shot Mr. Baxter."

Lord Emsworth's pince-nez flew from his nose. Without them he could see only indistinctly, but he continued to stare at the butler, and in his eyes there appeared an expression which was a blend of several emotions. Amazement would have been the chief of these, had it not been exceeded by affection. He did not speak, but his eyes said, "My brother!"

"With Master George's air gun, m'lord, which her ladyship left in my custody. I regret to say, m'lord, that upon receipt of the weapon I went out into the grounds and came upon Mr. Baxter walking near the shrubbery. I tried to resist the temptation, m'lord, but it was too keen. I was seized with an urge which I have not experienced since I was a small lad, and, in short, I—"

"Plugged him?"

"Yes, m'lord."

Lord Emsworth could put two and two together.

"So that's what he was talking about in the library. That's what made him change his mind and send me that note. . . . How far was he away when you shot him?"

"A matter of a few feet, m'lord. I endeavoured to conceal myself behind a tree, but he turned very sharply, and I was so convinced that he had detected me that I felt I had no alternative but to resign my situation before he could make his report to you, m'lord."

"And I thought you were leaving because my sister Connie shot you!"

"Her ladyship did not shoot me, m'lord. It is true that the weapon exploded accidentally in her ladyship's hand, but the bullet passed me harmlessly."

Lord Emsworth snorted.

"And she said she was a good shot! Can't even hit a sitting butler at six feet. Listen to me, Beach. I want no more of this nonsense of you resigning. Bless my soul, how do you suppose I could get on without you? How long have you been here?"

"Eighteen years, m'lord."

"Eighteen years! And you talk of resigning! Of all the dashed, absurd ideas!"

"But I fear, m'lord, when her ladyship learns — "

"Her ladyship won't learn. Baxter won't tell her. Baxter's gone."

"Gone, m'lord?"

"Gone forever."

"But I understood, m'lord — "

"Never mind what you understood. He's gone. A few feet away, did you say?"

"M'lord?"

"Did you say Baxter was only a few feet away when you got him?"

"Yes, m'lord."

"Ah!" said Lord Emsworth.

He took the gun absently from the table and absently slipped a slug into the breach. He was feeling pleased and proud, as champions do whose pre-eminence is undisputed. Connie had missed a mark like Beach — practically a haystack — at six feet. Beach had plugged Baxter, true, and so had young George — but only with the muzzle of the gun almost touching the fellow. It had been left for him, Clarence, ninth Earl of Emsworth, to do the real shooting. . . .

A damping thought came to diminish his complacency. It was as if a voice had whispered in his ear the word "Fluke!" His jaw dropped a little, and he stood for a while, brooding. He felt flattened and discouraged.

Had it been merely a fluke, that superb shot from the library window? Had he been mistaken in supposing that the ancient skill still lingered? Would he — which was what the voice was hinting — under similar conditions miss nine times out of ten?

A stuttering, sputtering noise broke in upon his reverie. He raised his eyes to the window. Out in the stableyard, Rupert Baxter was starting up his motor bicycle.

"Mr. Baxter, m'lord."

"I see him."

An overwhelming desire came upon Lord Emsworth to put this thing to the test, to silence forever that taunting voice.

"How far away would you say he was, Beach?"

"Fully twenty yards, m'lord."

"Watch!" said Lord Emsworth.

Into the sputtering of the bicycle there cut a soft pop. It was followed by a sharp howl. Rupert Baxter, who had been leaning on the handle bars, rose six inches with his hand to his thigh.

"There!" said Lord Emsworth.

Baxter had ceased to rub his thigh. He was a man of intelligence, and he realised that anyone on the premises of Blandings Castle who wasted time hanging about and rubbing thighs was simply asking for it. To one trapped in this inferno of a Blandings Castle instant flight was the only way of winning to safety. The sputtering rose to a crescendo, diminished, died away altogether. Rupert Baxter had gone on, touring England.

Lord Emsworth was still gazing out of the window, raptly, as if looking at the X which marked the spot. For a long moment Beach stood staring reverently at his turned back. Then, as if performing some symbolic rite in keeping with the dignity of the scene, he reached for his glass of port and raised it in a silent toast.

Peace reigned in the butler's pantry. The sweet air of the summer evening poured in through the open window. It was as if Nature had blown the All Clear.

Blandings Castle was itself again.

UKRIDGE
STARTS
A
BANK
ACCOUNT

EXCEPT THAT HE WAS QUITE WELL DRESSED AND plainly prosperous, the man a yard or two ahead of me as I walked along Piccadilly looked exactly like my old friend Stanley Featherstonehaugh Ukridge, and I was musing on these odd resemblances and speculating idly as to what my little world would be like if there were two of him in it, when he stopped to peer into a tobacconist's window and I saw that it was Ukridge. It was months since I had seen that battered man of wrath, and though my guardian angel whispered to me that it would mean parting with a loan of five or even ten shillings if I made my presence known, I tapped him on the shoulder.

Usually if you tap Ukridge on the shoulder, he leaps at least six inches into the air, a guilty conscience making him feel that the worst has happened and his sins have found him out, but now he merely beamed, as if being tapped by me had made his day.

"Corky, old horse!" he cried. "The very man I wanted to see. Come in here while I buy one of those cigarette lighters, and then you must have a bite of lunch with me. And when

I say lunch, I don't mean the cup of coffee and roll and butter to which you are accustomed, but something more on the lines of a Babylonian orgy."

We went into the shop, and he paid for the lighter from a wallet stuffed with currency.

"And now," he said, "that lunch of which I was speaking. The Ritz is handy."

It was perhaps tactless of me, but when we had seated ourselves and he had ordered spaciously, I started to probe the mystery of this affluence of his. It occurred to me that he might have gone to live again with his aunt, the wealthy novelist Miss Julia Ukridge, and I asked him if this was so. He said it was not.

"Then where did you get all that money?"

"Honest work, laddie, or anyway I thought it was honest when I took it on. The pay was good. Ten pounds a week and no expenses, for of course Percy attended to the household bills. Everything I got was velvet."

"Who was Percy?"

"My employer, and the job with which he entrusted me was selling antique furniture. It came about through my meeting Stout, my aunt's butler, in a pub, and the advice I would give to every young man starting life is always go into pubs, for you never know whether there won't be someone there who can do you a bit of good. For some minutes after entering the place I had been using all my eloquence and persuasiveness to induce Flossie, the barmaid, to chalk my refreshment up on the slate, my finances at the time being at a rather low ebb. It wasn't easy. I had to extend all my powers. But I won through at last, and I was returning to my seat with a well-filled flagon, when a bloke accosted me and with some surprise I saw it was my Aunt Julia's major domo.

" 'Hullo,' " I said. " 'Why aren't you butling?' "

It appeared that he no longer held office. Aunt Julia had given him the sack. This occasioned me no astonishment, for she is a confirmed sacker. You will probably recall that she has bunged me out of the home not once but many times. So

I just said "Tough luck" or something to that effect, and we chatted on this and that. He asked me where I was living now, and I told him, and after a pleasant quarter of an hour we parted, he to go and see his brother, or that's where he said he was going, I to trickle round to the Foreign Office and try to touch George Tupper for a couple of quid, which I was fortunately able to do, he luckily happening to be in amiable mood. Sometimes when you approach Tuppy for a small loan you find him all agitated because mysterious veiled women have been pinching his secret treaties, and on such occasions it is difficult to bend him to your will.

With this addition to my resources I was in a position to pay my landlady the trifling sum I owed her, so when she looked in on me that night as I sat smoking my pipe and wishing I could somehow accumulate a bit of working capital I met her eye without a tremor.

But she had not come to talk finance. She said there was a gentleman downstairs who wanted to see me, and I confess this gave me pause. What with the present world-wide shortage of money — affecting us all these days — I had been compelled to let one or two bills run up, and this might well be some creditor whom it would have been embarrassing to meet.

"What sort of man is he?" I asked, and she said he was husky in the voice, which didn't get me much further, and when she added that she had told him I was in, I said she had better send him up, and a few moments later in came a bloke who might have been Stout's brother. Which was as it should have been, for that was what he turned out to be.

"Evening," he said, and I could see why Mrs. Whatever-her-name-was had described him as husky. His voice was hoarse and muffled. Laryngitis or something, I thought.

"Name of Stout," he proceeded. "I think you know my brother Horace."

"Good Lord!" I said. "Is his name Horace?"

"That's right. And mine's Percy."

"Are you a butler, too?"

"Silver-ring bookie. Or was."

"You've retired?"

"For a while. Lost my voice calling the odds. And that brings me to what I've come about."

It was a strange story he had to relate. It seemed that a client of his had let his obligations pile up — a thing I've often wished bookies would let me do — till he owed this Percy a pretty considerable sum, and finally he had settled by handing over a lot of antique furniture. The stuff being no good to Percy, he was anxious to dispose of it if the price was right, and the way to make the price right, he felt, was to enlist the services of someone of persuasive eloquence — someone with the gift of the gab was the way he put it — to sell it for him. Because, of course, he couldn't do it himself, his bronchial cords having turned blue on him. And his brother Horace, having heard me in action, was convinced that they need seek no further. Any man, Horace said, who could persuade Flossie to give credit for two pints of mild and bitter was the man for Percy. He knew Flossie to be a girl of steel and iron, adamant to the most impassioned pleas, and he said that if he hadn't heard it with his own ears, he wouldn't have believed it possible.

"So how about it," Percy asked.

Well, you know me, Corky. First and foremost the level-headed man of business. What, I inquired, was there in it for me, and he said he would give me a commission. I said that I would prefer a salary, and when he suggested five pounds a week with board and lodging thrown in, it was all I could do to keep from jumping at it, for, as I told you, my financial position was not good. But I managed to sneer loftily, and in the end I got him up to ten.

"You say board and lodging," I said. "Where do I board and lodge?"

That, he said, was the most attractive part of the assignment. He wasn't going to take a shop in the metropolis but planned to exhibit his wares in a cottage equipped with honeysuckle, roses and all the fittings down in Kent. One followed his train of thought. Motorists would be passing to and fro in droves and the betting was that at least some of them, seeing the notice on the front gate "Antique furniture for sale. Genuine period. Guaranteed," would stop off and buy. My Aunt Julia is an aficionado of old furniture and I knew that she had often picked up some good stuff at these wayside emporia. The thing looked to me like a snip, and he said he thought so, too. For mark you, Corky, though you and I wouldn't be seen dead in a ditch with the average antique, there are squads of half-wits who value them highly — showing, I often say, that it takes all sorts to make a world. I told myself that this was going to be good, I slapped him on the back. He slapped me on the back. I shook his hand. He shook my hand. And — what made the whole thing a real love feast — he slipped me an advance of five quid. And the following afternoon found me at Rosemary Cottage in the neighborhood of Tunbridge Wells, all eagerness to get my nose down to it.

My rosy expectations were fulfilled. For solid comfort there is nothing to beat a jolly bachelor establishment. Women have their merits, of course, but if you are to live the good life, you don't want them around the home. They are always telling you to wipe your boots and they don't like you dining in your shirt sleeves. At Rosemary Cottage we were hampered by none of these restrictions. Liberty Hall about sums it up.

We were a happy little community. Percy had a fund of good stories garnered from his years on the turf, while Horace, though less effervescent as a conversationalist, played the harmonica with considerable skill, a thing I didn't know butlers ever did. The other member of our group was a substantial character named Erb, who was attached to Percy in the capacity of what is called a minder. In case the term is new to you, it meant that if you owed Percy a fiver on the two o'clock at Plumpton and didn't brass up pretty quick, you got Erb on the back of your neck. He was one of those strong silent men who don't speak till they're spoken to, and not often then, but he was fortunately able to play a fair game of bridge, so we had a four for after supper. Erb was vice-president in charge of the cooking, and I never wish to bite better pork chops than the ones he used to serve up. They melted in the mouth.

Yes, it was an idyllic life, and we lived it to the full. The only thing that cast a shadow was the fact that business might have been brisker. I sold a few of the ghastly objects, but twice I let promising prospects get away from me, and this made me uneasy. I didn't want to get Percy thinking that in entrusting the selling end of the business to me he might have picked the wrong man. With a colossal sum like ten quid a week at stake it behooved me to do some quick thinking, and it wasn't long before I spotted where the trouble lay. My patter lacked the professional note.

You know how it is when you're buying old furniture. You expect the fellow who's selling it to weigh in with a lot of abstruse stuff which doesn't mean a damn thing to you but which you know ought to be there. It's much the same as when you're buying a car. If you aren't handed plenty of applesauce about springs and cam shafts and differential gears and sprockets, you suspect a trap and tell the chap you'll think it over and let him know.

And fortunately I was in a position to correct this flaw in my technique without difficulty. Aunt Julia had shelves of books about old furniture which I could borrow and bone up on, thus acquiring the necessary double talk, so next morning I set out for The Cedars, Wimbledon Common, full of zeal and the will to win.

I was sorry to be informed by Horace's successor on my arrival that she was in bed with a nasty cold, but he took my name up and came back to say that she could give me five minutes — not longer, because she was expecting the doctor. So I went up and found her sniffing eucalyptus and sneezing a good deal, plainly in rather poor shape. But her sufferings had not impaired her spirit, for the first thing she said to me was that she wouldn't give me a penny, and I was pained to see that that matter of the ormolu clock still rankled. What ormolu clock? Oh, just one which, needing a bit of capital at the time, I pinched from one of the spare rooms, little thinking that its absence would ever be noticed. I hastened to disabuse her of the idea that I had come in the hope of making a touch, and the strain that had threatened to mar the conversation became eased.

"Though I did come to borrow something, Aunt Julia," I said. "Do you mind if I take two or three books of yours about antique furniture? I'll return them shortly."

She sneezed skeptically.

"Or pawn them," she said. "Since when have you been interested in antique furniture?"

"I'm selling it."

"You're *selling* it?" she exclaimed like an echo in the Swiss mountains. "Do you mean you are working in a shop?"

"Well, not exactly a shop. We conduct our business at a cottage — Rosemary Cottage, to be exact — on the roadside not far from Tunbridge Wells. In this way we catch the motoring trade. The actual selling is in my hands and so far I've done pretty well, but I have not been altogether satisfied with my work. I feel I need more technical stuff, and last night it occurred to me that if I read a few of your books I'd be able to make my sales talk more convincing. So if you will allow me to take a selection from your library — "

She sneezed again, but this time more amiably. She said that if I was really doing some genuine work, she would certainly be delighted to help me, adding in rather poor taste, I thought, that it was about time I stopped messing about and wasting my life as I had been doing. I could have told her, of course, that there is not a moment of the day, except possibly when relaxing over a mild and bitter at the pub, when I am not pondering some vast scheme which will bring me wealth and power, but it didn't seem humane to argue with a woman suffering from a nasty cold.

84

"Tomorrow, if I am well enough," she said, "I will come and see your stock myself."

"Will you really? That'll be fine."

"Or perhaps the day after tomorrow. But it's an extraordinary coincidence that you should be selling antique furniture, because — "

"Yes, it was odd that I should have happened to run into Stout."

"Stout? You mean my butler?"

"Your late butler. He gave me to understand that you had sacked him."

She sneezed grimly.

"I certainly did. Let me tell you what happened."

"No, let me tell *you* what happened," I said, and I related the circumstances of my meeting with Horace, prudently changing the pub to a milk bar. "I had been having an argument with a fellow at the next table," I concluded, "and my eloquence so impressed him that he asked me if I would come down to Rosemary Cottage and sell this antique furniture. He has a brother who recently acquired a lot of it."

"What!"

She sat up in bed, her eyes, though watery, flashing with all the old fire. It was plain that she was about to say something of significance, but before she could speak the door opened and the medicine man appeared, and thinking they were best alone I pushed off and got the books and legged it for the great open spaces.

There was a telephone booth at the end of the road, and I went to it and rang up Percy. These long-distance calls run into money, but I felt that he ought to have the good news without delay, no matter what the expense.

It was Horace who answered the phone, and I slipped him the tidings of great joy.

"I've just been seeing my aunt," I said.

"Oh?" he said.

"She's got a nasty cold," I said.

"Ah," he said, and I seemed to detect a note of gratification in his voice, as if he was thinking well of Heaven for having given her a sharp lesson which would teach her to be more careful in future how she went about giving good men the bum's rush.

"But she thinks she'll be all right tomorrow," I said, "and the moment the sniffles have ceased and the temperature has returned to normal she's coming down here to inspect our stock. I don't need to tell you what this means. Next to her novels what she loves most in this world is old furniture. It is to her what catnip is to a cat. Confront her with some chair on which nobody could sit with any comfort, and provided it was made by Chippendale, if I've got the name right, the sky's the limit. She's quite likely to buy everything we've got, paying a prince's ransom for each article. I've been with her to sales and with my own eyes have observed her flinging the cash about like a drunken sailor. I know what you're thinking, of course. You feel that after what has passed between you it will be painful for you to meet her again, but you must clench your teeth and stick it like a man. We're all working for the good of the show, so . . . Hullo? Hullo? Are you there?"

He wasn't. He had hung up. Mysterious, I thought, and most disappointing to one who, like myself, had been expecting paeans of joy. However, I was much too bucked to worry about the peculiar behavior of butlers, and feeling that the occasion called for something in the nature of a celebration I went to the Foreign Office, gave George Tupper his two quid back and took him out to lunch.

It wasn't a very animated lunch, because Tuppy hardly said a word. He seemed dazed. I've noticed the same thing before in fellows to whom I've repaid a small loan. They get a sort of stunned look, as if they had passed through some great spiritual experience. Odd. But it took more than a silent Tuppy to damp my jocund mood, and I was feeling on top of my form when an hour or two later I crossed the threshold of Rosemary Cottage.

"Yoo-hoo!" I cried. "I'm back."

I expected shouts of welcome — not, of course, from Erb, but certainly from Horace and Percy. Instead of which, complete silence reigned. They might all have gone for a walk, but that didn't seem likely, because while Percy sometimes enjoyed a little exercise, Horace and Erb hadn't set a foot outdoors since we'd been there. And it was as I stood puzzling over this that I noticed that except for a single table — piecrust tables the things are called — all the furniture had gone, too. I don't mind telling you, Corky, that it baffled me. I could make nothing of it, and I was still making nothing of it when I had that feeling you get sometimes that you are not alone, and, turning, I saw that I had company. Standing beside me was a policeman.

There have been times, I will not conceal it from you, when such a spectacle would have chilled me to the marrow, for you never know what may not ensue once the Force starts popping up, and it just shows how crystal clear my conscience was that I didn't quail but greeted him with a cheery "Good evening, officer."

"Good evening, sir," he responded courteously. "Is this Rosemary Cottage?"

"Nothing but. Anything I can do for you?"

"I've come on behalf of Miss Julia Ukridge."

It seemed strange to me that Aunt Julia should have dealings with the police, but aunts notoriously do the weirdest things, so I received the information with a polite "Oh, really?" — adding that she was linked to me by ties of blood, being indeed the sister of my late father, and he said "Was that so?" and expressed the opinion that it was a small world, a sentiment in which I concurred.

"She was talking of looking me up here," I said.

"So I understood, sir. But she was unable to come herself, so she sent her maid with the list. She has a nasty cold."

"Probably caught it from my aunt."

"Sir?"

"You said the maid had a nasty cold."

"No, sir, it's Miss Ukridge who has the nasty cold."

"Ah, now we have got it straight. What did she send the maid for?"

"To bring us the list of the purloined objects."

I don't know how it is with you, Corky, but the moment anyone starts talking about purloined objects in my presence I get an uneasy feeling. It was with not a little goose-flesh running down my spine that I gazed at the officer.

"Purloined objects?"

"A number of valuable pieces of furniture. Antiques they call them."

"Oh, my aunt!"

"Yes, sir, they were her property. They were removed from her residence on Wimbledon Common during her absence. She states that she had gone to Brussels to attend one of these conferences where writers assemble, she being a writer, I understand, and she left her butler in charge of the house. When she came back, the valuable pieces of antique furniture weren't there. The butler, questioned, stated that he had taken the afternoon off and gone to the dog races and nobody more surprised than himself when he returned and found the objects had been purloined. He was dismissed, of course, but that didn't help Miss Ukridge's bereavement much. Just locking the stable door after the milk has been spilt, as you might say. And there till this morning the matter rested. But this morning, on information received, the lady was led to suspect that the purloined objects were in this Rosemary Cottage, and she got in touch with the local police, who got in touch with us. She thinks, you see, that the butler did it. Worked in with an accomplice, I mean to say, and the two of them got away with the purloined objects, no doubt in a plain van."

I believe I once asked you, Corky, if during a political discussion in a pub you had ever suddenly been punched on the nose, and if I remember rightly you replied in the negative. But I have been — twice — and on each occasion I was conscious of feeling dazed and stunned, like George Tupper when I paid him back the two quid he had lent me and took him to lunch. The illusion that the roof had fallen in and landed on top of my head was extraordinarily vivid. Drinking the constable in with a horrified gaze, I seemed to be looking at two constables, both doing the shimmy.

For his words had removed the scales from my eyes, and I saw Horace and Percy no longer as pleasant business associates but as what they were, a wolf in butler's clothing and a bookie who did not know the difference between right and wrong. Yes, yes, as you say, I have sometimes been compelled by circumstances to pinch an occasional trifle like a clock from my aunt, but there is a sharp line drawn between swiping a clock and getting away with a houseful of assorted antique furniture. No doubt they had done it precisely as the constable had said, and it must have been absurdly simple. Nothing to it. No, Corky, you are wrong. I do *not* wish I had thought of it myself. I would have scorned such an action, even though knowing the stuff was fully insured and my aunt would be far better off without it.

"The only thing is," the officer was proceeding, "I don't see any antique furniture here. There's that table, but it's not on the list. And if there had been antique furniture here, you'd have noticed it. Looks to me as if they'd sent me to the wrong place," he said, and with a word of regret that I had been troubled he mounted his bicycle and pedaled off.

He left me, as you can readily imagine, with my mind in a turmoil, and you are probably thinking that what was giving me dark circles under the eyes was the discovery that I had been lured by a specious bookie into selling hot furniture and so rendering myself liable to a sharp sentence as an accessory or whatever they call it, but it wasn't. That was bad enough, but what was worse was the realization that my employer had gone off owing me six weeks' salary. You see, when we had made that gentleman's agreement of ours, he had said that if it was all the same to me, he would prefer to

Ukridge Starts a Bank Account 89

pay me in a lump sum at the end of my term of office instead of week by week, and I had seen no objection. Foolish of me, of course. I cannot impress it on you too strongly, Corky old horse, that if anyone comes offering you money, you should grab it at once and not assent to any suggestion of payment at some later date. Only so can you be certain of trousering the stuff.

So, as I say, I stood there draining the bitter cup, and while I was thus engaged a car stopped in the road outside and a man came up the garden path.

He was a tall man with gray hair and a funny sort of twist to his mouth, as if he had just swallowed a bad oyster and was wishing he hadn't.

"I see you advertise antique furniture," he said. "Where do you keep it?"

I was just about to tell him it had all gone, when he spotted the piecrust table.

"This looks a nice piece," he said, and as he spoke I saw in his eye the unmistakable antique-furniture-collector's gleam which I had so often seen in my Aunt Julia's at sales, and I quivered from hair to shoe sole.

You have often commented on my lightning brain and ready resource, Corky . . . well, if it wasn't you, it was somebody else . . . and I don't suppose I've ever thought quicker than I did then. In a sort of blinding flash it came to me that if I could sell Percy's piecrust table for what he owed me, the thing would be a stand-off and my position stabilized.

"You bet it's a nice piece," I said, and proceeded to give him the works. I was inspired, I doubt if I have ever, not even when pleading with Flossie that credit was the lifeblood of commerce, talked more persuasively. The golden words simply flowed out, and I could see that I had got him going. It seemed but a moment before he had produced his checkbook and was writing me a check for sixty pounds.

"Who shall I make it out to?" he asked, and I said S. F. Ukridge, and he did so and told me where to send the table

— somewhere in the Mayfair district of London — and we parted on cordial terms.

And not ten minutes after he had driven off, who should show up but Percy. Yes, Percy in person, the last bloke I had expected to see. I don't think I described him to you did I, but his general appearance was that of a clean-shaven Santa Claus, and he was looking now more like Santa Claus than ever. Bubbling over with good will and *joie de vivre*. He couldn't have been chirpier if he had just seen the heavily backed favorite in the big race stub its toe on a fence and come a purler.

"Hullo, cocky," he said. "So you got back."

Well, you might suppose that after what I had heard from the rozzer I would have started right away to reproach him for his criminal activities and to urge him to give his better self a chance to guide him, but I didn't — partly because it's never any use trying to jerk a bookie's better self to the surface, but principally because I wanted to lose no time in putting our financial affairs on a sound basis. First things first has always been my motto.

"You!" I said. "I thought you had skipped."

Have you ever seen a bookie cut to the quick? I hadn't till then. He took it big. There's a word my aunt is fond of using in her novels when the hero has said the wrong thing to the heroine and made her hot under the collar. She — what is it? — "bridled," that's the word I mean. Percy bridled.

"Who, me?" he said. "Without paying you your money? What do you think I am — dishonest?"

I apologized. I said that naturally when I returned and found him gone and all the furniture removed it had started a train of thought.

"Well, I had to get the stuff away before your aunt arrived, didn't I? How much do I owe you? Sixty quid, isn't it? Here you are," he said, pulling out a wallet the size of an elephant. "What's that you've got there?"

And I'm blowed if in my emotion at seeing him again I hadn't forgotten all about the twisted-lip man's check. I endorsed it with a hasty fountain pen and pushed it across. He eyed it with some surprise.

"What's this?"

I may have smirked a bit, for I was not a little proud of my recent triumph of salesmanship.

"I just sold the piecrust table to a man who came by in a car."

"Good boy," said Percy. "I knew I hadn't made a mistake in making you vice-president in charge of sales. I've had that table on my hands for months. Took it for a bad debt. How much did you get for it?" He looked at the check. "Sixty quid? Splendid. I only got forty."

"Eh?"

"From the chap I sold it to this morning."

"You sold it to somebody this morning?"

"That's right."

"Then which of them gets it?"

"Why, your chap, of course. He paid more. We've got to do the honest thing."

"And you'll give your chap his money back?"

"Now don't be silly," said Percy, and would probably have gone on to reproach me further, but at this moment we had another visitor, a gaunt, lean, spectacled popper-in who looked as if he might be a professor or something on that order.

"I see you advertise antique furniture," he said. "I would like to look at ... Ah," he said, spotting the table. He nuzzled it a good deal and turned it upside down and once or twice looked as if he were going to smell it.

"Beautiful," he said. "A lovely bit of work."

"You can have it for eighty quid," said Percy.

The professor smiled one of those gentle smiles.

"I fear it is hardly worth that. When I called it beautiful and lovely, I was alluding to Tansy's workmanship. Ike Tansy, possibly the finest forger of old furniture we have today. At a glance I would say that this was an example of his middle period."

Percy blew a few bubbles.

"You mean it's a fake? But I was told —"

"Whatever you were told, your informant was mistaken. And may I add that if you persist in this policy of yours of advertising and selling forgeries as genuine antiques, you are liable to come into uncomfortable contact with the Law. It would be wise to remove that notice you have at your gate. Good evening, gentlemen, good evening."

He left behind him what you might call a strained silence, broken after a moment or so by Percy saying, "Cor!"

"This calls for thought," he said, "We've sold that table."

"Yes."

"Twice."

"Yes."

"And got the money for it."

"Yes."

"And it's a fake."

"Yes."

"And we passed it off as genuine."

"Yes."

"And it seems there's a law against that."

"Yes."

"We'd better go to the pub and talk it over."

"Yes."

"You be walking on. There's something I want to attend to in the kitchen. By the way, got any matches? I've used all mine."

I gave him a box and strolled on, deep in thought, and presently he joined me, seeming deep in thought, too. We sat on a stile, both of us plunged in meditation, and then he suddenly uttered an exclamation.

"What a lovely sunset," he said, "and how peculiar that the sun's setting in the east. I've never known it to do that before. Why, strike me pink, I believe the cottage is on fire."

And, Corky, he was perfectly accurate. It was.

Ukridge broke off his narrative, reached for his wallet and laid it on the table preparatory to summoning the waiter to bring the bill. I ventured a question.

"The cottage was reduced to ashes?"

"It was."

"The piecrust table, too?"

"Yes, I think it must have burned briskly."

"A bit of luck for you."

"Very fortunate. Very fortunate."

"Percy was probably careless with those matches."

"One feels he must have been. But he certainly brought about the happy ending. Percy's happy. He's made a good thing out of it. I'm happy. I've made a good thing out of it, too. Aunt Julia has the insurance money, so she also is happy, provided of course that her nasty cold has now yielded to treatment. I doubt if the insurance blokes are happy, but we must always remember that the more cash these insurance firms get taken off them, the better it is for them. It makes them more spiritual."

"How about the two owners of the table?"

"Oh, they've probably forgotten the whole thing by now. Money means nothing to fellows like that. The fellow I sold it to was driving a Rolls Royce. So looking on the episode from the broad viewpoint . . . I beg your pardon?"

"I said 'Good afternoon, Mr. Ukridge,'" said the man who had suddenly appeared at our table, and I saw Ukridge's jaw fall like an express lift going down. And I wasn't surprised, for this was a tall man with gray hair and a curiously twisted mouth. His eyes, as they bored into Ukridge, were bleak.

"I've been looking for you for a long time and hoping to meet you again. I'll trouble you for sixty pounds."

"I haven't got sixty pounds."

"Spent some of it, eh? Then let's see what you *have* got," said the man, turning the contents of the wallet out on the tablecloth and counting it in an efficient manner. "Fifty-eight pounds, six and threepence. That's near enough."

"But who's going to pay for my lunch?"

"Ah, that we shall never know," said the man.

But I knew, and it was with a heavy heart that I reached in my hip pocket for the thin little bundle of pound notes which I had been hoping would last me for another week.

THE
PURITY
OF
THE
TURF

WHEN THE THING WAS OVER, I MADE MY MIND UP.

"Jeeves," I said.

"Sir?"

"Never again! The strain is too great. I don't say I shall chuck betting altogether: if I get hold of a good thing for one of the big races no doubt I shall have my bit on as aforetime: but you won't catch me mixing myself up with one of these minor country meetings again. They're too hot."

"I think perhaps you are right, sir," said Jeeves.

It was young Bingo Little who lured me into the thing. About the third week of my visit at Twing Hall he blew into my bedroom one morning while I was toying with a bit of breakfast and thinking of this and that.

"Bertie!" he said, in an earnest kind of voice.

I decided to take a firm line from the start. Young Bingo, if you remember, was at a pretty low ebb at about this juncture. He had not only failed to put his finances on a sound basis over the recent Sermon Handicap, but had also discovered that Lady Cynthia Wick loved another. These things had jarred the unfortunate mutt, and he had developed a habit of dropping in on me at all hours and decanting his anguished soul on me. I could stand this all right after dinner, and even after lunch; but before breakfast, no. We Woosters are amiability itself, but there is a limit.

"Now look here, old friend," I said. "I know your bally heart is broken and all that, and at some future time I shall be delighted to hear all about it, but — "

"I didn't come to talk about that."

"No? Good egg!"

"The past," said young Bingo, "is dead. Let us say no more about it."

"Right-o!"

"I have been wounded to the very depths of my soul, but don't speak about it."

"I won't."

"Ignore it. Forget it."

"Absolutely!"

I hadn't seen him so dashed reasonable for weeks.

"What I came to see you about this morning, Bertie," he said, fishing a sheet of paper out of his pocket, "was to ask if you would care to come in on another little flutter."

If there is one thing we Woosters are simply dripping with, it is sporting blood. I bolted the rest of my sausage, and sat up and took notice.

"Proceed," I said. "You interest me strangely, old bird."

Bingo laid the paper on the bed.

"On Monday week," he said, "you may or may not know, the annual village school-treat takes place. Lord Wickhammersley lends the Hall grounds for the purpose. There will be games, and a conjuror, and coconut shies, and tea in a tent. And also sports."

"I know. Cynthia was telling me."

Young Bingo winced.

"Would you mind not mentioning that name? I am not made of marble."

"Sorry!"

"Well, as I was saying, this jamboree is slated for Monday week. The question is, Are we on?"

"How do you mean, 'Are we on'?"

"I am referring to the sports. Steggles did so well out of the Sermon Handicap that he has decided to make a book on these sports. Punters can be accommodated at ante-post odds or starting price, according to their preference."

Steggles, I don't know if you remember, was one of the gang of youths who were reading for some examination or other with old Heppenstall down at the Vicarage. He was the fellow who had promoted the Sermon Handicap. A bird of considerable enterprise and vast riches, being the only son of one of the biggest bookies in London, but no pal of mine. I never liked the chap. He was a ferret-faced egg with a shifty eye and not a few pimples. On the whole, a nasty growth.

"I think we ought to look into it," said young Bingo.

I pressed the bell.

"I'll consult Jeeves. I don't touch any sporting proposition without his advice. Jeeves," I said, as he drifted in, "rally round."

"Sir?"

"Stand by. We want your advice."

"Very good, sir."

"State your case, Bingo."

Bingo stated his case.

"What about it, Jeeves?" I said. "Do we go in?"

Jeeves pondered to some extent.

"I am inclined to favour the idea, sir."

That was good enough for me. "Right," I said. "Then we will form a syndicate and bust the Ring. I supply the money, you supply the brains, and Bingo — what do you supply, Bingo?"

"If you will carry me, and let me settle up later," said young Bingo, "I think I can put you in the way of winning a parcel on the Mothers' Sack Race."

"All right. We will put you down as Inside Information. Now, what are the events?"

Bingo reached for his paper and consulted it.

"Girls' Under Fourteen Fifty-Yard Dash seems to open the proceedings."

"Anything to say about that, Jeeves?"

"No, sir. I have no information."

"What's the next?"

"Boys' and Girls' Mixed Animal Potato Race, All Ages."

This was a new one to me. I had never heard of it at any of the big meetings.

"What's that?"

"Rather sporting," said young Bingo. "The competitors enter in couples, each couple being assigned an animal cry and a potato. For instance, let's suppose that you and Jeeves entered. Jeeves would stand at a fixed point holding a potato. You would have your head in a sack, and you would grope about trying to find Jeeves and making a noise like a cat; Jeeves also making a noise like a cat. Other competitors would be making noises like cows and pigs and dogs, and so on, and groping about for *their* potato-holders, who would also be making noises like cows and pigs and dogs and so on — "

I stopped the poor fish.

"Jolly if you're fond of animals," I said, "but on the whole — "

"Precisely, sir," said Jeeves. "I wouldn't touch it."

"Too open, what?"

"Exactly, sir. Very hard to estimate form."

"Carry on, Bingo. Where do we go from there?"

"Mothers' Sack Race."

"Ah! that's better. This is where you know something."

"A gift for Mrs. Penworthy, the tobacconist's wife," said Bingo, confidently. "I was in at her shop yesterday, buying cigarettes, and she told me she had won three times at fairs in Worcestershire. She only moved to these parts a short time

The Purity of the Turf 99

ago, so nobody knows about her. She promised me she would keep herself dark, and I think we could get a good price."

"Risk a tenner each way, Jeeves, what?"

"I think so, sir."

"Girls' Open Egg and Spoon Race," read Bingo.

"How about that?"

"I doubt if it would be worth while to invest, sir," said Jeeves. "I am told it is a certainty for last year's winner, Sarah Mills, who will doubtless start an odds-on favourite."

"Good, is she?"

"They tell me in the village that she carries a beautiful egg, sir."

"Then there's the Obstacle Race," said Bingo. "Risky, in my opinion. Like betting on the Grand National. Fathers' Hat-Trimming Contest — another speculative event. That's all, except the Choir Boys' Hundred Yards Handicap, for a pewter mug presented by the vicar — open to all whose voices have not broken before the second Sunday in Epiphany. Willie Chambers won last year, in a canter, receiving fifteen yards. This time he will probably be handicapped out of the race. I don't know what to advise."

"If I might make a suggestion, sir."

I eyed Jeeves with interest. I don't know that I'd ever seen him look so nearly excited.

"You've got something up your sleeve?"

"I have, sir."

"Red-hot?"

"That precisely describes it, sir. I think I may confidently assert that we have the winner of the Choir Boys' Handicap under this very roof, sir. Harold, the page-boy."

"Page-boy? Do you mean the tubby little chap in buttons one sees bobbing about here and there? Why, dash it, Jeeves, nobody has a greater respect for your knowledge of form than I have, but I'm hanged if I can see Harold catching the judge's eye. He's practically circular, and every time I've seen him he's been leaning up against something half-asleep."

"He receives thirty yards, sir, and could win from scratch. The boy is a flier."

"How do you know?"

Jeeves coughed, and there was a dreamy look in his eye.

"I was as much astonished as yourself, sir, when I first became aware of the lad's capabilities. I happened to pursue him one morning with the intention of fetching him a clip on the side of the head — "

"Great Scott, Jeeves! You!"

"Yes, sir. The boy is of an outspoken disposition, and had made an opprobrious remark respecting my personal appearance."

"What did he say about your appearance?"

"I have forgotten, sir," said Jeeves, with a touch of austerity. "But it was opprobrious. I endeavoured to correct him, but he out-distanced me by yards, and made good his escape."

"But, I say, Jeeves, this is sensational. And yet — if he's such a sprinter, why hasn't anybody in the village found it out? Surely he plays with the other boys?"

"No, sir. As his lordship's page-boy, Harold does not mix with the village lads."

"Bit of a snob, what?"

"He is somewhat acutely alive to the existence of class distinctions, sir."

"You're absolutely certain he's such a wonder?" said Bingo. "I mean, it wouldn't do to plunge unless you're sure."

"If you desire to ascertain the boy's form by personal inspection, sir, it will be a simple matter to arrange a secret trial."

"I'm bound to say I should feel easier in my mind," I said.

"Then if I may take a shilling from the money on your dressing-table — "

"What for?"

"I propose to bribe the lad to speak slightingly of the second footman's squint, sir. Charles is somewhat sensitive on the point, and should undoubtedly make the lad extend himself. If you will be at the first-floor passage-window, overlooking the back-door, in half an hour's time — "

I don't know when I've dressed in such a hurry. As a rule, I'm what you might call a slow and careful dresser: I like to linger over the tie and see that the trousers are just so; but this morning I was all worked up. I just shoved on my things anyhow, and joined Bingo at the window with a quarter of an hour to spare.

The passage-window looked down on to a broad sort of paved courtyard, which ended after about twenty yards in an archway through a high wall. Beyond this archway you got on to a strip of the drive, which curved round for another thirty yards or so till it was lost behind a thick shrubbery. I put myself in the stripling's place and thought what steps I would take with a second footman after me. There was only one thing to do — leg it for the shrubbery and take cover; which meant that at least fifty yards would have to be covered — an excellent test. If good old Harold could fight off the second footman's challenge long enough to allow him to reach the bushes, there wasn't a choirboy in England who could give him thirty yards in the hundred. I waited, all of a twitter, for what seemed hours, and then suddenly there was a confused noise without and something round and blue and buttony shot through the back-door and buzzed for the archway like a mustang. And about two seconds later out came the second footman, going his hardest.

There was nothing to it. Absolutely nothing. The field never had a chance. Long before the footman reached the half-way mark, Harold was in the bushes, throwing stones. I came away from the window thrilled to the marrow; and when I met Jeeves on the stairs I was so moved that I nearly grasped his hand.

"Jeeves," I said, "no discussion! The Wooster shirt goes on this boy!"

"Very good, sir," said Jeeves.

The worst of these country meetings is that you can't plunge as heavily as you would like when you get a good thing, because it alarms the Ring. Steggles, though pimpled, was, as I have indicated, no chump, and if I had invested all I wanted to he would have put two and two together. I managed to get a good solid bet down for the syndicate, however, though it did make him look thoughtful. I heard in the next few days that he had been making searching inquiries in the village concerning Harold; but nobody could tell him anything, and eventually he came to the conclusion, I suppose, that I must be having a long shot on the strength of that thirty yards start. Public opinion wavered between Jimmy Goode, receiving ten yards, at seven-to-two, and Alexander Bartlett, with six yards start, at eleven-to-four. Willie Chambers, scratch, was offered to the public at two-to-one, but found no takers.

We were taking no chances on the big event, and directly we had got our money on at a nice hundred-to-twelve Harold was put into strict training. It was a wearing business, and I can understand now why most of the big trainers are grim, silent men, who look as though they had suffered. The kid wanted constant watching. It was no good talking to him about honour and glory and how proud his mother would be when he wrote and told her he had won a real cup — the moment blighted Harold discovered that training meant knocking off pastry, taking exercise, and keeping away from the cigarettes, he was all against it, and it was only by unceasing vigilance that we managed to keep him in any shape at all. It was the diet that was the stumbling block. As far as exercise went, we could generally arrange for a sharp dash every morning with the assistance of the second footman. It ran into money, of course, but that couldn't be helped. Still, when a kid has simply to wait till the butler's back is turned to have the run of the pantry and has only to nip into the smoking-room to collect a handful of the best Turkish, training becomes a rocky job. We could only hope that on the day his natural stamina would pull him through.

And then one evening young Bingo came back from the links with a disturbing story. He had been in the habit of giving Harold mild exercise in the afternoons by taking him out as a caddie.

At first he seemed to think it humorous, the poor chump! He bubbled over with merry mirth as he began his tale.

"I say, rather funny this afternoon," he said. "You ought to have seen Steggles's face!"

"Seen Steggles's face? What for?"

"When he saw young Harold sprint, I mean."

I was filled with a grim foreboding of an awful doom.

"Good heavens! You didn't let Harold sprint in front of Steggles?"

Young Bingo's jaw dropped.

"I never thought of that," he said gloomily. "It wasn't my fault. I was playing a round with Steggles, and after we'd finished we went into the club-house for a drink, leaving Harold with the clubs outside. In about five minutes we came out, and there was the kid on the gravel practising swings with Steggles's driver and a stone. When he saw us coming, the kid dropped the club and was over the horizon like a streak. Steggles was absolutely dumbfounded. And I must say it was a revelation even to me. The kid certainly gave of his best. Of course, it's a nuisance in a way; but I don't see, on second thoughts," said Bingo, brightening up, "that it matters. We're on at a good price. We've nothing to lose by the kid's form becoming known. I take it he will start odds on, but that doesn't affect us."

I looked at Jeeves. Jeeves looked at me.

"It affects us all right if he doesn't start at all."

"Precisely, sir."

"What do you mean?" asked Bingo.

"If you ask me," I said, "I think Steggles will try to noble him before the race."

"Good Lord! I never thought of that." Bingo blenched. "You don't think he would really do it?"

"I think he would have a jolly good try. Steggles is a bad man. From now on, Jeeves, we must watch Harold like hawks."

"Undoubtedly, sir."

"Ceaseless vigilance, what?"

"Precisely, sir."

"You wouldn't care to sleep in his room, Jeeves?"

"No, sir, I should not."

"No, nor would I, if it comes to that. But dash it all," I said, "we're letting ourselves get rattled! We're losing our nerve. This won't do. How can Steggles possibly get at Harold, even if he wants to?"

There was no cheering young Bingo up. He's one of those birds who simply leap at the morbid view, if you give them half a chance.

"There are all sorts of ways of nobbling favourites," he said, in a sort of death-bed voice. "You ought to read some of these racing novels. In 'Pipped on the Post', Lord Jasper Mauleverer as near as a toucher outed Bonny Betsy by bribing the head-lad to slip a cobra into her stable the night before the Derby!"

"What are the chances of a cobra biting Harold, Jeeves?"

"Slight, I should imagine, sir. And in such an event, knowing the boy as intimately as I do, my anxiety would be entirely for the snake."

"Still, unceasing vigilance, Jeeves."

"Most certainly, sir."

I must say I got a bit fed with young Bingo in the next few days. It's all very well for a fellow with a big winner in his stable to exercise proper care, but in my opinion Bingo overdid it. The blighter's mind appeared to be absolutely saturated with racing fiction; and in stories of that kind, as far as I could make out, no horse is ever allowed to start in a race without at least a dozen attempts to put it out of action. He stuck to Harold like a plaster. Never let the unfortunate kid out of his sight. Of course, it meant a lot to the poor old egg if he could collect on this race, because it would give him enough money to chuck his tutoring job and get back to London; but all the same, he needn't have woken me up at three in the morning twice running — once to tell me we ought to cook Harold's food ourselves to prevent doping; the other time to say that he had heard mysterious noises in the shrubbery. But he reached the limit, in my opinion, when he insisted on my going to evening service on Sunday, the day before the sports.

"Why on earth?" I said, never being much of a lad for evensong.

"Well, I can't go myself. I shan't be here. I've got to go to London to-day with young Egbert." Egbert was Lord Wickhammersley's son, the one Bingo was tutoring. "He's going for a visit down in Kent, and I've got to see him off at Charing Cross. It's an infernal nuisance. I shan't be back till Monday afternoon. In fact, I shall miss most of the sports, I expect. Everything, therefore, depends on you, Bertie."

"But why should either of us go to evening service?"

"Ass! Harold sings in the choir, doesn't he?"

"What about it? I can't stop him dislocating his neck over a high note, if that's what you're afraid of."

"Fool! Steggles sings in the choir, too. There may be dirty work after the service."

"What absolute rot!"

"Is it?" said young Bingo. "Well, let me tell you that in 'Jenny, the Girl Jockey,' the villain kidnapped the boy who was to ride the favourite the night before the big race, and he was the only one who understood and could control the horse, and if the heroine hadn't dressed up in riding things and — "

"Oh, all right, all right. But, if there's any danger, it seems to me the simplest thing would be for Harold not to turn out on Sunday evening."

"He must turn out. You seem to think the infernal kid is a monument of rectitude, beloved by all. He's got the shakiest reputation of any kid in the village. His name is as near being mud as it can jolly well stick. He's played hookey from the choir so often that the vicar told him, if one more thing happened, he would fire him out. Nice chumps we should look if he was scratched the night before the race!"

Well, of course, that being so, there was nothing for it but to toddle along.

There's something about evening service in a country church that makes a fellow feel drowsy and peaceful. Sort of end-of-a-perfect-day feeling. Old Heppenstall, the vicar, was up in the pulpit, and he has a kind of regular, bleating delivery that assists thought. They had left the door open, and the air was full of a mixed scent of trees and honeysuckle and mildew and villagers' Sunday clothes. As far as the eye could reach, you could see farmers propped up in restful attitudes, breathing heavily; and the children in the congregation who had fidgeted during the earlier part of the proceedings were now lying back in a surfeited sort of coma. The last rays of the setting sun shone through the stained-glass windows, birds were twittering in the trees, the women's dresses crackled gently in the stillness. Peaceful. That's what I'm driving at. I felt peaceful. Everybody felt peaceful. And that is why the explosion, when it came, sounded like the end of all things.

I call it an explosion, because that was what it seemed like when it broke loose. One moment a dreamy hush was all over the place, broken only by old Heppenstall talking about our duty to our neighbors; and then, suddenly, a sort of piercing, shrieking squeal that got you right between the eyes and ran all the way down your spine and out at the soles of the feet.

"EE-ee-ee-ee-ee! Oo-ee! Ee-ee-ee-ee!"

It sounded like about six hundred pigs having their tails twisted simultaneously, but it was simply the kid Harold, who appeared to be having some species of fit. He was jumping up and down and slapping at the back of his neck. And about every other second he would take a deep breath and give out another of the squeals.

Well, I mean, you can't do that sort of thing in the middle of the sermon during evening service without exciting remark. The congregation came out of its trance with a jerk, and climbed on the pews to get a better view. Old Heppenstall stopped in the middle of a sentence and spun round. And a couple of vergers with great presence of mind bounded up the aisle like leopards, collected Harold, still squealing, and marched him out. They disappeared into the vestry, and I grabbed my hat and legged it round to the stage-door, full of apprehension and what not. I couldn't think what the deuce could have happened, but somewhere dimly behind the proceedings there seemed to me to lurk the hand of the blighter Steggles.

By the time I got there and managed to get someone to open the door, which was locked, the service seemed to be over. Old Heppenstall was standing in the middle of a crowd of choir-boys and vergers and sextons and what not, putting the wretched Harold through it with no little vim. I had come in at the tail-end of what must have been a fairly fruity oration.

"Wretched boy! How dare you — "

"I got a sensitive skin!"

"This is no time to talk about your skin — "

"Somebody put a beetle down my back!"

"Absurd!"

"I felt it wriggling — "

"Nonsense!"

"Sounds pretty thin, doesn't it?" said someone at my side.

It was Steggles, dash him. Clad in a snowy surplice or cassock, or whatever they call it, and wearing an expression of grave concern, the blighter had the cold, cynical crust to look me in the eyeball without a blink.

"Did you put a beetle down his neck?" I cried.

"Me!" said Steggles. "Me!"

Old Heppenstall was putting on the black cap.

"I do not credit a word of your story, wretched boy! I have warned you before, and now the time has come to act. You cease from this moment to be a member of my choir. Go, miserable child!"

Steggles plucked at my sleeve.

"In that case," he said, "those bets, you know — I'm afraid you lose your money, dear old boy. It's a pity you didn't put it on S.P. I always think S.P.'s the only safe way."

I gave him one look. Not a bit of good, of course.

"And they talk about the Purity of the Turf!" I said. And I meant it to sting, by Jove!

Jeeves received the news bravely, but I think the man was a bit rattled beneath the surface.

"An ingenious young gentleman, Mr. Steggles, sir."

"A bally swindler, you mean."

"Perhaps that would be a more exact description. However, these things will happen on the Turf, and it is useless to complain."

"I wish I had your sunny disposition, Jeeves!"

Jeeves bowed.

"We now rely, then, it would seem, sir, almost entirely on Mrs. Penworthy. Should she justify Mr. Little's encomiums and show real class in the Mothers' Sack Race, our gains will just balance our losses."

"Yes; but that's not much consolation when you've been looking forward to a big win."

"It is just possible that we may still find ourselves on the right side of the ledger after all, sir. Before Mr. Little left, I persuaded him to invest a small sum for the syndicate of which you were kind enough to make me a member, sir, on the Girls' Egg and Spoon Race."

"On Sarah Mills?"

"No, sir. On a long-priced outsider. Little Prudence Baxter, sir, the child of his lordship's head gardener. Her father assures me she has a very steady hand. She is accustomed to bring him his mug of beer from the cottage each afternoon, and he informs me she has never spilled a drop."

Well, that sounded as though young Prudence's control was good. But how about speed? With seasoned performers like Sarah Mills entered, the thing practically amounted to a classic race, and in these big events you must have speed.

"I am aware that it is what is termed a long shot, sir. Still, I thought it judicious."

"You backed her for a place, too, of course?"

"Yes, sir. Each way."

"Well, I suppose it's all right. I've never known you make a bloomer yet."

"Thank you very much, sir."

I'm bound to say that, as a general rule, my idea of a large afternoon would be to keep as far away from a village school-treat as possible. A sticky business. But with such grave issues toward, if you know what I mean, I sank my prejudices on this occasion and rolled up. I found the proceedings about as scaly as I had expected. It was a warm day, and the Hall grounds were a dense, practically liquid mass of peasantry. Kids seethed to and fro. One of them, a small girl of sorts, grabbed my hand and hung on to it as I dove my way through the jam to where the Mothers' Sack Race was to finish. We hadn't been introduced, but she seemed to think I would do as well as anyone else to talk to about the rag-doll she had won in the Lucky Dip, and she rather spread herself on the topic.

"I'm going to call it Gertrude," she said. "And I shall undress it every night and put it to bed, and wake it up in the morning and dress it, and put it to bed at night, and wake it up next morning and dress it — "

"I say, old thing," I said, "I don't want to hurry you and all that, but you couldn't condense it a bit, could you? I'm rather anxious to see the finish of this race. The Wooster fortunes are by way of hanging on it."

"I'm going to run in a race soon," she said, shelving the doll for the nonce and descending to ordinary chitchat.

"Yes?" I said. Distrait, if you know what I mean, and trying to peer through the chinks in the crowd.

"What race is that?"

"Egg'n Spoon."

"No, really? Are you Sarah Mills?"

"Na-ow!" Registering scorn. "I'm Prudence Baxter."

Naturally this put our relations on a different footing. I gazed at her with considerable interest. One of the stable. I must say she didn't look much of a flier. She was short and round. Bit out of condition, I thought.

"I say," I said, "that being so, you mustn't dash about in the hot sun and take the edge off yourself. You must conserve your energies, old friend. Sit down here in the shade."

"Don't want to sit down."

"Well, take it easy, anyhow."

The kid flitted to another topic like a butterfly hovering from flower to flower.

"I'm a good girl," she said.

"I bet you are. I hope you're a good egg-and-spoon racer, too."

"Harold's a bad boy. Harold squealed in church and isn't allowed to come to the treat. I'm glad," continued this ornament of her sex, wrinkling her nose virtuously, "because he's a bad boy. He pulled my hair Friday. Harold isn't coming to the treat! Harold isn't coming to the treat! Harold isn't coming to the treat!" she chanted, making a regular song of it.

"Don't rub it in, my dear old gardener's daughter," I pleaded. "You don't know it, but you've hit on rather a painful subject."

"Ah, Wooster, my dear fellow! So you have made friends with this little lady?"

It was old Heppenstall, beaming pretty profusely. Life and soul of the party.

"I am delighted, my dear Wooster," he went on, "quite delighted at the way you young men are throwing yourselves into the spirit of this little festivity of ours."

"Oh, yes?" I said.

"Oh, yes! Even Rupert Steggles. I must confess that my opinion of Rupert Steggles has materially altered for the better this afternoon."

Mine hadn't. But I didn't say so.

"I had always considered Rupert Steggles, between ourselves, a rather self-centered youth, by no means the kind who would put himself out to further the enjoyment of his fellows. And yet twice within the last half-hour I have observed him escorting Mrs. Penworthy, our worthy tobacconist's wife, to the refreshment-tent."

I left him standing. I shook off the clutching hand of the Baxter kid and hared it rapidly to the spot where the Mothers' Sack Race was just finishing. I had a horrid presentiment that there had been more dirty work at the cross-roads. The first person I ran into was young Bingo. I grabbed him by the arm.

"Who won?"

"I don't know. I didn't notice." There was bitterness in the chappie's voice. "It wasn't Mrs. Penworthy, dash her! Bertie, that hound Steggles is nothing more nor less than one of our leading snakes. I don't know how he heard about her, but he must have got on to it that she was dangerous. Do you know what he did? He lured that miserable woman into the refreshment-tent five minutes before the race, and brought her out so weighed down with cake and tea that she blew up in the first twenty yards. Just rolled over and lay there! Well, thank goodness we still have Harold!"

I gaped at the poor chump.

"Harold! Haven't you heard?"

"Heard?" Bingo turned a delicate green. "Heard what? I haven't heard anything. I only arrived five minutes ago.

Came here straight from the station. What has happened? Tell me!"

I slipped him the information. He stared at me for a moment in a ghastly sort of way, then with a hollow groan tottered away and was lost in the crowd. A nasty knock, poor chap. I didn't blame him for being upset.

They were clearing the decks now for the Egg and Spoon Race, and I thought I might as well stay where I was and watch the finish. Not that I had much hope. Young Prudence was a good conversationalist, but she didn't seem to me to be the build for a winner.

As far as I could see through the mob, they got off to a good start. A short, red-haired child was making the running, with a freckled blonde second and Sarah Mills lying up an easy third. Our nominee was straggling along with the field, well behind the leaders. It was not hard even as early as this to spot the winner. There was a grace, a practised precision, in the way Sarah Mills held her spoon that told its own story. She was cutting out a good pace, but her egg didn't even wobble. A natural egg-and-spooner, if ever there was one.

Class will tell. Thirty yards from the tape, the red-haired kid tripped over her feet and shot her egg on to the turf. The freckled blonde fought gamely, but she had run herself out half-way down the straight, and Sarah Mills came past and home on a tight rein by several lengths, a popular winner. The blonde was second. A sniffing female in blue gingham beat a pie-faced kid in pink for the place-money, and Prudence Baxter, Jeeves's long shot, was either fifth or sixth, I couldn't see which.

And then I was carried along with the crowd to where old Heppenstall was going to present the prizes. I found myself standing next to the man Steggles.

"Hallo, old chap!" he said, very bright and cheery. "You've had a bad day, I'm afraid."

I looked at him with silent scorn. Lost on the blighter, of course.

"It's not been a good meeting for any of the big punters,"

he went on. "Poor old Bingo Little went down badly over that Egg and Spoon Race."

I hadn't been meaning to chat with the fellow, but I was startled.

"How do you mean badly?" I said. "We — he only had a small bet on."

"I don't know what you call small. He had thirty quid each way on the Baxter kid."

The landscape reeled before me.

"What!"

"Thirty quid at ten to one. I thought he must have heard something, but apparently not. The race went by the form-book all right."

I was trying to do sums in my head. I was just in the middle of working out the syndicate's losses, when old Heppenstall's voice came sort of faintly to me out of the distance. He had been pretty fatherly and debonair when ladling out the prizes for the other events, but now he had suddenly grown all pained and grieved. He peered sorrowfully at the multitude.

"With regard to the Girls' Egg and Spoon Race, which has just concluded," he said, "I have a painful duty to perform. Circumstances have arisen which it is impossible to ignore. It is not too much to say that I am stunned."

He gave the populace about five seconds to wonder why he was stunned, then went on.

"Three years ago, as you are aware, I was compelled to expunge from the list of events at this annual festival the Fathers' Quarter-Mile, owing to reports coming to my ears of wagers taken and given on the result at the village inn and a strong suspicion that on at least one occasion the race had actually been sold by the speediest runner. That unfortunate occurrence shook my faith in human nature, I admit — but still there was one event at least which I confidently expected to remain untainted by the miasma of Professionalism. I allude to the Girls' Egg and Spoon Race. It seems, alas, that I was too sanguine."

He stopped again, and wrestled with his feelings.

"I will not weary you with the unpleasant details. I will merely say that before the race was run a stranger in our midst, the manservant of one of the guests at the Hall — I will not specify with more particularity — approached several of the competitors and presented each of them with five shillings on condition that they — er — finished. A belated sense of remorse has led him to confess to me what he did, but it is too late. The evil is accomplished, and retribution must take its course. It is no time for half-measures. I must be firm. I rule that Sarah Mills, Jane Parker, Bessie Clay, and Rosie Jukes, the first four to pass the winning-post, have forfeited their amateur status and are disqualified, and this handsome work-bag, presented by Lord Wickhammersley, goes, in consequence, to Prudence Baxter. Prudence, step forward!"

THE
SMILE
THAT
WINS

THE CONVERSATION IN THE BAR-PARLOUR OF THE
Anglers' Rest had turned to the subject of the regrettably low
standard of morality prevalent among the nobility and
landed gentry of Great Britain.

Miss Postlethwaite, our erudite barmaid, had brought the
matter up by mentioning that in the novelette which she was
reading a viscount had just thrown a family solicitor over a
cliff.

"Because he had found out his guilty secret," explained
Miss Postlethwaite, polishing a glass a little severely, for she
was a good woman. "It was his guilty secret this solicitor had
found out, so the viscount threw him over a cliff. I suppose,
if one did but know, that sort of thing is going on all the
time."

Mr. Mulliner nodded gravely.

"So much so," he agreed, "that I believe that whenever a
family solicitor is found in two or more pieces at the bottom
of a cliff, the first thing the Big Four at Scotland Yard do is
make a round-up of all the viscounts in the neighbourhood."

"Baronets are worse than viscounts," said a Pint of Stout vehemently. "I was done down by one only last month over the sale of a cow."

"Earls are worse than baronets," insisted a Whisky Sour. "I could tell you something about earls."

"How about O.B.E.'s?" demanded a Mild and Bitter. "If you ask me, O.B.E.'s want watching, too."

Mr. Mulliner sighed.

"The fact is," he said, "reluctant though one may be to admit it, the entire British aristocracy is seamed and honey-combed with immorality. I venture to assert that, if you took a pin and jabbed it down anywhere in the pages of *Debrett's Peerage,* you would find it piercing the name of someone who was going about the place with a conscience as tender as a sunburned neck. If anything were needed to prove my assertion, the story of my nephew, Adrian Mulliner, the de-tective, would do it."

"I didn't know you had a nephew who was a detective," said the Whisky Sour.

Oh, yes. He has retired now, but at one time he was as keen an operator as anyone in the profession. After leaving Oxford and trying his hand at one or two uncongenial tasks, he had found his niche as a member of the firm of Widgery and Boon, Investigators, of Albemarle Street. And it was during his second year with this old-established house that he met and loved Lady Millicent Shipton-Bellinger, younger daugh-ter of the fifth Earl of Brangbolton.

It was the Adventure of the Missing Sealyham that brought the young couple together. From the purely professional standpoint, my nephew has never ranked this among his greatest triumphs of retiocination; but, considering what it led to, he might well, I think, be justified in regarding it as the most important case of his career. What happened was that he met the animal straying in the park, deduced from the name and address on its collar that it belonged to Lady

Millicent Shipton-Bellinger, of 18A, Upper Brook Street, and took it thither at the conclusion of his stroll and restored it.

"Child's-play" is the phrase with which, if you happen to allude to it, Adrian Mulliner will always airily dismiss this particular investigation; but Lady Millicent could not have displayed more admiration and enthusiasm had it been the supremest masterpiece of detective work. She fawned on my nephew. She invited him in to tea, consisting of buttered toast, anchovy sandwiches and two kinds of cake; and at the conclusion of the meal they parted on terms which, even at that early stage in their acquaintance, were something warmer than those of mere friendship.

Indeed, it is my belief that the girl fell in love with Adrian as instantaneously as he with her. On him, it was her radiant blonde beauty that exercised the spell. She, on her side, was fascinated, I fancy, not only by the regularity of his features, which, as is the case with all the Mulliners, was considerable, but also by the fact that he was dark and thin and wore an air of inscrutable melancholy.

This, as a matter of fact, was due to the troublesome attacks of dyspepsia from which he had suffered since boyhood; but to the girl it naturally seemed evidence of a great and romantic soul. Nobody, she felt, could look so grave and sad, had he not hidden deeps in him.

One can see the thing from her point of view. All her life she had been accustomed to brainless juveniles who eked out their meagre eyesight with monocles and, as far as conversation was concerned, were a spent force after they had asked her if she had seen the Academy or did she think she would prefer a glass of lemonade. The effect on her of a dark, keen-eyed man like Adrian Mulliner, who spoke well and easily of footprints, psychology and the underworld, must have been stupendous.

At any rate, their love ripened rapidly. It could not have been two weeks after their first meeting when Adrian, as he was giving her lunch one day at the Senior Bloodstain, the detectives' club in Rupert Street, proposed and was accepted. And for the next twenty-four hours, one is safe in saying, there was in the whole of London, including the outlying suburban districts, no happier private investigator than he.

Next day, however, when he again met Millicent for lunch, he was disturbed to perceive on her beautiful face an emotion which his trained eye immediately recognized as anguish.

"Oh, Adrian," said the girl brokenly. "The worst has happened. My father refuses to hear of our marrying. When I told him we were engaged, he said 'Pooh!' quite a number of times, and added that he had never heard such dashed nonsense in his life. You see, ever since my Uncle Joe's trouble in nineteen-twenty-eight, father has had a horror of detectives."

"I don't think I have met your Uncle Joe."

"You will have the opportunity next year. With the usual allowance for good conduct he should be with us again about July. And there is another thing."

"Not another?"

"Yes. Do you know Sir Jasper Addleton, O.B.E.?"

"The financier?"

"Father wants me to marry him. Isn't it awful!"

"I have certainly heard more enjoyable bits of news," agreed Adrian. "This wants a good deal of careful thinking over."

The process of thinking over his unfortunate situation had the effect of rendering excessively acute the pangs of Adrian Mulliner's dyspepsia. During the past two weeks the ecstasy of being with Millicent and deducing that she loved him had caused a complete cessation of the attacks; but now they began again, worse than ever. At length, after a sleepless night during which he experienced all the emotions of one who has carelessly swallowed a family of scorpions, he sought a specialist.

The specialist was one of those keen, modern minds who disdain the outworn formulæ of the more conservative mass of the medical profession. He examined Adrian carefully, then sat back in his chair, with the tips of his fingers touching.

"Smile!" he said.

"Eh?" said Adrian.

"Smile, Mr. Mulliner."

"Did you say smile?"

"That's it. Smile."

"But," Adrian pointed out, "I've just lost the only girl I ever loved."

"Well, that's fine," said the specialist, who was a bachelor. "Come on, now, if you please. Start smiling."

Adrian was a little bewildered.

"Listen," he said. "What *is* all this about smiling? We started, if I recollect, talking about my gastric juices. Now, in some mysterious way, we seem to have got on to the subject of smiles. How do you mean — smile? I never smile. I haven't smiled since the butler tripped over the spaniel and upset the melted butter on my Aunt Elizabeth, when I was a boy of twelve."

The specialist nodded.

"Precisely. And that is why your digestive organs trouble you. Dyspepsia," he proceeded, "is now recognized by the progressive element of the profession as purely mental. We do not treat it with drugs and medicines. Happiness is the only cure. Be gay, Mr. Mulliner. Be cheerful. And, if you can't do that, at any rate smile. The mere exercise of the risible muscles is in itself beneficial. Go out now and make a point, whenever you have a spare moment, of smiling."

"Like this?" said Adrian.

"Wider than that."

"How about this?"

"Better," said the specialist, "but still not quite so elastic as one could desire. Naturally, you need practice. We must expect the muscles to work rustily for a while at their unaccustomed task. No doubt things will brighten by and by."

He regarded Adrian thoughtfully.

"Odd," he said. "A curious smile, yours, Mr. Mulliner. It

reminds me a little of the Mona Lisa's. It has the same underlying note of the sardonic and the sinister. It virtually amounts to a leer. Somehow it seems to convey the suggestion that you know all. Fortunately, my own life is an open book, for all to read, and so I was not discommoded. But I think it would be better if, for the present, you endeavoured not to smile at invalids or nervous persons. Good morning, Mr. Mulliner. That will be five guineas, precisely."

On Adrian's face, as he went off that afternoon to perform the duties assigned to him by his firm, there was no smile of any description. He shrank from the ordeal before him. He had been told off to guard the wedding-presents at a reception in Grosvenor Square, and naturally anything to do with weddings was like a sword through his heart. His face, as he patrolled the room where the gifts were laid out, was drawn and forbidding. Hitherto, at these functions, it had always been his pride that nobody could tell that he was a detective. To-day, a child could have recognized his trade. He looked like Sherlock Holmes.

To the gay throng that surged about him he paid little attention. Usually tense and alert on occasions like this, he now found his mind wandering. He mused sadly on Millicent. And suddenly — the result, no doubt, of these gloomy meditations, though a glass of wedding champagne may have contributed its mite — there shot through him, starting at about the third button of his neat waistcoat, a pang of dyspepsia so keen that he felt the pressing necessity of doing something about it immediately.

With a violent effort he contorted his features into a smile. And, as he did so, a stout, bluff man of middle age, with a red face and a grey moustache, who had been hovering near one of the tables, turned and saw him.

"Egad!" he muttered, paling.

Sir Sutton Hartley-Wesping, Bart. — for the red-faced man was he — had had a pretty good afternoon. Like all baronets who attend Society wedding-receptions, he had been going round the various tables since his arrival, pocketing here a fish-slice, there a jewelled egg-boiler, until now he had taken on about all the cargo his tonnage would warrant, and was thinking of strolling off to the pawnbroker's in the Euston Road, with whom he did most of his business. At the sight of Adrian's smile, he froze where he stood, appalled.

We have seen what the specialist thought of Adrian's smile. Even to him, a man of clear and limpid conscience, it had seemed sardonic and sinister. We can picture, then, the effect it must have had on Sir Sutton Hartley-Wesping.

At all costs, he felt, he must conciliate this leering man. Swiftly removing from his pockets a diamond necklace, five fish-slices, ten cigarette-lighters and a couple of egg-boilers, he placed them on the table and came over to Adrian with a nervous little laugh.

"How *are* you, my dear fellow?" he said.

Adrian said that he was quite well. And so, indeed, he was. The specialist's recipe had worked like magic. He was mildly surprised at finding himself so cordially addressed by a man whom he did not remember ever having seen before, but he attributed this to the magnetic charm of his personality.

"That's fine," said the Baronet heartily. "That's capital. That's splendid. Er — by the way — I fancied I saw you smile just now."

"Yes," said Adrian. "I did smile. You see — "

"Of course I see. Of course, my dear fellow. You detected the joke I was playing on our good hostess, and you were amused because you understood that there is no animus, no *arrière-pensée*, behind these little practical pleasantries — nothing but good, clean fun, at which nobody would have laughed more heartily than herself. And now, what are you doing this weekend, my dear old chap? Would you care to run down to my place in Sussex?"

"Very kind of you," began Adrian doubtfully. He was not quite sure that he was in the mood for strange week-ends.

"Here is my card, then. I shall expect you on Friday. Quite

a small party. Lord Brangbolton, Sir Jasper Addleton, and a few more. Just loafing about, you know, and a spot of bridge at night. Splendid. Capital. See you, then, on Friday."

And, carelessly dropping another egg-boiler on the table as he passed, Sir Sutton disappeared.

Any doubts which Adrian might have entertained as to accepting the Baronet's invitation had vanished as he heard the names of his fellow-guests. It always interests a fiancé to meet his fiancée's father and his fiancée's prospective fiancé. For the first time since Millicent had told him the bad news, Adrian became almost cheerful. If, he felt, this baronet had taken such a tremendous fancy to him at first sight, why might it not happen that Lord Brangbolton would be equally drawn to him — to the extent, in fact, of overlooking his profession and welcoming him as a son-in-law?

He packed, on the Friday, with what was to all intents and purposes a light heart.

A fortunate chance at the very outset of his expedition increased Adrian's optimism. It made him feel that Fate was fighting on his side. As he walked down the platform of Victoria Station, looking for an empty compartment in the train which was to take him to his destination, he perceived a tall, aristocratic old gentleman being assisted into a first-class carriage by a man of butlerine aspect. And in the latter he recognized the servitor who had admitted him to 18A, Upper Brook Street, when he visited the house after solving the riddle of the missing Sealyham. Obviously, then, the white-haired, dignified passenger could be none other than Lord Brangbolton. And Adrian felt that if on a long train journey he failed to ingratiate himself with the old buster, he had vastly mistaken his amiability and winning fascination of manner.

He leaped in, accordingly, as the train began to move, and the Earl, glancing up from his paper, jerked a thumb at the door.

"Get out, blast you!" he said. "Full up."

As the compartment was empty but for themselves, Adrian made no move to comply with the request. Indeed, to alight now, to such an extent had the train gathered speed, would have been impossible. Instead, he spoke cordially.

"Lord Brangbolton, I believe?"

"Go to hell," said his lordship.

"I fancy we are to be fellow-guests at Wesping Hall this week-end."

"What of it?"

"I just mentioned it."

"Oh?" said Lord Brangbolton. "Well, since you're here, how about a little flutter?"

As is customary with men of his social position, Millicent's father always travelled with a pack of cards. Being gifted by nature with considerable manual dexterity, he usually managed to do well with these on race-trains.

"Ever played Persian Monarchs?" he asked, shuffling.

"I think not," said Adrian.

"Quite simple," said Lord Brangbolton. "You just bet a quid or whatever it may be that you can cut a higher card than the other fellow, and, if you do, you win, and, if you don't, you don't."

Adrian said it sounded a little like Blind Hooky.

"It is like Blind Hooky," said Lord Brangbolton. "Very like Blind Hooky. In fact, if you can play Blind Hooky, you can play Persian Monarchs."

By the time they alighted at Wesping Parva Adrian was twenty pounds on the wrong side of the ledger. The fact, however, did not prey upon his mind. On the contrary, he was well satisfied with the progress of events. Elated with his winnings, the old Earl had become positively cordial, and Adrian resolved to press his advantage home at the earliest opportunity.

Arrived at Wesping Hall, accordingly, he did not delay. Shortly after the sounding of the dressing-gong he made his way to Lord Brangbolton's room and found him in his bath.

"Might I have a word with you, Lord Brangbolton?" he said.

"You can do more than that," replied the other, with marked amiability. "You can help me find the soap."

"Have you lost the soap?"

"Yes. Had it a minute ago, and now it's gone."

"Strange," said Adrian.

"Very strange," agreed Lord Brangbolton. "Makes a fellow think a bit, that sort of thing happening. My own soap, too. Brought it with me."

Adrian considered.

"Tell me exactly what occurred," he said. "In your own words. And tell me everything, please, for one never knows when the smallest detail may not be important."

His companion marshalled his thoughts.

"My name," he began, "is Reginald Alexander Montacute James Bramfylde Tregennis Shipton-Bellinger, fifth Earl of Brangbolton. On the sixteenth of the present month — to-day, in fact — I journeyed to the house of my friend Sir Sutton Hartley-Wesping, Bart. — here, in short — with the purpose of spending the week-end there. Knowing that Sir Sutton likes to have his guests sweet and fresh about the place, I decided to take a bath before dinner. I unpacked my soap and in a short space of time had lathered myself thoroughly from the neck upwards. And then, just as I was about to get at my right leg, what should I find but that the soap had disappeared. Nasty shock it gave me, I can tell you."

Adrian had listened to this narrative with the closest attention. Certainly the problem appeared to present several points of interest.

"It looks like an inside job," he said thoughtfully. "It could scarcely be the work of a gang. You would have noticed a gang. Just give me the facts briefly once again, if you please."

"Well, I was here, in the bath, as it might be, and the soap was here — between my hands, as it were. Next moment it was gone."

"Are you sure you have omitted nothing?"

Lord Brangbolton reflected.

"Well, I was singing, of course."

A tense look came into Adrian's face.

"Singing what?"

" 'Sonny Boy.' "

Adrian's face cleared.

"As I suspected," he said, with satisfaction. "Precisely as I had supposed. I wonder if you are aware, Lord Brangbolton, that in the singing of that particular song the muscles unconsciously contract as you come to the final 'boy'? Thus — 'I still have you, sonny BOY.' You observe? It would be impossible for anyone, rendering the number with the proper gusto, not to force his hands together at this point, assuming that they were in anything like close juxtaposition. And if there were any slippery object between them, such as a piece of soap, it would inevitably shoot sharply upwards and fall" — he scanned the room keenly — "outside the bath on the mat. As, indeed," he concluded, picking up the missing object and restoring it to its proprietor, "it did."

Lord Brangbolton gaped.

"Well, dash my buttons," he cried, "if that isn't the smartest bit of work I've seen in a month of Sundays!"

"Elementary," said Adrian with a shrug.

"You ought to be a detective."

Adrian took the cue.

"I am a detective," he said. "My name is Mulliner."

For an instant the words did not appear to have made any impression. The aged peer continued to beam through the soap-suds. Then suddenly his geniality vanished with an ominous swiftness.

"Mulliner? Did you say Mulliner?"

"I did."

"You aren't by any chance the feller — "

" — who loves your daughter Millicent with a fervour he cannot begin to express? Yes, Lord Brangbolton, I am. And I am hoping that I may receive your consent to the match."

A hideous scowl had darkened the Earl's brow. His fingers, which were grasping a loofah, tightened convulsively.

"Oh?" he said. "You are, are you? You imagine, do you, that I propose to welcome a blighted footprint-and-cigar-ash inspector into my family? It is your idea, is it, that I shall acquiesce in the union of my daughter to a dashed feller who goes about the place on his hands and knees with a magnifying-glass, picking up small objects and putting them carefully away in his pocket-book? I seem to see myself! Why, rather than permit Millicent to marry a bally detective — "

"What is your objection to detectives?"

"Never you mind what's my objection to detectives. Marry my daughter, indeed! I like your infernal cheek. Why, you couldn't keep her in lipsticks."

Adrian preserved his dignity.

"I admit that my services are not so amply remunerated as I could wish, but the firm hint at a rise next Christmas — "

"Tchah!" said Lord Brangbolton. "Pshaw! If you are interested in my daughter's matrimonial arrangements, she is going, as soon as he gets through with this Bramah-Yamah Gold Mines flotation of his, to marry my old friend Jasper Addleton. As for you, Mr. Mulliner, I have only two words to say to you. One is POP, the other is OFF. And do it now."

Adrian sighed. He saw that it would be hopeless to endeavour to argue with the haughty old man in his present mood.

"So be it, Lord Brangbolton," he said quietly.

And, affecting not to notice the nail-brush which struck him smartly on the back of the head, he left the room.

The food and drink provided for his guests by Sir Sutton Hartley-Wesping at the dinner which began some half-hour later were all that the veriest gourmet could have desired; but Adrian gulped them down, scarcely tasting them. His whole attention was riveted on Sir Jasper Addleton, who sat immediately opposite him.

And the more he examined Sir Jasper, the more revolting seemed the idea of his marrying the girl he loved.

Of course, an ardent young fellow inspecting a man who is going to marry the girl he loves is always a stern critic. In the peculiar circumstances Adrian would, no doubt, have looked askance at a John Barrymore or a Ronald Colman. But, in the case of Sir Jasper, it must be admitted that he had quite reasonable grounds for his disapproval.

In the first place, there was enough of the financier to make two financiers. It was as if Nature, planning a financier, had said to itself: "We will do this thing well. We will not skimp," with the result that, becoming too enthusiastic, it had overdone it. And then, in addition to being fat, he was also bald and goggle-eyed. And, if you overlooked his baldness and the goggly protuberance of his eyes, you could not get away from the fact that he was well advanced in years. Such a man, felt Adrian, would have been better employed in pricing burial-lots in Kensal Green Cemetery than in forcing his unwelcome attentions on a sweet young girl like Millicent: and as soon as the meal was concluded he approached him with cold abhorrence.

"A word with you," he said, and led him out on to the terrace.

The O.B.E., as he followed him into the cool night air, seemed surprised and a little uneasy. He had noticed Adrian scrutinizing him closely across the dinner table, and if there is one thing a financier who has just put out a prospectus of a gold mine dislikes, it is to be scrutinized closely.

"What do you want?" he asked nervously.

Adrian gave him a cold glance.

"Do you ever look in a mirror, Sir Jasper?" he asked curtly.

"Frequently," replied the financier, puzzled.

"Do you ever weigh yourself?"

"Often."

"Do you ever listen while your tailor is toiling round you with the tape-measure and calling out the score to his assistant?"

"I do."

"Then," said Adrian, "and I speak in the kindest spirit of disinterested friendship, you must have realized that you are an overfed old bohunkus. And how you ever got the idea that you were a fit mate for Lady Millicent Shipton-Bellinger frankly beats me. Surely it must have occurred to you what a priceless ass you will look, walking up the aisle with that young and lovely girl at your side? People will mistake you for an elderly uncle taking his niece to the Zoo."

The O.B.E. bridled.

"Ho!" he said.

"It is no use saying 'Ho!' " said Adrian. "You can't get out of it with any 'Ho's.' When all the talk and argument have died away, the fact remains that, millionaire though you be, you are a nasty-looking, fat, senile millionaire. If I were you, I should give the whole thing a miss. What do you want to get married for, anyway? You are much happier as you are. Besides, think of the risks of a financier's life. Nice it would be for that sweet girl suddenly to get a wire from you telling her not to wait dinner for you as you had just started a seven-year stretch at Dartmoor!"

An angry retort had been trembling on Sir Jasper's lips during the early portion of this speech, but at these concluding words it died unspoken. He blenched visibly, and stared at the speaker with undisguised apprehension.

"What do you mean?" he faltered.

"Never mind," said Adrian.

He had spoken, of course, purely at a venture, basing his remarks on the fact that nearly all O.B.E.'s who dabble in High Finance go to prison sooner or later. Of Sir Jasper's actual affairs he knew nothing.

"Hey, listen!" said the financier.

But Adrian did not hear him. I have mentioned that during dinner, preoccupied with his thoughts, he had bolted his food. Nature now took its toll. An acute spasm suddenly ran through him, and with a brief "Ouch!" of pain he doubled up and began to walk round in circles.

Sir Jasper clicked his tongue impatiently.

"This is no time for doing the Astaire pom-pom dance," he said sharply. "Tell me what you meant by that stuff you were talking about prison."

Adrian had straightened himself. In the light of the moon which flooded the terrace with its silver beams, his clean-cut face was plainly visible. And with a shiver of apprehension Sir Jasper saw that it wore a sardonic, sinister smile — a smile which, it struck him, was virtually tantamount to a leer.

I have spoken of the dislike financiers have for being scrutinized closely. Still more vehemently do they object to being leered at. Sir Jasper reeled, and was about to press his question when Adrian, still smiling, tottered off into the shadows and was lost to sight.

The financier hurried into the smoking-room, where he knew there would be the materials for a stiff drink. A stiff drink was what he felt an imperious need of at the moment. He tried to tell himself that that smile could not really have had the inner meaning which he had read into it; but he was still quivering nervously as he entered the smoking-room.

As he opened the door, the sound of an angry voice smote his ears. He recognized it as Lord Brangbolton's.

"I call it dashed low," his lordship was saying in his high-pitched tenor.

Sir Jasper gazed in bewilderment. His host, Sir Sutton Hartley-Wesping, was standing backed against the wall, and Lord Brangbolton, tapping him on the shirt-front with a piston-like forefinger, was plainly in the process of giving him a thorough ticking off.

"What's the matter?" asked the financier.

"I'll tell you what's the matter," cried Lord Brangbolton. "This hound here has got down a detective to watch his guests. A dashed fellow named Mulliner. So much," he said bitterly, "for our boasted English hospitality. Egad!" he went on, still tapping the baronet round and about the diamond solitaire. "I call it thoroughly low. If I have a few of my society chums down to my little place for a visit, naturally I chain up the hair-brushes and tell the butler to count the spoons every night, but I'd never dream of going so far as to employ beastly detectives. One has one's code. *Noblesse,* I mean to say, *oblige,* what, what?"

"But, listen," pleaded the Baronet. "I keep telling you. I had to invite the fellow here. I thought that if he had eaten my bread and salt, he would not expose me."

"How do you mean, expose you?"

Sir Sutton coughed.

"Oh, it was nothing. The merest trifle. Still, the man undoubtedly could have made things unpleasant for me, if he had wished. So, when I looked up and saw him smiling at me in that frightful sardonic, knowing way — "

Sir Jasper Addleton uttered a sharp cry.

"Smiling!" He gulped. "Did you say smiling?"

"Smiling," said the Baronet, "is right. It was one of those smiles that seem to go clean through you and light up all your inner being as if with a searchlight."

Sir Jasper gulped again.

"Is this fellow — this smiler fellow — is he a tall, dark, thin chap?"

"That's right. He sat opposite you at dinner."

"And he's a detective?"

"He is," said Lord Brangbolton. "As shrewd and smart a detective," he added grudgingly, "as I ever met in my life. The way he found that soap . . . Feller struck me as having some sort of a sixth sense, if you know what I mean, dash and curse him. I hate detectives," he said with a shiver. "They give me the creeps. This one wants to marry my daughter, Millicent, of all the dashed nerve!"

"See you later," said Sir Jasper. And with a single bound he was out of the room and on his way to the terrace. There was, he felt, no time to waste. His florid face, as he galloped along, was twisted and ashen. With one hand he drew from his inside pocket a cheque-book, with the other from his trouser-pocket a fountain-pen.

Adrian, when the financier found him, was feeling a good

deal better. He blessed the day when he had sought the specialist's advice. There was no doubt about it, he felt, the man knew his business. Smiling might make the cheek-muscles ache, but it undoubtedly did the trick as regarded the pangs of dyspepsia.

For a brief while before Sir Jasper burst onto the terrace, waving fountain-pen and cheque-book, Adrian had been giving his face a rest. But now, the pain in his cheeks having abated, he deemed it prudent to resume the treatment. And so it came about that the financier, hurrying towards him, was met with a smile so meaning, so suggestive, that he stopped in his tracks and for a moment could not speak.

"Oh, there you are!" he said, recovering at length. "Might I have a word with you in private, Mr. Mulliner?"

Adrian nodded, beaming. The financier took him by the coat-sleeve and led him across the terrace. He was breathing a little stertorously.

"I've been thinking things over," he said, "and I've come to the conclusion that you were right."

"Right?" said Adrian.

"About me marrying. It wouldn't do."

"No?"

"Positively not. Absurd. I can see it now. I'm too old for the girl."

"Yes."

"Too bald."

"Exactly."

"And too fat."

"Much too fat," agreed Adrian. This sudden change of heart puzzled him, but none the less the other's words were as music to his ears. Every syllable the O.B.E. had spoken had caused his heart to leap within him like a young lamb in springtime, and his mouth curved in a smile.

Sir Jasper, seeing it, shied like a frightened horse. He patted Adrian's arm feverishly.

"So I have decided," he said, "to take your advice and —if I recall your expression—give the thing a miss."

"You couldn't do better," said Adrian heartily.

"Now, if I were to remain in England in these circumstances," proceeded Sir Jasper, "there might be unpleasantness. So I propose to go quietly away at once to some remote spot — say, South America. Don't you think I am right?" he asked, giving the cheque-book a twitch.

"Quite right," said Adrian.

"You won't mention this little plan of mine to anyone? You will keep it as just a secret between ourselves? If, for instance, any of your cronies at Scotland Yard should express curiosity as to my whereabouts, you will plead ignorance?"

"Certainly."

"Capital!" said Sir Jasper, relieved. "And there is one other thing. I gather from Brangbolton that you are anxious to marry Lady Millicent yourself. And, as by the time of the wedding I shall doubtless be in — well, Callao is a spot that suggests itself off-hand, I would like to give you my little wedding-present now."

He scribbled hastily in his cheque-book, tore out a page and handed it to Adrian.

"Remember!" he said. "Not a word to anyone!"

"Quite," said Adrian.

He watched the financier disappear in the direction of the garage, regretting that he could have misjudged a man who so evidently had much good in him. Presently the sound of a motor engine announced that the other was on his way. Feeling that one obstacle, at least, between himself and his happiness had been removed, Adrian strolled indoors to see what the rest of the party were doing.

It was a quiet, peaceful scene that met his eyes as he wandered into the library. Overruling the request of some of the members of the company for a rubber of bridge, Lord Brangbolton had gathered them together at a small table and was initiating them into his favourite game of Persian Monarchs.

"It's perfectly simple, dash it," he was saying. "You just take the pack and cut. You bet — let us say ten pounds

— that you will cut a higher card than the feller you're cutting against. And if you do, you win, dash it. And, if you don't, the other dashed feller wins. Quite clear, what?"

Somebody said that it sounded a little like Blind Hooky.

"It is like Blind Hooky," said Lord Brangbolton. "Very like Blind Hooky. In fact, if you can play Blind Hooky, you can play Persian Monarchs."

They settled down to their game, and Adrian wandered about the room, endeavouring to still the riot of emotion which his recent interview with Sir Jasper Addleton had aroused in his bosom. All that remained for him to do now, he reflected, was by some means or other to remove the existing prejudice against him from Lord Brangbolton's mind.

It would not be easy, of course. To begin with, there was the matter of his straitened means.

He suddenly remembered that he had not yet looked at the cheque which the financier had handed him. He pulled it out of his pocket.

And, having glanced at it, Adrian Mulliner swayed like a poplar in a storm.

Just what he had expected, he could not have said. A fiver, possibly. At the most, a tenner. Just a trifling gift, he had imagined, with which to buy himself a cigarette-lighter, a fish-slice, or an egg-boiler.

The cheque was for a hundred thousand pounds.

So great was the shock that, as Adrian caught sight of himself in the mirror opposite to which he was standing, he scarcely recognized the face in the glass. He seemed to be seeing it through a mist. Then the mist cleared, and he saw not only his own face clearly, but also that of Lord Brangbolton, who was in the act of cutting against his left-hand neighbour, Lord Knubble of Knopp.

And, as he thought of the effect this sudden accession of wealth must surely have on the father of the girl he loved, there came into Adrian's face a sudden, swift smile.

And simultaneously from behind him he heard a gasping

exclamation, and, looking in the mirror, he met Lord Brangbolton's eyes. Always a little prominent, they were now almost prawn-like in their convexity.

Lord Knubble of Knopp had produced a banknote from his pocket and was pushing it along the table.

"Another ace!" he exclaimed. "Well I'm dashed!"

Lord Brangbolton had risen from his chair.

"Excuse me," he said in a strange, croaking voice. "I just want to have a little chat with my friend, my dear old friend, Mulliner here. Might I have a word in private with you, Mr. Mulliner?"

There was silence between the two men until they had reached a corner of the terrace out of earshot of the library window. Then Lord Brangbolton cleared his throat.

"Mulliner," he began, "or, rather — what is your Christian name?"

"Adrian."

"Adrian, my dear fellow," said Lord Brangbolton, "my memory is not what it should be, but I seem to have a distinct recollection that, when I was in my bath before dinner, you said something about wanting to marry my daughter Millicent."

"I did," replied Adrian. "And, if your objections to me as a suitor were mainly financial, let me assure you that, since we last spoke, I have become a wealthy man."

"I never had any objections to you, Adrian, financial or otherwise," said Lord Brangbolton, patting his arm affectionately. "I have always felt that the man my daughter married ought to be a fine, warm-hearted young fellow like you. For you, Adrian," he proceeded, "are essentially warm-hearted. You would never dream of distressing a father-in-law by mentioning any . . . any little . . . well, in short, I saw from your smile in there that you had noticed that I was introducing into that game of Blind Hooky — or, rather, Persian Monarchs — certain little — shall I say variations, designed to give it additional interest and excitement, and I feel sure that you would scorn to embarrass a father-in-law by. . . . Well, to cut a long story short, my boy, take Millicent and with her a father's blessing."

He extended his hand. Adrian clasped it warmly.

"I am the happiest man in the world," he said, smiling.

Lord Brangbolton winced.

"Do you mind not doing that?" he said.

"I only smiled," said Adrian.

"I know," said Lord Brangbolton.

Little remains to be told. Adrian and Millicent were married three months later at a fashionable West End church. All Society was there. The presents were both numerous and costly, and the bride looked charming. The service was conducted by the Very Reverend the Dean of Bittlesham.

It was in the vestry afterwards, as Adrian looked at Millicent and seemed to realize for the first time that all his troubles were over and that this lovely girl was indeed his, for better or worse, that a full sense of his happiness swept over the young man.

All through the ceremony he had been grave, as befitted a man at the most serious point of his career. But now, fizzing as if with some spiritual yeast, he clasped her in his arms and over her shoulder his face broke into a quick smile.

He found himself looking into the eyes of the Dean of Bittlesham. A moment later he felt a tap on his arm.

"Might I have a word with you in private, Mr. Mulliner?" said the Dean in a low voice.

THE
PURIFICATION
OF
RODNEY
SPELVIN

IT WAS AN AFTERNOON ON WHICH ONE WOULD
have said that all Nature smiled. The air was soft and balmy;
the links, fresh from the rains of spring, glistened in the
pleasant sunshine; and down on the second tee young Clifford Wimple, in a new suit of plus-fours, had just sunk two
balls in the lake, and was about to sink a third. No element,
in short, was lacking that might be supposed to make for
quiet happiness.

And yet on the forehead of the Oldest Member, as he sat
beneath the chestnut tree on the terrace overlooking the
ninth green, there was a peevish frown; and his eye, gazing
down at the rolling expanse of turf, lacked its customary
genial benevolence. His favourite chair, consecrated to his
private and personal use by unwritten law, had been occupied by another. That is the worst of a free country —
liberty so often degenerates into licence.

The Oldest Member coughed.

"I trust," he said, "you find that chair comfortable?"

The intruder, who was the club's hitherto spotless secretary, glanced up in a goofy manner.

"Eh?"

"That chair — you find it fits snugly to the figure?"

"Chair? Figure? Oh, you mean this chair? Oh yes."

"I am gratified and relieved," said the Oldest Member.

There was a silence.

"Look here," said the secretary, "what would you do in a case like this? You know I'm engaged?"

"I do. And no doubt your *fiancée* is missing you. Why not go in search of her?"

"She's the sweetest girl on earth."

"I should lose no time."

"But jealous. And just now I was in my office, and that Mrs. Pettigrew came in to ask if there was any news of the purse which she lost a couple of days ago. It had just been brought to my office, so I produced it; whereupon the infernal woman, in a most unsuitably girlish manner, flung her arms round my neck and kissed me on my bald spot. And at that moment Adela came in. Death," said the secretary, "where is thy sting?"

The Oldest Member's pique melted. He had a feeling heart.

"Most unfortunate. What did you say?"

"I hadn't time to say anything. She shot out too quick."

The Oldest Member clicked his tongue sympathetically.

"These misunderstandings between young and ardent hearts are very frequent," he said. "I could tell you at least fifty cases of the same kind. The one which I will select is the story of Jane Packard, William Bates, and Rodney Spelvin."

"You told me that the other day. Jane Packard got engaged to Rodney Spelvin, the poet, but the madness passed and she married William Bates, who was a golfer."

"This is another story of the trio."

"You told me that one, too. After Jane Packard married

William Bates she fell once more under the spell of Spelvin, but repented in time."

"This is still another story. Making three in all."

The secretary buried his face in his hands.

"Oh, well," he said, "go ahead. What does anything matter now?"

"First," said the Oldest Member, "let us make ourselves comfortable. Take this chair. It is easier than the one in which you are sitting."

"No, thanks."

"I insist."

"Oh, all right."

"Woof!" said the Oldest Member, settling himself luxuriously.

With an eye now full of kindly good-will, he watched young Clifford Wimple play his fourth. Then, as the silver drops flashed up into the sun, he nodded approvingly and began.

The story which I am about to relate (said the Oldest Member) begins at a time when Jane and William had been married some seven years. Jane's handicap was eleven, William's twelve, and their little son, Braid Vardon, had just celebrated his sixth birthday.

Ever since that dreadful time, two years before, when, lured by the glamour of Rodney Spelvin, she had taken a studio in the artistic quarter, dropped her golf, and practically learned to play the ukelele, Jane had been unremitting in her efforts to be a good mother and to bring up her son on the strictest principles. And, in order that his growing mind might have every chance, she had invited William's younger sister, Anastatia, to spend a week or two with them and put the child right on the true functions of the mashie. For Anastatia had reached the semifinals of the last Ladies' Open Championship and, unlike many excellent players, had the knack of teaching.

On the evening on which this story opens the two women were sitting in the drawing-room, chatting. They had finished tea; and Anastatia, with the aid of a lump of sugar, a spoon, and some crumbled cake, was illustrating the method by which she had got out of the rough on the fifth at Squashy Hollow.

"You're wonderful!" said Jane, admiringly. "And such a good influence for Braid! You'll give him his lesson to-morrow afternoon as usual?"

"I shall have to make it the morning," said Anastatia. "I've promised to meet a man in town in the afternoon."

As she spoke there came into her face a look so soft and dreamy that it aroused Jane as if a bradawl had been driven into her leg. As, her history has already shown, there was a strong streak of romance in Jane Bates.

"Who is he?" she asked, excitedly.

"A man I met last summer," said Anastatia.

And she sighed with such abandon that Jane could no longer hold in check her womanly nosiness.

"Do you love him?" she cried.

"Like bricks," whispered Anastatia.

"Does he love you?"

"Sometimes I think so."

"What's his name?"

"Rodney Spelvin."

"What!"

"Oh, I know he writes the most awful bilge," said Anastatia, defensively, misinterpreting the yowl of horror which had proceeded from Jane. "All the same, he's a darling."

Jane could not speak. She stared at her sister-in-law aghast. Although she knew that if you put a driver in her hands she could paste the ball into the next county, there always seemed to her something fragile and helpless about Anastatia. William's sister was one of those small, rose-leaf girls with big blue eyes to whom good men instinctively want to give a stroke a hole and on whom bad men automatically prey. And when Jane reflected that Rodney Spelvin had to all intents and purposes preyed upon herself, who stood five foot seven in her shoes and, but for an innate love of animals, could have felled an ox with a blow, she shuddered at the thought of how he would prey on this innocent half-portion.

"You really love him?" she quavered.

"If he beckoned to me in the middle of a medal round, I would come to him," said Anastatia.

Jane realised that further words were useless. A sickening sense of helplessness obsessed her. Something ought to be done about this terrible thing, but what could she do? She was so ashamed of her past madness that not even to warn this girl could she reveal that she had once been engaged to Rodney Spelvin herself; that he had recited poetry on the green while she was putting; and that, later, he had hypnotised her into taking William and little Braid to live in a studio full of samovars. These revelations would no doubt open Anastatia's eyes, but she could not make them.

And then, suddenly, Fate pointed out a way.

It was Jane's practice to go twice a week to the cinema palace in the village; and two nights later she set forth as usual and took her place just as the entertainment was about to begin.

At first she was only mildly interested. The title of the picture, *Tried in the Furnace,* had suggested nothing to her. Being a regular patron of the silver screen, she knew that it might quite easily turn out to be an educational film on the subject of clinker-coal. But as the action began to develop she found herself leaning forward in her seat, blindly crushing a caramel between her fingers. For scarcely had the operator started to turn the crank when inspiration came to her.

Of the main plot of *Tried in the Furnace* she retained, when finally she reeled out into the open air, only a confused recollection. It had something to do with money not bringing happiness or happiness not bringing money, she could not remember which. But the part which remained graven upon her mind was the bit where Gloria Gooch goes by night to the apartments of the libertine, to beg him to spare her sister, whom he has entangled in his toils.

Jane saw her duty clearly. She must go to Rodney Spelvin and conjure him by the memory of their ancient love to spare Anastatia.

It was not the easiest of tasks to put this scheme into operation. Gloria Gooch, being married to a scholarly man who spent nearly all his time in a library a hundred yards long, had been fortunately situated in the matter of paying visits to libertines; but for Jane the job was more difficult. William expected her to play a couple of rounds with him in the morning and another in the afternoon, which rather cut into her time. However, Fate was still on her side, for one morning at breakfast William announced that business called him to town.

"Why don't you come too?" he said.

Jane started.

"No. No, I don't think I will, thanks."

"Give you lunch somewhere."

"No. I want to stay here and do some practice-putting."

"All right. I'll try to get back in time for a round in the evening."

Remorse gnawed at Jane's vitals. She had never deceived William before. She kissed him with even more than her usual fondness when he left to catch the ten-forty-five. She waved to him till he was out of sight; then, bounding back into the house, leaped at the telephone and, after a series of conversations with the Marks-Morris Glue Factory, the Poor Pussy Home for Indigent Cats, and Messrs. Oakes, Oakes, and Parbury, dealers in fancy goods, at last found herself in communication with Rodney Spelvin.

"Rodney?" she said, and held her breath, fearful at this breaking of a two years' silence and yet loath to hear another strange voice say "Wadnumjerwant?" "Is that you, Rodney?"

"Yes. Who is that?"

"Mrs. Bates. Rodney, can you give me lunch at the Alcazar to-day at one?"

"Can I!" Not even the fact that some unknown basso had got on the wire and was asking if that was Mr. Bootle could blur the enthusiasm in his voice. "I should say so!"

"One o'clock, then," said Jane. His enthusiastic response had relieved her. If by merely speaking she could stir him so, to bend him to her will when they met face to face would be pie.

"One o'clock," said Rodney.

Jane hung up the receiver and went to her room to try on hats.

The impression came to Jane, when she entered the lobby of the restaurant and saw him waiting, that Rodney Spelvin looked somehow different from the Rodney she remembered. His handsome face had a deeper and more thoughtful expression, as if he had been through some ennobling experience.

"Well, here I am," she said, going to him and affecting a jauntiness which she did not feel.

He looked at her, and there was in his eyes that unmistakable goggle which comes to men suddenly addressed in a public spot by women whom, to the best of their recollection, they do not know from Eve.

"How are you?" he said. He seemed to pull himself together. "You're looking splendid."

"You're looking fine," said Jane.

"You're looking awfully well," said Rodney.

"You're looking awfully well," said Jane.

"You're looking fine," said Rodney.

There was a pause.

"You'll excuse my glancing at my watch," said Rodney. "I have an appointment to lunch with — er — somebody here, and it's past the time."

"But you're lunching with me," said Jane, puzzled.

"With you?"

The Purification of Rodney Spelvin 143

"Yes. I rang you up this morning."

Rodney gaped.

"Was it you who 'phoned? I thought you said 'Miss Bates.' "

"No, Mrs. Bates."

"Mrs. Bates?"

"Mrs. Bates."

"Of course. You're Mrs. Bates."

"Had you forgotten me?" said Jane, in spite of herself a little piqued.

"Forgotten you, dear lady! As if I could!" said Rodney, with a return of his old manner. "Well, shall we go in and have lunch?"

"All right," said Jane.

She felt embarrassed and ill at ease. The fact that Rodney had obviously succeeded in remembering her only after the effort of a lifetime seemed to her to fling a spanner into the machinery of her plans at the very outset. It was going to be difficult, she realised, to conjure him by the memory of their ancient love to spare Anastatia; for the whole essence of the idea of conjuring any one by the memory of their ancient love is that the party of the second part should be aware that there ever was such a thing.

At the luncheon-table conversation proceeded fitfully. Rodney said that this morning he could have sworn it was going to rain, and Jane said she had thought so, too, and Rodney said that now it looked as if the weather might hold up, and Jane said Yes, didn't it? and Rodney said he hoped the weather would hold up because rain was such a nuisance, and Jane said Yes, wasn't it? Rodney said yesterday had been a nice day, and Jane said Yes, and Rodney said that it seemed to be getting a little warmer, and Jane said Yes, and Rodney said that summer would be here at any moment now, and Jane said Yes, wouldn't it? and Rodney said he hoped it would not be too hot this summer, but that, as a matter of fact, when you came right down to it, what one minded was not so much the heat as the humidity, and Jane said Yes, didn't one?

In short, by the time they rose and left the restaurant, not a word had been spoken that could have provoked the censure of the sternest critic. Yet William Bates, catching sight of them as they passed down the aisle, started as if he had been struck by lightning. He had happened to find himself near the Alcazar at lunch-time and had dropped in for a chop; and, peering round the pillar which had hidden his table from theirs, he stared after them with saucer-like eyes.

"Oh, dash it!" said William.

This William Bates, I have indicated in my previous references to him, was not an abnormally emotional or temperamental man. Built physically on the lines of a motor-lorry, he had much of that vehicle's placid and even phlegmatic outlook on life. Few things had the power to ruffle William, but, unfortunately, it so happened that one of these things was Rodney Spelvin. He had never been able entirely to overcome his jealousy of this man. It had been Rodney who had come within an ace of scooping Jane from him in the days when she had been Miss Packard. It had been Rodney who had temporarily broken up his home some years later by persuading Jane to become a member of the artistic set. And now, unless his eyes jolly well deceived him, this human gumboil was once more busy on his dastardly work. Too dashed thick, was William's view of the matter; and he gnashed his teeth in such a spasm of resentful fury that a man lunching at the next table told the waiter to switch off the electric fan, as it had begun to creak unendurably.

Jane was reading in the drawing-room when William reached home that night.

"Had a nice day?" asked William.

"Quite nice," said Jane.

"Play golf?" asked William.

"Just practised," said Jane.

"Lunch at the club?"

"Yes."

"I thought I saw that bloke Spelvin in town," said William.

Jane wrinkled her forehead.

"Spelvin? Oh, you mean Rodney Spelvin? Did you? I see he's got a new book coming out."

"You never run into him these days, do you?"

"Oh no. It must be two years since I saw him."

"Oh?" said William. "Well, I'll be going upstairs and dressing."

It seemed to Jane, as the door closed, that she heard a curious clicking noise, and she wondered for a moment if little Braid had got out of bed and was playing with the Mah-Jongg counters. But it was only William gnashing his teeth.

There is nothing sadder in this life than the spectacle of a husband and wife with practically identical handicaps drifting apart; and to dwell unnecessarily on such a spectacle is, to my mind, ghoulish. It is not my purpose, therefore, to weary you with a detailed description of the hourly widening of the breach between this once ideally united pair. Suffice it to say that within a few days of the conversation just related the entire atmosphere of this happy home had completely altered. On the Tuesday, William had excused himself from the morning round on the plea that he had promised Peter Willard a match, and Jane said What a pity! On Tuesday afternoon William said that his head ached, and Jane said Isn't that too bad? On Wednesday morning William said he had lumbago, and Jane, her sensitive feelings now deeply wounded, said Oh, had he? After that, it came to be agreed between them by silent compact that they should play together no more.

Also, they began to avoid one another in the house. Jane would sit in the drawing-room, while William retired down the passage to his den. In short, if you had added a couple of ikons and a photograph of Trotsky, you would have had a *mise en scène* which would have fitted a Russian novel like the paper on the wall.

One evening, about a week after the beginning of this tragic state of affairs, Jane was sitting in the drawing-room, trying to read *Braid on Taking Turf.* But the print seemed blurred and the philosophy too metaphysical to be grasped. She laid the book down and stared sadly before her.

Every moment of these black days had affected Jane like a stymie on the last green. She could not understand how it was that William should have come to suspect, but that he did suspect was plain; and she writhed on the horns of a dilemma. All she had to do to win him back again was to go to him and tell him of Anastatia's fatal entanglement. But what would happen then? Undoubtedly he would feel it his duty as a brother to warn the girl against Rodney Spelvin; and Jane instinctively knew that William warning any one against Rodney Spelvin would sound like a private of the line giving his candid opinion of the sergeant-major.

Inevitably, in this case, Anastatia, a spirited girl and deeply in love, would take offence at his words and leave the house. And if she left the house, what would be the effect on little Braid's mashie-play? Already, in less than a fortnight, the gifted girl had taught him more about the chip-shot from ten to fifteen yards off the green than the local pro had been able to do in two years. Her departure would be absolutely disastrous.

What it amounted to was that she must sacrifice her husband's happiness or her child's future; and the problem of which was to get the loser's end was becoming daily more insoluble.

She was still brooding on it when the postman arrived with the evening mail, and the maid brought the letters into the drawing-room.

Jane sorted them out. There were three for William, which she gave to the maid to take to him in his den. There were two for herself, both bills. And there was one for Anastatia, in the well-remembered handwriting of Rodney Spelvin.

Jane placed this letter on the mantel-piece, and stood looking at it like a cat at a canary. Anastatia was away for the day, visiting friends who lived a few stations down the line; and every womanly instinct in Jane urged her to get hold of a kettle and steam the gum off the envelope. She had almost made up her mind to disembowel the thing and write "Opened in error" on it, when the telephone suddenly went off like a bomb and nearly startled her into a decline. Coming at that moment it sounded like the Voice of Conscience.

"Hullo?" said Jane.

"Hullo!" replied a voice.

Jane clucked like a hen with uncontrollable emotion. It was Rodney.

"Is that you?" asked Rodney

"Yes," said Jane.

And so it was, she told herself.

"Your voice is like music," said Rodney.

This may or may not have been the case, but at any rate it was exactly like every other female voice when heard on the telephone. Rodney prattled on without a suspicion.

"Have you got my letter yet?"

"No," said Jane. She hesitated. "What was in it?" she asked, tremulously.

"It was to ask you to come to my house to-morrow at four."

"To your house!" faltered Jane.

"Yes. Everything is ready. I will send the servants out, so that we shall be quite alone. You will come, won't you?"

The room was shimmering before Jane's eyes, but she regained command of herself with a strong effort.

"Yes," she said. "I will be there."

She spoke softly, but there was a note of menace in her voice. Yes, she would indeed be there. From the very moment when this man had made his monstrous proposal, she had been asking herself what Gloria Gooch would have done in a crisis like this. And the answer was plain. Gloria Gooch, if her sister-in-law was intending to visit the apartments of a libertine, would have gone there herself to save the poor child from the consequences of her infatuated folly.

"Yes," said Jane, "I will be there."

"You have made me the happiest man in the world," said

Rodney. "I will meet you at the corner of the street at four, then." He paused. "What is that curious clicking noise?" he asked.

"I don't know," said Jane. "I noticed it myself. Something wrong with the wire, I suppose."

"I thought it was somebody playing the castanets. Until to-morrow, then, good-bye."

"Good-bye."

Jane replaced the receiver. And William, who had been listening to every word of the conversation on the extension in his den, replaced his receiver, too.

Anastatia came back from her visit late that night. She took her letter, and read it without comment. At breakfast next morning she said that she would be compelled to go into town that day.

"I want to see my dressmaker," she said.

"I'll come, too," said Jane. "I want to see my dentist."

"So will I," said William. "I want to see my lawyer."

"That will be nice," said Anastatia, after a pause.

"Very nice," said Jane, after another pause.

"We might all lunch together," said Anastatia. "My appointment is not till four."

"I should love it," said Jane. "My appointment is at four, too."

"So is mine," said William.

"What a coincidence!" said Jane, trying to speak brightly.

"Yes," said William. He may have been trying to speak brightly, too; but, if so, he failed. Jane was too young to have seen Salvini in "Othello," but, had she witnessed that great tragedian's performance, she could not have failed to be struck by the resemblance between his manner in the pillow scene and William's now.

"Then shall we all lunch together?" said Anastatia.

"I shall lunch at my club," said William, curtly.

"William seems to have a grouch," said Anastatia.

"Ha!" said William.

The Purification of Rodney Spelvin 149

He raised his fork and drove it with sickening violence at his sausage.

So Jane had a quiet little woman's lunch at a confectioner's alone with Anastatia. Jane ordered a tongue-and-lettuce sandwich, two macaroons, marsh-mallows, ginger-ale and cocoa; and Anastatia ordered pineapple chunks with whipped cream, tomatoes stuffed with beetroot, three dill pickles, a raspberry nut sundae, and hot chocolate. And, while getting outside this garbage, they talked merrily, as women will, of every subject but the one that really occupied their minds. When Anastatia got up and said good-bye with a final reference to her dressmaker, Jane shuddered at the depths of deceit to which the modern girl can sink.

It was now about a quarter to three, so Jane had an hour to kill before going to the rendezvous. She wandered about the streets, and never had time appeared to her to pass so slowly, never had a city been so congested with hard-eyed and suspicious citizens. Every second person she met seemed to glare at her as if he or she had guessed her secret.

The very elements joined in the general disapproval. The sky had turned a sullen grey, and faraway thunder muttered faintly, like an impatient golfer held up on the tee by a slow foursome. It was a relief when at length she found herself at the back of Rodney Spelvin's house, standing before the scullery window, which it was her intention to force with the pocket-knife won in happier days as second prize in a competition at a summer hotel for those with handicaps above eighteen.

But the relief did not last long. Despite the fact that she was about to enter this evil house with the best motives, a sense of almost intolerable guilt oppressed her. If William should ever get to know of this! Wow! felt Jane.

How long she would have hesitated before the window, one cannot say. But at this moment, glancing guiltily round, she happened to catch the eye of a cat which was sitting on a near-by wall, and she read in this cat's eye such cynical derision that the urge came upon her to get out of its range as quickly as possible. It was a cat that had manifestly seen a lot of life, and it was plainly putting an entirely wrong construction on her behaviour. Jane shivered, and, with a quick jerk prised the window open and climbed in.

It was two years since she had entered this house, but once she had reached the hall she remembered its topography perfectly. She mounted the stairs to the large studio sitting-room on the first floor, the scene of so many Bohemian parties in that dark period of her artistic life. It was here, she knew, that Rodney would bring his victim.

The studio was one of those dim, over-ornamented rooms which appeal to men like Rodney Spelvin. Heavy curtains hung in front of the windows. One corner was cut off by a high-backed Chesterfield. At the far end was an alcove, curtained like the windows. Once Jane had admired this studio, but now it made her shiver. It seemed to her one of those nests in which, as the sub-title of "Tried in the Furnace" had said, only eggs of evil are hatched. She paced the thick carpet restlessly, and suddenly there came to her the sound of footsteps on the stairs.

Jane stopped, every muscle tense. The moment had arrived. She faced the door, tight-lipped. It comforted her a little in this crisis to reflect that Rodney was not one of those massive Ethel M. Dell libertines who might make things unpleasant for an intruder. He was only a welter-weight egg of evil; and, if he tried to start anything, a girl of her physique would have little or no difficulty in knocking the stuffing out of him.

The footsteps reached the door. The handle turned. The door opened. And in strode William Bates, followed by two men in bowler hats.

"Ha!" said William.

Jane's lips parted, but no sound came from them. She staggered back a pace or two. William, advancing into the centre of the room, folded his arms and gazed at her with burning eyes.

"So," said William, and the words seemed forced like drops of vitriol from between his clenched teeth, "I find you here, dash it!"

Jane choked convulsively. Years ago, when an innocent child, she had seen a conjurer produce a rabbit out of a top-hat which an instant before had been conclusively proved to be empty. The sudden apparition of William affected her with much the same sensations as she had experienced then.

"How-ow-ow — ?" she said.

"I beg your pardon?" said William, coldly.

"How-ow-ow — ?"

"Explain yourself," said William.

"How-ow-ow did you get here? And who-oo-oo are these men?"

William seemed to become aware for the first time of the presence of his two companions. He moved a hand in a hasty gesture of introduction.

"Mr. Reginald Brown and Mr. Cyril Delancey — my wife," he said, curtly.

The two men bowed slightly and raised their bowler hats.

"Pleased to meet you," said one.

"Most awfully charmed," said the other.

"They are detectives," said William.

"Detectives!"

"From the Quick Results Agency," said William. "When I became aware of your clandestine intrigue, I went to the agency and they gave me their two best men."

"Oh, well," said Mr. Brown, blushing a little.

"Most frightfully decent of you to put it that way," said Mr. Delancey.

William regarded Jane sternly.

"I knew you were going to be here at four o'clock," he said.

"I overheard you making the assignation on the telephone."

"Oh, William!"

"Woman," said William, "where is your paramour?"

"Really, really," said Mr. Delancey, deprecatingly.

"Keep it clean," urged Mr. Brown.

"Your partner in sin, where is he? I am going to take him and tear him into little bits and stuff him down his throat and make him swallow himself."

"Fair enough," said Mr. Brown.

"Perfectly in order," said Mr. Delancey.

Jane uttered a stricken cry.

"William," she screamed, "I can explain all."

"All?" said Mr. Delancey.

"All?" said Mr. Brown.

"All," said Jane.

"All?" said William.

"All," said Jane.

William sneered bitterly.

"I'll bet you can't," he said.

"I'll bet I can," said Jane.

"Well?"

"I came here to save Anastatia."

"Anastatia?"

"Anastatia."

"My sister?"

"Your sister."

"His sister Anastatia," explained Mr. Brown to Mr. Delancey in an undertone.

"What from?" asked William.

"From Rodney Spelvin. Oh, William, can't you understand?"

"No, I'm dashed if I can."

"I, too," said Mr. Delancey, "must confess myself a little fogged. And you, Reggie?"

"Completely, Cyril," said Mr. Brown, removing his bowler

hat with a puzzled frown, examining the maker's name, and putting it on again.

"The poor child is infatuated with this man."

"With the bloke Spelvin?"

"Yes. She is coming here with him at four o'clock."

"Important," said Mr. Brown, producing a notebook and making an entry.

"Important, if true," agreed Mr. Delancey.

"But I heard you making the appointment with the bloke Spelvin over the 'phone," said William.

"He thought I was Anastatia. And I came here to save her."

William was silent and thoughtful for a few moments.

"It all sounds very nice and plausible," he said, "but there's just one thing wrong. I'm not a very clever sort of bird, but I can see where your story slips up. If what you say is true, where is Anastatia?"

"Just coming in now," whispered Jane. "Hist!"

"Hist, Reggie!" whispered Mr. Delancey.

They listened. Yes, the front door had banged, and feet were ascending the staircase.

"Hide!" said Jane, urgently.

"Why?" said William.

"So that you can overhear what they say and jump out and confront them."

"Sound," said Mr. Delancey.

"Very sound," said Mr. Brown.

The two detectives concealed themselves in the alcove. William retired behind the curtains in front of the window. Jane dived behind the Chesterfield. A moment later the door opened.

Crouching in her corner, Jane could see nothing, but every word that was spoken came to her ears; and with every syllable her horror deepened.

"Give me your things," she heard Rodney say, "and then we'll go upstairs."

Jane shivered. The curtains by the window shook. From

the direction of the alcove there came a soft scratching sound, as the two detectives made an entry in their notebooks.

For a moment after this there was silence. Then Anastatia uttered a sharp, protesting cry.

"Ah, no, no! Please, please!"

"But why not?" came Rodney's voice.

"It is wrong — wrong."

"I can't see why."

"It is, it is! You must not do that. Oh, please, please don't hold so tight."

There was a swishing sound, and through the curtains before the window a large form burst. Jane raised her head above the Chesterfield.

William was standing there, a menacing figure. The two detectives had left the alcove and were moistening their pencils. And in the middle of the room stood Rodney Spelvin, stooping slightly and grasping Anastatia's parasol in his hands.

"I don't get it," he said. "Why is it wrong to hold the dam' thing tight?" He looked up and perceived his visitors. "Ah, Bates," he said, absently. He turned to Anastatia again. "I should have thought that the tighter you held it, the more force you would get into the shot."

"But don't you see, you poor zimp," replied Anastatia, "that you've got to keep the ball straight. If you grip the shaft as if you were a drowning man clutching at a straw and keep your fingers under like that, you'll pull like the dickens and probably land out of bounds or in the rough. What's the good of getting force into the shot if the ball goes in the wrong direction, you cloth-headed goof?"

"I see now," said Rodney, humbly. "How right you always are!"

"Look here," interrupted William, folding his arms. "What is the meaning of this?"

"You want to grip firmly but lightly," said Anastatia.

"Firmly but lightly," echoed Rodney.

"What is the meaning of this?"

"And with the fingers. Not with the palms."

"What is the meaning of this?" thundered William. "Anastatia, what are you doing in this man's rooms?"

"Giving him a golf lesson, of course. And I wish you wouldn't interrupt."

"Yes, yes," said Rodney, a little testily. "Don't interrupt, Bates, there's a good fellow. Surely you have things to occupy you elsewhere?"

"We'll go upstairs," said Anastatia, "where we can be alone."

"You will not go upstairs," barked William.

"We shall get on much better there," explained Anastatia. "Rodney has fitted up the top-floor back as an indoor practising room."

Jane darted forward with a maternal cry.

"My poor child, has the scoundrel dared to delude you by pretending to be a golfer? Darling, he is nothing of the kind."

Mr. Reginald Brown coughed. For some moments he had been twitching restlessly.

"Talking of golf," he said, "it might interest you to hear of a little experience I had the other day at Marshy Moor. I had got a nice drive off the tee, nothing record-breaking, you understand, but straight and sweet. And what was my astonishment on walking up to play my second to find — "

"A rather similar thing happened to me at Windy Waste last Tuesday," interrupted Mr. Delancey. "I had hooked my drive the merest trifle, and my caddie said to me, 'You're out of bounds.' 'I am not out of bounds,' I replied, perhaps a little tersely, for the lad had annoyed me by a persistent habit of sniffing. 'Yes, you are out of bounds,' he said. 'No, I am not out of bounds,' I retorted. Well, believe me or believe me not, when I got up to my ball — "

"Shut up!" said William.

"Just as you say, sir," replied Mr. Delancey, courteously.

Rodney Spelvin drew himself up, and in spite of her loathing for his villainy Jane could not help feeling what a noble and romantic figure he made. His face was pale, but his voice did not falter.

"You are right," he said. "I am not a golfer. But with the help of this splendid girl here, I hope humbly to be one some day. Ah, I know what you are going to say," he went on, raising a hand. "You are about to ask how a man who has wasted his life as I have done can dare to entertain the mad dream of ever acquiring a decent handicap. But never forget," proceeded Rodney, in a low, quivering voice, "that Walter J. Travis was nearly forty before he touched a club, and a few years later he won the British Amateur."

"True," murmured William.

"True, true," said Mr. Delancey and Mr. Brown. They lifted their bowler hats reverently.

"I am thirty-three years old," continued Rodney, "and for fourteen of those thirty-three years I have been writing poetry — aye, and novels with a poignant sex-appeal, and if ever I gave a thought to this divine game it was but to sneer at it. But last summer I saw the light."

"Glory! Glory!" cried Mr. Brown.

"One afternoon I was persuaded to try a drive. I took the club with a mocking, contemptuous laugh." He paused, and a wild light came into his eyes. "I brought off a perfect pip," he said, emotionally. "Two hundred yards and as straight as a whistle. And, as I stood there gazing after the ball, something seemed to run up my spine and bite me in the neck. It was the golf-germ."

"Always the way," said Mr. Brown. "I remember the first drive I ever made. I took a nice easy stance — "

"The first drive I made," said Mr. Delancey, "you won't believe this, but it's a fact, was a full — "

"From that moment," continued Rodney Spelvin, "I have had but one ambition — to somehow or other, cost what it might, get down into single figures." He laughed bitterly. "You see," he said, "I cannot even speak of this thing without splitting my infinitives. And even as I split my infinitives, so did I split my drivers. After that first heavenly slosh I didn't seem able to do anything right."

He broke off, his face working. William cleared his throat awkwardly.

"Yes, but dash it," he said, "all this doesn't explain why I find you alone with my sister in what I might call your lair."

"The explanation is simple," said Rodney Spelvin. "This sweet girl is the only person in the world who seems able to simply and intelligently and in a few easily understood words make clear the knack of the thing. There is none like her, none. I have been to pro after pro, but not one has been any good to me. I am a temperamental man, and there is a lack of sympathy and human understanding about these professionals which jars on my artist soul. They look at you as if you were a half-witted child. They click their tongues. They make odd Scotch noises. I could not endure the strain. And then this wonderful girl, to whom in a burst of emotion I had confided my unhappy case, offered to give me private lessons. So I went with her to some of those indoor practising places. But here, too, my sensibilities were racked by the fact that unsympathetic eyes observed me. So I fixed up a room here where we could be alone."

"And instead of going there," said Anastatia, "we are wasting half the afternoon talking."

William brooded for a while. He was not a quick thinker.

"Well, look here," he said at length, "this is the point. This is the nub of the thing. This is where I want you to follow me very closely. Have you asked Anastatia to marry you?"

"Marry me?" Rodney gazed at him, shocked. "Have I asked her to marry me? I, who am not worthy to polish the blade of her niblick! I, who have not even a thirty handicap, ask a girl to marry me who was in the semi-final of last year's

Ladies' Open! No, no, Bates, I may be a *vers-libre* poet, but I have some sense of what is fitting. I love her, yes. I love her with a fervour which causes me to frequently and for hours at a time lie tossing sleeplessly upon my pillow. But I would not dare to ask her to marry me."

Anastatia burst into a peal of girlish laughter.

"You poor chump!" she cried. "Is that what has been the matter all this time! I couldn't make out what the trouble was. Why, I'm crazy about you. I'll marry you any time you give the word."

Rodney reeled.

"What!"

"Of course I will."

"Anastatia!"

"Rodney!"

He folded her in his arms.

"Well, I'm dashed," said William. "It looks to me as if I had been making rather a lot of silly fuss about nothing. Jane, I wronged you."

"It was my fault."

"No, no!"

"Yes, yes."

"Jane!"

"William!"

He folded her in his arms. The two detectives, having entered the circumstances in their notebooks, looked at one another with moist eyes.

"Cyril!" said Mr. Brown.

"Reggie!" said Mr. Delancey.

Their hands met in a brotherly clasp.

"And so," concluded the Oldest Member, "all ended happily. The storm-tossed lives of William Bates, Jane Packard, and Rodney Spelvin came safely at long last into harbour. At the subsequent wedding William and Jane's present of a complete golfing outfit, including eight dozen new balls, a cloth cap, and a pair of spiked shoes, was generally admired by all who inspected the gifts during the reception."

"From that time forward the four of them have been inseparable. Rodney and Anastatia took a little cottage close to that of William and Jane, and rarely does a day pass without a close foursome between the two couples. William and Jane being steady tens and Anastatia scratch and Rodney a persevering eighteen, it makes an ideal match."

"What does?" asked the secretary, waking from his reverie.

"This one."

"Which?"

"I see," said the Oldest Member, sympathetically, "that your troubles, weighing on your mind, have caused you to follow my little narrative less closely than you might have done. Never mind, I will tell it again."

"The story" (said the Oldest Member) "which I am about to relate begins at a time when — "

WITHOUT
THE
OPTION

THE EVIDENCE WAS ALL IN. THE MACHINERY OF the law had worked without a hitch. And the beak, having adjusted a pair of pince-nez which looked as though they were going to do a nose dive any moment, coughed like a pained sheep and slipped us the bad news.

"The prisoner, Wooster," he said — and who can paint the shame and agony of Bertram at hearing himself so described? — "will pay a fine of five pounds."

"Oh, rather!" I said. "Absolutely! Like a shot!"

I was dashed glad to get the thing settled at such a reasonable figure. I gazed across what they call the sea of faces till I picked up Jeeves, sitting at the back. Stout fellow, he had come to see the young master through his hour of trial.

"I say, Jeeves," I sang out, "have you got a fiver? I'm a bit short."

"Silence!" bellowed some officious blighter.

"It's all right," I said; "just arranging the financial details. Got the stuff, Jeeves?"

"Yes, sir."

"Good egg!"

"Are you a friend of the prisoner?" asked the beak.

"I am in Mr. Wooster's employment, Your Worship, in the capacity of gentleman's personal gentleman."

"Then pay the fine to the clerk."

"Very good, Your Worship."

The beak gave a coldish nod in my direction, as much as to say that they might now strike the fetters from my wrists; and having hitched up the pince-nez once more, proceeded to hand poor old Sippy one of the nastiest looks ever seen in Bosher Street Police Court.

"The case of the prisoner Leon Trotzky — which," he said, giving Sippy the eye again, "I am strongly inclined to think an assumed and fictitious name — is more serious. He has been convicted of a wanton and violent assault upon the police. The evidence of the officer has proved that the prisoner struck him in the abdomen, causing severe internal pain, and in other ways interfered with him in the execution of his duties. I am aware that on the night following the annual aquatic contest between the Universities of Oxford and Cambridge a certain licence is traditionally granted by the authorities, but aggravated acts of ruffianly hooliganism like that of the prisoner Trotzky cannot be overlooked or palliated. He will serve a sentence of thirty days in the Second Division without the option of a fine."

"No, I say — here — hi — dash it all!" protested poor old Sippy.

"Silence!" bellowed the officious blighter.

"Next case," said the beak. And that was that.

The whole affair was most unfortunate. Memory is a trifle blurred; but as far as I can piece together the facts, what happened was more or less this:

Abstemious cove though I am as a general thing, there is one night in the year when, putting all other engagements aside, I am rather apt to let myself go a bit and renew my lost youth, as it were. The night to which I allude is the one following the annual aquatic contest between the Universities of Oxford and Cambridge; or, putting it another way,

Boat-Race Night. Then, if ever, you will see Bertram under the influence. And on this occasion, I freely admit, I had been doing myself rather juicily, with the result that when I ran into old Sippy opposite the Empire I was in quite fairly bonhomous mood. This being so, it cut me to the quick to perceive that Sippy, generally the brightest of revellers, was far from being his usual sunny self. He had the air of a man with a secret sorrow.

"Bertie," he said as we strolled along toward Piccadilly Circus, "the heart bowed down by weight of woe to weakest hope will cling." Sippy is by way of being an author, though mainly dependent for the necessaries of life on subsidies from an old aunt who lives in the country, and his conversation often takes a literary turn. "But the trouble is that I have no hope to cling to, weak or otherwise. I am up against it, Bertie."

"In what way, laddie?"

"I've got to go to-morrow and spend three weeks with some absolutely dud — I will go further — some positively scaly friends of my Aunt Vera. She has fixed the thing up, and may a nephew's curse blister every bulb in her garden."

"Who are these hounds of hell?" I asked.

"Some people named Pringle. I haven't seen them since I was ten, but I remember them at that time striking me as England's premier warts."

"Tough luck. No wonder you've lost your morale."

"The world," said Sippy, "is very grey. How can I shake off this awful depression?"

It was then that I got one of those bright ideas one does get round about 11.30 on Boat-Race Night.

"What you want, old man," I said, "is a policeman's helmet."

"Do I, Bertie?"

"If I were you, I'd just step straight across the street and get that one over there."

"But there's a policeman inside it. You can see him distinctly."

"What does that matter?" I said. I simply couldn't follow his reasoning.

Sippy stood for a moment in thought.

"I believe you're absolutely right," he said at last. "Funny I never thought of it before. You really recommend me to get that helmet?"

"I do, indeed."

"Then I will," said Sippy, brightening up in the most remarkable manner.

So there you have the posish, and you can see why, as I left the dock a free man, remorse gnawed at my vitals. In his twenty-fifth year, with life opening out before him and all that sort of thing, Oliver Randolph Sipperley had become a jailbird, and it was all my fault. It was I who had dragged that fine spirit down into the mire, so to speak, and the question now arose: What could I do to atone?

Obviously the first move must be to get in touch with Sippy and see if he had any last messages and what not. I pushed about a bit, making inquiries, and presently found myself in a little dark room with whitewashed walls and a wooden bench. Sippy was sitting on the bench with his head in his hands.

"How are you, old lad?" I asked in a hushed, bedside voice.

"I'm a ruined man," said Sippy, looking like a poached egg.

"Oh, come," I said, "it's not so bad as all that. I mean to say, you had the swift intelligence to give a false name. There won't be anything about you in the papers."

"I'm not worrying about the papers. What's bothering me is, how can I go and spend three weeks with the Pringles, starting to-day, when I've got to sit in a prison cell with a ball and chain on my ankle?"

"But you said you didn't want to go."

"It isn't a question of wanting, fathead. I've got to go. If I don't my aunt will find out where I am. And if she finds out that I am doing thirty days, without the option, in the lowest dungeon beneath the castle moat — well, where shall I get off?"

I saw his point.

"This is not a thing we can settle for ourselves," I said gravely. "We must put our trust in a higher power. Jeeves is the man we must consult."

And having collected a few of the necessary data, I shook his hand, patted him on the back and tooled off home to Jeeves.

"Jeeves," I said, when I had climbed outside the pick-me-up which he had thoughtfully prepared against my coming, "I've got something to tell you; something important; something that vitally affects one whom you have always regarded with — one whom you have always looked upon — one whom you have — well, to cut a long story short, as I'm not feeling quite myself — Mr. Sipperley."

"Yes, sir?"

"Jeeves, Mr. Souperley is in the sip."

"Sir?"

"I mean, Mr. Sipperley is in the soup."

"Indeed, sir?"

"And all owing to me. It was I who, in a moment of mistaken kindness, wishing only to cheer him up and give him something to occupy his mind, recommended him to pinch that policeman's helmet."

"Is that so, sir?"

"Do you mind not intoning the responses, Jeeves?" I said. "This is a most complicated story for a man with a headache to have to tell, and if you interrupt you'll make me lose the thread. As a favour to me, therefore, don't do it. Just nod every now and then to show that you're following me."

I closed my eyes and marshalled the facts.

"To start with then, Jeeves, you may or may not know that Mr. Sipperley is practically dependent on his Aunt Vera."

"Would that be Miss Sipperley of the Paddock, Beckley-on-the-Moor, in Yorkshire, sir?"

"Yes. Don't tell me you know her!"

"Not personally, sir. But I have a cousin residing in the village who has some slight acquaintance with Miss Sipperley. He has described her to me as an imperious and quick-tempered old lady. . . . But I beg your pardon, sir, I should have nodded."

"Quite right, you should have nodded. Yes, Jeeves, you should have nodded. But it's too late now."

I nodded myself. I hadn't had my eight hours the night before, and what you might call a lethargy was showing a tendency to steal over me from time to time.

"Yes, sir?" said Jeeves.

"Oh — ah — yes," I said, giving myself a bit of a hitch up. "Where had I got to?"

"You were saying that Mr. Sipperley is practically dependent upon Miss Sipperley, sir."

"Was I?"

"You were, sir."

"You're perfectly right; so I was. Well, then, you can readily understand, Jeeves, that he has got to take jolly good care to keep in with her. You get that?"

Jeeves nodded.

"Now mark this closely: The other day she wrote to old Sippy, telling him to come down and sing at her village concert. It was equivalent to a royal command, if you see what I mean, so Sippy couldn't refuse in so many words. But he had sung at her village concert once before and had got the bird in no uncertain manner, so he wasn't playing any return dates. You follow so far, Jeeves?"

Jeeves nodded.

"So what did he do, Jeeves? He did what seemed to him at the moment a rather brainy thing. He told her that, though he would have been delighted to sing at her village concert, by a most unfortunate chance an editor had commissioned him to write a series of articles on the colleges of Cambridge and he was obliged to pop down there at once and would be away for quite three weeks. All clear up to now?"

Jeeves inclined the coco-nut.

"Whereupon, Jeeves, Miss Sipperley wrote back, saying that she quite realised that work must come before pleasure — pleasure being her loose way of describing the act of singing songs at the Beckley-on-the-Moor concert and getting the laugh from the local toughs; but that, if he was going to Cambridge, he must certainly stay with her friends, the Pringles, at their house just outside the town. And she dropped them a line telling them to expect him on the twenty-eighth, and they dropped another line saying right-ho, and the thing was settled. And now Mr. Sipperley is in the jug, and what will be the ultimate outcome or upshot? Jeeves, it is a problem worthy of your great intellect. I rely on you."

"I will do my best to justify your confidence, sir."

"Carry on, then. And meanwhile pull down the blinds and bring a couple more cushions and heave that small chair this way so that I can put my feet up, and then go away and brood and let me hear from you in — say, a couple of hours, or maybe three. And if anybody calls and wants to see me, inform them that I am dead."

"Dead, sir?"

"Dead. You won't be so far wrong."

It must have been well toward evening when I woke up with a crick in my neck but otherwise somewhat refreshed. I pressed the bell.

"I looked in twice, sir," said Jeeves, "but on each occasion you were asleep and I did not like to disturb you."

"The right spirit, Jeeves. . . . Well?"

"I have been giving close thought to the little problem which you indicated, sir, and I can see only one solution."

"One is enough. What do you suggest?"

"That you go to Cambridge in Mr. Sipperley's place, sir."

I stared at the man. Certainly I was feeling a good deal better than I had been a few hours before; but I was far from being in a fit condition to have rot like this talked to me.

"Jeeves," I said sternly, "pull yourself together. This is mere babble from the sickbed."

"I fear I can suggest no other plan of action, sir, which will extricate Mr. Sipperley from his dilemma."

"But think! Reflect! Why, even I, in spite of having had a disturbed night and a most painful morning with the minions of the law, can see that the scheme is a loony one. To put the finger on only one leak in the thing, it isn't me these people want to see; it's Mr. Sipperley. They don't know me from Adam."

"So much the better, sir. For what I am suggesting is that you go to Cambridge, affecting actually to be Mr. Sipperley."

This was too much.

"Jeeves," I said, and I'm not half sure there weren't tears in my eyes, "surely you can see for yourself that this is pure banana-oil. It is not like you to come into the presence of a sick man and gibber."

"I think the plan I have suggested would be practicable, sir. While you were sleeping, I was able to have a few words with Mr. Sipperley, and he informed me that Professor and Mrs. Pringle have not set eyes upon him since he was a lad of ten."

"No, that's true. He told me that. But even so, they would be sure to ask him questions about my aunt — or rather his aunt. Where would I be then?"

"Mr. Sipperley was kind enough to give me a few facts respecting Miss Sipperley, sir, which I jotted down. With these, added to what my cousin has told me of the lady's habits, I think you would be in a position to answer any ordinary question."

There is something dashed insidious about Jeeves. Time and again since we first came together he has stunned me with some apparently drivelling suggestion or scheme or ruse or plan of campaign, and after about five minutes has convinced me that it is not only sound but fruity. It took nearly a quarter of an hour to reason me into this particular one, it being considerably the weirdest to date; but he did it. I was holding out pretty firmly, when he suddenly clinched the thing.

"I would certainly suggest, sir," he said, "that you left London as soon as possible and remained hid for some little time in some retreat where you would not be likely to be found."

"Eh? Why?"

"During the last hour Mrs. Spenser Gregson has been on the telephone three times, sir, endeavouring to get into communication with you."

"Aunt Agatha!" I cried, paling beneath my tan.

"Yes, sir. I gathered from her remarks that she had been reading in the evening paper a report of this morning's proceedings in the police court."

I hopped from the chair like a jack rabbit of the prairie. If Aunt Agatha was out with her hatchet, a move was most certainly indicated.

"Jeeves," I said, "this is a time for deeds, not words. Pack —and that right speedily."

"I have packed, sir."

"Find out when there is a train for Cambridge."

"There is one in forty minutes, sir."

"Call a taxi."

"A taxi is at the door, sir."

"Good!" I said. "Then lead me to it."

The Maison Pringle was quite a bit of a way out of Cambridge, a mile or two down the Trumpington Road; and when I arrived everybody was dressing for dinner. So it wasn't till I had shoved on the evening raiment and got down to the drawing-room that I met the gang.

"Hullo-ullo!" I said, taking a deep breath and floating in.

I tried to speak in a clear and ringing voice, but I wasn't feeling my chirpiest. It is always a nervous job for a diffident and unassuming bloke to visit a strange house for the first time; and it doesn't make the thing any better when he goes there pretending to be another fellow. I was conscious of a rather pronounced sinking feeling, which the appearance of the Pringles did nothing to allay.

Sippy had described them as England's premier warts, and it looked to me as if he might be about right. Professor Pringle was a thinnish, baldish, dyspeptic-lookingish cove with an eye like a haddock, while Mrs. Pringle's aspect was that of one who had had bad news round about the year 1900 and never really got over it. And I was just staggering under the impact of these two when I was introduced to a couple of ancient females with shawls all over them.

"No doubt you remember my mother?" said Professor Pringle mournfully, indicating Exhibit A.

"Oh — ah!" I said, achieving a bit of a beam.

"And my aunt," sighed the prof, as if things were getting worse and worse.

"Well, well, well!" I said shooting another beam in the direction of Exhibit B.

"They were saying only this morning that they remembered you," groaned the prof, abandoning all hope.

There was a pause. The whole strength of the company gazed at me like a family group out of one of Edgar Allan Poe's less cheery yarns, and I felt my *joie de vivre* dying at the roots.

"I remember Oliver," said Exhibit A. She heaved a sigh. "He was such a pretty child. What a pity! What a pity!"

Tactful, of course, and calculated to put the guest completely at his ease.

"I remember Oliver," said Exhibit B, looking at me in much the same way as the Bosher Street beak had looked at Sippy before putting on the black cap. "Nasty little boy! He teased my cat."

"Aunt Jane's memory is wonderful, considering that she will be eighty-seven next birthday," whispered Mrs. Pringle with mournful pride.

"What did you say?" asked the Exhibit suspiciously.

"I said your memory was wonderful."

"Ah!" The dear old creature gave me another glare. I could see that no beautiful friendship was to be looked for by Bertram in this quarter. "He chased my Tibby all over the garden, shooting arrows at her from a bow."

At this moment a cat strolled out from under the sofa and

made for me with its tail up. Cats always do take to me, which made it all the sadder that I should be saddled with Sippy's criminal record. I stooped to tickle it under the ear, such being my invariable policy, and the Exhibit uttered a piercing cry.

"Stop him! Stop him!"

She leaped forward, moving uncommonly well for one of her years, and having scooped up the cat, stood eyeing me with bitter defiance, as if daring me to start anything. Most unpleasant.

"I like cats," I said feebly.

It didn't go. The sympathy of the audience was not with me. And conversation was at what you might call a low ebb, when the door opened and a girl came in.

"My daughter Heloise," said the prof moodily, as if he hated to admit it.

I turned to mitt the female, and stood there with my hand out, gaping. I can't remember when I've had such a nasty shock.

I suppose everybody has had the experience of suddenly meeting somebody who reminded them frightfully of some fearful person. I mean to say, by way of an example, once when I was golfing in Scotland I saw a woman come into the hotel who was the living image of my Aunt Agatha. Probably a very decent sort, if I had only waited to see, but I didn't wait. I legged it that evening, utterly unable to stand the spectacle. And on another occasion I was driven out of a thoroughly festive night club because the head waiter reminded me of my Uncle Percy.

Well, Heloise Pringle, in the most ghastly way, resembled Honoria Glossop.

I think I may have told you before about this Glossop scourge. She was the daughter of Sir Roderick Glossop, the loony doctor, and I had been engaged to her for about three weeks, much against my wishes, when the old boy most fortunately got the idea that I was off my rocker and put the bee on the proceedings. Since then the mere thought of her had been enough to make me start out of my sleep with a loud cry. And this girl was exactly like her.

"Er — how are you?" I said.

"How do you do?"

Her voice put the lid on it. It might have been Honoria herself talking. Honoria Glossop has a voice like a lion tamer making some authoritative announcement to one of the troupe, and so had this girl. I backed away convulsively and sprang into the air as my foot stubbed itself against something squashy. A sharp yowl rent the air, followed by an indignant cry, and I turned to see Aunt Jane, on all fours, trying to put things right with the cat, which had gone to earth under the sofa. She gave me a look, and I could see that her worst fears had been realised.

At this juncture dinner was announced — not before I was ready for it.

"Jeeves," I said, when I got him alone that night, "I am no faint-heart, but I am inclined to think that this binge is going to prove a shade above the odds."

"You are not enjoying your visit, sir?"

"I am not, Jeeves. Have you seen Miss Pringle?"

"Yes, sir, from a distance."

"The best way to see her. Did you observe her keenly?"

"Yes, sir."

"Did she remind you of anybody?"

"She appeared to me to bear a remarkable likeness to her cousin, Miss Glossop, sir."

"Her cousin! You don't mean to say she's Honoria Glossop's cousin!"

"Yes, sir. Mrs. Pringle was a Miss Blatherwick — the younger of two sisters, the elder of whom married Sir Roderick Glossop."

"Great Scott! That accounts for the resemblance."

"Yes, sir."

"And what a resemblance, Jeeves! She even talks like Miss Glossop."

"Indeed, sir? I have not yet heard Miss Pringle speak."

"You have missed little. And what it amounts to, Jeeves, is that, though nothing will induce me to let old Sippy down, I can see that this visit is going to try me high. At a pinch, I could stand the prof and wife. I could even make the effort of a lifetime and bear up against Aunt Jane. But to expect a man to mix daily with the girl Heloise — and to do it, what is more, on lemonade, which is all there was to drink at dinner — is to ask too much of him. What shall I do, Jeeves?"

"I think that you should avoid Miss Pringle's society as much as possible."

"The same great thought had occurred to me," I said.

It is all very well, though, to talk airily about avoiding a female's society; but when you are living in the same house with her, and she doesn't want to avoid you, it takes a bit of doing. It is a peculiar thing in life that the people you most particularly want to edge away from always seem to cluster round like a poultice. I hadn't been twenty-four hours in the place before I perceived that I was going to see a lot of this pestilence.

She was one of those girls you're always meeting on the stairs and in passages. I couldn't go into a room without seeing her drift in a minute later. And if I walked in the garden she was sure to leap out at me from a laurel bush or the onion bed or something. By about the tenth day I had begun to feel absolutely haunted.

"Jeeves," I said, "I have begun to feel absolutely haunted."

"Sir?"

"This woman dogs me. I never seem to get a moment to myself. Old Sippy was supposed to come here to make a study of the Cambridge colleges, and she took me round about fifty-seven this morning. This afternoon I went to sit in the garden, and she popped up through a trap and was in my midst. This evening she cornered me in the morning-room. It's getting so that, when I have a bath, I wouldn't be a bit surprised to find her nestling in the soap dish."

"Extremely trying, sir."

"Dashed so. Have you any remedy to suggest?"

"Not at the moment, sir. Miss Pringle does appear to be distinctly interested in you, sir. She was asking me questions this morning respecting your mode of life in London."

"What?"

"Yes, sir."

I stared at the man in horror. A ghastly thought had struck me. I quivered like an aspen.

At lunch that day a curious thing had happened. We had just finished mangling the cutlets and I was sitting back in my chair, taking a bit of an easy before being allotted my slab of boiled pudding, when, happening to look up, I caught the girl Heloise's eye fixed on me in what seemed to me a rather rummy manner. I didn't think much about it at the time, because boiled pudding is a thing you have to give your undivided attention to if you want to do yourself justice; but now, recalling the episode in the light of Jeeves's words, the full sinister meaning of the thing seemed to come home to me.

Even at the moment, something about that look had struck me as oddly familiar, and now I suddenly saw why. It had been the identical look which I had observed in the eye of Honoria Glossop in the days immediately preceding our engagement — the look of a tigress that has marked down its prey.

"Jeeves, do you know what I think?"

"Sir?"

I gulped slightly.

"Jeeves," I said, "listen attentively. I don't want to give the impression that I consider myself one of those deadly coves who exercise an irresistible fascination over one and all and can't meet a girl without wrecking her peace of mind in the first half-minute. As a matter of fact, it's rather the other way with me, for girls on entering my presence are mostly inclined to give me the raised eyebrow and the twitching upper lip. Nobody, therefore, can say that I am a man who's likely to take alarm unnecessarily. You admit that, don't you?"

"Yes, sir."

"Nevertheless, Jeeves, it is a known scientific fact that there is a particular style of female that does seem strangely attracted to the sort of fellow I am."

"Very true, sir."

"I mean to say, I know perfectly well that I've got, roughly speaking, half the amount of brain a normal bloke ought to possess. And when a girl comes along who has about twice the regular allowance, she too often makes a bee line for me with the love light in her eyes. I don't know how to account for it, but it is so."

"It may be Nature's provision for maintaining the balance of the species, sir."

"Very possibly. Anyway, it has happened to me over and over again. It was what happened in the case of Honoria Glossop. She was notoriously one of the brainiest women of her year at Girton, and she just gathered me in like a bull pup swallowing a piece of steak."

"Miss Pringle, I am informed, sir, was an even more brilliant scholar than Miss Glossop."

"Well, there you are! Jeeves, she looks at me."

"Yes, sir?"

"I keep meeting her on the stairs and in passages."

"Indeed, sir?"

"She recommends me books to read, to improve my mind."

"Highly suggestive, sir."

"And at breakfast this morning, when I was eating a sausage, she told me I shouldn't, as modern medical science held that a four-inch sausage contained as many germs as a dead rat. The maternal touch, you understand; fussing over my health."

"I think we may regard that, sir, as practically conclusive."

I sank into a chair, thoroughly pipped.

"What's to be done, Jeeves?"

"We must think, sir."

"You think. I haven't the machinery."

"I will most certainly devote my very best attention to the

matter, sir, and will endeavour to give satisfaction."

Well, that was something. But I was ill at ease. Yes, there is no getting away from it, Bertram was ill at ease.

Next morning we visited sixty-three more Cambridge colleges, and after lunch I said I was going to my room to lie down. After staying there for half an hour to give the coast time to clear, I shoved a book and smoking materials in my pocket, and climbing out of a window, shinned down a convenient water-pipe into the garden. My objective was the summer-house, where it seemed to me that a man might put in a quiet hour or so without interruption.

It was extremely jolly in the garden. The sun was shining, the crocuses were all to the mustard and there wasn't a sign of Heloise Pringle anywhere. The cat was fooling about on the lawn, so I chirruped to it and it gave a low gargle and came trotting up. I had just got it in my arms and was scratching it under the ear when there was a loud shriek from above, and there was Aunt Jane half out of the window. Dashed disturbing.

"Oh, right-ho," I said.

I dropped the cat, which galloped off into the bushes, and dismissing the idea of bunging a brick at the aged relative, went on my way, heading for the shrubbery. Once safely hidden there, I worked round till I got to the summer-house. And, believe me, I had hardly got my first cigarette nicely under way when a shadow fell on my book and there was young Sticketh-Closer-Than-a-Brother in person.

"So there you are," she said.

She seated herself by my side, and with a sort of gruesome playfulness jerked the gasper out of the holder and heaved it through the door.

"You're always smoking," she said, a lot too much like a lovingly chiding young bride for my comfort. "I wish you wouldn't. It's so bad for you. And you ought not to be sitting out here without your light overcoat. You want someone to look after you."

"I've got Jeeves."

She frowned a bit.

"I don't like him," she said.

"Eh? Why not?"

"I don't know. I wish you would get rid of him."

My flesh absolutely crept. And I'll tell you why. One of the first things Honoria Glossop had done after we had become engaged was to tell me she didn't like Jeeves and wanted him shot out. The realisation that this girl resembled Honoria not only in body but in blackness of soul made me go all faint.

"What are you reading?"

She picked up my book and frowned again. The thing was one I had brought down from the old flat in London, to glance at in the train — a fairly zippy effort in the detective line called *The Trail of Blood*. She turned the pages with a nasty sneer.

"I can't understand you liking nonsense of this — " She stopped suddenly. "Good gracious!"

"What's the matter?"

"Do you know Bertie Wooster?"

And then I saw that my name was scrawled right across the title page, and my heart did three back somersaults.

"Oh — er — well — that is to say — well, slightly."

"He must be a perfect horror. I'm surprised that you can make a friend of him. Apart from anything else, the man is practically an imbecile. He was engaged to my Cousin Honoria at one time, and it was broken off because he was next door to insane. You should hear my Uncle Roderick talk about him!"

I wasn't keen.

"Do you see much of him?"

"A goodish bit."

"I saw in the paper the other day that he was fined for making a disgraceful disturbance in the street."

"Yes, I saw that."

She gazed at me in a foul, motherly way.

"He can't be a good influence for you," she said. "I do wish you would drop him. Will you?"

"Well —" I began. And at this point old Cuthbert, the cat, having presumably found it a bit slow by himself in the bushes, wandered in with a matey expression on his face and jumped on my lap. I welcomed him with a good deal of cordiality. Though but a cat, he did make a sort of third at this party; and he afforded a good excuse for changing the conversation.

"Jolly birds, cats," I said.

She wasn't having any.

"Will you drop Bertie Wooster?" she said, absolutely ignoring the cat *motif.*

"It would be so difficult."

"Nonsense! It only needs a little will power. The man surely can't be so interesting a companion as all that. Uncle Roderick says he is an invertebrate waster."

I could have mentioned a few things that I thought Uncle Roderick was, but my lips were sealed, so to speak.

"You have changed a great deal since we last met," said the Pringle disease reproachfully. She bent forward and began to scratch the cat under the other ear. "Do you remember, when we were children together, you used to say that you would do anything for me?"

"Did I?"

"I remember once you cried because I was cross and wouldn't let you kiss me."

I didn't believe it at the time, and I don't believe it now. Sippy is in many ways a good deal of a chump, but surely even at the age of ten he cannot have been such a priceless ass as that. I think the girl was lying, but that didn't make the position of affairs any better. I edged away a couple of inches and sat staring before me, the old brow beginning to get slightly bedewed.

And then suddenly — well, you know how it is, I mean. I suppose everyone has had that ghastly feeling at one time or another of being urged by some overwhelming force to do some absolutely blithering act. You get it every now and then when you're in a crowded theatre, and something seems to be egging you on to shout "Fire!" and see what happens. Or you're talking to someone and all at once you feel, "Now, suppose I suddenly biffed this bird in the eye!"

Well, what I'm driving at is this, at this juncture, with her shoulder squashing against mine and her back hair tickling my nose, a perfectly loony impulse came sweeping over me to kiss her.

"No, really?" I croaked.

"Have you forgotten?"

She lifted the old onion and her eyes looked straight into mine. I could feel myself skidding. I shut my eyes. And then from the doorway there spoke the most beautiful voice I had ever heard in my life:

"Give me that cat!"

I opened my eyes. There was good old Aunt Jane, that queen of her sex, standing before me, glaring at me as if I were a vivisectionist and she had surprised me in the middle of an experiment. How this pearl among women had tracked me down I don't know, but there she stood, bless her dear, intelligent old soul, like the rescue party in the last reel of a motion picture.

I didn't wait. The spell was broken and I legged it. As I went, I heard that lovely voice again.

"He shot arrows at my Tibby from a bow," said this most deserving and excellent octogenarian.

For the next few days all was peace. I saw comparatively little of Heloise. I found the strategic value of that water-pipe outside my window beyond praise. I seldom left the house now by any other route. It seemed to me that, if only the luck held like this, I might after all be able to stick this visit out for the full term of the sentence.

But meanwhile, as they used to say in the movies—

The whole family appeared to be present and correct as I came down to the drawing-room a couple of nights later. The

Prof, Mrs. Prof, the two Exhibits and the girl Heloise were scattered about at intervals. The cat slept on the rug, the canary in its cage. There was nothing, in short, to indicate that this was not just one of our ordinary evenings.

"Well, well, well!" I said cheerily. "Hullo-ullo-ullo!"

I always like to make something in the nature of an entrance speech, it seeming to me to lend a chummy tone to the proceedings.

The girl Heloise looked at me reproachfully.

"Where have you been all day?" she asked.

"I went to my room after lunch."

"You weren't there at five."

"No. After putting in a spell of work on the good old colleges I went for a stroll. Fellow must have exercise if he means to keep fit."

"Mens sana in corpore sano," observed the prof.

"I shouldn't wonder," I said cordially.

At this point, when everything was going as sweet as a nut and I was feeling on top of my form, Mrs. Pringle suddenly soaked me on the base of the skull with a sandbag. Not actually, I don't mean. No, no. I speak figuratively, as it were.

"Roderick is very late," she said.

You may think it strange that the sound of that name should have sloshed into my nerve centres like a half-brick. But, take it from me, to a man who has had any dealings with Sir Roderick Glossop there is only one Roderick in the world — and that is one too many.

"Roderick?" I gurgled.

"My brother-in-law, Sir Roderick Glossop, comes to Cambridge to-night," said the prof. "He lectures at St. Luke's to-morrow. He is coming here to dinner."

And while I stood there, feeling like the hero when he discovers that he is trapped in the den of the Secret Nine, the door opened.

"Sir Roderick Glossop," announced the maid or some such person, and in he came.

One of the things that get this old crumb so generally

disliked among the better element of the community is the fact that he has a head like the dome of St. Paul's and eyebrows that want bobbing or shingling to reduce them to anything like reasonable size. It is a nasty experience to see this bald and bushy bloke advancing on you when you haven't prepared the strategic railways in your rear.

As he came into the room I backed behind a sofa and commended my soul to God. I didn't need to have my hand read to know that trouble was coming to me through a dark man.

He didn't spot me at first. He shook hands with the prof and wife, kissed Heloise and waggled his head at the Exhibits.

"I fear I am somewhat late," he said. "A slight accident on the road, affecting what my chauffeur termed the — "

And then he saw me lurking on the outskirts and gave a startled grunt, as if I hurt him a good deal internally.

"This — " began the prof, waving in my direction.

"I am already acquainted with Mr. Wooster."

"This," went on the prof, "is Miss Sipperley's nephew, Oliver. You remember Miss Sipperley?"

"What do you mean?" barked Sir Roderick. Having had so much to do with loonies has given him a rather sharp and authoritative manner on occasion. "This is that wretched young man, Bertram Wooster. What is all this nonsense about Olivers and Sipperleys?"

The prof was eyeing me with some natural surprise. So were the others. I beamed a bit weakly.

"Well, as a matter of fact — " I said.

The prof was wrestling with the situation. You could hear his brain buzzing.

"He said he was Oliver Sipperley," he moaned.

"Come here!" bellowed Sir Roderick. "Am I to understand that you have inflicted yourself on this household under the pretence of being the nephew of an old friend?"

It seemed a pretty accurate description of the facts.

"Well — er — yes," I said.

Sir Roderick shot an eye at me. It entered the body somewhere about the top stud, roamed around inside for a bit and went out at the back.

"Insane! Quite insane, as I knew from the first moment I saw him."

"What did he say?" asked Aunt Jane.

"Roderick says this young man is insane," roared the prof.

"Ah!" said Aunt Jane, nodding. "I thought so. He climbs down water-pipes."

"Does what?"

"I've seen him — ah, many a time!"

Sir Roderick snorted violently.

"He ought to be under proper restraint. It is abominable that a person in his mental condition should be permitted to roam the world at large. The next stage may quite easily be homicidal."

It seemed to me that, even at the expense of giving old Sippy away, I must be cleared of this frightful charge. After all, Sippy's number was up anyway.

"Let me explain," I said. "Sippy asked me to come here."

"What do you mean?"

"He couldn't come himself, because he was jugged for biffing a cop on Boat-Race Night."

Well, it wasn't easy to make them get the hang of the story, and even when I'd done it it didn't seem to make them any chummier towards me. A certain coldness about expresses it, and when dinner was announced I counted myself out and pushed off rapidly to my room. I could have done with a bit of dinner, but the atmosphere didn't seem just right.

"Jeeves," I said, having shot in and pressed the bell, "we're sunk."

"Sir?"

"Hell's foundations are quivering and the game is up."

He listened attentively.

"The contingency was one always to have been anticipated as a possibility, sir. It only remains to take the obvious step."

"What's that?"

"Go and see Miss Sipperley, sir."

"What on earth for?"

"I think it would be judicious to apprise her of the facts yourself, sir, instead of allowing her to hear of them through the medium of a letter from Professor Pringle. That is to say, if you are still anxious to do all in your power to assist Mr. Sipperley."

"I can't let Sippy down. If you think it's any good — "

"We can but try it, sir. I have an idea, sir, that we may find Miss Sipperley disposed to look leniently upon Mr. Sipperley's misdemeanour."

"What makes you think that?"

"It is just a feeling that I have, sir."

"Well, if you think it would be worth trying — How do we get there?"

"The distance is about a hundred and fifty miles, sir. Our best plan would be to hire a car."

"Get it at once," I said.

The idea of being a hundred and fifty miles away from Heloise Pringle, not to mention Aunt Jane and Sir Roderick Glossop, sounded about as good to me as anything I had ever heard.

The Paddock, Beckley-on-the-Moor, was about a couple of parasangs from the village, and I set out for it next morning, after partaking of a hearty breakfast at the local inn, practically without a tremor. I suppose when a fellow has been through it as I had in the last two weeks his system becomes hardened. After all, I felt, whatever this aunt of Sippy's might be like, she wasn't Sir Roderick Glossop, so I was that much on velvet from the start.

The Paddock was one of those medium-sized houses with a goodish bit of very tidy garden and a carefully rolled gravel drive curving past a shrubbery that looked as if it had just come back from the dry cleaner — the sort of house you take one look at and say to yourself, "Somebody's aunt lives there." I pushed on up the drive, and as I turned the bend I observed in the middle distance a woman messing about by

a flower-bed with a trowel in her hand. If this wasn't the
female I was after, I was very much mistaken, so I halted,
cleared the throat and gave tongue.

"Miss Sipperley?"

She had had her back to me, and at the sound of my voice
she executed a sort of leap or bound, not unlike a barefoot
dancer who steps on a tin-tack halfway through the Vision of
Salome. She came to earth and goggled at me in a rather
goofy manner. A large, stout female with a reddish face.

"Hope I didn't startle you," I said.

"Who are you?"

"My name's Wooster. I'm a pal of your nephew, Oliver."

Her breathing had become more regular.

"Oh?" she said. "When I heard your voice I thought you
were someone else."

"No, that's who I am. I came up here to tell you about
Oliver."

"What about him?"

I hesitated. Now that we were approaching what you
might call the nub, or crux, of the situation, a good deal of my
breezy confidence seemed to have slipped from me.

"Well, it's rather a painful tale, I must warn you."

"Oliver isn't ill? He hasn't had an accident?"

She spoke anxiously, and I was pleased at this evidence of
human feeling. I decided to shoot the works with no more
delay.

"Oh, no, he isn't ill," I said; "and as regards having accidents, it depends on what you call an accident. He's in
chokey."

"In what?"

"In prison."

"In prison!"

"It was entirely my fault. We were strolling along on Boat-
Race Night and I advised him to pinch a policeman's helmet."

"I don't understand."

"Well, he seemed depressed, don't you know; and rightly

or wrongly, I thought it might cheer him up if he stepped across the street and collared a policeman's helmet. He thought it a good idea, too, so he started doing it, and the man made a fuss and Oliver sloshed him."

"Sloshed him?"

"Biffed him — smote him a blow — in the stomach."

"My nephew Oliver hit a policeman in the stomach?"

"Absolutely in the stomach. And next morning the beak sent him to the bastille for thirty days without the option."

I was looking at her a bit anxiously all this while to see how she was taking the thing, and at this moment her face seemed suddenly to split in half. For an instant she appeared to be all mouth, and then she was staggering about the grass, shouting with laughter and waving the trowel madly.

It seemed to me a bit of luck for her that Sir Roderick Glossop wasn't on the spot. He would have been calling for the strait-waistcoat in the first half-minute.

"You aren't annoyed?" I said.

"Annoyed?" She chuckled happily. "I've never heard such a splendid thing in my life."

I was pleased and relieved. I had hoped the news wouldn't upset her too much, but I had never expected it to go with such a roar as this.

"I'm proud of him," she said.

"That's fine."

"If every young man in England went about hitting policemen in the stomach, it would be a better country to live in."

I couldn't follow her reasoning, but everything seemed to be all right; so after a few more cheery words I said good-bye and legged it.

"Jeeves," I said when I got back to the inn, "everything's fine. But I am far from understanding why."

"What actually occurred when you met Miss Sipperley, sir?"

"I told her Sippy was in the jug for assaulting the police. Upon which she burst into hearty laughter, waved her trowel in a pleased manner and said she was proud of him."

"I think I can explain her apparently eccentric behaviour, sir. I am informed that Miss Sipperley has had a good deal of annoyance at the hands of the local constable during the past two weeks. This has doubtless resulted in a prejudice on her part against the force as a whole."

"Really? How was that?"

"The constable has been somewhat over-zealous in the performance of his duties, sir. On no fewer than three occasions in the last ten days he has served summonses upon Miss Sipperley — for exceeding the speed limit in her car; for allowing her dog to appear in public without a collar; and for failing to abate a smoky chimney. Being in the nature of an autocrat, if I may use the term, in the village, Miss Sipperley has been accustomed to do these things in the past with impunity, and the constable's unexpected zeal has made her somewhat ill-disposed to policemen as a class and consequently disposed to look upon such assaults as Mr. Sipperley's in a kindly and broadminded spirit."

I saw his point.

"What an amazing bit of luck, Jeeves!"

"Yes, sir."

"Where did you hear all this?"

"My informant was the constable himself, sir. He is my cousin."

I gaped at the man. I saw, so to speak, all.

"Good Lord, Jeeves! You didn't bribe him?"

"Oh, no, sir. But it was his birthday last week, and I gave him a little present. I have always been fond of Egbert, sir."

"How much?"

"A matter of five pounds, sir."

I felt in my pocket.

"Here you are," I said. "And another fiver for luck."

"Thank you very much, sir."

"Jeeves," I said, "you move in a mysterious way your wonders to perform. You don't mind if I sing a bit, do you?"

"Not at all, sir," said Jeeves.

THE
ROMANCE
OF
A
BULB-SQUEEZER

SOMEBODY HAD LEFT A COPY OF AN ILLUSTRATED
weekly paper in the bar-parlour of the Anglers' Rest; and,
glancing through it, I came upon the ninth full-page photograph of a celebrated musical comedy actress that I had seen
since the preceding Wednesday. This one showed her looking archly over her shoulder with a rose between her teeth,
and I flung the periodical from me with a stifled cry.

"Tut, tut!" said Mr. Mulliner, reprovingly. "You must not
allow these things to affect you so deeply. Remember, it is not
actresses' photographs that matter, but the courage which
we bring to them."

He sipped his hot Scotch.

I wonder if you have ever reflected (he said gravely) what
life must be like for the men whose trade it is to make these
pictures? Statistics show that the two classes of the community which least often marry are milkmen and fashionable
photographers — milkmen because they see women too
early in the morning, and fashionable photographers because
their days are spent in an atmosphere of feminine loveliness
so monotonous that they become surfeited and morose. I

know of none of the world's workers whom I pity more sincerely than the fashionable photographer; and yet — by one of those strokes of irony which make the thoughtful man waver between sardonic laughter and sympathetic tears — it is the ambition of every youngster who enters the profession some day to become one.

At the outset of his career, you see, a young photographer is sorely oppressed by human gargoyles; and gradually this begins to prey upon his nerves.

"Why is it," I remember my cousin Clarence saying, after he had been about a year in the business, "that all these misfits want to be photographed? Why do men with faces which you would have thought they would be anxious to hush up wish to be strewn about the country on whatnots and in albums? I started out full of ardour and enthusiasm, and my eager soul is being crushed. This morning the Mayor of Tooting East came to make an appointment. He is coming to-morrow afternoon to be taken in his cocked hat and robes of office; and there is absolutely no excuse for a man with a face like that perpetuating his features. I wish to goodness I was one of those fellows who only take camera portraits of beautiful women."

His dream was to come true sooner than he had imagined. Within a week the great test-case of Biggs v. Mulliner had raised my cousin Clarence from an obscure studio in West Kensington to the position of London's most famous photographer.

You possibly remember the case? The events that led up to it were, briefly, as follows: —

Jno. Horatio Biggs, O.B.E., the newly-elected Mayor of Tooting East, alighted from a cab at the door of Clarence Mulliner's studio at four-ten on the afternoon of June the seventeenth. At four-eleven he went in. And at four-sixteen and a half he was observed shooting out of a first-floor window, vigorously assisted by my cousin, who was prodding him in the seat of the trousers with the sharp end of a photographic tripod. Those who were in a position to see stated that Clarence's face was distorted by a fury scarcely human.

Naturally the matter could not be expected to rest there. A week later the case of Biggs *v.* Mulliner had begun, the plaintiff claiming damages to the extent of ten thousand pounds and a new pair of trousers. And at first things looked very black for Clarence.

It was the speech of Sir Joseph Bodger, K.C., briefed for the defence, that turned the scale.

"I do not," said Sir Joseph, addressing the jury on the second day, "propose to deny the charges which have been brought against my client. We freely admit that on the seventeenth inst. we did jab the defendant with our tripod in a manner calculated to cause alarm and despondency. But, gentlemen, we plead justification. The whole case turns upon one question. Is a photographer entitled to assault — either with or, as the case may be, without a tripod — a sitter who, after being warned that his face is not up to the minimum standard requirements, insists upon remaining in the chair and moistening the lips with the tip of the tongue? Gentlemen, I say Yes!

"Unless you decide in favour of my client, gentlemen of the jury, photographers — debarred by law from the privilege of rejecting sitters — will be at the mercy of anyone who comes along with the price of a dozen photographs in his pocket. You have seen the plaintiff, Biggs. You have noted his broad, slab-like face, intolerable to any man of refinement and sensibility. You have observed his walrus moustache, his double chin, his protruding eyes. Take another look at him, and then tell me if my client was not justified in chasing him with a tripod out of that sacred temple of Art and Beauty, his studio.

"Gentlemen, I have finished. I leave my client's fate in your hands with every confidence that you will return the only verdict that can conceivably issue from twelve men of your obvious intelligence, your manifest sympathy, and your superb breadth of vision."

Of course, after that there was nothing to it. The jury

decided in Clarence's favour without leaving the box; and the crowd waiting outside to hear the verdict carried him shoulder-high to his house, refusing to disperse until he had made a speech and sung Photographers never, never, never shall be slaves. And next morning every paper in England came out with a leading article commending him for having so courageously established, as it had not been established since the days of Magna Charta, the fundamental principle of the Liberty of the Subject.

The effect of this publicity on Clarence's fortunes was naturally stupendous. He had become in a flash the best-known photographer in the United Kingdom, and was now in a position to realise that vision which he had of taking the pictures of none but the beaming and the beautiful. Every day the loveliest ornaments of Society and the Stage flocked to his studio; and it was with the utmost astonishment, therefore, that, calling upon him one morning on my return to England after an absence of two years in the East, I learned that Fame and Wealth had not brought him happiness.

I found him sitting moodily in his studio, staring with dull eyes at a camera-portrait of a well-known actress in a bathing-suit. He looked up listlessly as I entered.

"Clarence!" I cried, shocked at his appearance, for there were hard lines about his mouth and wrinkles on a forehead that once had been smooth as alabaster. "What is wrong?"

"Everything," he replied, "I'm fed up."

"What with?"

"Life. Beautiful women. This beastly photography business."

I was amazed. Even in the East rumours of his success had reached me, and on my return to London I found that they had not been exaggerated. In every photographers' club in the Metropolis, from the Negative and Solution in Pall Mall to the humble public-houses frequented by the men who do your pictures while you wait on the sands at seaside resorts, he was being freely spoken of as the logical successor to the

Presidency of the Amalgamated Guild of Bulb-Squeezers.

"I can't stick it much longer," said Clarence, tearing the camera-portrait into a dozen pieces with a dry sob and burying his face in his hands. "Actresses nursing their dolls! Countesses simpering over kittens! Film stars among their books! In ten minutes I go to catch a train at Waterloo. I have been sent for by the Duchess of Hampshire to take some studies of Lady Monica Southbourne in the castle grounds."

A shudder ran through him. I patted him on the shoulder. I understood now.

"She has the most brilliant smile in England," he whispered.

"Come, come!"

"Coy yet roguish, they tell me."

"It may not be true."

"And I bet she will want to be taken offering a lump of sugar to her dog, and the picture will appear in *The Sketch* and *Tatler* as 'Lady Monica Southbourne and Friend.'"

"Clarence, this is morbid."

He was silent for a moment.

"Ah, well," he said, pulling himself together with a visible effort, "I have made my sodium sulphite, and I must lie in it."

I saw him off in a cab. The last view I had of him was of his pale, drawn profile. He looked, I thought, like an aristocrat of the French Revolution being borne off to his doom on a tumbril. How little he guessed that the only girl in the world lay waiting for him round the corner.

No, you are wrong. Lady Monica did not turn out to be the only girl in the world. If what I said caused you to expect that, I misled you. Lady Monica proved to be all his fancy had pictured her. In fact even more. Not only was her smile coy yet roguish, but she had a sort of coquettish droop of the left eyelid of which no one had warned him. And, in addition to her two dogs, which she was portrayed in the act of feeding with two lumps of sugar, she possessed a totally unforeseen pet monkey, of which he was compelled to take no fewer than eleven studies.

The Romance of a Bulb-Squeezer 191

No, it was not Lady Monica who captured Clarence's heart, but a girl in a taxi whom he met on his way to the station.

It was in a traffic jam at the top of Whitehall that he first observed this girl. His cab had become becalmed in a sea of omnibuses, and, chancing to look to the right, he perceived within a few feet of him another taxi, which had been heading for Trafalgar Square. There was a face at its window. It turned towards him, and their eyes met.

To most men it would have seemed an unattractive face. To Clarence, surfeited with the coy, the beaming, and the delicately-chiselled, it was the most wonderful thing he had ever looked at. All his life, he felt, he had been searching for something on these lines. That snub nose — those freckles — that breadth of cheek-bone — the squareness of that chin. And not a dimple in sight. He told me afterwards that his only feeling at first was one of incredulity. He had not believed that the world contained women like this. And then the traffic jam loosened up and he was carried away.

It was as he was passing the Houses of Parliament that the realisation came to him that the strange bubbly sensation that seemed to start from just above the lower left side-pocket of his waistcoat was not, as he had at first supposed, dyspepsia, but love. Yes, love had come at long last to Clarence Mulliner; and for all the good it was likely to do him, he reflected bitterly, it might just as well have been the dyspepsia for which he had mistaken it. He loved a girl whom he would probably never see again. He did not know her name or where she lived or anything about her. All he knew was that he would cherish her image in his heart for ever, and that the thought of going on with the old dreary round of photographing lovely women with coy yet roguish smiles was almost more than he could bear.

However, custom is strong; and a man who has once allowed the bulb-squeezing habit to get a grip of him cannot cast it off in a moment. Next day Clarence was back in his studio, diving into the velvet nose-bag as of yore and telling peeresses to watch the little birdie just as if nothing had happened. And if there was now a strange haunting look of pain in his eyes, nobody objected to that. Indeed, inasmuch as the grief which gnawed at his heart had the effect of deepening and mellowing his camera-side manner to an almost sacerdotal unctuousness, his private sorrows actually helped his professional prestige. Women told one another that being photographed by Clarence Mulliner was like undergoing some wonderful spiritual experience in a noble cathedral; and his appointment-book became fuller than ever.

So great now was his reputation that to anyone who had had the privilege of being taken by him, either full face or in profile, the doors of Society opened automatically. It was whispered that his name was to appear in the next Birthday Honours List and at the annual banquet of the Amalgamated Bulb-Squeezers, when Sir Godfrey Stooge, the retiring President, in proposing his health, concluded a glowingly eulogistic speech with the words, "Gentlemen, I give you my destined successor, Mulliner the Liberator!" five hundred frantic photographers almost shivered the glasses on the table with their applause.

And yet he was not happy. He had lost the only girl he had ever loved and without her what was Fame? What was Affluence? What were the highest Honours in the Land?

These were the questions he was asking himself one night as he sat in his library, sombrely sipping a final whisky-and-soda before retiring. He had asked them once and was going to ask them again, when he was interrupted by the sound of some one ringing at the front-door bell.

He rose, surprised. It was late for callers. The domestic staff had gone to bed, so he went to the door and opened it. A shadowy figure was standing on the steps.

"Mr. Mulliner?"

"I am Mr. Mulliner."

The man stepped past him into the hall. And, as he did so, Clarence saw that he was wearing over the upper half of his face a black velvet mask.

"I must apologise for hiding my face, Mr. Mulliner," the visitor said, as Clarence led him to the library.

"Not at all," replied Clarence, courteously. "No doubt it is all for the best."

"Indeed?" said the other, with a touch of asperity. "If you really want to know, I am probably as handsome a man as there is in London. But my mission is one of such extraordinary secrecy that I dare not run the risk of being recognised." He paused, and Clarence saw his eyes glint through the holes in the mask as he directed a rapid gaze into each corner of the library. "Mr. Mulliner, have you any acquaintance with the ramifications of international secret politics?"

"I have."

"And you are a patriot?"

"I am."

"Then I can speak freely. No doubt you are aware Mr. Mulliner, that for some time past this country and a certain rival Power have been competing for the friendship and alliance of a certain other Power?"

"No," said Clarence, "they didn't tell me that."

"Such is the case. And the President of this Power — "

"Which one?"

"The second one."

"Call it B."

"The President of Power B. is now in London. He arrived incognito, travelling under the assumed name of J. J. Shubert: and the representatives of Power A., to the best of our knowledge, are not yet aware of his presence. This gives us just the few hours necessary to clinch this treaty with Power B. before Power A. can interfere. I ought to tell you, Mr. Mulliner, that if Power B. forms an alliance with this country, the supremacy of the Anglo-Saxon race will be secured for hundreds of years. Whereas if Power A. gets hold of Power B., civilisation will be thrown into the melting-pot. In the

eyes of all Europe — and when I say all Europe I refer particularly to Powers C., D., and E. — this nation would sink to
the rank of a fourth-class Power."

"Call it Power F.," said Clarence.

"It rests with you, Mr. Mulliner, to save England."

"Great Britain," corrected Clarence. He was half Scotch
on his mother's side. "But how? What can I do about it?"

"The position is this. The President of Power B. has an
overwhelming desire to have his photograph taken by Clarence Mulliner. Consent to take it, and our difficulties will be
at an end. Overcome with gratitude, he will sign the treaty,
and the Anglo-Saxon race will be safe."

Clarence did not hesitate. Apart from the natural gratification that he was doing the Anglo-Saxon race a bit of good,
business was business; and if the President took a dozen of
the large size finished in silver wash it would mean a nice
profit.

"I shall be delighted," he said.

"Your patriotism," said the visitor, "will not go unre-
warded. It will be gratefully noted in the Very Highest Circles."

Clarence reached for his appointment-book.

"Now, let me see. Wednesday? — No, I'm full up Wednesday. Thursday? — No. Suppose the President looks in at my
studio between four and five on Friday?"

The visitor uttered a gasp.

"Good heavens, Mr. Mulliner," he exclaimed, "surely you
do not imagine that, with the vast issues at stake, these things
can be done openly and in daylight? If the devils in the pay
of Power A. were to learn that the President intended to
have his photograph taken by you, I would not give a straw
for your chances of living an hour."

"Then what do you suggest?"

"You must accompany me now to the President's suite at
the Milan Hotel. We shall travel in a closed car, and God send
that these fiends did not recognise me as I came here. If they
did, we shall never reach that car alive. Have you, by any

The Romance of a Bulb-Squeezer 195

chance, while we have been talking, heard the hoot of an owl?"

"No," said Clarence. "No owls."

"Then perhaps they are nowhere near. The fiends always imitate the hoot of an owl."

"A thing," said Clarence, "which I tried to do when I was a small boy and never seemed able to manage. The popular idea that owls say 'Tu-whit, tu-whoo' is all wrong. The actual noise they make is something far more difficult and complex, and it was beyond me."

"Quite so." The visitor looked at his watch. "However, absorbing as these reminiscences of your boyhood days are, time is flying. Shall we be making a start?"

"Certainly."

"Then follow me."

It appeared to be holiday-time for fiends, or else the night shift had not yet come on, for they reached the car without being molested. Clarence stepped in, and his masked visitor, after a keen look up and down the street, followed him.

"Talking of my boyhood —" began Clarence.

The sentence was never completed. A soft wet pad was pressed over his nostrils: the air became a-reek with the sickly fumes of chloroform: and Clarence knew no more.

When he came to, he was no longer in the car. He found himself lying on a bed in a room in a strange house. It was a medium-sized room with scarlet wall-paper, simply furnished with a wash-hand stand, a chest of drawers, two cane-bottomed chairs, and a "God Bless Our Home" motto framed in oak. He was conscious of a severe headache, and was about to rise and make for the water-bottle on the wash-stand when, to his consternation, he discovered that his arms and legs were shackled with stout cord.

As a family, the Mulliners have always been noted for their reckless courage; and Clarence was no exception to the rule. But for an instant his heart undeniably beat a little faster. He saw now that his masked visitor had tricked him. Instead of being a representative of His Majesty's Diplomatic Service (a most respectable class of men), he had really been all along a fiend in the pay of Power A.

No doubt he and his vile associates were even now chuckling at the ease with which their victim had been duped. Clarence gritted his teeth and struggled vainly to loose the knots which secured his wrists. He had fallen back exhausted when he heard the sound of a key turning and the door opened. Somebody crossed the room and stood by the bed, looking down on him.

The new-comer was a stout man with a complexion that matched the wall-paper. He was puffing slightly, as if he had found the stairs trying. He had broad, slab-like features; and his face was split in the middle by a walrus moustache. Somewhere and in some place, Clarence was convinced, he had seen this man before.

And then it all came back to him. An open window with a pleasant summer breeze blowing in; a stout man in a cocked hat trying to climb through this window; and he, Clarence, doing his best to help him with the sharp end of a tripod. It was Jno. Horatio Biggs, the Mayor of Tooting East.

A shudder of loathing ran through Clarence.

"Traitor!" he cried.

"Eh?" said the Mayor.

"If anybody had told me that a son of Tooting, nursed in the keen air of freedom which blows across the Common, would sell himself for gold to the enemies of his country, I would never have believed it. Well, you may tell your employers — "

"What employers?"

"Power A."

"Oh, that?" said the Mayor. "I am afraid my secretary, whom I instructed to bring you to this house, was obliged to romance a little in order to ensure your accompanying him, Mr. Mulliner. All that about Power A. and Power B. was just his little joke. If you want to know why you were brought here — "

The Romance of a Bulb-Squeezer 197

Clarence uttered a low groan.

"I have guessed your ghastly object, you ghastly object," he said quietly. "You want me to photograph you."

The Mayor shook his head.

"Not myself. I realise that that can never be. My daughter."

"Your daughter?"

"My daughter."

"Does she take after you?"

"People tell me there is a resemblance."

"I refuse," said Clarence.

"Think well, Mr. Mulliner."

"I have done all the thinking that is necessary. England — or, rather, Great Britain — looks to me to photograph only her fairest and loveliest; and though, as a man, I admit that I loathe beautiful women, as a photographer I have a duty to consider that is higher than any personal feelings. History has yet to record an instance of a photographer playing his country false, and Clarence Mulliner is not the man to supply the first one. I decline your offer."

"I wasn't looking on it exactly as an offer," said the Mayor, thoughtfully. "More as a command, if you get my meaning."

"You imagine that you can bend a lens-artist to your will and make him false to his professional reputation?"

"I was thinking of having a try."

"Do you realise that, if my incarceration here were known, ten thousand photographers would tear this house brick from brick and you limb from limb?"

"But it isn't," the Mayor pointed out. "And that, if you follow me, is the whole point. You came here by night in a closed car. You could stay here for the rest of your life, and no one would be any the wiser. I really think you had better reconsider, Mr. Mulliner."

"You have had my answer."

"Well, I'll leave you to think it over. Dinner will be served at seven-thirty. Don't bother to dress."

At half-past seven precisely the door opened again and the Mayor reappeared, followed by a butler bearing on a silver salver a glass of water and a small slice of bread. Pride urged Clarence to reject the refreshment, but hunger overcame pride. He swallowed the bread which the butler offered him in small bits in a spoon and drank the water.

"At what hour would the gentleman desire breakfast sir?" asked the butler.

"Now," said Clarence, for his appetite, always healthy, seemed to have been sharpened by the trials which he had undergone.

"Let us say nine o'clock," suggested the Mayor. "Put aside another slice of that bread, Meadows. And no doubt Mr. Mulliner would enjoy a glass of this excellent water."

For perhaps half an hour after his host had left him, Clarence's mind was obsessed to the exclusion of all other thoughts by a vision of the dinner he would have liked to be enjoying. All we Mulliners have been good trenchermen, and to put a bit of bread into it after it had been unoccupied for a whole day was to offer to Clarence's stomach an insult which it resented with an indescribable bitterness. Clarence's only emotion for some considerable time, then, was that of hunger. His thoughts centred themselves on food. And it was to this fact, oddly enough, that he owed his release.

For, as he lay there in a sort of delirium, picturing himself getting outside a medium-cooked steak smothered in onions, with grilled tomatoes and floury potatoes on the side, it was suddenly borne in upon him that this steak did not taste quite so good as other steaks which he had eaten in the past. It was tough and lacked juiciness. It tasted just like rope.

And then, his mind clearing, he saw that it actually was rope. Carried away by the anguish of hunger, he had been chewing the cord which bound his hands; and he now discovered that he had bitten into it quite deeply.

A sudden flood of hope poured over Clarence Mulliner.

The Romance of a Bulb-Squeezer 199

Carrying on at this rate, he perceived, he would be able ere long to free himself. It only needed a little imagination. After a brief interval to rest his aching jaws, he put himself deliberately into that state of relaxation which is recommended by the apostles of Suggestion.

"I am entering the dining-room of my club," murmured Clarence. "I am sitting down. The waiter is handing me the bill of fare. I have selected roast duck with green peas and new potatoes, lamb cutlets with Brussels sprouts, fricassee of chicken, porterhouse steak, boiled beef and carrots, leg of mutton, haunch of mutton, mutton chops, curried mutton, veal, kidneys sauté, spaghetti Caruso, and eggs and bacon, fried on both sides. The waiter is now bringing my order. I have taken up my knife and fork. I am beginning to eat."

And, murmuring a brief grace, Clarence flung himself on the rope and set to.

Twenty minutes later he was hobbling about the room, restoring the circulation to his cramped limbs.

Just as he had succeeded in getting himself nicely limbered up, he heard the key turning in the door.

Clarence crouched for the spring. The room was quite dark now, and he was glad of it, for darkness well fitted the work which lay before him. His plans, conceived on the spur of the moment, were necessarily sketchy, but they included jumping on the Mayor's shoulders and pulling his head off. After that, no doubt, other modes of self-expression would suggest themselves.

The door opened. Clarence made his leap. And he was just about to start on the programme as arranged, when he discovered with a shock that this was no O.B.E. that he was being rough with, but a woman. And no photographer worthy of the name will ever lay a hand upon a woman, save to raise her chin and tilt it a little more to the left.

"I beg your pardon!" he cried.

"Don't mention it," said his visitor, in a low voice. "I hope I didn't disturb you."

"Not at all," said Clarence.

There was a pause.

"Rotten weather," said Clarence, feeling that it was for him, as the male member of the sketch, to keep the conversation going.

"Yes, isn't it?"

"A lot of rain we've had this summer."

"Yes. It seems to get worse every year."

"Doesn't it?"

"So bad for tennis."

"And cricket."

"And polo."

"And garden parties."

"I hate rain."

"So do I."

"Of course, we may have a fine August."

"Yes, there's always that."

The ice was broken, and the girl seemed to become more at her ease.

"I came to let you out," she said. "I must apologise for my father. He loves me foolishly and has no scruples where my happiness is concerned. He has always yearned to have me photographed by you, but I cannot consent to allow a photographer to be coerced into abandoning his principles. If you will follow me, I will let you out by the front door."

"It's awfully good of you," said Clarence, awkwardly. As any man of nice sentiment would have been, he was embarrassed. He wished that he could have obliged this kind-hearted girl by taking her picture, but a natural delicacy restrained him from touching on this subject. They went down the stairs in silence.

On the first landing a hand was placed on his in the darkness and the girl's voice whispered in his ear.

"We are just outside father's study," he heard her say. "We must be as quiet as mice."

"As what?" said Clarence.

"Mice."

"Oh, rather," said Clarence, and immediately bumped into what appeared to be a pedestal of some sort.

These pedestals usually have vases on top of them, and it was revealed to Clarence a moment later that this one was no exception. There was a noise like ten simultaneous dinner-services coming apart in the hands of ten simultaneous parlour-maids; and then the door was flung open, the landing became flooded with light, and the Mayor of Tooting East stood before them. He was carrying a revolver and his face was dark with menace.

"Ha!" said the Mayor.

But Clarence was paying no attention to him. He was staring open-mouthed at the girl. She had shrunk back against the wall, and the light fell full upon her.

"You!" cried Clarence.

"This—" began the Mayor.

"You! At last!"

"This is a pretty—"

"Am I dreaming?"

"This is a pretty state of af—"

"Ever since that day I saw you in the cab I have been scouring London for you. To think that I have found you at last!"

"This is a pretty state of affairs," said the Mayor, breathing on the barrel of his revolver and polishing it on the sleeve of his coat. "My daughter helping the foe of her family to fly —"

"Flee, father," corrected the girl, faintly.

"Flea or fly — this is no time for arguing about insects. Let me tell you—"

Clarence interrupted him indignantly.

"What do you mean," he cried, "by saying that she took after you?"

"She does."

"She does not. She is the loveliest girl in the world, while you look like Lon Chaney made up for something. See for yourself." Clarence led them to the large mirror at the head of the stairs. "Your face — if you can call it that — is one of those beastly blobby squashy sort of faces — "

"Here!" said the Mayor.

" — whereas hers is simply divine. Your eyes are bulbous and goofy — "

"Hey!" said the Mayor.

" — while hers are sweet and soft and intelligent. Your ears — "

"Yes, yes," said the Mayor, petulantly. "Some other time, some other time. Then am I to take it, Mr. Mulliner — "

"Call me Clarence."

"I refuse to call you Clarence."

"You will have to very shortly, when I am your son-in-law." The girl uttered a cry. The Mayor uttered a louder cry.

"My son-in-law!"

"That," said Clarence, firmly, "is what I intend to be — and speedily." He turned to the girl. "I am a man of volcanic passions, and now that love has come to me there is no power in heaven or earth that can keep me from the object of my love. It will be my never-ceasing task — er — "

"Gladys," prompted the girl.

"Thank you. It will be my never-ceasing task, Gladys, to strive daily to make you return that love — "

"You need not strive, Clarence," she whispered, softly. "It is already returned."

Clarence reeled.

"Already?" he gasped.

"I have loved you since I saw you in that cab. When we were torn asunder, I felt quite faint."

"So did I. I was in a daze. I tipped my cabman at Waterloo three half-crowns. I was aflame with love."

"I can hardly believe it."

"Nor could I, when I found out. I thought it was three-pence. And ever since that day — "

The Mayor coughed.

"Then am I to take it — er — Clarence," he said, "that

your objections to photographing my daughter are removed?"

Clarence laughed happily.

"Listen," he said, "and I'll show you the sort of son-in-law I am. Ruin my professional reputation though it may, I will take a photograph of you too!"

"Me!"

"Absolutely. Standing beside her with the tips of your fingers on her shoulder. And what's more, you can wear your cocked hat."

Tears had begun to trickle down the Mayor's cheeks.

"My boy!" he sobbed, brokenly. "My boy!"

And so happiness came to Clarence Mulliner at last. He never became President of the Bulb-Squeezers, for he retired from business the next day, declaring that the hand that had snapped the shutter when taking the photograph of his dear wife should never snap it again for sordid profit. The wedding, which took place some six weeks later, was attended by almost everybody of any note in Society or on the Stage; and was the first occasion on which a bride and bridegroom had ever walked out of church beneath an arch of crossed tripods.

AUNT
AGATHA
TAKES
THE
COUNT

"JEEVES," I SAID, "WE'VE BACKED A WINNER."

"Sir?"

"Coming to this place, I mean. Here we are in a topping hotel, with fine weather, good cooking, golf, bathing, gambling of every variety, and my Aunt Agatha miles away on the other side of the English Channel. I ask you, what could be sweeter?"

I had had to leg it, if you remember, with considerable speed from London because my Aunt Agatha was on my track with a hatchet as the result of the breaking-off of my engagement to Honoria Glossop. The thing hadn't been my fault, but I couldn't have convinced Aunt Agatha of that if I'd argued for a week: so it had seemed to me that the judicious course to pursue was to buzz briskly off while the buzzing was good. I was standing now at the window of the extremely decent suite which I'd taken at the Hotel Splendide at Roville on the French coast, and, as I looked down at the people popping to and fro in the sunshine, and reflected that in about a quarter of an hour I was due to lunch with a girl who was the exact opposite of Honoria Glossop in every way, I felt dashed uplifted. Gay, genial, happy-go-lucky, and devil-may-care, if you know what I mean.

I had met this girl — Aline Hemmingway her name was — for the first time on the train coming from Paris. She was going to Roville to wait there for a brother who was due to arrive from England. I had helped her with her baggage, got into conversation, had a bite of dinner with her in the restaurant-car, and the result was we had become remarkably chummy. I'm a bit apt, as a rule, to give the modern girl a miss, but there was something different about Aline Hemmingway.

I turned round, humming a blithe melody, and Jeeves shied like a startled mustang.

I had rather been expecting some such display of emotion on the man's part, for I was trying out a fairly fruity cummerbund that morning — one of those silk contrivances, you know, which you tie round your waist, something on the order of a sash, only more substantial. I had seen it in a shop the day before and hadn't been able to resist it, but I'd known all along that there might be trouble with Jeeves. It was a pretty brightish scarlet.

"I beg your pardon, sir," he said, in a sort of hushed voice. "You are surely not proposing to appear in public in that thing?"

"What, Cuthbert the Cummerbund?" I said in a careless, debonair way, passing it off. "Rather!"

"I should not advise it, sir, really I shouldn't."

"Why not?"

"The effect, sir, is loud in the extreme."

I tackled the blighter squarely. I mean to say, nobody knows better than I do that Jeeves is a mastermind and all that, but, dash it, a fellow must call his soul his own. You can't be a serf to your valet.

"You know, the trouble with you, Jeeves," I said, "is that you're too — what's the word I want? — too bally insular.

You can't realise that you aren't in Piccadilly all the time. In a place like this, simply dripping with the gaiety and *joie-de-vivre* of France, a bit of colour and a touch of the poetic is expected of you. Why, last night at the Casino I saw a fellow in a full evening suit of yellow velvet."

"Nevertheless, sir — "

"Jeeves," I said, firmly, "my mind is made up. I'm in a foreign country; it's a corking day; God's in his heaven and all's right with the world and this cummerbund seems to me to be called for."

"Very good, sir," said Jeeves, coldly.

Dashed upsetting, this sort of thing. If there's one thing that gives me the pip, it's unpleasantness in the home; and I could see that relations were going to be pretty fairly strained for a while. I suppose the old brow must have been a bit furrowed or something, for Aline Hemmingway spotted that things were wrong directly we sat down to lunch.

"You seem depressed, Mr. Wooster," she said. "Have you been losing money at the Casino?"

"No," I said. "As a matter of fact, I won quite a goodish sum last night."

"But something is the matter. What is it?"

"Well, to tell you the truth," I said, "I've just had rather a painful scene with my man, and it's shaken me a bit. He doesn't like this cummerbund."

"Why, I've just been admiring it. I think it's very becoming."

"No, really?"

"It has rather a Spanish effect."

"Exactly what I thought myself. Extraordinary you should have said that. A touch of the hidalgo, what? Sort of Vincente y Blasco What's-his-name stuff. The jolly old hidalgo off to the bull-fight, what?"

"Yes. Or a corsair of the Spanish Main."

"Absolutely! I say, you know, you have bucked me up. It's a rummy thing about you — how sympathetic you are, I mean. The ordinary girl you meet to-day is all bobbed hair and gaspers, but you — "

I was about to continue in this strain, when somebody halted at our table, and the girl jumped up.

"Sidney!" she cried.

The chappie who had anchored in our midst was a small, round cove with a face rather like a sheep. He wore pince-nez, his expression was benevolent, and he had on one of those collars which button at the back. A parson, in fact.

"Well, my dear," he said, beaming pretty freely, "here I am at last."

"Are you very tired?"

"Not at all. A most enjoyable journey, in which tedium was rendered impossible by the beauty of the scenery through which we passed and the entertaining conversation of my fellow-travellers. But may I be presented to this gentleman?" he said, peering at me through the pince-nez.

"This is Mr. Wooster," said the girl, "who was very kind to me coming from Paris. Mr. Wooster, this is my brother."

We shook hands, and the brother went off to get a wash.

"Sidney's such a dear," said the girl. "I know you'll like him."

"Seems a topper."

"I do hope he will enjoy his stay here. It's so seldom he gets a holiday. His vicar overworks him dreadfully."

"Vicars are the devil, what?"

"I wonder if you will be able to spare any time to show him round the place? I can see he's taken such a fancy to you. But, of course, it would be a bother, I suppose, so — "

"Rather not. Only too delighted." For half a second I thought of patting her hand, then I felt I'd better wait a bit. "I'll do anything, absolutely anything."

"It's awfully kind of you."

"For you," I said, "I would — "

At this point the brother returned, and the conversation became what you might call general.

After lunch I fairly curvetted back to my suite, with a most extraordinary braced sensation going all over me like a rash.

"Jeeves," I said, "you were all wrong about that cummerbund. It went like a breeze from the start."

"Indeed, sir?"

"Made an absolutely outstanding hit. The lady I was lunching with admired it. Her brother admired it. The waiter looked as if he admired it. Well, anything happened since I left?"

"Yes, sir. Mrs. Gregson has arrived at the hotel."

A fellow I know who went shooting, and was potted by one of his brother-sportsmen in mistake for a rabbit, once told me that it was several seconds before he realised that he had contributed to the day's bag. For about a tenth of a minute everything seemed quite O.K., and then suddenly he got it. It was just the same with me. It took about five seconds for this fearful bit of news to sink in.

"What!" I yelled. "Aunt Agatha here?"

"Yes, sir."

"She can't be."

"I have seen her, sir."

"But how did she get here?"

"The Express from Paris has just arrived, sir."

"But, I mean, how the dickens did she know I was here?"

"You left a forwarding-address at the flat for your correspondence, sir. No doubt Mrs. Gregson obtained it from the hall-porter."

"But I told the chump not to give it away to a soul."

"That would hardly baffle a lady of Mrs. Gregson's forceful personality, sir."

"Jeeves, I'm in the soup."

"Yes, sir."

"Right up to the hocks!"

"Yes, sir."

"What shall I do?"

"I fear I have nothing to suggest, sir."

I eyed the man narrowly. Dashed aloof his manner was. I saw what was the matter, of course. He was still brooding over that cummerbund.

"I shall go for a walk, Jeeves," I said.

"Yes, sir?"

"A good long walk."

"Very good, sir."

"And if — er — if anybody asks for me, tell 'em you don't know when I'll be back."

To people who don't know my Aunt Agatha I find it extraordinarily difficult to explain why it is that she has always put the wind up me to such a frightful extent. I mean, I'm not dependent on her financially, or anything like that. It's simply personality, I've come to the conclusion. You see, all through my childhood and when I was a kid at school she was always able to turn me inside out with a single glance, and I haven't come out from under the 'fluence yet. We run to height a bit in our family, and there's about five-foot-nine of Aunt Agatha, topped off with a beaky nose, an eagle eye, and a lot of grey hair, and the general effect is pretty formidable.

Her arrival in Roville at this juncture had made things more than a bit complicated for me. What to do? Leg it quick before she could get hold of me, would no doubt have been the advice most fellows would have given me. But the situation wasn't as simple as that. I was in much the same position as the cat on the garden wall who, when on the point of becoming matey with the cat next door, observes the bootjack sailing through the air. If he stays where he is, he gets it in the neck; if he biffs, he has to start all over again where he left off. I didn't like the prospect of being collared by Aunt Agatha, but on the other hand I simply barred the notion of leaving Roville by the night-train and parting from Aline Hemmingway. Absolutely a man's crossroads, if you know what I mean.

I prowled about the neighbourhood all the afternoon and evening, then I had a bit of dinner at a quiet restaurant in the town and trickled cautiously back to the hotel. Jeeves was popping about in the suite.

"There is a note for you, sir," he said, "on the mantelpiece."

The blighter's manner was still so cold and unchummy that I bit the bullet and had a dash at being airy.

"A note, eh?"

"Yes, sir. Mrs. Gregson's maid brought it shortly after you had left."

"Tra-la-la!" I said.

"Precisely, sir."

I opened the note.

"She wants me to look in on her after dinner some time."

"Yes, sir?"

"Jeeves," I said, "mix me a stiffish brandy-and-soda."

"Yes, sir."

"Stiffish, Jeeves. Not too much soda, but splash the brandy about a bit."

"Very good, sir."

He shimmered off into the background to collect the materials, and just at that moment there was a knock at the door.

I'm bound to say it was a shock. My heart stood still, and I bit my tongue.

"Come in," I bleated.

But it wasn't Aunt Agatha after all. It was Aline Hemmingway, looking rather rattled, and her brother, looking like a sheep with a secret sorrow.

"Oh, Mr. Wooster!" said the girl, in a sort of gasping way.

"Oh, what-ho!" I said. "Won't you come in? Take a seat or two."

"I don't know how to begin."

"Eh?" I said. "Is anything up?"

"Poor Sidney — it was my fault — I ought never to have let him go there alone."

At this point the brother, who had been standing by wrapped in the silence, gave a little cough, like a sheep caught in the mist on a mountain-top.

"The fact is, Mr. Wooster," he said. "I have been gambling at the Casino."

"Oh!" I said. "Did you click?"

He sighed heavily.

"If you mean, was I successful, I must answer in the negative. I rashly persisted in the view that the colour red, having appeared no fewer than seven times in succession, must inevitably at no distant date give place to black. I was in error. I lost my little all, Mr. Wooster."

"Tough luck," I said.

"I left the Casino, and returned to the hotel. There I encountered one of my parishioners, a Colonel Musgrave, who chanced to be holiday-making over here. I — er — induced him to cash me a cheque for one hundred pounds on my bank in London."

"Well, that was all to the good, what?" I said, hoping to induce the poor egg to look on the bright side. "I mean bit of luck finding someone to slip it into, first crack out of the box."

"On the contrary, Mr. Wooster, it did but make matters worse. I burn with shame as I make the confession, but I went back to the Casino and lost the entire sum."

"I say!" I said. "You *are* having a night out!"

"And," concluded the chappie, "the most lamentable feature of the whole affair is that I have no funds in the bank to meet the cheque, when presented."

I'm free to confess that I gazed at him with no little interest and admiration. Never in my life before had I encountered a curate so genuinely all to the mustard. Little as he might look like one of the lads of the village, he certainly appeared to be the real tabasco.

"Colonel Musgrave," he went on, gulping somewhat, "is not a man who would be likely to overlook the matter. He is a hard man. He will expose me to my vic-ah. My vic-ah is a hard man. I shall be ruined if Colonel Musgrave presents that cheque, and he leaves for England to-night."

"Mr. Wooster," the girl burst out, "won't you, won't you help us? Oh, do say you will. We must have the money to get back that cheque from Colonel Musgrave before nine o'clock — he leaves on the nine-twenty. I was at my wits' end what to do, when I remembered how kind you had always been and how you had told me at lunch that you had won some money at the Casino last night. Mr. Wooster, will you lend it to us, and take these as security?" And, before I knew what she was doing, she had dived into her bag, produced a case, and opened it. "My pearls," she said. "I don't know what they are worth — they were a present from my poor father — but I know they must be worth ever so much more than the amount we want."

Dashed embarrassing. Made me feel like a pawnbroker. More than a touch of popping the watch about the whole business.

"No, I say, really," I protested, the haughty old spirit of the Woosters kicking like a mule at the idea. "There's no need of any security, you know, or any rot of that kind. I mean to say, among pals, you know, what? Only too glad the money'll come in useful."

And I fished it out and pushed it across. The brother shook his head.

"Mr. Wooster," he said, "we appreciate your generosity, your beautiful, heartening confidence in us, but we cannot permit this."

"What Sidney means," said the girl, "is that you really don't know anything about us, when you come to think of it. You mustn't risk lending all this money without any security at all to two people who, after all, are almost strangers."

"Oh, don't say that!"

"I do say it. If I hadn't thought that you would be quite businesslike about this, I would never have dared to come to you. If you will just give me a receipt, as a matter of form — "

"Oh, well."

I wrote out the receipt and handed it over feeling more or less of an ass.

"Here you are," I said.

The girl took the piece of paper, shoved it in her bag, grabbed the money and slipped it to brother Sidney, and then, before I knew what was happening, she had darted at me, kissed me, and legged it from the room.

I don't know when I've been so rattled. The whole thing was so dashed sudden and unexpected. Through a sort of mist I could see that Jeeves had appeared from the background and was helping the brother on with his coat; and then the brother came up to me and grasped my hand.

"I can't thank you sufficiently, Mr. Wooster!"

"Oh, right-ho!"

"You have saved my good name. 'Good name in man or woman, dear my lord,' " he said, massaging the fin with some fervour, " 'is the immediate jewel of their souls. Who steals my purse steals trash. 'Twas mine, 'tis his, and has been slave to thousands. But he that filches from me my good name robs me of that which not enriches him and makes me poor indeed.' I thank you from the bottom of my heart. Good night, Mr. Wooster."

"Good night, old thing," I said.

"Your brandy-and-soda, sir," said Jeeves, as the door shut.

I blinked at him.

"Oh, there you are!"

"Yes, sir."

"Rather a sad affair, Jeeves."

"Yes, sir."

"Lucky I happened to have all that money handy."

"Well — er — yes, sir."

"You speak as though you didn't think much of it."

"It is not my place to criticize your actions, sir, but I will venture to say that I think you behaved a little rashly."

"What, lending that money?"

"Yes, sir. These fashionable French watering-places are notoriously infested by dishonest characters."

This was a bit too thick.

"Now, look here, Jeeves," I said, "I can stand a lot, but when it comes to your casting asp-whatever-the-word-is on the sweetest girl in the world and a bird in Holy Orders — "

"Perhaps I am over-suspicious, sir. But I have seen a great deal of these resorts. When I was in the employment of Lord Frederick Ranelagh, shortly before I entered your service, his lordship was very neatly swindled by a criminal known, I believe, by the sobriquet of Soapy Sid, who scraped acquaintance with us in Monte Carlo with the assistance of a female accomplice. I have never forgotten the circumstance."

"I don't want to butt in on your reminiscences, Jeeves," I said coldly, "but you're talking through your hat. How can there have been anything fishy about this business? They've left me the pearls, haven't they? Very well, then, think before you speak. You had better be tooling down to the desk now and having these things shoved in the hotel safe." I picked up the case and opened it. "Oh, Great Scot!"

The bally thing was empty!

"Oh, my Lord!" I said, staring, "don't tell me there's been dirty work at the cross-roads, after all!"

"Precisely, sir. It was in exactly the same manner that Lord Frederick was swindled on the occasion to which I have alluded. While his female accomplice was gratefully embracing his lordship, Soapy Sid substituted a duplicate case for the one containing the pearls, and went off with the jewels, the money, and the receipt. On the strength of the receipt he subsequently demanded from his lordship the return of the pearls, and his lordship, not being able to produce them, was obliged to pay a heavy sum in compensation. It is a simple but effective ruse."

I felt as if the bottom had dropped out of things with a jerk. I mean to say, Aline Hemmingway, you know. What I mean is, if Love hadn't actually awakened in my heart, there's no doubt it was having a jolly good stab at it, and the thing was only a question of days. And all the time — well, I mean, dash it, you know.

"Soapy Sid? Sid! *Sidney!* Brother Sidney! Why, by Jove, Jeeves, do you think that parson was Soapy Sid?"

"Yes, sir."

"But it seems so extraordinary. Why, his collar buttoned at the back — I mean, he would have deceived a bishop. Do you really think he was Soapy Sid?"

"Yes, sir. I recognised him directly he came into the room."

I stared at the blighter.

"You recognised him?"

"Yes, sir."

"Then, dash it all," I said, deeply moved, "I think you might have told me."

"I thought it would save disturbance and unpleasantness if I merely abstracted the case from the man's pocket as I assisted him with his coat, sir. Here it is."

He laid another case on the table beside the dud one, and, by Jove, you couldn't tell them apart. I opened it, and there were the good old pearls, as merry and bright as dammit, smiling up at me. I gazed feebly at the man. I was feeling a bit overwrought.

"Jeeves," I said, "you're an absolute genius!"

"Yes, sir."

Relief was surging over me in great chunks by now. I'd almost forgotten that a woman had toyed with my heart and thrown it away like a worn-out tube of tooth-paste and all that sort of thing. What seemed to me the important item was the fact that, thanks to Jeeves, I was not going to be called on to cough up several thousand quid.

"It looks to me as though you had saved the old home. I mean, even a chappie endowed with the immortal rind of dear old Sid is hardly likely to have the nerve to come back and retrieve these little chaps."

"I should imagine not, sir."

"Well, then — Oh, I say, you don't think they are just paste or anything like that?"

"No, sir. These are genuine pearls, and extremely valuable."

"Well, then dash it, I'm on velvet. Absolutely reclining on the good old plush! I may be down a hundred quid, but I'm up a jolly good string of pearls. Am I right or wrong?"

"Hardly that, sir. I think that you will have to restore the pearls."

"What! To Sid? Not while I have my physique!"

"No, sir. To their rightful owner."

"But who is their rightful owner?"

"Mrs. Gregson, sir."

"What! How do you know?"

"It was all over the hotel an hour ago that Mrs. Gregson's pearls had been abstracted. The man Sid travelled from Paris in the same train as Mrs. Gregson, and no doubt marked them down. I was speaking to Mrs. Gregson's maid shortly before you came in, and she informed me that the manager of the hotel is now in Mrs. Gregson's suite."

"And having a devil of a time, what?"

"So I should be disposed to imagine, sir."

The situation was beginning to unfold before me.

"I'll go and give them back to her, eh? It'll put me one up, what?"

"If I might make the suggestion, sir, I think it would strengthen your position if you were to affect to discover the pearls in Mrs. Gregson's suite — say, in a bureau drawer."

"I don't see why."

"I think I am right, sir."

"Well, I stand on you. If you say so. I'll be popping, what?"

"The sooner the better, sir."

Long before I reached Aunt Agatha's lair I could tell that the hunt was up. Divers chappies in hotel uniform and not a few chambermaids of sorts were hanging about in the corridor, and through the panels I could hear a mixed assortment of voices, with Aunt Agatha's topping the lot. I knocked, but no one took any notice, so I trickled in. Among those present I noticed a chambermaid in hysterics, Aunt Agatha with her hair bristling, and a whiskered cove who looked like a bandit, as no doubt he was, being the proprietor of the hotel.

"Oh, hallo," I said. "I got your note, Aunt Agatha."

She waved me away. No welcoming smile for Bertram.

"Oh don't bother me now," she snapped, looking at me as if I were more or less the last straw.

"Something up?"

"Yes, yes, yes! I've lost my pearls."

"Pearls? Pearls? Pearls?" I said. "No, really? Dashed annoying. Where did you see them last?"

"What *does* it matter where I saw them last? They have been stolen."

Here Wilfred the Whisker-King, who seemed to have been taking a rest between rounds, stepped into the ring again and began to talk rapidly in French. Cut to the quick he seemed. The chambermaid whooped in the corner.

"Sure you've looked everywhere?" I asked.

"Of course I've looked everywhere."

"Well, you know, I've often lost a collar-stud and — "

"Do try not to be so maddening, Bertie! I have enough to bear without your imbecilities. Oh, be quiet! Be quiet!" she shouted. And such was the magnetism of what Jeeves called her forceful personality that Wilfred subsided as though he had run into a wall. The chambermaid continued to go strong.

"I say," I said, "I think there's something the matter with this girl. Isn't she crying or something?"

"She stole my pearls! I am convinced of it."

This started the whisker-specialist off again, and I left them at it and wandered off on a tour round the room. I slipped the pearls out of the case and decanted them into a drawer. By the time I'd done this and had leisure to observe the free-for-all once more, Aunt Agatha had reached the frozen grande-dame stage and was putting the Last of the Bandits through it in the voice she usually reserves for snubbing waiters in restaurants.

"I tell you, my good man, for the hundredth time, that I have searched thoroughly — everywhere. Why you should imagine that I have overlooked so elementary — "

"I say," I said, "don't want to interrupt you and all that sort of thing, but aren't these the little chaps?"

I pulled them out of the drawer and held them up.

"These look like pearls, what?"

I don't know when I've had a more juicy moment. It was one of those occasions about which I shall prattle to my grand-children — if I ever have any, which at the moment of going to press seems more or less of a hundred-to-one shot. Aunt Agatha simply deflated before my eyes. It reminded me of when I once saw some intrepid aeronauts letting the gas out of a balloon.

"Where — where — where?" she gurgled.

"In this drawer. They'd slid under some paper."

"Oh!" said Aunt Agatha, and there was a bit of silence.

I dug out my entire stock of manly courage, breathed a short prayer, and let her have it right in the thorax.

"I must say, Aunt Agatha, dash it," I said, crisply, "I think you have been a little hasty, what? I mean to say, giving this poor man here so much anxiety and worry and generally biting him in the gizzard. You've been very, very unjust to this poor man!"

"Yes, yes," chipped in the poor man.

"And this unfortunate girl, what about her? Where does she get off? You've accused her of pinching the things on absolutely no evidence. I think she would be jolly well advised to bring an action for — for whatever it is, and soak you for substantial damages."

"Mais oui, mais oui, c'est trop fort!" shouted the Bandit Chief, backing me up like a good 'un. And the chambermaid looked up inquiringly, as if the sun was breaking the clouds.

"I shall recompense her," said Aunt Agatha, feebly.

"If you take my tip, you jolly well will, and that eftsoons or right speedily. She's got a cast-iron case, and if I were her I wouldn't take a cent under twenty quid. But what gives me the pip most is the way you've abused this poor man and tried to give his hotel a bad name — "

"Yes, by damn! It's too bad!" cried the whiskered marvel. "You careless old woman! You give my hotel bad names, would you or wasn't it? To-morrow you leave my hotel."

And more to the same effect, all good, ripe stuff. And presently, having said his say, he withdrew, taking the chambermaid with him, the latter with a crisp tenner clutched in a vicelike grip. I suppose she and the bandit split it outside. A French hotel-manager wouldn't be likely to let real money wander away from him without counting himself in on the division.

I turned to Aunt Agatha, whose demeanour was now rather like that of one who, picking daisies on the railway, has just caught the down-express in the small of the back.

"There was something you wished to speak to me about?" I said.

"No, no. Go away, go away."

"You said in your note — "

"Yes, yes, never mind. Please go away, Bertie. I wish to be alone."

"Oh, right-ho!" I said. "Right-ho! right-ho!" And back to the good old suite.

"Ten o'clock, a clear night, and all's well, Jeeves," I said, breezing in.

"I am gratified to hear it, sir."

"If twenty quid would be any use to you, Jeeves — ?"

"I am much obliged, sir."

There was a pause. And then — well, it was a wrench, but I did it. I unstripped the cummerbund and handed it over.

"Do you wish me to press this, sir?"

I gave the thing one last longing look. It had been very dear to me.

"No," I said, "take it away; give it to the deserving poor. I shall never wear it again."

"Thank you very much, sir," said Jeeves.

THE
FIERY
WOOING
OF
MORDRED

THE PINT OF LAGER BREATHED HEAVILY THROUGH his nose.

"Silly fathead!" he said. "Ash-trays in every nook and cranny of the room — ash-trays staring you in the eye wherever you look — and he has to go and do a fool thing like that."

He was alluding to a young gentleman with a vacant, fish-like face who, leaving the bar-parlour of the Anglers' Rest a few moments before, had thrown his cigarette into the waste-paper basket, causing it to burst into a cheerful blaze. Not one of the little company of amateur fire-fighters but was ruffled. A Small Bass with a high blood pressure had had to have his collar loosened, and the satin-clad bosom of Miss Postlethwaite, our emotional barmaid, was still heaving.

Only Mr. Mulliner seemed disposed to take a tolerant view of what had occurred.

"In fairness to the lad," he pointed out, sipping his hot Scotch and lemon, "we must remember that our bar-parlour contains no grand piano or priceless old walnut table, which to the younger generation are the normal and natural repositories for lighted cigarette-ends. Failing these, he, of course, selected the waste-paper basket. Like Mordred."

"Like who?" asked a Whisky and Splash.

"Whom," corrected Miss Postlethwaite.

The Whisky and Splash apologized.

"A nephew of mine. Mordred Mulliner, the poet."

"Mordred," murmured Miss Postlethwaite pensively. "A sweet name."

"And one," said Mr. Mulliner, "that fitted him admirably, for he was a comely lovable sensitive youth with large, fawn-like eyes, delicately chiselled features and excellent teeth. I mention these teeth, because it was owing to them that the train of events started which I am about to describe."

"He bit somebody?" queried Miss Postlethwaite, groping.

"No. But if he had had no teeth he would not have gone to the dentist's that day, and if he had not gone to the dentist's he would not have met Annabelle."

"Annabelle whom?"

"Who," corrected Miss Postlethwaite.

"Oh, shoot," said the Whisky and Splash.

"Annabelle Sprockett-Sprockett, the only daughter of Sir Murgatroyd and Lady Sprockett-Sprockett of Smattering Hall, Worcestershire. Impractical in many ways," said Mr. Mulliner, "Mordred never failed to visit his dentist every six months, and on the morning on which my story opens he had just seated himself in the empty waiting-room and was turning the pages of a three-months-old copy of the *Tatler* when the door opened and there entered a girl at the sight of whom — or who, if our friend here prefers it — something seemed to explode on the left side of his chest like a bomb. The *Tatler* swam before his eyes, and when it solidified again he realized that love had come to him at last."

Most of the Mulliners have fallen in love at first sight, but few with so good an excuse as Mordred. She was a singularly beautiful girl, and for a while it was this beauty of hers that enchained my nephew's attention to the exclusion of all else. It was only after he had sat gulping for some minutes like a dog with a chicken bone in its throat that he detected the sadness in her face. He could see now that her eyes, as she listlessly perused her four-months-old copy of *Punch,* were heavy with pain.

His heart ached for her, and as there is something about the atmosphere of a dentist's waiting-room which breaks down the barriers of conventional etiquette he was emboldened to speak.

"Courage!" he said. "It may not be so bad, after all. He may just fool about with that little mirror thing of his, and decide that there is nothing that needs to be done."

For the first time she smiled — faintly, but with sufficient breadth to give Mordred another powerful jolt.

"I'm not worrying about the dentist," she explained. "My trouble is that I live miles away in the country and only get a chance of coming to London about twice a year for about a couple of hours. I was hoping that I should be able to put in a long spell of window-shopping in Bond Street, but now I've got to wait goodness knows how long I don't suppose I shall have time to do a thing. My train goes at one-fifteen."

All the chivalry in Mordred came to the surface like a leaping trout.

"If you would care to take my place —"

"Oh, I couldn't."

"Please. I shall enjoy waiting. It will give me an opportunity of catching up with my reading."

"Well, if you really wouldn't mind —"

Considering that Mordred by this time was in the market to tackle dragons on her behalf or to climb the loftiest peak of the Alps to supply her with edelweiss, he was able to assure her that he did not mind. So in she went, flashing at him a shy glance of gratitude which nearly doubled him up, and he lit a cigarette and fell into a reverie. And presently she came out and he sprang to his feet, courteously throwing his cigarette into the waste-paper basket.

She uttered a cry. Mordred recovered the cigarette.

"Silly of me," he said, with a deprecating laugh. "I'm always doing that. Absent-minded. I've burned two flats already this year."

She caught her breath.

"Burned them to the ground?"

"Well, not to the ground. They were on the top floor."

"But you burned them?"

"Oh, yes. I burned them."

"Well, well!" She seemed to muse. "Well, good-bye, Mr. —"

"Mulliner. Mordred Mulliner."

"Good-bye, Mr. Mulliner, and thank you so much."

"Not at all, Miss —"

"Sprockett-Sprockett."

"Not at all, Miss Sprockett-Sprockett. A pleasure."

She passed from the room, and a few minutes later he was lying back in the dentist's chair, filled with an infinite sadness. This was not due to any activity on the part of the dentist, who had just said with a rueful sigh that there didn't seem to be anything to do this time, but to the fact that his life was now a blank. He loved this beautiful girl, and he would never see her more. It was just another case of ships that pass in the waiting-room.

Conceive his astonishment, therefore, when by the afternoon post next day he received a letter which ran as follows:

Smattering Hall,
Lower Smattering-on-the-Wissel,
Worcestershire.

Dear Mr. Mulliner,

My little girl has told me how very kind you were to her at the dentist's to-day. I cannot tell you how grateful she was. She does so love to walk down Bond Street and breathe on the jewellers' windows, and but for you she would have had to go another six months without her little treat.

I suppose you are a very busy man, like everybody in London, but if you can spare the time it would give my

The Fiery Wooing of Mordred 225

*husband and myself so much pleasure if you could run down
and stay with us for a few days — a long week-end, or even
longer if you can manage it.*

> *With best wishes,*
> *Yours sincerely,*
> *Aurelia Sprockett-Sprockett.*

Mordred read this communication six times in a minute
and a quarter and then seventeen times rather more slowly
in order to savour any *nuance* of it that he might have overlooked. He took it that the girl must have got his address from
the dentist's secretary on her way out, and he was doubly
thrilled — first, by this evidence that one so lovely was as
intelligent as she was beautiful, and secondly because the
whole thing seemed to him so frightfully significant. A girl,
he meant to say, does not get her mother to invite fellows to
her country home for long week-ends (or even longer if they
can manage it) unless such fellows have made a pretty substantial hit with her. This, he contended, stood to reason.

He hastened to the nearest post-office, despatched a tele-
gram to Lady Sprockett-Sprockett assuring her that he would
be with her on the morrow, and returned to his flat to pack
his effects. His heart was singing within him. Apart from
anything else, the invitation could not have come at a more
fortunate moment, for what with musing on his great love
while smoking cigarettes he had practically gutted his little
nest on the previous evening, and while it was still habitable
in a sense there was no gainsaying the fact that all those
charred sofas and things struck a rather melancholy note and
he would be glad to be away from it all for a few days.

It seemed to Mordred, as he travelled down on the following afternoon, that the wheels of the train, clattering
over the metals, were singing "Sprockett-Sprockett" —
not "Annabelle," of course, for he did not yet know her
name — and it was with a whispered "Sprockett-Sprockett" on his lips that he alighted at the little station of

Smattering-cum-Blimpstead-in-the-Vale, which, as his hostess's note-paper had informed him, was where you got off for the Hall. And when he perceived that the girl herself had come to meet him in a two-seater car the whisper nearly became a shout.

For perhaps three minutes, as he sat beside her, Mordred remained in this condition of ecstatic bliss. Here he was, he reflected, and here she was — here, in fact, they both were — together, and he was just about to point out how jolly this was and — if he could work it without seeming to rush things too much — to drop a hint to the effect that he could wish this state of affairs to continue through all eternity, when the girl drew up outside a tobacconist's.

"I won't be a minute," she said. "I promised Biffy I would bring him back some cigarettes."

A cold hand seemed to lay itself on Mordred's heart.

"Biffy?"

"Captain Biffing, one of the men at the Hall. And Guffy wants some pipe-cleaners."

"Guffy?"

"Jack Guffington. I expect you know his name, if you are interested in racing. He was third in last year's Grand National."

"Is he staying at the Hall, too?"

"Yes."

"You have a large house-party?"

"Oh, not so very. Let me see. There's Billy Biffing, Jack Guffington, Ted Prosser, Freddie Boot — he's the tennis champion of the county, Tommy Mainprice, and — oh, yes, Algy Fripp — the big-game hunter, you know."

The hand on Mordred's heart, now definitely iced, tightened its grip. With a lover's sanguine optimism, he had supposed that this visit of his was going to be just three days of jolly sylvan solitude with Annabelle Sprockett-Sprockett. And now it appeared that the place was unwholesomely crowded with his fellow men. And what fellow men! Big-game hunters . . . Tennis champions . . . Chaps who rode in

Grand Nationals . . . He could see them in his mind's eye —lean, wiry, riding-breeched and flannel-trousered young Apollos, any one of them capable of cutting out his weight in Clark Gables.

A faint hope stirred within him.

"You have also, of course, with you Mrs. Biffing, Mrs. Guffington, Mrs. Prosser, Mrs. Boot, Mrs. Mainprice and Mrs. Algernon Fripp?"

"Oh, no, they aren't married."

"None of them?"

"No."

The faint hope coughed quietly and died.

"Ah," said Mordred.

While the girl was in the shop, he remained brooding. The fact that not one of these blisters should be married filled him with an austere disapproval. If they had had the least spark of civic sense, he felt, they would have taken on the duties and responsibilities of matrimony years ago. But no. Intent upon their selfish pleasures, they had callously remained bachelors. It was this spirit of *laissez-faire*, Mordred considered, that was eating like a canker into the soul of England.

He was aware of Annabelle standing beside him.

"Eh?" he said, starting.

"I was saying: Have you plenty of cigarettes?"

"Plenty, thank you."

"Good. And of course there will be a box in your room. Men always like to smoke in their bedrooms, don't they? As a matter of fact, two boxes — Turkish and Virginian. Father put them there specially."

"Very kind of him," said Mordred mechanically.

He relapsed into a moody silence, and they drove off.

It would be agreeable (said Mr. Mulliner) if, having shown you my nephew so gloomy, so apprehensive, so tortured with dark forebodings at this juncture, I were able now to state that the hearty English welcome of Sir Murgatroyd and Lady Sprockett-Sprockett on his arrival at the Hall cheered him up and put new life into him. Nothing, too, would give me greater pleasure than to say that he found, on encountering the dreaded Biffies and Guffies, that they were negligible little runts with faces incapable of inspiring affection in any good woman.

But I must adhere rigidly to the facts. Genial, even effusive, though his host and hostess showed themselves, their cordiality left him cold. And, so far from his rivals being weeds, they were one and all models of manly beauty, and the spectacle of their obvious worship of Annabelle cut my nephew like a knife.

And on top of all this there was Smattering Hall itself.

Smattering Hall destroyed Mordred's last hope. It was one of those vast edifices, so common throughout the countryside of England, whose original founders seem to have budgeted for families of twenty-five or so and a domestic staff of not less than a hundred. "Home isn't home," one can picture them saying to themselves, "unless you have plenty of elbow room." And so this huge, majestic pile had come into being. Romantic persons, confronted with it, thought of knights in armour riding forth to the Crusades. More earthy individuals felt that it must cost a packet to keep up. Mordred's reaction on passing through the front door was a sort of sick sensation, a kind of settled despair.

How, he asked himself, even assuming that by some miracle he succeeded in fighting his way to her heart through all these Biffies and Guffies, could he ever dare to take Annabelle from a home like this? He had quite satisfactory private means, of course, and would be able, when married, to give up the bachelor flat and spread himself to something on a bigger scale — possibly, if sufficiently *bijou,* even a desirable residence in the Mayfair district. But after Smattering Hall would not Annabelle feel like a sardine in the largest of London houses?

Such were the dark thoughts that raced through Mordred's brain before, during and after dinner. At eleven o'clock he pleaded fatigue after his journey, and Sir Murgatroyd accompanied him to his room, anxious, like a good host, to see that everything was comfortable.

"Very sensible of you to turn in early," he said, in his bluff, genial way. "So many young men ruin their health with late hours. Now you, I imagine, will just get into a dressing-gown and smoke a cigarette or two and have the light out by twelve. You have plenty of cigarettes? I told them to see that you were well supplied. I always think the bedroom smoke is the best one of the day. Nobody to disturb you, and all that. If you want to write letters or anything, there is lots of paper, and here is the waste-paper basket, which is always so necessary. Well, good night, my boy, good night."

The door closed, and Mordred, as foreshadowed, got into a dressing-gown and lit a cigarette. But though, having done this, he made his way to the writing-table, it was not with any idea of getting abreast of his correspondence. It was his purpose to compose a poem to Annabelle Sprockett-Sprockett. He had felt it seething within him all the evening, and sleep would be impossible until it was out of his system.

Hitherto, I should mention, my nephew's poetry, for he belonged to the modern fearless school, had always been stark and rhymeless and had dealt principally with corpses and the smell of cooking cabbage. But now, with the moonlight silvering the balcony outside, he found that his mind had become full of words like "love" and "dove" and "eyes" and "summer skies."

> *Blue eyes,* wrote Mordred . . .
> *Sweet lips,* wrote Mordred . . .
> *Oh, eyes like skies of summer blue . . .*
> *Oh, love . . .*
> *Oh, dove . . .*
> *Oh, lips . . .*

With a muttered ejaculation of chagrin he tore the sheet across and threw it into the waste-paper basket.

Blue eyes that burn into my soul,
  Sweet lips that smile my heart away,
Pom-pom, pom-pom, pom something whole (Goal?)
  And tiddly-iddly-umpty-ay (Gay? Say? Happy day?)

Blue eyes into my soul that burn,
  Sweet lips that smile away my heart,
Oh, something something turn or yearn
  And something something something part.

You burn into my soul, blue eyes,
  You smile my heart away, sweet lips,
Short long short long of summer skies
  And something something something trips. (Hips?
    Ships? Pips?)

He threw the sheet into the waste-paper basket and rose with a stifled oath. The waste-paper basket was nearly full now, and still his poet's sense told him that he had not achieved perfection. He thought he saw the reason for this. You can't just sit in a chair and expect inspiration to flow — you want to walk about and clutch your hair and snap your fingers. It had been his intention to pace the room, but the moonlight pouring in through the open window called to him. He went out on to the balcony. It was but a short distance to the dim, mysterious lawn. Impulsively he dropped from the stone balustrade.

The effect was magical. Stimulated by the improved conditions, his Muse gave quick service, and this time he saw at once that she had rung the bell and delivered the goods. One turn up and down the lawn, and he was reciting as follows:

TO ANNABELLE

Oh, lips that smile! Oh, eyes that shine
  Like summer skies, or stars above!
Your beauty maddens me like wine,
  Oh, umpty-pumpty-tumty love!

And he was just wondering, for he was a severe critic of his own work, whether that last line couldn't be polished up a bit, when his eye was attracted by something that shone like summer skies or stars above and, looking more closely, he perceived that his bedroom curtains were on fire.

Now, I will not pretend that my nephew Mordred was in every respect the cool-headed man of action, but this happened to be a situation with which use had familiarized him. He knew the procedure.

"Fire!" he shouted.

A head appeared in an upstairs window. He recognized it as that of Captain Biffing.

"Eh?" said Captain Biffing.

"Fire!"

"What?"

"Fire!" vociferated Mordred. "F for Francis, I for Isabel . . ."

"Oh, fire?" said Captain Biffing. "Right ho."

And presently the house began to discharge its occupants.

In the proceedings which followed, Mordred, I fear, did not appear to the greatest advantage. This is an age of specialization, and if you take the specialist off his own particular ground he is at a loss. Mordred's genius, as we have seen, lay in the direction of starting fires. Putting them out called for quite different qualities, and these he did not possess. On the various occasions of holocausts at his series of flats, he had never attempted to play an active part, contenting himself with going downstairs and asking the janitor to step up and see what he could do about it. So now, though under the bright eyes of Annabelle Sprockett-Sprockett he would have given much to be able to dominate the scene, the truth is that the Biffies and Guffies simply played him off the stage.

His heart sank as he noted the hideous efficiency of these young men. They called for buckets. They formed a line. Freddie Boot leaped lissomely on to the balcony, and Algy Fripp, mounted on a wheel-barrow, handed up to him the necessary supplies. And after Mordred, trying to do his bit, had tripped up Jack Guffington and upset two buckets over Ted Prosser, he was advised in set terms to withdraw into the background and stay there.

It was a black ten minutes for the unfortunate young man. One glance at Sir Murgatroyd's twisted face as he watched the operations was enough to tell him how desperately anxious the fine old man was for the safety of his ancestral home and how bitter would be his resentment against the person who had endangered it. And the same applied to Lady Sprockett-Sprockett and Annabelle. Mordred could see the anxiety in their eyes, and the thought that ere long those eyes must be turned accusingly on him chilled him to the marrow.

Presently Freddie Boot emerged from the bedroom to announce that all was well.

"It's out," he said, jumping lightly down. "Anybody know whose room it was?"

Mordred felt a sickening qualm, but the splendid Mulliner courage sustained him. He stepped forward, white and tense.

"Mine," he said.

He became the instant centre of attention. The six young men looked at him.

"Yours?"

"Oh, yours, was it?"

"What happened?"

"How did it start?"

"Yes, how did it start?"

"Must have started somehow, I mean," said Captain Biffing, who was a clear thinker. "I mean to say, must have, don't you know, what?"

Mordred mastered his voice.

"I was smoking, and I suppose I threw my cigarette into the waste-paper basket, and as it was full of paper . . ."

"Full of paper? Why was it full of paper?"

"I had been writing a poem."

There was a stir of bewilderment.

"A what?" said Ted Prosser.

"Writing a what?" said Jack Guffington.

"Writing a *poem?*" asked Captain Biffing of Tommy Mainprice.

"That's how I got the story," said Tommy Mainprice, plainly shaken.

"Chap was writing a poem," Freddie Boot informed Algy Fripp.

"You mean the chap writes poems?"

"That's right. Poems."

"Well, I'm dashed!"

"Well, I'm blowed!"

Their now unconcealed scorn was hard to bear. Mordred chafed beneath it. The word "poem" was flitting from lip to lip, and it was only too evident that, had there been an "s" in the word, those present would have hissed it. Reason told him that these men were mere clods, Philistines, fatheads who would not recognize the rare and the beautiful if you handed it to them on a skewer, but that did not seem to make it any better. He knew that he should be scorning them, but it is not easy to go about scorning people in a dressing-gown, especially if you have no socks on and the night breeze is cool around the ankles. So, as I say, he chafed. And finally, when he saw the butler bend down with pursed lips to the ear of the cook, who was a little hard of hearing, and after a contemptuous glance in his direction speak into it, spacing his syllables carefully, something within him seemed to snap.

"I regret, Sir Murgatroyd," he said, "that urgent family business compels me to return to London immediately. I shall be obliged to take the first train in the morning."

Without another word he went into the house.

In the matter of camping out in devastated areas my nephew had, of course, become by this time an old hand. It was rarely nowadays that a few ashes and cinders about the place disturbed him. But when he had returned to his bedroom one look was enough to assure him that nothing practical in the way of sleep was to be achieved here. Apart from the unpleasant, acrid smell of burned poetry, the apartment, thanks to the efforts of Freddie Boot, had been converted into a kind of inland sea. The carpet was awash, and on the bed only a duck could have made itself at home.

And so it came about that some ten minutes later Mordred Mulliner lay stretched upon a high-backed couch in the library, endeavouring by means of counting sheep jumping through a gap in a hedge to lull himself into unconsciousness.

But sleep refused to come. Nor in his heart had he really thought that it would. When the human soul is on the rack, it cannot just curl up and close its eyes and expect to get its eight hours as if nothing had happened. It was all very well for Mordred to count sheep, but what did this profit him when each sheep in turn assumed the features and lineaments of Annabelle Sprockett-Sprockett and, what was more, gave him a reproachful glance as it drew itself together for the spring?

Remorse gnawed him. He was tortured by a wild regret for what might have been. He was not saying that with all these Biffies and Guffies in the field he had ever had more than a hundred to eight chance of winning that lovely girl, but at least his hat had been in the ring. Now it was definitely out. Dreamy Mordred may have been — romantic — impractical — but he had enough sense to see that the very worst thing you can do when you are trying to make a favourable impression on the adored object is to set fire to her childhood home, every stick and stone of which she has no doubt worshipped since they put her into rompers.

He had reached this point in his meditations, and was about to send his two hundred and thirty-second sheep at the gap, when with a suddenness which affected him much as an explosion of gelignite would have done, the lights flashed on. For an instant, he lay quivering, then, cautiously poking his head round the corner of the couch, he looked to see who his visitors were.

It was a little party of three that had entered the room. First came Sir Murgatroyd, carrying a tray of sandwiches. He was followed by Lady Sprockett-Sprockett with a syphon and glasses. The rear was brought up by Annabelle, who was bearing a bottle of whisky and two dry ginger ales.

So evident was it that they were assembling here for purposes of a family council that, but for one circumstance, Mordred, to whom anything in the nature of eavesdropping was as repugnant as it has always been to all the Mulliners, would have sprung up with a polite "Excuse me" and taken his blanket elsewhere. This circumstance was the fact that on lying down he had kicked his slippers under the couch, well out of reach. The soul of modesty, he could not affront Annabelle with the spectacle of his bare toes.

So he lay there in silence, and silence, broken only by the swishing of soda-water and the *whoosh* of opened ginger-ale bottles, reigned in the room beyond.

Then Sir Murgatroyd spoke.

"Well, that's that," he said, bleakly.

There was a gurgle as Lady Sprockett-Sprockett drank ginger ale. Then her quiet, well-bred voice broke the pause.

"Yes," she said, "it is the end."

"The end," agreed Sir Murgatroyd heavily. "No good trying to struggle on against luck like ours. Here we are and here we have got to stay, mouldering on in this blasted barrack of a place which eats up every penny of my income when, but for the fussy interference of that gang of officious, ugly nitwits, there would have been nothing left of it but a pile of ashes, with a man from the Insurance Company standing on it with his fountain-pen, writing cheques. Curse those imbeciles! Did you see that young Fripp with those buckets?"

"I did, indeed," sighed Lady Sprockett-Sprockett.

"Annabelle," said Sir Murgatroyd sharply.

"Yes, Father?"

"It has seemed to me lately, watching you with a father's eye, that you have shown signs of being attracted by young Algernon Fripp. Let me tell you that if ever you allow yourself to be ensnared by his insidious wiles, or by those of William Biffing, John Guffington, Edward Prosser, Thomas

Mainprice or Frederick Boot, you will do so over my dead body. After what occurred to-night, those young men shall never darken my door again. They and their buckets! To think that we could have gone and lived in London . . ."

"In a nice little flat . . ." said Lady Sprockett-Sprockett.

"Handy for my club . . ."

"Convenient for the shops . . ."

"Within a stone's throw of the theatres . . ."

"Seeing all our friends . . ."

"Had it not been," said Sir Murgatroyd, summing up, "for the pestilential activities of these Guffingtons, these Biffings, these insufferable Fripps, men who ought never to be trusted near a bucket of water when a mortgaged country-house has got nicely alight. I did think," proceeded the stricken old man, helping himself to a sandwich, "that when Annabelle, with a ready intelligence which I cannot overpraise, realized this young Mulliner's splendid gifts and made us ask him down here, the happy ending was in sight. What Smattering Hall has needed for generations has been a man who throws his cigarette-ends into waste-paper baskets. I was convinced that here at last was the angel of mercy we required."

"He did his best, Father."

"No man could have done more," agreed Sir Murgatroyd cordially. "The way he upset those buckets and kept getting entangled in people's legs. Very shrewd. It thrilled me to see him. I don't know when I've met a young fellow I liked and respected more. And what if he is a poet? Poets are all right. Why, dash it, I'm a poet myself. At the last dinner of the Loyal Sons of Worcestershire I composed a poem which, let me tell you, was pretty generally admired. I read it out to the boys over the port, and they cheered me to the echo. It was about a young lady of Bewdley, who sometimes behaved rather rudely . . ."

"Not before Mother, Father."

"Perhaps you're right. Well, I'm off to bed. Come along, Aurelia. You coming, Annabelle?"

"Not yet, Father. I want to stay and think."

"Do what?"

"Think."

"Oh, think? Well, all right."

"But, Murgatroyd," said Lady Sprockett-Sprockett, "is there no hope? After all, there are plenty of cigarettes in the house, and we could always give Mr. Mulliner another waste-paper basket. . . ."

"No good. You heard him say he was leaving by the first train to-morrow. When I think that we shall never see that splendid young man again . . . Why, hullo, hullo, hullo, what's this? Crying, Annabelle?"

"Oh, Mother!"

"My darling, what is it?"

A choking sob escaped the girl.

"Mother, I love him! Directly I saw him in the dentist's waiting-room, something seemed to go all over me, and I knew that there could be no other man for me. And now . . ."

"Hi!" cried Mordred, popping up over the side of the couch like a jack-in-the-box.

He had listened with growing understanding to the conversation which I have related, but had shrunk from revealing his presence because, as I say, his toes were bare. But this was too much. Toes or no toes, he felt that he must be in this.

"You love me, Annabelle?" he cried.

His sudden advent had occasioned, I need scarcely say, a certain reaction in those present. Sir Murgatroyd had leaped like a jumping bean. Lady Sprockett-Sprockett had quivered like a jelly. As for Annabelle, her lovely mouth was open to the extent of perhaps three inches, and she was staring like one who sees a vision.

"You really love me, Annabelle?"

"Yes, Mordred."

"Sir Murgatroyd," said Mordred formally, "I have the honour to ask you for your daughter's hand. I am only a poor poet . . ."

"How poor?" asked the other, keenly.

"I was referring to my Art," explained Mordred. "Financially, I am nicely fixed. I could support Annabelle in modest comfort."

"Then take her, my boy, take her. You will live, of course"
— the old man winced — "in London?"

"Yes. And so shall you."

Sir Murgatroyd shook his head.

"No, no, that dream is ended. It is true that in certain circumstances I had hoped to do so, for the insurance, I may mention, amounts to as much as a hundred thousand pounds, but I am resigned now to spending the rest of my life in this infernal family vault. I see no reprieve."

"I understand," said Mordred, nodding. "You mean you have no paraffin in the house?"

Sir Murgatroyd started.

"Paraffin?"

"If," said Mordred, and his voice was very gentle and winning, "there had been paraffin on the premises, I think it possible that to-night's conflagration, doubtless imperfectly quenched, might have broken out again, this time with more serious results. It is often this way with fires. You pour buckets of water on them and think they are extinguished, but all the time they have been smouldering unnoticed, to break out once more in — well, in here, for example."

"Or the billiard-room," said Lady Sprockett-Sprockett.

"*And* the billiard-room," corrected Sir Murgatroyd.

"And the billiard-room," said Mordred. "And possibly — who knows? — in the drawing-room, dining-room, kitchen, servants' hall, butler's pantry and the usual domestic offices, as well. Still, as you say you have no paraffin . . ."

"My boy," said Sir Murgatroyd, in a shaking voice, "what gave you the idea that we have no paraffin? How did you fall into this odd error? We have gallons of paraffin. The cellar is full of it."

"And Annabelle will show you the way to the cellar — in case you thought of going there," said Lady Sprockett-

Sprockett. "Won't you, dear?"

"Of course, Mother. You will like the cellar, Mordred, darling. Most picturesque. Possibly, if you are interested in paraffin, you might also care to take a look at our little store of paper and shavings, too."

"My angel," said Mordred, tenderly, "you think of everything."

He found his slippers, and hand in hand they passed down the stairs. Above them, they could see the head of Sir Murgatroyd, as he leaned over the banisters. A box of matches fell at their feet like a father's benediction.

UKRIDGE'S
ACCIDENT
SYNDICATE

"HALF A MINUTE, LADDIE," SAID UKRIDGE. AND, gripping my arm, he brought me to a halt on the outskirts of the little crowd which had collected about the church door.

It was a crowd such as may be seen any morning during the London mating-season outside any of the churches which nestle in the quiet squares between Hyde Park and the King's Road, Chelsea.

It consisted of five women of cooklike aspect, four nurse-maids, half a dozen men of the non-producing class who had torn themselves away for the moment from their normal task of propping up the wall of the Bunch of Grapes publichouse on the corner, a costermonger with a barrow of vegetables, divers small boys, eleven dogs, and two or three purposeful-looking young fellows with cameras slung over their shoulders. It was plain that a wedding was in progress — and, arguing from the presence of the camera-men and the line of smart motor-cars along the kerb, a fairly fashionable wedding. What was not plain — to me — was why Ukridge, stern-est of bachelors, had desired to add himself to the spectators.

"What," I enquired, "is the thought behind this? Why are

we interrupting our walk to attend the obsequies of some perfect stranger?"

Ukridge did not reply for a moment. He seemed plunged in thought. Then he uttered a hollow, mirthless laugh —a dreadful sound like the last gargle of a dying moose.

"Perfect stranger, my number eleven foot!" he responded, in his coarse way. "Do you know who it is who's getting hitched up in there?"

"Who?"

"Teddy Weeks."

"Teddy Weeks? Teddy Weeks? Good Lord!" I exclaimed. "Not really?"

And five years rolled away.

It was at Barolini's Italian restaurant in Beak Street that Ukridge evolved his great scheme. Barolini's was a favourite resort of our little group of earnest strugglers in the days when the philanthropic restaurateurs of Soho used to supply four courses and coffee for a shilling and sixpence; and there were present that night, besides Ukridge and myself, the following men-about-town: Teddy Weeks, the actor, fresh from a six-weeks' tour with the Number Three "Only a Shop-Girl" Company; Victor Beamish, the artist, the man who drew that picture of the O-So-Eesi Piano-Player in the advertisement pages of the *Piccadilly Magazine;* Bertram Fox, author of *Ashes of Remorse,* and other unproduced motion-picture scenarios; and Robert Dunhill, who, being employed at a salary of eighty pounds per annum by the New Asiatic Bank, represented the sober, hard-headed commercial element. As usual, Teddy Weeks had collared the conversation, and was telling us once again how good he was and how hardly treated by a malignant fate.

There is no need to describe Teddy Weeks. Under another and a more euphonious name he has long since made his personal appearance dreadfully familiar to all who read the illustrated weekly papers. He was then, as now, a sickeningly handsome young man, possessing precisely the same melting eyes, mobile mouth, and corrugated hair so esteemed by the theatre-going public to-day. And yet, at this period of his career he was wasting himself on minor touring companies of the kind which open at Barrow-in-Furness and jump to Bootle for the second half of the week. He attributed this, as Ukridge was so apt to attribute his own difficulties, to lack of capital.

"I have everything," he said, querulously, emphasising his remarks with a coffee-spoon. "Looks, talent, personality, a beautiful speaking-voice — everything. All I need is a chance. And I can't get that because I have no clothes fit to wear. These managers are all the same, they never look below the surface, they never bother to find out if a man has genius. All they go by are his clothes. If I could afford to buy a couple of suits from a Cork Street tailor, if I could have my boots made to order by Moykoff instead of getting them ready-made and second-hand at Moses Brothers', if I could once contrive to own a decent hat, a really good pair of spats, and a gold cigarette-case, all at the same time, I could walk into any manager's office in London and sign up for a West-end production to-morrow."

It was at this point that Freddie Lunt came in. Freddie, like Robert Dunhill, was a financial magnate in the making and an assiduous frequenter of Barolini's; and it suddenly occurred to us that a considerable time had passed since we had last seen him in the place. We enquired the reason for this aloofness.

"I've been in bed," said Freddie, "for over a fort-night."

The statement incurred Ukridge's stern disapproval. That great man made a practice of never rising before noon, and on one occasion, when a carelessly-thrown match had burned a hole in his only pair of trousers, had gone so far as to remain between the sheets for forty-eight hours; but sloth on so majestic a scale as this shocked him.

"Lazy young devil," he commented severely. "Letting the golden hours of youth slip by like that when you ought to have been bustling about and making a name for yourself."

Freddie protested himself wronged by the imputation.

"I had an accident," he explained. "Fell off my bicycle and sprained an ankle."

"Tough luck," was our verdict.

"Oh, I don't know," said Freddie. "It wasn't bad fun getting a rest. And of course there was the fiver."

"What fiver?"

"I got a fiver from the *Weekly Cyclist* for getting my ankle sprained."

"You — *what?*" cried Ukridge, profoundly stirred — as ever — by a tale of easy money. "Do you mean to sit there and tell me that some dashed paper paid you five quid simply because you sprained your ankle? Pull yourself together, old horse. Things like that don't happen."

"It's quite true."

"Can you show me the fiver?"

"No; because if I did you would try to borrow it."

Ukridge ignored this slur in dignified silence.

"Would they pay a fiver to *anyone* who sprained his ankle?" he asked, sticking to the main point.

"Yes. If he was a subscriber."

"I knew there was a catch in it," said Ukridge, moodily.

"Lots of weekly papers are starting this wheeze," proceeded Freddie. "You pay a year's subscription and that entitles you to accident insurance."

We were interested. This was in the days before every daily paper in London was competing madly against its rivals in the matter of insurance and offering princely bribes to the citizens to make a fortune by breaking their necks. Nowadays papers are paying as high as two thousand pounds for a genuine corpse and five pounds a week for a mere dislocated spine; but at that time the idea was new and it had an attractive appeal.

"How many of these rags are doing this?" asked Ukridge. You could tell from the gleam in his eyes that that great brain was whirring like a dynamo. "As many as ten?"

"Yes, I should think so. Quite ten."

"Then a fellow who subscribed to them all and then sprained his ankle would get fifty quid?" said Ukridge, reasoning acutely.

"More if the injury was more serious," said Freddie, the expert. "They have a regular tariff. So much for a broken arm, so much for a broken leg, and so forth."

Ukridge's collar leaped off its stud and his pince-nez wobbled drunkenly as he turned to us.

"How much money can you blokes raise?" he demanded.

"What do you want it for?" asked Robert Dunhill, with a banker's caution.

"My dear old horse, can't you see? Why, my gosh, I've got the idea of the century. Upon my Sam, this is the giltest-edged scheme that was ever hatched. We'll get together enough money and take out a year's subscription for every one of these dashed papers."

"What's the good of that?" said Dunhill, coldly unenthusiastic.

They train bank clerks to stifle emotion, so that they will be able to refuse overdrafts when they become managers. "The odds are we should none of us have an accident of any kind, and then the money would be chucked away."

"Good heavens, ass," snorted Ukridge, "you don't suppose I'm suggesting that we should leave it to chance, do you? Listen! Here's the scheme. We take out subscriptions for all these papers, then we draw lots, and the fellow who gets the fatal card or whatever it is goes out and breaks his leg and draws the loot, and we split it up between us and live on it in luxury. It ought to run into hundreds of pounds."

A long silence followed. Then Dunhill spoke again. His was a solid rather than a nimble mind.

"Suppose he couldn't break his leg?"

"My gosh!" cried Ukridge, exasperated. "Here we are in the twentieth century, with every resource of modern civilisation at our disposal, with opportunities for getting our legs broken opening about us on every side — and you ask a silly question like that! Of course he could break his leg. Any ass

Ukridge's Accident Syndicate 245

can break a leg. It's a little hard! We're all infernally broke — personally, unless Freddie can lend me a bit of that fiver till Saturday, I'm going to have a difficult job pulling through. We all need money like the dickens, and yet, when I point out this marvellous scheme for collecting a bit, instead of fawning on me for my ready intelligence you sit and make objections. It isn't the right spirit. It isn't the spirit that wins."

"If you're as hard up as that," objected Dunhill, "how are you going to put in your share of the pool?"

A pained, almost a stunned, look came into Ukridge's eyes. He gazed at Dunhill through his lop-sided pince-nez as one who speculates as to whether his hearing has deceived him.

"Me?" he cried. "Me? I like that! Upon my Sam, that's rich! Why, damme, if there's any justice in the world, if there's a spark of decency and good feeling in your bally bosoms, I should think you would let me in free for suggesting the idea. It's a little hard! I supply the brains and you want me to cough up cash as well. My gosh, I didn't expect this. This hurts me, by George! If anybody had told me that an old pal would — "

"Oh, all right," said Robert Dunhill. "All right, all right, all right. But I'll tell you one thing. If you draw the lot it'll be the happiest day of my life."

"I shan't," said Ukridge. "Something tells me that I shan't."

Nor did he. When, in a solemn silence broken only by the sound of a distant waiter quarrelling with the cook down a speaking-tube, we had completed the drawing, the man of destiny was Teddy Weeks.

I suppose that even in the springtime of Youth, when broken limbs seems a lighter matter than they become later in life, it can never be an unmixedly agreeable thing to have to go out into the public highways and try to make an accident happen to one. In such circumstances the reflection that you are thereby benefiting your friends brings but slight balm. To Teddy Weeks it appeared to bring no balm at all. That he was experiencing a certain disinclination to sacrifice himself for the public good became more and more evident as the days went by and found him still intact. Ukridge, when he called upon me to discuss the matter, was visibly perturbed. He sank into a chair beside the table at which I was beginning my modest morning meal, and, having drunk half my coffee, sighed deeply.

"Upon my Sam," he moaned, "it's a little disheartening. I strain my brain to think up schemes for getting us all a bit of money just at the moment when we are all needing it most, and when I hit on what is probably the simplest and yet ripest notion of our time, this blighter Weeks goes and lets me down by shirking his plain duty. It's just my luck that a fellow like that should have drawn the lot. And the worst of it is, laddie, that, now we've started with him, we've got to keep on. We can't possibly raise enough money to pay yearly subscriptions for anybody else. It's Weeks or nobody."

"I suppose we must give him time."

"That's what he says," grunted Ukridge, morosely, helping himself to toast. "He says he doesn't know how to start about it. To listen to him, you'd think that going and having a trifling accident was the sort of delicate and intricate job that required years of study and special preparation. Why, a child of six could do it on his head at five minutes' notice. The man's so infernally particular. You make helpful suggestions, and instead of accepting them in a broad, reasonable spirit of co-operation he comes back at you every time with some frivolous objection. He's so dashed fastidious. When we were out last night, we came on a couple of navvies scrapping. Good hefty fellows, either of them capable of putting him in hospital for a month. I told him to jump in and start separating them, and he said no; it was a private dispute which was none of his business, and he didn't feel justified in interfering. Finicky, I call it. I tell you, laddie, this blighter is a broken reed. He has got cold feet. We did wrong to let him into the drawing at all. We might have known that a fellow like that would never give results. No conscience. No sense of esprit de corps. No notion of putting himself out to the most trifling extent for the benefit of the community. Haven't you any more marmalade, laddie?"

"I have not."

"Then I'll be going," said Ukridge, moodily. "I suppose," he added, pausing at the door, "you couldn't lend me five bob?"

"How did you guess?"

"Then I'll tell you what," said Ukridge, ever fair and reasonable; "you can stand me dinner to-night." He seemed cheered up for the moment by this happy compromise, but gloom descended on him again. His face clouded. "When I think," he said, "of all the money that's locked up in that poor faint-hearted fish, just waiting to be released, I could sob. Sob, laddie, like a little child. I never liked that man — he has a bad eye and waves his hair. Never trust a man who waves his hair, old horse."

Ukridge's pessimism was not confined to himself. By the end of a fortnight, nothing having happened to Teddy Weeks worse than a slight cold which he shook off in a couple of days, the general consensus of opinion among his apprehensive colleagues in the Syndicate was that the situation had become desperate. There were no signs whatever of any return on the vast capital which we had laid out, and meanwhile meals had to be bought, landladies paid, and a reasonable supply of tobacco acquired. It was a melancholy task in these circumstances to read one's paper of a morning.

All over the inhabited globe, so the well-informed sheet gave one to understand, every kind of accident was happening every day to practically everybody in existence except Teddy Weeks. Farmers in Minnesota were getting mixed up with reaping-machines, peasants in India were being bisected by crocodiles; iron girders from skyscrapers were falling hourly on the heads of citizens in every town from Philadelphia to San Francisco; and the only people who were not down with ptomaine poisoning were those who had walked over cliffs, driven motors into walls, tripped over manholes, or assumed on too slight evidence that the gun was not loaded. In a crippled world, it seemed, Teddy Weeks walked alone, whole and glowing with health. It was one of those grim, ironical, hopeless, grey, despairful situations which the Russian novelists love to write about, and I could not find it in me to blame Ukridge for taking direct action in this crisis. My only regret was that bad luck caused so excellent a plan to miscarry.

My first intimation that he had been trying to hurry matters on came when he and I were walking along the King's Road one evening, and he drew me into Markham Square, a dismal backwater where he had once had rooms.

"What's the idea?" I asked, for I disliked the place.

"Teddy Weeks lives here," said Ukridge. "In my old rooms." I could not see that this lent any fascination to the place. Every day and in every way I was feeling sorrier and sorrier that I had been foolish enough to put money which I could ill spare into a venture which had all the earmarks of a wash-out, and my sentiments towards Teddy Weeks were cold and hostile.

"I want to enquire after him."

"Enquire after him? Why?"

"Well, the fact is, laddie, I have an idea that he has been bitten by a dog."

"What makes you think that?"

"Oh, I don't know," said Ukridge, dreamily. "I've just got the idea. You know how one gets ideas."

The mere contemplation of this beautiful event was so inspiring that for awhile it held me silent. In each of the ten journals in which we had invested dog-bites were specifically recommended as things which every subscriber ought to have. They came about half-way up the list of lucrative accidents, inferior to a broken rib or a fractured fibula, but better value than an ingrowing toe-nail. I was gloating happily over the picture conjured up by Ukridge's words when an exclamation brought me back with a start to the realities of life. A revolting sight met my eyes. Down the street came ambling the familiar figure of Teddy Weeks, and one glance at his elegant person was enough to tell us that our hopes had been built on sand. Not even a toy Pomeranian had chewed this man.

"Hallo, you fellows!" said Teddy Weeks.

"Hallo!" we responded, dully.

"Can't stop," said Teddy Weeks. "I've got to fetch a doctor."

"A doctor?"

"Yes. Poor Victor Beamish. He's been bitten by a dog."

Ukridge and I exchanged weary glances. It seemed as if Fate was going out of its way to have sport with us. What was the good of a dog biting Victor Beamish? What was the good of a hundred dogs biting Victor Beamish? A dog-bitten Victor Beamish had no market value whatever.

"You know that fierce brute that belongs to my landlady," said Teddy Weeks. "The one that always dashes out into the area and barks at people who come to the front door." I remembered. A large mongrel with wild eyes and flashing fangs, badly in need of a haircut. I had encountered it once in the street, when visiting Ukridge, and only the presence of the latter, who knew it well and to whom all dogs were as brothers, had saved me from the doom of Victor Beamish. "Somehow or other he got into my bedroom this evening. He was waiting there when I came home. I had brought Beamish back with me, and the animal pinned him by the leg the moment I opened the door."

"Why didn't he pin you?" asked Ukridge, aggrieved.

"What I can't make out," said Teddy Weeks, "is how on earth the brute came to be in my room. Somebody must have put him there. The whole thing is very mysterious."

"Why didn't he pin you?" demanded Ukridge again.

"Oh, I managed to climb on to the top of the wardrobe while he was biting Beamish," said Teddy Weeks. "And then the landlady came and took him away. But I can't stop here talking. I must go and get that doctor."

We gazed after him in silence as he tripped down the street. We noted the careful manner in which he paused at the corner to eye the traffic before crossing the road, the wary way in which he drew back to allow a truck to rattle past.

"You heard that?" said Ukridge, tensely. "He climbed on to the top of the wardrobe!"

"Yes."

"And you saw the way he dodged that excellent truck?"

"Yes."

"Something's got to be done," said Ukridge, firmly. "The man has got to be awakened to a sense of his responsibilities."

Next day a deputation waited on Teddy Weeks.

Ukridge was our spokesman, and he came to the point with admirable directness.

"How about it?" asked Ukridge.

"How about what?" replied Teddy Weeks, nervously, avoiding his accusing eye.

"When do we get action?"

"Oh, you mean that accident business?"

"Yes."

"I've been thinking about that," said Teddy Weeks.

Ukridge drew the mackintosh which he wore indoors and out of doors and in all weathers more closely around him. There was in the action something suggestive of a member of the Roman Senate about to denounce an enemy of the State. In just such a manner must Cicero have swished his toga as he took a deep breath preparatory to assailing Clodius. He toyed for a moment with the ginger-beer wire which held his pince-nez in place, and endeavoured without success to button his collar at the back. In moments of emotion Ukridge's collar always took on a sort of temperamental jumpiness which no stud could restrain.

"And about time you *were* thinking about it," he boomed, sternly.

We shifted appreciatively in our seats, all except Victor Beamish, who had declined a chair and was standing by the mantelpiece. "Upon my Sam, it's about time you were thinking about it. Do you realise that we've invested an enormous sum of money in you on the distinct understanding that we could rely on you to do your duty and get immediate results? Are we to be forced to the conclusion that you are so yellow and few in the pod as to want to evade your honourable obligations? We thought better of you, Weeks. Upon my Sam, we thought better of you. We took you for a two-fisted, enterprising, big-souled, one hundred-per-cent he-man who would stand by his friends to the finish."

"Yes, but—"

"Any bloke with a sense of loyalty and an appreciation of what it meant to the rest of us would have rushed out and found some means of fulfilling his duty long ago. You don't even grasp at the opportunities that come your way. Only yesterday I saw you draw back when a single step into the road would have had a truck bumping into you."

"Well, it's not so easy to let a truck bump into you."

"Nonsense. It only requires a little ordinary resolution. Use your imagination, man. Try to think that a child has fallen down in the street—a little golden-haired child," said Ukridge, deeply affected. "And a dashed great cab or something comes rolling up. The kid's mother is standing on the pavement, helpless, her hands clasped in agony. 'Dammit,' she cries, "will no one save my darling?' 'Yes, by George,' you shout, '*I* will.' And out you jump and the thing's over in half a second. I don't know what you're making such a fuss about."

"Yes, but—" said Teddy Weeks.

"I'm told, what's more, it isn't a bit painful. A sort of dull shock, that's all."

"Who told you that?"

"I forget. Someone."

"Well, you can tell him from me that he's an ass," said Teddy Weeks, with asperity.

"All right. If you object to being run over by a truck there are lots of other ways. But, upon my Sam, it's pretty hopeless suggesting them. You seem to have no enterprise at all. Yesterday, after I went to all the trouble to put a dog in your room, a dog which would have done all the work for you—all that you had to do was stand still and let him use his own judgment — what happened? You climbed on to — "

Victor Beamish interrupted, speaking in a voice husky with emotion.

"Was it you who put that damned dog in the room?"

"Eh?" said Ukridge. "Why, yes. But we can have a good talk about all that later on," he proceeded, hastily. "The point at the moment is how the dickens we're going to persuade this poor worm to collect our insurance money for us. Why, damme, I should have thought you would have — "

"All I can say — " began Victor Beamish, heatedly.

"Yes, yes," said Ukridge; "some other time. Must stick to business now, laddie. I was saying," he resumed, "that I should have thought you would have been as keen as mustard to put the job through for your own sake. You're always beefing that you haven't any clothes to impress managers with. Think of all you can buy with your share of the swag once you have summoned up a little ordinary determination and seen the thing through. Think of the suits, the boots, the hats, the spats. You're always talking about your dashed career, and how all you need to land you in a West-end production is good clothes. Well, here's your chance to get them."

His eloquence was not wasted. A wistful look came into Teddy Weeks's eye, such a look as must have come into the eye of Moses on the summit of Pisgah. He breathed heavily. You could see that the man was mentally walking along Cork Street, weighing the merits of one famous tailor against another.

"I'll tell you what I'll do," he said, suddenly. "It's no use asking me to put this thing through in cold blood. I simply can't do it. I haven't the nerve. But if you fellows will give me a dinner to-night with lots of champagne I think it will key me up to it."

A heavy silence fell upon the room. Champagne! The word was like a knell.

"How on earth are we going to afford champagne?" said Victor Beamish.

"Well, there it is," said Teddy Weeks. "Take it or leave it."

"Gentlemen," said Ukridge, "it would seem that the company requires more capital. How about it, old horses? Let's get together in a frank, business-like cards-on-the-table spirit, and see what can be done. I can raise ten bob."

"What!" cried the entire assembled company, amazed. "How?"

"I'll pawn a banjo."

"You haven't got a banjo."

"No, but George Tupper has, and I know where he keeps it."

Started in this spirited way, the subscriptions came pouring in. I contributed a cigarette-case, Bertram Fox thought his landlady would let him owe for another week, Robert Dunhill had an uncle in Kensington who, he fancied, if tactfully approached, would be good for a quid, and Victor Beamish said that if the advertisement-manager of the O-So-Eesi Piano-Player was churlish enough to refuse an advance of five shillings against future work he misjudged him sadly. Within a few minutes, in short, the Lightning Drive had produced the impressive total of two pounds six shillings, and we asked Teddy Weeks if he thought that he could get adequately keyed up within the limits of that sum.

"I'll try," said Teddy Weeks.

So, not unmindful of the fact that that excellent hostelry supplied champagne at eight shillings the quart bottle, we fixed the meeting for seven o'clock at Barolini's.

Considered as a social affair, Teddy Weeks's keying-up dinner was not a success. Almost from the start I think we all found it trying. It was not so much the fact that he was drinking deeply of Barolini's eight-shilling champagne while we, from lack of funds, were compelled to confine ourselves to meaner beverages; what really marred the pleasantness of the function was the extraordinary effect the stuff had on Teddy. What was actually in the champagne supplied to Barolini and purveyed by him to the public, such as were reckless enough to drink it, at eight shillings the bottle remains a secret between its maker and his Maker; but three glasses of it were enough to convert Teddy Weeks from a mild and rather oily young man into a truculent swashbuckler.

He quarrelled with us all. With the soup he was tilting at Victor Beamish's theories of Art; the fish found him ridiculing Bertram Fox's views on the future of the motion-picture; and by the time the leg of chicken with dandelion salad arrived — or, as some held, string salad — opinions varied on this point — the hell-brew had so wrought on him that he had begun to lecture Ukridge on his mis-spent life and was urging him in accents audible across the street to go out and get a job and thus acquire sufficient self-respect to enable him to look himself in the face in a mirror without wincing. Not, added Teddy Weeks with what we all thought uncalled-for offensiveness, that any amount of self-respect was likely to do that. Having said which, he called imperiously for another eight bobs'-worth.

We gazed at one another wanly. However excellent the end towards which all this was tending, there was no denying that it was hard to bear. But policy kept us silent. We recognised that this was Teddy Weeks's evening and that he must be humoured. Victor Beamish said meekly that Teddy had cleared up a lot of points which had been troubling him for a long time. Bertram Fox agreed that there was much in what Teddy had said about the future of the close-up. And even Ukridge, though his haughty soul was seared to its foundations by the latter's personal remarks, promised to take his homily to heart and act upon it at the earliest possible moment.

"You'd better!" said Teddy Weeks, belligerently, biting off the end of one of Barolini's best cigars. "And there's another thing — don't let me hear of your coming and sneaking people's socks again."

"Very well, laddie," said Ukridge, humbly.

"If there is one person in the world that I despise," said

Teddy, bending a red-eyed gaze on the offender, "it's a snock-seeker — a seek-snocker — a — well, you know what I mean."

We hastened to assure him that we knew what he meant and he relapsed into a lengthy stupor, from which he emerged three-quarters of an hour later to announce that he didn't know what we intended to do, but that he was going. We said that we were going too, and we paid the bill and did so.

Teddy Weeks's indignation on discovering us gathered about him upon the pavement outside the restaurant was intense, and he expressed it freely. Among other things, he said — which was not true — that he had a reputation to keep up in Soho.

"It's all right, Teddy, old horse," said Ukridge, soothingly. "We just thought you would like to have all your old pals round you when you did it."

"Did it? Did what?"

"Why, had the accident."

Teddy Weeks glared at him truculently. Then his mood seemed to change abruptly, and he burst into a loud and hearty laugh.

"Well, of all the silly ideas!" he cried, amusedly. "I'm not going to have an accident. You don't suppose I ever seriously intended to have an accident, do you? It was just my fun." Then, with another sudden change of mood, he seemed to become a victim to an acute unhappiness. He stroked Ukridge's arm affectionately, and a tear rolled down his cheek. "Just my fun," he repeated. "You don't mind my fun, do you?" he asked, pleadingly. "You like my fun, don't you? All my fun. Never meant to have an accident at all. Just wanted dinner." The gay humour of it all overcame his sorrow once more. "Funniest thing ever heard," he said cordially. "Didn't want accident, wanted dinner. Dinner daxident, danner dixident," he added, driving home his point. "Well, good night all," he said, cheerily. And, stepping off the kerb on to a banana-skin, was instantly knocked ten feet by a passing lorry.

"Two ribs and an arm," said the doctor five minutes later, superintending the removal proceedings. "Gently with that stretcher."

It was two weeks before we were informed by the authorities of Charing Cross Hospital that the patient was in a condition to receive visitors. A whip-round secured the price of a basket of fruit, and Ukridge and I were deputed by the shareholders to deliver it with their compliments and kind enquiries.

"Hallo!" we said in a hushed, bedside manner when finally admitted to his presence.

"Sit down, gentlemen," replied the invalid.

I must confess even in that first moment to having experienced a slight feeling of surprise. It was not like Teddy Weeks to call us gentlemen. Ukridge, however, seemed to notice nothing amiss.

"Well, well, well," he said, buoyantly. "And how are you, laddie? We've brought you a few fragments of fruit."

"I am getting along capitally," replied Teddy Weeks, still in that odd precise way which had made his opening words strike me as curious. "And I should like to say that in my opinion England has reason to be proud of the alertness and enterprise of her great journals. The excellence of their reading-matter, the ingenuity of their various competitions, and, above all, the go-ahead spirit which has resulted in this accident insurance scheme are beyond praise. Have you got that down?" he enquired.

Ukridge and I looked at each other. We had been told that Teddy was practically normal again, but this sounded like delirium.

"Have we got that down, old horse?" asked Ukridge, gently.

Teddy Weeks seemed surprised.

"Aren't you reporters?"

"How do you mean, reporters?"

"I thought you had come from one of these weekly papers that have been paying me insurance money, to interview me," said Teddy Weeks.

Ukridge and I exchanged another glance. An uneasy glance this time. I think that already a grim foreboding had begun to cast its shadow over us.

"Surely you remember me, Teddy, old horse?" said Ukridge, anxiously.

Teddy Weeks knit his brow, concentrating painfully.

"Why, of course," he said at last. "You're Ukridge, aren't you?"

"That's right. Ukridge."

"Of course. Ukridge."

"Yes. Ukridge. Funny your forgetting me!"

"Yes," said Teddy Weeks. "It's the effect of the shock I got when that thing bowled me over. I must have been struck on the head, I suppose. It has had the effect of rendering my memory rather uncertain. The doctors here are very interested. They say it is a most unusual case. I can remember some things perfectly, but in some ways my memory is a complete blank."

"Oh, but I say, old horse," quavered Ukridge. "I suppose you haven't forgotten about that insurance, have you?"

"Oh, no, I remember that."

Ukridge breathed a relieved sigh.

"I was a subscriber to a number of weekly papers," went on Teddy Weeks. "They are paying me insurance money now."

"Yes, yes, old horse," cried Ukridge. "But what I mean is you remember the Syndicate, don't you?"

Teddy Weeks raised his eyebrows.

"Syndicate? What Syndicate?"

"Why, when we all got together and put up the money to pay for the subscriptions to these papers and drew lots, to choose which of us should go out and have an accident and collect the money. And you drew it, don't you remember?"

Utter astonishment, and a shocked astonishment at that, spread itself over Teddy Weeks's countenance. The man seemed outraged.

"I certainly remember nothing of the kind," he said, severely. "I cannot imagine myself for a moment consenting to become a party to what from your own account would appear to have been a criminal conspiracy to obtain money under false pretences from a number of weekly papers."

"But, laddie — "

"However," said Teddy Weeks, "if there is any truth in this story, no doubt you have documentary evidence to support it."

Ukridge looked at me. I looked at Ukridge. There was a long silence.

"Shift-ho, old horse?" said Ukridge, sadly. "No use staying on here."

"No," I replied, with equal gloom. "May as well go."

"Glad to have seen you," said Teddy Weeks, "and thanks for the fruit."

The next time I saw the man he was coming out of a manager's office in the Haymarket. He had on a new Homburg hat of a delicate pearl grey, spats to match, and a new blue flannel suit, beautifully cut, with an invisible red twill. He was looking jubilant, and, as I passed him, he drew from his pocket a gold cigarette-case.

It was shortly after that, if you remember, that he made a big hit as the juvenile lead in that piece at the Apollo and started on his sensational career as a *matinée* idol.

Inside the church the organ had swelled into the familiar music of the Wedding March. A verger came out and opened the doors. The five cooks ceased their reminiscences of other and smarter weddings at which they had participated. The camera-men unshipped their cameras. The costermonger moved his barrow of vegetables a pace forward. A dishevelled and unshaven man at my side uttered a disapproving growl.

"Idle rich!" said the dishevelled man.

Out of the church came a beauteous being, leading attached to his arm another being, somewhat less beauteous.

There was no denying the spectacular effect of Teddy
Weeks. He was handsomer than ever. His sleek hair, gor-
geously waved, shone in the sun, his eyes were large and
bright; his lissome frame, garbed in faultless morning-coat
and trousers, was that of an Apollo. But his bride gave the
impression that Teddy had married money. They paused in
the doorway, and the camera-men became active and fussy.

"Have you got a shilling, laddie?" said Ukridge in a low,
level voice.

"Why do you want a shilling?"

"Old horse," said Ukridge, tensely, "it is of the utmost vital
importance that I have a shilling here and now."

I passed it over. Ukridge turned to the dishevelled man,
and I perceived that he held in his hand a large rich tomato
of juicy and over-ripe appearance.

"Would you like to earn a bob?" Ukridge said.

"Would I!" replied the dishevelled man.

Ukridge sank his voice to a hoarse whisper.

The camera-men had finished their preparations. Teddy
Weeks, his head thrown back in that gallant way which has
endeared him to so many female hearts, was exhibiting his
celebrated teeth. The cooks, in undertones, were making
adverse comments on the appearance of the bride.

"Now, please," said one of the camera-men.

Over the heads of the crowd, well and truly aimed,
whizzed a large juicy tomato. It burst like a shell full between
Teddy Weeks's expressive eyes, obliterating them in scarlet
ruin. It spattered Teddy Weeks's collar, it dripped on Teddy
Weeks's morning-coat. And the dishevelled man turned
abruptly and raced off down the street.

Ukridge grasped my arm. There was a look of deep content
in his eyes.

"Shift-ho?" said Ukridge.

Arm-in-arm, we strolled off in the pleasant June sunshine.

INDISCRETIONS
OF
ARCHIE

IT SEEMED TO ARCHIE, AS HE SURVEYED HIS POSI-
tion at the end of the first month of his married life, that all
was for the best in the best of all possible worlds. In their
attitude towards America, visiting Englishmen almost invariably incline to extremes, either detesting all that therein is
or else becoming enthusiasts on the subject of the country,
its climate, and its institutions. Archie belonged to the second
class. He liked America and got on splendidly with Ameri-
cans from the start. He was a friendly soul, a mixer; and in
New York, that city of mixers, he found himself at home. The
atmosphere of good-fellowship and the open-hearted hospitality of everybody he met appealed to him. There were
moments when it seemed to him as though New York had
simply been waiting for him to arrive before giving the word
to let the revels commence.

Nothing, of course, in this world is perfect; and, rosy as
were the glasses through which Archie looked on his new
surroundings, he had to admit that there was one flaw,
one fly in the ointment, one individual caterpillar in the

salad. Mr. Daniel Brewster, his father-in-law, remained consistently unfriendly. Indeed, his manner towards his new relative became daily more and more a manner which would have caused gossip on the plantation if Simon Legree had exhibited it in his relations with Uncle Tom. And this in spite of the fact that Archie, as early as the third morning of his stay, had gone to him and in the most frank and manly way had withdrawn his criticism of the Hotel Cosmopolis, giving it as his considered opinion that the Hotel Cosmopolis on closer inspection appeared to be a good egg, one of the best and brightest, and a bit of all right.

"A credit to you, old thing," said Archie cordially.

"Don't call me old thing!" growled Mr. Brewster.

"Right-o, old companion!" said Archie amiably.

Archie, a true philosopher, bore this hostility with fortitude, but it worried Lucille.

"I do wish father understood you better," was her wistful comment when Archie had related the conversation.

"Well, you know," said Archie, "I'm open for being understood any time he cares to take a stab at it."

"You must try and make him fond of you."

"But how? I smile winsomely at him and what not, but he doesn't respond."

"Well, we shall have to think of something. I want him to realise what an angel you are. You *are* an angel, you know."

"No, really?"

"Of course you are."

"It's a rummy thing," said Archie, pursuing a train of thought which was constantly with him, "the more I see of you, the more I wonder how you can have a father like—I mean to say, what I mean to say is, I wish I had known your mother; she must have been frightfully attractive."

"What would really please him, I know," said Lucille, "would be if you got some work to do. He loves people who work."

"Yes?" said Archie doubtfully. "Well, you know, I heard

him interviewing that chappie behind the desk this morning, who works like the dickens from early morn to dewy eve, on the subject of a mistake in his figures; and, if he loved him, he dissembled it all right. Of course, I admit that so far I haven't been one of the toilers, but the dashed difficult thing is to know how to start. I'm nosing round, but the openings for a bright young man seem so scarce."

"Well, keep on trying. I feel sure that, if you could only find something to do, it doesn't matter what, father would be quite different."

It was possibly the dazzling prospect of making Mr. Brewster quite different that stimulated Archie. He was strongly of the opinion that any change in his father-in-law must inevitably be for the better. A chance meeting with James B. Wheeler, the artist, at the Pen-and-Ink Club seemed to open the way.

To a visitor to New York who has the ability to make himself liked it almost appears as though the leading industry in that city was the issuing of two-weeks' invitation-cards to clubs. Archie since his arrival had been showered with these pleasant evidences of his popularity; and he was now an honorary member of so many clubs of various kinds that he had not time to go to them all. There were the fashionable clubs along Fifth Avenue to which his friend Reggie van Tuyl, son of his Florida hostess, had introduced him. There were the businessmen's clubs of which he was made free by more solid citizens. And, best of all, there were the Lambs', the Players', the Friars', the Coffee-House, the Pen-and-Ink, and the other resorts of the artist, the author, the actor, and the Bohemian. It was in these that Archie spent most of his time, and it was here that he made the acquaintance of J. B. Wheeler, the popular illustrator.

To Mr. Wheeler, over a friendly lunch, Archie had been confiding some of his ambitions to qualify as the hero of one of the Get-on-or-get-out-young-man-step-lively-books.

"You want a job?" said Mr. Wheeler.

"I want a job," said Archie.

Mr. Wheeler consumed eight fried potatoes in quick succession. He was an able trencherman.

"I always looked on you as one of our leading lilies of the field," he said. "Why this anxiety to toil and spin?"

"Well, my wife, you know, seems to think it might put me one up with the jolly old dad if I did something."

"And you're not particular what you do, so long as it has the outer aspect of work?"

"Anything in the world, laddie, anything in the world."

"Then come and pose for a picture I'm doing," said J. B. Wheeler. "It's for a magazine cover. You're just the model I want, and I'll pay you at the usual rates. Is it a go?"

"Pose?"

"You've only got to stand still and look like a chunk of wood. You can do that, surely?"

"I can do that," said Archie.

"Then come along down to my studio to-morrow."

"Right-o!" said Archie.

"I say, old thing!"

Archie spoke plaintively. Already he was looking back ruefully to the time when he had supposed that an artist's model had a soft job. In the first five minutes muscles which he had not been aware that he possessed had started to ache like neglected teeth. His respect for the toughness and durability of artists' models was now solid. How they acquired the stamina to go through this sort of thing all day and then bound off to Bohemian revels at night was more than he could understand.

"Don't wobble, confound you!" snorted Mr. Wheeler.

"Yes, but, my dear old artist," said Archie, "what you don't seem to grasp—what you appear not to realise—is that I'm getting a crick in the back."

"You weakling! You miserable, invertebrate worm. Move an inch and I'll murder you, and come and dance on your grave every Wednesday and Saturday. I'm just getting it."

"It's in the spine that it seems to catch me principally."

"Be a man, you faint-hearted string-bean!" urged J. B. Wheeler. "You ought to be ashamed of yourself. Why, a girl who was posing for me last week stood for a solid hour on one leg, holding a tennis racket over her head and smiling brightly withal."

"The female of the species is more india-rubbery than the male," argued Archie.

"Well, I'll be through in a few minutes. Don't weaken. Think how proud you'll be when you see yourself on all the bookstalls."

Archie sighed, and braced himself to the task once more. He wished he had never taken on this binge. In addition to his physical discomfort, he was feeling a most awful chump. The cover on which Mr. Wheeler was engaged was for the August number of the magazine, and it had been necessary for Archie to drape his reluctant form in a two-piece bathing suit of a vivid lemon colour; for he was supposed to be representing one of those jolly dogs belonging to the best families who dive off floats at exclusive seashore resorts. J. B. Wheeler, a stickler for accuracy, had wanted him to remove his socks and shoes; but there Archie had stood firm. He was willing to make an ass of himself, but not a silly ass.

"All right," said J. B. Wheeler, laying down his brush. "That will do for to-day. Though, speaking without prejudice and with no wish to be offensive, if I had had a model who wasn't a weak-kneed, jelly-backboned son of Belial, I could have got the darned thing finished without having to have another sitting."

"I wonder why you chappies call this sort of thing 'sitting,' " said Archie, pensively, as he conducted tentative experiments in osteopathy on his aching back. "I say, old thing, I could do with a restorative, if you have one handy. But, of course, you haven't, I suppose," he added, resignedly. Abstemious as a rule, there were moments when Archie found the Eighteenth Amendment somewhat trying.

J. B. Wheeler shook his head.

"You're a little previous," he said. "But come round in

another day or so, and I may be able to do something for you." He moved with a certain conspirator-like caution to a corner of the room, and, lifting to one side a pile of canvases, revealed a stout barrel, which he regarded with a fatherly and benignant eye. "I don't mind telling you that, in the fullness of time, I believe this is going to spread a good deal of sweetness and light."

"Oh, ah," said Archie, interested. "Home-brew, what?"

"Made with these hands. I added a few more raisins yesterday, to speed things up a bit. There is much virtue in your raisin. And, talking of speeding things up, for goodness' sake try to be a bit more punctual to-morrow. We lost an hour of good daylight to-day."

"I like that! I was here on the absolute minute. I had to hang about on the landing waiting for you."

"Well, well, that doesn't matter," said J. B. Wheeler, impatiently, for the artist soul is always annoyed by petty details. "The point is that we were an hour late in getting to work. Mind you're here to-morrow at eleven sharp."

It was, therefore, with a feeling of guilt and trepidation that Archie mounted the stairs on the following morning; for in spite of his good resolutions he was half an hour behind time. He was relieved to find that his friend had also lagged by the wayside. The door of the studio was ajar, and he went in, to discover the place occupied by a lady of mature years, who was scrubbing the floor with a mop. He went into the bedroom and donned his bathing suit. When he emerged, ten minutes later, the charwoman had gone, but J. B. Wheeler was still absent. Rather glad of the respite, he sat down to kill time by reading the morning paper, whose sporting page alone he had managed to master at the breakfast table.

There was not a great deal in the paper to interest him. The usual bond-robbery had taken place on the previous day, and the police were reported hot on the trail of the Master-Mind who was alleged to be at the back of these financial operations. A messenger named Henry Babcock had been arrested and was expected to become confidential. To one who, like Archie, had never owned a bond, the story made little appeal. He turned with more interest to a cheery half-column on the activities of a gentleman in Minnesota who, with what seemed to Archie, as he thought of Mr. Daniel Brewster, a good deal of resource and public spirit, had recently beaned his father-in-law with the family meat-axe. It was only after he had read this through twice in a spirit of gentle approval that it occurred to him that J. B. Wheeler was uncommonly late at the tryst. He looked at his watch, and found that he had been in the studio three-quarters of an hour.

Archie became restless. Long-suffering old bean though he was, he considered this a bit thick. He got up and went out on to the landing, to see if there were any signs of the blighter. There were none. He began to understand now what had happened. For some reason or other the bally artist was not coming to the studio at all that day. Probably he had called up the hotel and left a message to this effect, and Archie had just missed it. Another man might have waited to make certain that his message had reached its destination, but not woollen-headed Wheeler, the most casual individual in New York. Thoroughly aggrieved, Archie turned back to the studio to dress and go away.

His progress was stayed by a solid, forbidding slab of oak. Somehow or other, since he had left the room, the door had managed to get itself shut.

"Oh, dash it!" said Archie.

The mildness of the expletive was proof that the full horror of the situation had not immediately come home to him. His mind in the first few moments was occupied with the problem of how the door had got that way. He could not remember shutting it. Probably he had done it unconsciously. As a child, he had been taught by sedulous elders that the little gentleman always closed doors behind him, and presumably his subconscious self was still under the influence. And then, suddenly, he realised that this infernal, officious ass of a sub-conscious self had deposited him right in the gumbo. Behind that closed door, unattainable as youthful ambition, lay his gent's heather-mixture with the green twill, and here he was, out in the world, alone, in a lemon-coloured bathing suit.

In all crises of human affairs there are two broad courses open to a man. He can stay where he is or he can go else-where. Archie, leaning on the banisters, examined these alternatives narrowly. If he stayed where he was he would have to spend the night on this dashed landing. If he legged it, in this kit, he would be gathered up by the constabulary before he had gone a hundred yards. He was no pessimist, but he was reluctantly forced to the conclusion that he was up against it.

It was while he was musing with a certain tenseness on these things that the sound of footsteps came to him from below. But almost in the first instant the hope that this might be J. B. Wheeler, the curse of the human race, died away. Whoever was coming up the stairs was running, and J. B. Wheeler never ran upstairs. He was not one of your lean, haggard, spiritual-looking geniuses. He made a large income with his brush and pencil, and spent most of it in creature comforts. This couldn't be J. B. Wheeler.

It was not. It was a tall, thin man whom he had never seen before. He appeared to be in a considerable hurry. He let himself into the studio on the floor below, and vanished without even waiting to shut the door.

He had come and disappeared in almost record time, but, brief though his passing had been, it had been long enough to bring consolation to Archie. A sudden bright light had been vouchsafed to Archie, and he now saw an admirably ripe and fruity scheme for ending his troubles. What could be simpler than to toddle down one flight of stairs and in an easy and debonair manner ask the chappie's permission to use his telephone? And what could be simpler, once he was at the 'phone, than to get in touch with somebody at the

Cosmopolis who would send down a few trousers and what not in a kit bag. It was a priceless solution, thought Archie, as he made his way downstairs. Not even embarrassing, he meant to say. This chappie, living in a place like this, wouldn't bat an eyelid at the spectacle of a fellow trickling about the place in a bathing suit. They would have a good laugh about the whole thing.

"I say, I hate to bother you—dare say you're busy and all that sort of thing—but would you mind if I popped in for half a second and used your 'phone?'"

That was the speech, the extremely gentlemanly and well-phrased speech, which Archie had prepared to deliver the moment the man appeared. The reason he did not deliver it was that the man did not appear. He knocked, but nothing stirred.

"I say!"

Archie now perceived that the door was ajar, and that on an envelope attached with a tack to one of the panels was the name "Elmer M. Moon." He pushed the door a little farther open and tried again.

"Oh, Mr. Moon! Mr. Moon!" He waited a moment. "Oh, Mr. Moon! Mr. Moon! Are you there, Mr. Moon?"

He blushed hotly. To his sensitive ear the words had sounded exactly like the opening line of the refrain of a vaudeville song-hit. He decided to waste no further speech on a man with such an unfortunate surname until he could see him face to face and get a chance of lowering his voice a bit. Absolutely absurd to stand outside a chappie's door singing song-hits in a lemon-coloured bathing suit. He pushed the door open and walked in; and his subconscious self, always the gentleman, closed it gently behind him.

"Up!" said a low, sinister, harsh, unfriendly, and unpleasant voice.

"Eh?" said Archie, revolving sharply on his axis.

He found himself confronting the hurried gentleman who had run upstairs. This sprinter had produced an automatic pistol, and was pointing it in a truculent manner at his head. Archie stared at his host, and his host stared at him.

"Put your hands up," he said.

"Oh, right-o! Absolutely!" said Archie. "But I mean to say — "

The other was drinking him in with considerable astonishment. Archie's costume seemed to have made a powerful impression upon him.

"Who the devil are you?" he enquired.

"Me? Oh, my name's — "

"Never mind your name. What are you doing here?"

"Well, as a matter of fact, I popped in to ask if I might use your 'phone. You see — "

A certain relief seemed to temper the austerity of the other's gaze. As a visitor, Archie, though surprising, seemed to be better than he had expected.

"I don't know what to do with you," he said, meditatively.

"If you'd just let me toddle to the 'phone — "

"Likely!" said the man. He appeared to reach a decision. "Here, go into that room."

He indicated with a jerk of his head the open door of what was apparently a bedroom at the farther end of the studio.

"I take it," said Archie, chattily, "that all this may seem to you not a little rummy."

"Get on!"

"I was only saying — "

"Well, I haven't time to listen. Get a move on!"

The bedroom was in a state of untidiness which eclipsed anything which Archie had ever witnessed. The other appeared to be moving house. Bed, furniture, and floor were covered with articles of clothing. A silk shirt wreathed itself about Archie's ankles as he stood gaping, and, as he moved farther into the room, his path was paved with ties and collars.

"Sit down!" said Elmer M. Moon, abruptly.

"Right-o! Thanks," said Archie, "I suppose you wouldn't like me to explain, and what not, what?"

"No!" said Mr. Moon. "I haven't got your spare time. Put your hands behind that chair."

Archie did so, and found them immediately secured by what felt like a silk tie. His assiduous host then proceeded to fasten his ankles in a like manner. This done, he seemed to feel that he had done all that was required of him, and he returned to the packing of a large suitcase which stood by the window.

"I say!" said Archie.

Mr. Moon, with the air of a man who has remembered something which he had overlooked, shoved a sock in his guest's mouth and resumed his packing. He was what might be called an impressionist packer. His aim appeared to be speed rather than neatness. He bundled his belongings in, closed the bag with some difficulty, and, stepping to the window, opened it. Then he climbed out on to the fire-escape, dragged the suit-case after him, and was gone.

Archie, left alone, addressed himself to the task of freeing his prisoned limbs. The job proved much easier than he had expected. Mr. Moon, that hustler, had wrought for the moment, not for all time. A practical man, he had been content to keep his visitor shackled merely for such a period as would permit him to make his escape unhindered. In less than ten minutes Archie, after a good deal of snake-like writhing, was pleased to discover that the thingummy attached to his wrists had loosened sufficiently to enable him to use his hands. He untied himself and got up.

He now began to tell himself that out of evil cometh good. His encounter with the elusive Mr. Moon had not been an agreeable one, but it had had this solid advantage, that it had left him right in the middle of a great many clothes. And Mr. Moon, whatever his moral defects, had the one excellent quality of taking about the same size as himself. Archie, casting a covetous eye upon a tweed suit which lay on the bed, was on the point of climbing into the trousers when on the outer door of the studio there sounded a forceful knocking.

"Open up here!"

Archie bounded silently out into the other room and stood listening tensely. He was not a naturally querulous man, but he did feel at this point that Fate was picking on him with a somewhat undue severity.

"In th' name av th' Law!"

There are times when the best of us lose our heads. At this juncture Archie should undoubtedly have gone to the door, opened it, explained his presence in a few well-chosen words, and generally have passed the whole thing off with ready tact. But the thought of confronting a posse of police in his present costume caused him to look earnestly about him for a hiding-place.

Up against the farther wall was a settee with a high, arching back, which might have been put there for that special purpose. He inserted himself behind this, just as a splintering crash announced that the Law, having gone through the formality of knocking with its knuckles, was now getting busy with an axe. A moment later the door had given way, and the room was full of trampling feet. Archie wedged himself against the wall with the quiet concentration of a clam nestling in its shell, and hoped for the best.

It seemed to him that his immediate future depended for better or for worse entirely on the native intelligence of the Force. If they were the bright, alert men he hoped they were, they would see all that junk in the bedroom and, deducing from it that their quarry had stood not upon the order of his going but had hopped it, would not waste time in searching a presumably empty apartment. If, on the other hand, they were the obtuse, flat-footed persons who occasionally find their way into the ranks of even the most enlightened constabularies, they would undoubtedly shift the settee and drag him into a publicity from which his modest soul shrank. He was enchanted, therefore, a few moments later, to hear a gruff voice state that th' mutt had beaten it down th' fire-escape. His opinion of the detective abilities of the New York police force rose with a bound.

There followed a brief council of war, which, as it took place in the bedroom, was inaudible to Archie except as a distant growling noise. He could distinguish no words, but, as it was succeeded by a general trampling of large boots in the direction of the door and then by silence, he gathered that the pack, having drawn the studio and found it empty, had decided to return to other and more profitable duties. He gave them a reasonable interval for removing themselves, and then poked his head cautiously over the settee.

All was peace. The place was empty. No sound disturbed the stillness.

Archie emerged. For the first time in this morning of disturbing occurrences he began to feel that God was in his heaven and all right with the world. At last things were beginning to brighten up a bit, and life might be said to have taken on some of the aspects of a good egg. He stretched himself, for it is cramping work lying under settees, and, proceeding to the bedroom, picked up the tweed trousers again.

Clothes had a fascination for Archie. Another man, in similar circumstances, might have hurried over his toilet; but Archie, faced by a difficult choice of ties, rather strung the thing out. He selected a specimen which did great credit to the taste of Mr. Moon, evidently one of our snappiest dressers, found that it did not harmonise with the deeper meaning of the tweed suit, removed it, chose another, and was adjusting the bow and admiring the effect, when his attention was diverted by a slight sound which was half a cough and half a sniff; and, turning, found himself gazing into the clear blue eyes of a large man in uniform, who had stepped into the room from the fire-escape. He was swinging a substantial club in a negligent sort of way, and he looked at Archie with a total absence of bonhomie.

"Ah!" he observed.

"Oh, *there* you are!" said Archie, subsiding weakly against the chest of drawers. He gulped. "Of course, I can see you're thinking all this pretty tolerably weird and all that," he proceeded, in a propitiatory voice.

The policeman attempted no analysis of his emotions. He opened a mouth which a moment before had looked incapable of being opened except with the assistance of powerful machinery, and shouted a single word.

"Cassidy!"

A distant voice gave tongue in answer. It was like alligators roaring to their mates across lonely swamps.

There was a rumble of footsteps in the region of the stairs, and presently there entered an even larger guardian of the Law than the first exhibit. He, too, swung a massive club, and, like his colleague, he gazed frostily at Archie.

"God save Ireland!" he remarked.

The words appeared to be more in the nature of an expletive than a practical comment on the situation. Having uttered them, he draped himself in the doorway like a colossus, and chewed gum.

"Where ja get him?" he enquired, after a pause.

"Found him in here attimpting to disguise himself."

"I told Cap. he was hiding somewheres, but he would have it that he'd beat it down th' escape," said the gum-chewer, with the sombre triumph of the underling whose sound advice has been overruled by those above him. He shifted his wholesome (or, as some say, unwholesome) morsel to the other side of his mouth, and for the first time addressed Archie directly. "Ye're pinched!" he observed.

Archie started violently. The bleak directness of the speech roused him with a jerk from the dream-like state into which he had fallen. He had not anticipated this. He had assumed that there would be a period of tedious explanations to be gone through before he was at liberty to depart to the cosy little lunch for which his interior had been sighing wistfully this long time past; but that he should be arrested had been outside his calculations. Of course, he could put everything right eventually; he could call witnesses to his character and the purity of his intentions; but in the meantime the whole dashed business would be in all the papers, embellished with all those unpleasant flippancies to which your newspaper reporter is so prone to stoop when he sees half a chance. He would feel a frightful chump. Chappies would rot him about it, to the most fearful extent. Old Brewster's name would come into it, and he could not disguise it from himself that his father-in-law, who liked his name in the papers as little as possible, would be sorer than a sunburned neck.

"No, I say, you know! I mean, I mean to say!"

"Pinched!" repeated the rather larger policeman.

"And annything ye say," added his slightly smaller colleague, "will be used agenst ya 't the trial."

"And if ya try t'escape," said the first speaker, twiddling his club, "ya'll getja block knocked off."

And, having sketched out this admirably clear and neatly constructed scenario, the two relapsed into silence. Officer Cassidy restored his gum to circulation. Officer Donahue frowned sternly at his boots.

"But, I say," said Archie, "it's all a mistake, you know. Absolutely a frightful error, my dear old constables. I'm not the lad you're after at all. The chappie you want is a different sort of fellow altogether. Another blighter entirely."

New York policemen never laugh when on duty. There is probably something in the regulations against it. But Officer Donahue permitted the left corner of his mouth to twitch slightly, and a momentary muscular spasm disturbed the calm of Officer Cassidy's granite features, as a passing breeze ruffles the surface of some bottomless lake.

"That's what they all say!" observed Officer Donahue.

"It's no use tryin' that line of talk," said Officer Cassidy. "Babcock's squealed."

"Sure. Squealed 's morning," said Officer Donahue.

Archie's memory stirred vaguely.

"Babcock?" he said. "Do you know, that name seems familiar to me, somehow. I'm almost sure I've read it in the paper or something."

"Ah, cut it out!" said Officer Cassidy, disgustedly. The two constables exchanged a glance of austere disapproval. This hypocrisy pained them. "Read it in th' paper or something!"

"By Jove! I remember now. He's the chappie who was arrested in that bond business. For goodness' sake, my dear, merry old constables," said Archie, astounded, "you surely aren't labouring under the impression that I'm the Master-Mind they were talking about in the paper? Why, what an absolutely priceless notion! I mean to say, I ask you, what! Frankly, laddies, do I look like a Master-Mind?"

Officer Cassidy heaved a deep sigh, which rumbled up from his interior like the first muttering of a cyclone.

"If I'd known," he said, regretfully, "that this guy was going to turn out a ruddy Englishman, I'd have taken a slap at him with m' stick and chanced it!"

Officer Donahue considered the point well taken.

"Ah!" he said, understandingly. He regarded Archie with an unfriendly eye. "I know th' sort well! Trampling on th' face av th' poor!"

"Ya c'n trample on the poor man's face," said Officer Cassidy, severely; "but don't be surprised if one day he bites you in the leg!"

"But, my dear old sir," protested Archie, "I've never trampled —"

"One of these days," said Officer Donahue, moodily, "the Shannon will flow in blood to the sea!"

"Absolutely! But —"

Officer Cassidy uttered a glad cry.

"Why couldn't we hit him a lick," he suggested, brightly, "an' tell th' Cap. he resisted us in th' exercise of our jooty?"

An instant gleam of approval and enthusiasm came into Officer Donahue's eyes. Officer Donahue was not a man who got these luminous inspirations himself, but that did not prevent him appreciating them in others and bestowing commendation in the right quarter. There was nothing petty or grudging about Officer Donahue.

"Ye're the lad with the head, Tim!" he exclaimed admiringly.

"It just sorta came to me," said Mr. Cassidy, modestly.

"It's a great idea, Timmy!"

"Just happened to think of it," said Mr. Cassidy, with a coy gesture of self-effacement.

Archie had listened to the dialogue with growing uneasiness. Not for the first time since he had made their acquaintance, he became vividly aware of the exceptional physical gifts of these two men. The New York police force demands from those who would join its ranks an extremely high standard of stature and sinew, but it was obvious that jolly old Donahue and Cassidy must have passed in first shot without any difficulty whatever.

"I say, you know," he observed, apprehensively.

And then a sharp and commanding voice spoke from the outer room.

"Donahue! Cassidy! What the devil does this mean?"

Archie had a momentary impression that an angel had fluttered down to his rescue. If this was the case, the angel had assumed an effective disguise—that of a police captain. The new arrival was a far smaller man than his subordinates —so much smaller that it did Archie good to look at him. For a long time he had been wishing that it were possible to rest his eyes with the spectacle of something of a slightly less out-size nature than his two companions.

"Why have you left your posts?"

The effect of the interruption on the Messrs. Cassidy and Donahue was pleasingly instantaneous. They seemed to shrink to almost normal proportions, and their manner took on an attractive deference.

Officer Donahue saluted.

"If ye plaze, sorr — "

Officer Cassidy also saluted, simultaneously.

"'Twas like this, sorr — "

The captain froze Officer Cassidy with a glance and, leaving him congealed, turned to Officer Donahue.

"Oi wuz standing on th' fire-escape, sorr," said Officer Donahue, in a tone of obsequious respect which not only delighted, but astounded Archie, who hadn't known he could talk like that, "accordin' to instructions, when I heard a suspicious noise. I crope in, sorr, and found this duck—found the accused, sorr—in front of th' mirror, examinin' himself. I then called to Officer Cassidy for assistance. We pinched—arrested um, sorr."

The captain looked at Archie. It seemed to Archie that he looked at him coldly and with contempt.

"Who is he?"

"The Master-Mind, sorr."

"The what?"

"The accused, sorr. The man that's wanted."

"You may want him. I don't," said the captain. Archie, though relieved, thought he might have put it more nicely. "This isn't Moon. It's not a bit like him."

"Absolutely not!" agreed Archie, cordially. "It's all a mistake, old companion, as I was trying to — "

"Cut it out!"

"Oh, right-o!"

"You've seen the photographs at the station. Do you mean to tell me you see any resemblance?"

"If ye plaze, sorr," said Officer Cassidy, coming to life.

"Well?"

"We thought he'd bin disguising himself, the way he wouldn't be recognised."

"You're a fool!" said the captain.

"Yes, sorr," said Officer Cassidy, meekly.

"So are you, Donahue."

"Yes, sorr."

Archie's respect for this chappie was going up all the time. He seemed to be able to take years off the lives of these massive blighters with a word. It was like the stories you read about lion-tamers. Archie did not despair of seeing Officer Donahue and his old college chum Cassidy eventually jumping through hoops.

"Who are you?" demanded the captain, turning to Archie.

"Well, my name is — "

"What are you doing here?"

"Well, it's rather a longish story, you know. Don't want to bore you, and all that."

"I'm here to listen. You can't bore *me*."

"Dashed nice of you to put it like that," said Archie, gratefully. "I mean to say, makes it easier and so forth. What I mean is, you know how rotten you feel telling the deuce of a long yarn and wondering if the party of the second part is wishing you would turn off the tap and go home. I mean — "

"If," said the captain, "you're reciting something, stop. If you're trying to tell me what you're doing here, make it shorter and easier."

Archie saw his point. Of course, time was money—the modern spirit of hustle—all that sort of thing.

"Well, it was this bathing suit, you know," he said.

"What bathing suit?"

"Mine, don't you know. A lemon-coloured contrivance. Rather bright and so forth, but in its proper place not altogether a bad egg. Well, the whole thing started, you know, with my standing on a bally pedestal sort of arrangement in a diving attitude—for the cover, you know. I don't know if you have ever done anything of that kind yourself, but it gives you a most fearful crick in the spine. However, that's rather beside the point, I suppose—don't know why I mentioned it. Well, this morning he was dashed late, so I went out — "

"What the devil are you talking about?"

Archie looked at him, surprised.

"Aren't I making it clear?"

"No."

"Well, you understand about the bathing suit, don't you? The jolly old bathing suit, you've grasped that, what?"

"No."

"Oh, I say," said Archie. "That's rather a nuisance. I mean to say, the bathing suit's what you might call the good old pivot of the whole dashed affair, you see. Well, you understand about the cover, what? You're pretty clear on the subject of the cover?"

"What cover?"

"Why, for the magazine."

"What magazine?"

"Now there you rather have me. One of these bright little periodicals, you know, that you see popping to and fro on the bookstalls."

"I don't know what you're talking about," said the captain. He looked at Archie with an expression of distrust and hostility. "And I'll tell you straight out I don't like the looks of you. I believe you're a pal of his."

"No longer," said Archie, firmly. "I mean to say, a chappie who makes you stand on a bally pedestal sort of arrangement and get a crick in the spine, and then doesn't turn up and leaves you biffing all over the countryside in a bathing suit — "

The reintroduction of the bathing suit motive seemed to have the worst effect on the captain. He flushed darkly.

"Are you trying to josh me? I've a mind to soak you!"

"If ye plaze, sorr," cried Officer Donahue and Officer Cassidy in chorus. In the course of their professional career they did not often hear their superior make many suggestions with which they saw eye to eye, but he had certainly, in their opinion, spoken a mouthful now.

"No, honestly, my dear old thing, nothing was farther from my thoughts — "

He would have spoken further, but at this moment the world came to an end. At least, that was how it sounded.

Somewhere in the immediate neighbourhood something went off with a vast explosion, shattering the glass in the window, peeling the plaster from the ceiling, and sending him staggering into the inhospitable arms of Officer Donahue.

The three guardians of the Law stared at one another.

"If ye plaze, sorr," said Officer Cassidy, saluting.

"Well?"

"May I spake, sorr?"

"Well?"

"Something's exploded, sorr!"

The information, kindly meant though it was, seemed to annoy the captain.

"What the devil did you think I thought had happened?" he demanded, with not a little irritation. "It was a bomb!"

Archie could have corrected this diagnosis, for already a faint but appealing aroma of an alcoholic nature was creeping into the room through a hole in the ceiling, and there had risen before his eyes the picture of J. B. Wheeler affectionately regarding that barrel of his on the previous morning in the studio upstairs. J. B. Wheeler had wanted quick results, and he had got them. Archie had long since ceased to regard J. B. Wheeler as anything but a tumour on the social system, but he was bound to admit that he had certainly done him a good turn now. Already these honest men, diverted by the superior attraction of this latest happening, appeared to have forgotten his existence.

"Sorr!" said Officer Donahue.

"Well?"

"It came from upstairs, sorr."

"Of course it came from upstairs. Cassidy!"

"Sorr?"

"Get down into the street, call up the reserves, and stand at the front entrance to keep the crowd back. We'll have the whole city here in five minutes."

"Right, sorr."

"Don't let anyone in."

"No, sorr."

"Well, see that you don't. Come along, Donahue, now. Look slippy."

"On the spot, sorr!" said Officer Donahue.

A moment later Archie had the studio to himself. Two minutes later he was picking his way cautiously down the fire-escape after the manner of the recent Mr. Moon. Archie had not seen much of Mr. Moon, but he had seen enough to know that in certain crises his methods were sound and should be followed. Elmer Moon was not a good man; his ethics were poor and his moral code shaky; but in the matter of legging it away from a situation of peril and discomfort he had no superior.